D0437692

The Mark
of the Golden Dragon

L. A. MEYER

The Mark
of the Golden Dragon

Being an Account
of the Further Adventures
of Jacky Faber,
Jewel of the East, Vexation of the West,
and Pearl of the South China Sea

HARCOURT
Houghton Mifflin Harcourt

Boston   New York   2011

Copyright © 2011 by L. A. Meyer

All rights reserved. For information about permission to reproduce selections
from this book, write to Permissions, Houghton Mifflin Harcourt Publishing
Company, 215 Park Avenue South, New York, New York 10003.

Harcourt is an imprint of Houghton Mifflin Harcourt Publishing Company.

www.hmhbooks.com

The text of this book is set in Minion.

Library of Congress Cataloging-in-Publication Data
Meyer, L. A. (Louis A.), 1942–
The mark of the golden dragon : being an account of the further adventures of
Jacky Faber, jewel of the East, vexation of the West, and pearl of the South China
Sea / L. A. Meyer.
p. cm.—(Bloody Jack adventure)
Summary: In 1807, having survived a typhoon in the East Indies, Jacky Faber
makes her way to London to seek a pardon for herself and her betrothed, Jaimy
Fletcher, who, posing as a highwayman, is trying to avenge her supposed death.
ISBN 978-0-547-51764-3
[1. Sex role—Fiction. 2. Seafaring life—Fiction. 3. Robbers and outlaws—Fiction. 4.
Sea stories. 5. London (England)—History—19th century—Fiction. 6. Great
Britain—History—George III, 1760-1820—Fiction. 7. Indonesia—History—19th
century—Fiction.] I. Title.
PZ7.M57172Mar 2011
[Fic]—dc22
2011009598

Manufactured in the United States of America
DOC 10 9 8 7 6 5 4 3 2
4500329423

For Annetje, the Feather in my Cap,
the Jewel in my Crown . . .

and for Mary and Joe and all of the Pankowskis
as well as for Dave and Bobbie and
all of the Lawrence clan

And finally, for the lads on The Hill . . .

Prologue

December 1807
Off the coast of Java
Onboard the *Lorelei Lee*

O God of Grace and Glory, we come before you this day in memory of our fallen shipmate. In your boundless compassion, console those of us who are left behind to mourn. Give us faith to see in death the gate of eternal life, so that in quiet confidence we may continue our course on Earth until by your call we are united with those who have gone before, through Jesus Christ our Lord. Amen.

Eternal Father whose arm doth sometimes calm the restless wave, and whose mighty arm doth at other times whip the sea into an angry froth, please accept into your loving arms the soul of our lost mate who in your greater wisdom you saw fit to take. We commend unto your divine presence our beloved comrade . . .

Jacky Faber.

Amen.

PART I

PART I

Chapter 1

My name is Jacky Faber and I am—by the grace of God, of Neptune, and of all the lesser gods—Owner and Captain of the *Lorelei Lee,* possibly the most beautiful brigantine bark ever to sail the seven seas. I am once again back in command of that fine ship. I am in my lovely cabin and my bottom is pressed back in its favorite chair at the head of my fine table, and grouped about that table are many of my dearest friends.

I've a glass of fine wine in my fist and my dearly beloved James Emerson Fletcher sits here beside me, his hand in mine. *Oh, Jaimy, finally!*

I am supremely happy.

Now a drop of Nelson's blood would not do us any harm,
No, a drop of Nelson's blood would not do us any harm . . .

Things are getting a mite rowdy here on the *Lorelei Lee* as we lift our glasses and bellow out the words to the song. My ship has been sailing in company with the *Cerberus* and HMS *Dart* back up the Strait of Malacca, with Sumatra to port and the Malay Archipelago to starboard, having left Australia, and all its meager charms, far behind.

Most of those in this northerly bound fleet had been condemned to servitude in the penal colony in New South Wales, but we managed, through various mutinies, battles, and some very welcome help from God, luck, and a Chinese pirate, to wriggle free of those bonds, and for that we are eternally grateful. I am, anyway.

Were we guilty of those crimes for which we were transported to the other side of the world? Well, the Irish lads were guilty mostly of merely being Irish. My own dear Jaimy Fletcher, former Lieutenant in His Majesty's Royal Navy and now in the eyes of that Service a vile pirate captain, was mainly guilty of merely being associated with me, false witness being brought against his good name.

My own guilt? Well, I'll let others decide that, but I won't stick around and wait for their decision. Oh, I suppose when I stand before the Pearly Gates, I'll have a few things to answer for, but I'd rather have God judge me and my actions than be judged by the King's ministers, who have not been all that kind in their treatment of my poor self. I do hope God will be more merciful than King George has proven to be.

No, a drop of Nelson's blood would not do us any harm,
And we'll all hang on behind!

Earlier we enjoyed much high hilarity over the pardons granted to all of us by Captain Bligh, Governor of New South Wales. This came about because my good Higgins, in securing the head money for each of the two hundred and fifty assorted female convicts we had delivered in good health to the colony, had also managed to cop a pile of the pardon forms. Using them, we had greatly delighted in granting ourselves absolution from all those various crimes for which we had been condemned. Captain Bligh—yes, *that* unfortunate Captain Bligh, formerly of the infamous *Bounty*—had signed the cargo manifest himself, so it was an easy thing for me to fake his signature on the pardons. I am quite good at forgery . . . among other things.

> *And we'll roll the golden chariot along,*
> *Yes, we'll roll the golden chariot along,*
> *We'll roll the old chariot along,*
> *And we'll all hang on behind.*

As we sing out the song, we linger over each "roll," making it "rrooooll" in time to the roll of the ship. Well, actually, the *Lee* is more wallowing than rolling, since we are essentially becalmed, which is why the captains of the *Dart* and *Cerberus* figured it was safe enough to leave their ships in the care of their junior officers and are now over here eating up my food, slugging down my wine, and eyeing me up, the dogs. I sit at the head of my table with Captain Fletcher on my right . . . and Captain Joseph Jared on my left.

So, yes, there are complications, for this Joseph Jared also has a claim on my affections—it was he who had befriended me when I was pressed into service on HMS *Wolverine* and who helped me in the eventual takeover of that unhappy ship and who protected me from harm in that vile French prison. Both Jaimy and Jared know how things lie between the three of us, and it makes for a bit of tension in the room.

Complications, complications . . .

I heave a sigh and think that if Joseph were not here right now, I'd be sitting in Jaimy's lap, and if Jaimy were not here, I'd probably be in Joseph's. Another heavy sigh. Just why my scrawny and much-scarred self should be such a source of covetous concern, I don't know . . . Men, I swear . . . I right now sit with my head mostly shaved 'cept for a braided pigtail hanging at the back of my shiny skull and a rather garish tattoo of a golden dragon resting on the back of my neck under said pigtail.

My Sailing Master, Enoch Lightner, a white bandage over his sightless eyes, is seated at the foot of the table, and he sings out the next verse in his lusty baritone.

Now, another winsome girl would not do us any harm,
No, another winsome lass would not do us any harm . . .

Arthur McBride, he who is Third Mate of the *Cerberus*, joins him, all the while leering at me over the rim of his wineglass.

Aye, one more winsome girl would not do us any harm,
And we'll all hang on behind!

The young Irish hound must know, given that both Jaimy and Joseph are here aboard, that he has absolutely no chance of getting into my knickers—or into my bed, for that matter—but he nevertheless gazes upon me with some heat as he sings the verse to finish up the song. I know that it was with great regret that he left his lovely and most attentive Chinese handmaidens behind him on Cheng Shih's *Divine Wind*. Sorry, mate, but for you, once again, the hair shirt of the monk.

I am not the only female aboard, because Ian McConnaughey sits midtable with his wife and my dear friend Mairead, in all her red-haired beauty, beaming at his side. 'Course Arthur McBride knows better than to try to touch *her*. In the past, he has never had such reservations about *me* even though for most of our acquaintance I have been his superior officer.

Ah, yes, the Jacky Faber bed . . . It is right over there, nicely made up by my servant, Lee Chi, with the best of silks and fine cottons, and I have seen covert male glances stealing over to look at it. *Don't think I don't see your eyes, or know your thoughts, you dogs.*

My Jolly Roger flag is draped at the foot of the bed and my gold-on-green silk Chinese dragon pennant floats over the top of it. I place my right hand on Jaimy's as we all sing out the song, but I do not place my left hand on Joseph's, even though I sort of want to. No, after all, we can't have a jealous male duel right here right now, and over my silly self, now, can we . . . ?

Complications, complications . . . Life used to be so simple . . .

Although we left the shores of Australia weeks ago, we continue to celebrate our deliverance from captivity. That is, some of us do, anyway—myself and my officers, and James Emerson Fletcher, Captain of the *Cerberus,* with his crew of recently freed Irish lads, many of whom were former crew members of my first ship, the bold, sleek, and ultimately doomed *Emerald.* Joseph Jared, Commander of the third ship in our fleet, HMS *Dart,* a neat and trim thirty-gun sloop of war, joins us in this celebration, but he is not a recently freed convict. Oh, no. He is, in fact, in charge of the Royal

Navy ship that was assigned to escort the East India Company's ship *Cerberus* to New South Wales and then bring her back. Therein lies a further complication because the *Cerberus* is no longer in the possession of the East India Company but is being held now by James Emerson Fletcher and his crew of Irish rogues.

It was what Mr. Yancy Beauregard Cantrell, renowned Mississippi gambler, used to call a "Mexican stand-off" ... all participants involved standing with guns pointing at each other's heads, waiting for someone to make the first deadly move. Something had to be done.

I called a conference. When all were gathered in my cabin, I said, "Gentlemen, please, we must come to some sort of agreement. Captain Jared, you may speak first . . ."

Jared stood and said, "Most of you are escaped convicts. I am honor bound to take you back . . ."

That got him a low growl from those present, who did, after all, outnumber him in the way of armed ships.

". . . however, I am open to suggestions." He sat back down.

Then my good and very intelligent John Higgins, the very soul of reason, spoke up:

"I know, Mr. Jared, how deeply you hold your concept of honor as a Royal Navy officer. However . . . consider this: Your initial duty was to escort the *Cerberus* to New South Wales, then back to England. Is that true?"

Jared nodded. "That was our mission."

Higgins fussed with some papers on the tabletop and continued.

"The *Cerberus* did, indeed, go to Australia and did discharge its cargo of felons as ordered. It is now ready to go back to England, under your protection, as per your original charter. So you have fulfilled your duty in that regard. Is that true?"

Jared considered this, and then said, "True."

"Now, as to the *Lorelei Lee* . . ." Higgins continued, "I believe, Captain Jared, there is nothing in your orders concerning that particular craft. Is that right?"

"Also true."

"Well, then, this is Faber Shipping Worldwide's modest proposal: That we all proceed back to European waters. Once there, the *Lorelei Lee* will go back to her home port of Boston, and the *Cerberus* and the *Dart* will go into British waters and any disputes between their respective captains will be settled there, and in an honorable fashion."

Higgins again paused and looked about. He cleared his throat.

"Ahem. There are further considerations: It is a long way back to England, and we are a formidable force—three swift ships, trained crews, and sixty-two guns, with powder and ball to match. It is to be expected that we will encounter many French and Spanish ships, and we are still at war with those nations . . . Prizes, Sirs . . . many rich prizes . . ."

There was a low growl of avarice all around the table, and the deal was done.

It was an uneasy truce, but, for now, it seems to be holding. Mr. Joseph Jared will have to make a decision when we get back to European waters—one of those "friendship versus duty" decisions—and I, for one, am not looking forward to the outcome.

Complications, complications . . .

• • •

"What means song, Memsahib? Who is Sahib Nelson and why do you sing of his dear blood?"

I look down into the deep dark eyes of Ravi, my little East Indian boy, gazing up at me. He is dressed in the white loincloth in which I first met him back on that street in Bombay. He holds a tray of full wineglasses, and eager hands reach out to grab their stems as he passes them around.

Grateful for a moment to deflect the ardent adult male gazes aimed in my direction, I direct my full attention to Ravi. I run my hand through his black locks and beam my present contentment down upon the little fellow. I am back in command of my lovely *Lorelei Lee,* Jaimy and all my friends are about me, and all's right with my watery world, for now. *So why not live in the moment,* I say. I want to throw my booted foot up on the table in sheer exuberant contentment, but I don't do it, being sort of a lady, and all.

"Well, young Sahib Ravi, it was like this," I say, scooping up the last glass on his tray and lifting it to my lips. "Several years ago there was a great naval battle off Cape Trafalgar, on the coast of Spain. It was between us Brits, with assorted Scots, Welsh, and Irishmen, against the might of Napoleon Bonaparte, Emperor of France. Over seventy warships were involved. All the men at this table were there and qualified to wear this medal—"

"Wasn't my fault you dumped me off back in London before the big fight!" laments Mairead, tossing her copper locks about in mock resentment. "Or I'da had a foine medal, too, like the one you wear, you brazen hussy!"

Laughter all around.

I grin and look down at the Trafalgar medal that rests

12

on the chest of my navy blue lieutenant's jacket, gold braid all around. True, I did get one of the medals that were struck to commemorate that great event, despite my being female, thanks to the efforts of Captain Trumbull, the officer who had relieved me of command of the HMS *Wolverine.*

"Yes, Mairead," I say. "And had you been on board, I'm sure the French would have been vanquished all the sooner!"

More laughter, but I'm not altogether kidding. Mairead *is* a fiery, fierce thing, and she would have given her best had she been there. I know it.

"Anyway, Ravi," I continue when the place subsides a bit. "This here gent"—and I pick up the medal and show him the man depicted there in profile—"was Admiral Lord Horatio Nelson, of the Royal Navy, and he led our fleet to victory that day against superior odds." I put the medal back flat upon my chest. "Had he not done so and we had been defeated, then Napoleon could have freely landed his troops on the east coast of England. At the best, there would have been many very bloody battles, and at the worst, we would all now be wearing French uniforms and Boney would be seated in Windsor Castle."

That gets a low growl from the Brits present.

"So, Ravi, to continue . . . At the end of the great battle, there was a French marine high up in the rigging of a French First-Rate man-of-war, and he shot down upon the officers who stood on the quarterdeck of HMS *Victory* and wounded Lord Nelson most severely."

Ravi's eyes grow wider and wider.

"And then, Missy Memsahib?"

"And then his men carried him down to his bed and laid him upon it, and there he died in great pain from a bullet in his spine, his last words being 'Come kiss me, Hardy, if you love me,' Captain Hardy being the commander of his flagship and his longtime friend, y'see."

"Very sad, Miss, but does not explain song," says the persistent Ravi.

"I'm getting to that, boy, just hold on. Ahem . . . So then, what to do with Lord Nelson's body? The naval officers present thought long and hard about it. He was much too important to be simply tossed over the side like any ordinary dead seaman. After all, he had saved Mother England herself, so it was decided that his body should be placed in a large cask and that cask be filled with rum to preserve his honored remains."

"Indian way much neater. Build fire, then *poof.*"

"I know, Ravi, but that is not our way," I continue. "And so it was done—Nelson's body was stripped down and placed in the cask, and the barrel was filled to the top with the best rum the ship had onboard, and HMS *Victory* headed back to England, bearing its sad burden."

"And so that is end of story, Missy?" asks Ravi. I can tell he is not totally satisfied with my explanation.

"Well, not quite, Ravi," I say. "There was one problem with the cask into which Nelson was put. There was a small spigot at the bottom . . ."

Snorts of suppressed laughter all around.

"So?" asks Ravi, mystified.

"So, my beautiful little boy." I chortle, gathering up the lad and hugging him to me. "When the ship got to England and the funeral was prepared and the cask was opened"—a bit of a pause here—"and when the cask was opened . . . the

body of Lord Nelson was still in there"—another pause—
"but the rum was not!"

Roars of laughter fill the cabin. *Well told, Jacky!*

"But what happened to it?" asks my innocent little lad.

"Uh . . . the *Victory*'s sailors had snuck down in the dark
of night and opened the spigot to pour themselves cups of
the rum, and they drank it till it was all gone."

Ravi pulls away from me, aghast. "But that is disgusting!"

I pull him back to me, shaking with laughter. "If you
think *that* is disgusting, Ravi, then you do not know British
sailors!"

More gales of raucous laughter.

"And so you see, little one, a cup of Nelson's blood is
another way of saying 'a cup of rum.' And sometimes having
a bit of a drink is called 'tapping the Admiral'! Now go do
your job and fill more cups with Nelson's blood and pass
them around!"

Ravi, thoroughly revolted, I am sure, to the depths of
his Hindu soul, scurries off to do his duty. I turn back to
the . . . situation . . . at hand. We are essentially becalmed
and so I have no real reason to deny Jaimy my bed this evening, and oh, I do so want it to be so . . . But what of Jared?
What of discipline?

Complications, complications . . .

While I'm dwelling on how I'm going to deal with this,
I notice that Lee Chi, who is usually a cheerful sort of Chinese
eunuch, is uncharacteristically nervous. He has been serving
the food under Higgins's watchful eye, but he has also gone
to the door several times to peer out, coming back each time
looking more worried. He was given to me by the Chinese

pirate Cheng Shih, who had, well . . . ahem . . . taken a bit of a shine to me when I was her prisoner on our way down to Botany Bay. *Quite a bit of a shine,* I recall with a slight blush coming to my cheeks.

It sure is hot in here, I'm thinking as I stick my finger in my collar and pull it away from my neck. I rather regret being dressed in my naval finery—heavy jacket, lacy shirt, tight britches, and black boots. But I do like to show off, especially with Jaimy by my side, and it's my duty as Grand Mistress of the Proceedings to look good and to sparkle and to be gay and so lend joy to all at my table.

I notice Lee Chi whispering something to Ravi, who has just come back into the cabin, and I break off telling a humorous story and motion for the lad to bring his tray to my side.

"What's up, Ravi?" I say, cutting my eyes to the Chinaman, who stands nervously in a corner. "What's wrong with Mr. Lee?"

"Sahib Lee teach me some of his words . . ."

"Yes, dear, go on," I say.

"He say *tai* means 'big' . . ."

I nod at that, anxious to get back into the high hilarity of the evening, however hot it is growing in here.

". . . and *phoon* means 'wind.'"

"So?"

I look up at Lee Chi and he points outside and says one word.

"Typhoon."

Uh-oh . . .

Chapter 2

The party is over.

"Get back to your ships!" I shout, yanking off my uniform and toeing off my boots. "There is a mighty storm to the west that's headed for us! Hurry!"

But I need not have said anything, for as soon as Joseph Jared sees that low line of pitch-black clouds forming up on the horizon, his leg is over the rail of the *Lee* and he is back in his launch, heading toward the *Dart*.

He is followed closely by Jaimy Fletcher, but not before I grab him, as I'm pulling off my dress trousers, and plant a good one on his mouth.

"Please be careful, Jaimy," I breathe in his ear. "Get down all the canvas you can and quickly! I have heard that tropical typhoons are just as bad as our hurricanes, maybe even worse, and—"

"I know what to do, dearest," he says, wrapping his arms about me and holding me to him. "I know what to do about my ship, but I do not know what to do about you."

"One more kiss, Jaimy, oh please . . ."

"Oh, God, how I wanted to—"

"I know, Jaimy, me, too! But now you must go."

I realize that I do not present an elegant picture, my pants now being around my ankles, yet oh, how I wish this moment could last!

But, alas, it cannot. Duty calls. He bows and says, "And you must tend to your own ship, I know that. Farewell, Jacky, we will come together again when this is over."

"God speed thee, love, and keep thee safe."

"One more . . ."

Oh, yes!

Then he is gone.

Deep breath, girl, and then collect yourself. All right . . . Done.

"Ravi! My Powder Monkey gear! Now!"

It is the simple light canvas pants and shirt with which I had outfitted my squad of convict girls on the *Lee* on those occasions when the ship ran into trouble and we needed powder brought up fast to the guns. One can move about real easy in that sort of gear, and that's what I need right now if I am to face this. So clad, with my shiv in its sheath up my sleeve, I run hatless and barefoot back up on deck.

"Mr. Lightner!" I shout to my Sailing Master. "Send all hands aloft to shorten sail!" And the sound of running feet pounds all around me.

Enoch has his drum and he pounds it to summon any laggards below. "All hands aloft to shorten sail!" he roars. "Take in all mains, topsails, and royals! Leave the fore jib and reef the spanker. Secure all deck gear!"

"Aye. That should give us bare steerageway, enough to keep her head into the weather," I say, coming up next to him. "We'll see how she holds. Well done, Enoch."

He nods, his hand on the forestay. He may be blind, but he can sense the oncoming weather and he can feel the sinews of the *Lorelei Lee* in the quivering of her lines.

We are joined by my First Mate, Mr. Seabrook, and my Second, Mr. Gibson, both very competent officers and both East India merchantmen. They were onboard when the *Lee* embarked from London as a convict ship, and I have kept them on to continue the running of it now. Mr. Hinckley, formerly Fourth Mate of the prison ship, elected to stay in Botany Bay to await another berth on a proper ship. He felt his naval career might be hampered by his having served on my *Lorelei Lee,* which often has cracked out the piratical skull and crossbones flag. Perhaps he is wise. We shall see.

We all watch the approaching storm with varying degrees of dread.

"I went through a typhoon back in ninety-nine," says Mr. Seabrook ominously. "When I was Fourth Mate on the *Carthage,* coming back from Singapore."

We all look to him to continue.

"Myself and three Filipina women were the only survivors," he says.

"Mr. Gibson, will you see that all the hatches are battened down securely?"

"Aye, Captain," says Mr. Gibson, hurrying off to his duty.

I look up at our now mostly bare poles. Only a few scraps of canvas are up forward, and the spanker over our heads back here on the quarterdeck is well reefed up. Those few sails, however, are not full, nor do they even flutter; we are dead calmed, and we wait in apprehensive silence for the storm to hit.

O Neptune, what have you in store for us poor souls?

"Try to hold her on course 020 degrees," I say to the helmsman, a man I know to be very good at his job.

"Aye, Captain," he says. "Soon as I get some wind."

Oh, you'll get wind, mate, just you wait.

We *all* wait . . . and wait . . .

I lift my long glass and note that the *Cerberus* and the *Dart* have each taken similar precautions in shortening sail and making ready for the blow. Both Jaimy and Jared are on their respective quarterdecks, and I know that they, too, wait.

The storm is high overhead now, with black clouds writhing and twisting about like the arms of demons from hell. All nonessential personnel have been ordered below, and still the watch above waits.

And then it comes. It starts with a quick puff of hot, wet air—enough to fill out our meager sails and give the helm some steerageway. The wind turns into a high unearthly whine, and as the storm slams into us for real, the *Lorelei Lee* heels hard over on her port side.

"I can't hold her, Sir!" screams the helmsman, clinging to his wheel.

"Bo'sun!" I yell at Tim Connell. "Two men to the helm!"

The wind has gone from dead stillness to over a hundred knots in a matter of seconds, clawing at every line, at every scrap of canvas, at every man on deck. Everything not securely tied down disappears instantly into the blackness. Torrents of rain come slashing at us, stinging and blinding us as we hang on for dear life. From out of the belly of the storm, enormous waves have suddenly built into towering mountains of black water. The *Lee* plunges and twists like a wild thing, but the three strong men now on the wheel manage to keep it from spinning . . . but not for long.

"The spanker!" shouts Enoch Lightner over the howl of the wind. "It's too much! We've got to get it down!"

"Drop the spanker, Bo'sun!" I order, clinging to the mizzenmast ratlines and pointing up to the sail overhead. "Get your top men up there! Get it down!"

But it is too late.

I was sure that the wind couldn't get any worse, but I was wrong. With the screech of a demented banshee, the storm doubles its fury and heels us over even further and then . . . *Horror!*

Close to starboard looms a wave that dwarfs all the others. It is at least fifty feet from deep bottom to wind-torn top. It rolls inexorably on and the *Lee* slides helplessly into the trough, yawing suddenly to her right, and then, as the body of the wave lifts us and passes on, way, *way* over to her other side. There she wallows, dangerously close to capsize and destruction.

The spanker hits the water and the belly of the sail fills with water, and as the *Lee* slowly rights herself, the added weight of the water is too much for the mizzenmast. With a sickening, splintering *crrraaack,* the mast splits and comes crashing down into the water on the port side.

"I've lost steerage!" cries the helmsman.

"It'll drag us down!" I screech. "Axes! Cut it away!"

The mizzen ratlines to which I had been clinging now lay flat across the deck, along with all the rest of the lines that had held up the now fallen aftermast.

Hand over hand I manage to get to the rack of axes

fixed to the side of the main hatch and pull one out. Other hands are at my side doing the same thing, and within moments, we are hacking away at the tangled mess.

No thinking, just cut, girl. Just swing and cut and swing and cut, else we are lost.

Neptune grants us a slight reprieve from the full intensity of the storm. *Must be getting close to the eye,* I'm thinkin', recalling hurricanes I had gone through in the Caribbean. *Maybe we'll be all right, maybe . . .*

Although my arm is aching, I swing my ax at one more line and that proves to be the last one holding the lost mast. The rigging, dragged by the drowned sail, begins to slide across the deck. When it falls into the sea, we will be able to regain some sort of steerage and so save ourselves. At least for the moment.

I put my fist into the small of my aching back and straighten up, then rub the rainwater from my eyes and gratefully watch the rigging go snaking over the side. *Now, we'll—*

At that moment, the galley hatchway opens and I see Ravi coming out, bearing cups of steaming coffee meant, no doubt, for me and the quarterdeck watch.

"No, Ravi!" I scream, but it is too late. Already he is on top of the squirming mass of lines, picking his way toward me. He slips and falls, his burden of coffee spilling out of the cups he still clutches in his hands.

Of course he cannot hear me above the roar of the wind, so I run to him and grab him by the scruff of his neck. "Get back below, you idiot!" and I thrust him toward the hatch.

Then I turn and begin picking my own way back to the quarterdeck. *Stupid kid, I'm gonna make his brown bottom turn red, I will, I'll . . .*

But I ain't gonna do that at all.

A large turnbuckle sliding off with the rest of the wreckage catches me at my ankle and I fall forward. Trying desperately to get up and flee to safety, my foot slips into a loop of line, which tightens around my leg, and I am pulled relentlessly to the edge. I try to untangle my leg but, *I can't, I can't.* It's just too tight, and there's the rail shattered by the fall of the mast, and I see Seabrook and Gibson rushing toward me but it's no good. I know it's no good. *Oh God, I'm gonna go over . . . I'm gonna die.*

And then arms are about me. But they are not the strong arms of any of my bully boys, no. They are the thin arms of tiny Ravi, who wails, *"Memsahib! Memsahib!"* as we are both dragged off the deck of the *Lorelei Lee* and plunged under the warm and, to us, suddenly very quiet waters of the South China Sea.

Chapter 3

James Emerson Fletcher
Captain, Cerberus
Off the Coast of Sumatra
In Company with Lorelei Lee
and HMS Dart
December 16, 1807

Jacky Faber
Lost to this World

Dear Jacky,

We held the funeral for you today. I assure you it was a most solemn, tearful crowd that stood at the rail of the *Lorelei Lee* as the words were said, commending your body to the sea and all that. Of course, your poor body was already drowned in the sea and there was no way to retrieve it— neither it nor the wonderful spirit that once dwelt therein— but Higgins had contrived a wreath of twined ropes, some strands white, some light brown, representing the tendrils of your hair, which seemed to suit the sad occasion.

We did look for you, Jacky, yes, for days on end we did, but could find no trace, and, eventually, we had to give up the search. Perhaps some landsman found your poor body and performed the terms of the Sailor's Contract—trading the golden ring in your ear for a proper burial on land. I do hope so, small comfort though it might bring to me in my grief and sorrow.

I do not have much to live for, Jacky, now that you are gone, but I know that I must keep on in this life—at least for a while. I will settle with Flashby and Bliffil, those two black-guards who sent you on this journey and whom I hold com-pletely and personally responsible for your death. Yes, my lust for revenge shall burn hot in my now cold heart and keep me alive till the day of reckoning.

The wind is fair, and I have responsibilities to both my people and yours, so I cannot let myself slip into the beck-oning depths of fatal melancholy into which I could easily slide, nor give ear to the sad songs of sirens into whose arms I could easily find solace.

I hope having your little fellow at your side as you went down lent you both some comfort. Yes, I have heard that we lost you in your vain attempt to save the boy. And yes, it was both reckless and noble of you to do so, but I do not in any way consider it a fair trade. I am sorry you lost your little lad, as I know you had great affection for him. I only wish now that some of that love could have been showered upon our own sons and daughters.

Enoch Lightner sang "O God, Our Help in Ages Past," and you may rest assured there was not a dry eye on any of the ships gathered in a rough circle for the sad event.

Were you watching and perhaps singing gleefully along?

I certainly hope so, but my faith in anything has become so strained. Perhaps you live on in another world . . . or perhaps the spark that was you was simply extinguished and that's all there is to it . . . I do not know, and might not ever know. None of us will . . . at least for now.

Your dear friend Mairead was, of course, devastated, as we all were, but she is bearing up—after all, she has responsibilities, too, being with child once again. Higgins, as well, soldiers on.

We will go to Bombay to resupply and refit the *Lorelei Lee*—it is the only British-controlled port in this area that can replace the mizzenmast of the *Lee* and effect the other repairs needed by our fleet. None came through unscathed by that terrible storm.

Rest in peace, Jacky. You will live forever in my heart, and in every corner of my mind,

Jaimy

Chapter 4

The sun is hot on my back as I awaken, my senses slowly returning to me. Something is wrong, and I realize that my face is pressed into . . . what? Sand? Yes . . . I lie on a beach, with my mouth full of grit. I open my eyes, blink several times, and then, groaning, force myself to my hands and knees. As I am half-buried in the sand, it comes to me that the tide must have ebbed and then come back in during the time I have lain here. Although I am groggy from the heat of the sun, and from my exertions the previous day and night, I am dimly able to sense that a certain East Indian boy kneels by my side. A certain very foolish East Indian boy . . .

"Is Memsahib all right?" he asks, fearful.

I gag and spit, trying, unsuccessfully, to clear my mouth of the grit.

"No?" he persists.

I find my voice.

"All right?" I choke. "All *right?* No, I'm not *all right.* I am definitely *not* all right, you little worm. Because of you, I am stuck here on some godforsaken beach, and all of my friends are quite sure that I am dead and rolling about on the bottom of the sea. Of course, I am *perfectly* all right with that. Why should I not be, you miserable little . . ."

The little fellow's big dark eyes well up with tears.

"Ravi is sorry and he will go now and bother Memsahib no more." He whimpers, turning away in sorrow.

"Oh, you'll go all right! By all your heathen gods, you'll trot your little brown ass down the beach *that* way." I point south, for we have landed in a shallow cove and cannot see very far along the shore. "And then you'll come back and report to me what's there on the other side of that outcropping." I struggle to my feet and aim a halfhearted kick at his retreating backside. "*That's* where you'll go!"

As I watch him run off, intent on his mission, I sink back down and sit with my head between my knees as I wail out my misery.

Damn, damn, damn, son of a bitch, damn! Oh, Lord, I don' wanna be here, cast away yet again! I want my ship. I want my friends . . . sniff . . . I jus' wanna . . . wanna go back to Boston! I just wanna go back to Amy and Randall and to the Pig and the Lawson Peabody and I'll never leave. No, I never, ever will. I swear it . . . sniff. If Jaimy finds out I'm still alive and he still wants me, he can come to Boston to get me, 'cause I ain't goin' to London ever again, no I ain't . . . sniff . . . But I know he won't be comin' for me, oh no, 'cause he's gotta think me dead, 'cause who could survive a storm like that, cast away on the roaring sea? Nobody, that's who. He'd be crazy to think otherwise . . . sniff . . . and though I know he'll be sad and melancholy for a while—poor Jaimy—I know, too, that he'll soon lift his head and cast his gaze about for someone to ease his pain. I know that for sure because I would do the same thing. Grief over a lost love is intense, but it only lasts so long. I wish you well, Jaimy, I really do. People always say in a case like this that life goes on . . . and it does . . . for those who are living . . . sniff. No matter what happens to you in the way of loss and grief, you still get hungry, and right now, I'm getting hungry . . . and thirsty . . . and damn, damn, son of a bitch, damn!

Yesterday, in the midst of the great typhoon, when Ravi and I both went over the side of the *Lorelei Lee* and into the angry, roiling sea, I managed to fall clear of the sinking tangle of rigging that had dragged us over the side. I bobbed up on the crest of a towering wave, and I had just enough light in the murkiness to see Ravi's head break the surface next to me. I lunged out and grasped him to me.

"Ahoy! Lads!" I had screamed into the howling storm. "I'm here! Here, lads! Help us!"

But the last sight I had of the *Lorelei Lee* was her broad stern yawing away from us, and all I got for that vain cry in the maelstrom was a choking mouthful of seawater. Another monster wave heaved up and the *Lee*—my ship, my love, and my last hope—was gone.

I sputtered and kicked and tried to stay up, but . . . *I can't, I can't . . .*

All right, Lord, take me, I prayed as I sank down into the water with Ravi wrapped around me. *I have had enough. I commend my body to the sea and my soul to thee . . .*

But then, just as I was about to suck in my final, fatal gulp of the salt, my foot struck something rough, something moving, something that felt . . . alive?

A shark? A whale . . . ? Oh, please, Lord, not that! Please let me be swallowed by your mighty sea and not by one of your fearsome beasts. Please, no!

But it was not a hungry, toothy mouth that brushed my leg, no. It was the rough rake of thick canvas and hard wood that propeled me and my young boy back to the surface. It was the once damned and now blessed mizzenmast. The spanker sail had trapped just enough air in its soggy billow to float and lift the entangled mast back up to the surface. The top of the mast thrust into the air and then fell to the side, the ballooning spanker hissing wetly next to it.

"Ravi!" I cried, gasping in the sweet air. "Here! Get up on the mast! Straddle it now!"

I grabbed the half-drowned boy by his loincloth to hoist him up, and then I clambered aboard myself, wrapping my legs around the wildly plunging mast and hanging on for dear life itself.

The raging sea continued to fling us about all night long, till I lost all sense of time and space. All I knew to do was to hang on and that is what I did. I dimly sensed that Ravi was doing the same, but I could no longer care. My rational mind, which had long since fled, would have known that the wood of this mast, though seasoned, would soon become water-logged and, feeling the pull of the iron rigging, would slowly sink, taking Ravi and me with it. But, trailing the rigging below it like the tentacles of a gigantic jellyfish, the mast stayed mercifully afloat, helped by what air was still trapped in the sail. It floated long enough, thanks be to God, till bright morning found us aground on this desolate beach.

I had stumbled off the mast and crawled up the beach,

and then, exhausted, flung myself face-down on the lovely warm sand and let blessed sleep take me away.

I rouse myself as Ravi comes pounding back up the beach to report on his scouting trip.

"Nothing there, Memsahib," he pants. "Only more beach and jungle." He glances, I think a bit uneasily, to the thick wall of forest that lies dark and somewhat foreboding off to our right. "What will we do, Memsahib?"

"Do?" I sigh, getting to my feet once again. "What we are going to do is march north till I find some sort of civilization in this godforsaken-heathen part of the world, and then we are going to make our way across goddamned Asia and goddamned Africa and the goddamned Atlantic Ocean and back to Boston, and *I swear* I will *never, ever* leave that part of the world, not for blood nor money!"

"I am sorry for getting dear Memsahib in pickle," he murmurs, head down.

Then, with a heavy sigh, I let all the resentment flow out of me. I am still alive, sucking air, and so is my dear little Ravi.

I relent and reach out to ruffle his hair. "Come on, you little heathen, let us get on with things. I'm sorry I yelled at you. Now let's get on with it."

My shirt is full of itchy sand and my pants are full of . . . what . . . ? Sand fleas? *Yuck!* I pull both off and wade into the water to rinse both myself and my meager garments free of the grit and the bugs.

"Tsk!" says Ravi. "Such immodesties."

"I should think you'd be used to my ways by now," I

retort, sinking beneath the now gentle surf and scrubbing off the sand. "I suspect you've probably got sand in your drawers, too, so get in here and rinse off."

"I have already cleansed myself in the holy waters of Mother Ocean."

"Well, good, as we've got some walking to do."

As I have done in similar circumstances in the past, I take an inventory of what I have and what I do not have.

What I have:

Self, body battered and bruised but still whole, and grateful for that;

Loose white shirt and cotton duck trousers, all warming and drying under the sun;

One fallen foremast from *Lorelei Lee*—useless now, but which did serve admirably as a raft;

Much tangled rope—possibly useful;

Large sodden sheet of canvas sail—also useful;

One sharp knife—my shiv, as it were, the one I had taken from Rooster Charlie on the day he died and which has been at my side ever since.

And . . . one very tiny Indian boy.

What I do not have:

I do not have hat, shoes, food, nor money. No, I did not wear my money belt when I was on the *Lee*. Why should I, as I was among friends? *Why not, indeed,* I think ruefully. No shoes is no problem, but no hat? How I shall hide my hair, I don't know, for I am sure to be the sole bearer of sandy blond locks within a radius of a thousand miles or more.

Further thought is required . . .

. . .

"All right, lad," I say, drawing out my shiv. "Let's do this." I wade up to the sail that lies quiet in the surf and begin a long cut in the fabric close to the spar to which it is attached.

"What is Memsahib doing?" asks Ravi.

"Well, I am going to cut out a piece about six foot by eight. With the rope that I'm also going to cut off, we'll make a tent to shelter us when we go to sleep at night back there in the woods."

He looks dubious at this but says nothing.

"And then I shall cut some smaller strips as I must fashion some sort of cap to hide my hair."

"Missy not have much hair, at least not on head . . ."

"Right. And what I do have is the wrong color, and I won't want to stand out."

"Ummm . . ."

I cut off some lengths of line and coil them into a loop. I also shear off some more canvas to use as blankets or ground covers, plus a bit more to use for whatever. I also sever a medium-sized iron turnbuckle and add it to our pile—it could come in handy should we need a club. When we leave here, we will not be able to come back and salvage any more from the mizzenmast.

This being done, I spread all out on the beach to dry. After an hour or so, I pull on my salty-stiff pants and shirt and roll up the canvas.

Using the rope, I fashion two backpacks and make us ready to go.

"All right, let us head north and see what awaits us there."

"Uh . . . Missy Memsahib," says Ravi, as I adjust the pack on his back.

"Yes?"

"We will sleep in jungle?"

"Yes. Why not? Where else?"

"Ummm . . . is all right . . . if Missy have good karma."

"Why would I need that?"

He looks again at the wall of jungle. "For there do tigers live."

Tigers?

Chapter 5

"Come on, Ravi, how can tigers be such a danger? Here? How can they sneak up on us? This is 1807, after all. Modern times."

We have been walking northward along the shore. There have been no signs of habitation as yet.

"Tiger do not know that, Memsahib. Many, many poor people in my country are eaten by tigers every year. Much horribles."

"Hmmm. Can these beasts swim?" I ask, looking toward the ocean. "Would a tiger chase you into the water? Cats don't usually like to get wet, you know."

"Little kitties, yes, but big tigers not seem to mind," says Ravi. "Many stories of them swimming in rivers to capture luckless peoples."

"Do you think one of them would chase us into the ocean?"

"Depends on how hungry tiger is. They very often hungry."

Hmmm . . . I can appreciate that, being rather hungry myself . . . and thirsty, which is much more worrying. We can live a long time without food, but not without fresh water—three days tops, if that.

We come to a large open flat area of beach, and I am gratified to see beneath my feet little round holes marking the presence of some lovely clams.

"Let us stop and refresh ourselves. Drop your pack and start digging here. Use your hands, as the mud is quite soft."

"Dig for what, Memsahib?"

"Clams. Something to eat. You'll see. Just follow those holes down and you'll find clams at the bottom. Roundish things, city boy, like rocks, but different. You'll see. Pile 'em up, and I'll be right back to open 'em and we shall eat . . . and, hopefully, drink."

The lad looks rather dubious, but he kneels down and bends to his task, clawing away at the muddy sand. I, on the other hand, shed my pack and head for the edge of the jungle, where I have spied a few palm trees bearing heavy bunches of coconuts and, possibly, a source of fresh water for us.

The trees are very long and very high, with no low branches on which to climb, so I whip out my shiv and cut about a six-foot length of line from my copious coils of rope and knot the ends together to form a loop around the base of the palm. Placing myself in the loop, I begin to walk up the slope of the tree, feet on trunk, and rope around my waist— two steps with my bare feet clutching the rough bark, and then move the rope up a few inches, settle back, and then do it again, inch by inch, till I reach the cluster of nuts at the top. When there, I take a moment to look out over the sea.

Stop that, girl. Ain't no one comin' to look for you this time.

Shaking such idle thoughts out of my head, I take my shiv and begin cutting the nuts off their very tough stems.

One falls, then another. There are lizards all over the place up here, but they seem harmless. Hope so, anyway. When six nuts have hit the ground, I go back down.

Ravi stands there.

"Missy Memsahib is very good at many things," he says, looking at the fallen nuts.

"Well, I have been around," I say by way of explanation as I hit the ground. "Here, let's see how you've done at the clamming."

He has been doing quite well, it seems. A pile of the creatures is heaped upon the sand, squirting out their juices in their clammy way.

"Here, Ravi, sit, and let us eat." I sink down and sit cross-legged and reach for the big clam that lies on top of the pile.

I slip the blade of my shiv into the shell and pull it around the edge, making the resident therein give up the fight, as well as the ghost, I suppose. I scrape along the bottom, and then the top of the shell, and lift up the whole thing to let its contents slide into my open mouth.

Ravi looks on aghast.

I chew lightly on the clam, but hard enough to rip open its fat belly and taste the sea, and then let it slip down my throat. Not bad—not as good as the oysters we used to get back in Boston, but, hey—not bad at all.

I open up the next clam.

"Here, Ravi. Your turn."

He blanches and his dusky face turns several shades paler than usual. He gulps, then says, "Eating living thing, Missy, not good."

"They are not living, you little fool, not since I cut them open."

He is not convinced.

"That unfortunate creature there is wiggling," he says, pointing at a still-moving part of the clam I hold out to him.

"There," I say, stabbing at the throbbing part with the point of my shiv till it stops its quivering. "Satisfied? Now eat it. You cannot be of use to me if you are half-starved. So do your duty. Remember, I am the President of Faber Shipping Worldwide and you are but a mere lowly employee, Seaman No-class Ravi."

"I am not a slave? I thought I was slave to you."

"No, you are not. I am completely against slavery in all its forms. However, I am ordering you to eat that clam, because I am bigger than you."

"As you wish, Memsahib. Ravi will risk his karma for you," he mumbles, tipping the clam shell up and his head back in imitation of me. He manages to get the clam down his throat without gagging.

"Um. Not too bad, Missy. Very slimy. Very salty."

"Yes, I know. We shall have some sweet water next, but here, have another."

He gets another one down and says, "Maybe now Ravi will come back as tiny clam in next life for eating of these poor creatures."

"Well, I am sure you would come back as a very pretty little clam, Ravi—lovely blue stripes on your shell and all. There are worse things, you know—you could come back as a British seaman."

He nods and we continue eating. Soon there is a pile of glistening empty shells. There are, however, a good number of uneaten clams, and those I wrap up in a small square of canvas for later eating, should we not find more on our trek north. I put a bit of soggy seaweed in with them and soak the whole thing down with seawater; they should keep. I shove them into Ravi's pack.

Then I turn to the coconuts. I sit down and take one of the green nuts into my lap. With my shiv, I begin hacking away at the husk at the top of the nut. It takes a while, but soon enough I've exposed one of the eyes of the hard inner shell. I poke in that soft eye with the point of my shiv and then lift the coconut up over Ravi's wondering head.

"Open up," I order. He does as I tip the nut and a stream of coconut milk comes pouring out of the punctured eye and into his open mouth.

He swallows and then gulps again. Doesn't take the picky little heathen long to appreciate *that* fine draft.

"Oh, Missy, that is so good!" he says, as the milk goes down his throat and the excess spills over his cheeks.

I then direct the stream into my own mouth.

Ummmm . . . yes, that is so, so good.

After we have gorged on the milk of three coconuts, we sling our packs onto our backs and continue our trek north. We could've set up a permanent camp back where we washed ashore, but ain't nobody gonna be comin' to look for us. In the eyes of those onboard my fleet, we are surely dead, so we must push north and trek onward. Which is what we do.

As we walk, a tune comes to my head, "The Rocky Road to Dublin," and I sing it out.

In the merry month of June from me home I started,
Left the girls of Kerry so sad and brokenhearted,
Saluted father dear, kissed me darling mother,
Drank a pint of beer, me grief and tears to smother,

Then off to reap the corn, leave where I was born,
And fright'ning all the dogs . . .
On the rocky road to Dublin!

One, two, three, four, five,
Hunt the hare and turn her
Down the rocky road
And all the ways to Dublin,
Whack-fol-lol-de-rah!

"Is nice song, Memsahib," says Ravi. "Though I do not understand meaning."

Thus encouraged, I continue.

In Donegal that night I rested limbs so weary,
Started by daylight next morning light and early.
Took a drop of the pure, to keep me heart from sinking,
That's an Irishman's cure
Whenever he's on to drinkin'.

One, two, three, four, five,
Hunt the hare and turn her
Down the rocky road
And all the ways to Dublin,
Whack-fol-lol-de-rah.

There is something about that tune that seems to fit in this foreign land. I don't know why, but it does. Sure wish I had my pennywhistle to try it out. We shall see . . . Maybe I'll find one out here, who knows.

I finish the last verse and feel Ravi bumping up next to me, so I put my arm on his shoulder.

"Are you happy, Ravi?" I ask.

"Yes, Missy. I am walking next to Missy Memsahib and she sings nice song. My belly is full of awful clam, but my tummy is silent. My karma is good. Yes. Sun shines and Ravi is happy at this moment."

"You have a good outlook on life, my lad," I say, smiling down upon him. "Others could learn from your example."

I hold my face up to the sun and think on this.

Yes . . . others like . . . Amy Trevelyne, my dear friend and most melancholy of girls. Yes, you shall soon hear of my demise. Will you be able to look upon the shining of the sun and other delightful things of this world, or will you fall fatally into gloom? Oh, I hope not, for I am not worthy of your grief, but I despair of that. Maybe the news will be long in coming to you. Maybe Ezra Pickering will be there to help you. I hope so . . .

"Look, Memsahib," says Ravi, pointing. We have just rounded yet another point and can see far along the shore to the north. "There is village up there!"

Sure enough, way off in the mist we can see some huts and boats pulled up on the beach.

I look at the sun, which is quickly setting, and say, "Right, Ravi, we shall go there tomorrow. Tonight we shall sleep here. Let us pitch camp. Right back there in the woods. There seems to be a bit of a clearing."

I stride in and pull my pack from my back. I open it and take out the large square of canvas and spread it out.

"What means Memsahib to do?" asks Ravi, his eyes a bit wide and looking fearfully about.

"Why, I'm going to set up our tent right here," I reply. "See, I'll string this rope from this tree to that tree, throw the canvas over it, and then cut some wooden stakes to hold down the corners. We will sleep very snug underneath it, and then tomorrow, we will go to that town to see what we shall see."

"Uh . . . would Memsahib mind too much if Ravi leave her side and sleep up in tree tonight?"

"Why, whatever for?"

Just then, from deep in the darkening jungle, comes this low rumble of a roar, which sends shivers up my spine, and I am suddenly a very small and frightened woodland creature.

"That is why, Missy," says Ravi, beginning to climb.

I am right behind him.

When we get to a good strong crotch in the tree, I look back down but see nothing.

"Can they climb trees?" I ask, my voice shaking. There was something in that growl that transported me from my modern state and shoved me cowering back to prehistoric times and into some dank, dark cave.

"Not far up," says Ravi. "They are too big. But they might try."

I take the canvas that would have been my tent, tie knots into each end, and attach ropes to them. Then I fasten those lines to strong branches and secure them as best I can, making a crude hammock.

"Get in here with me, Ravi, and let us hope for the best," I say, slipping into the fold of canvas.

He crawls in beside me and I hold him to me.

RRRRRROOOOWLLLLLLL.

The beast is right below us, circling about the base of the tree. Another low roar and the tree shakes and we know the tiger is trying the tree.

Ravi's arms tighten around me, and mine around him.

Oh, how I hope my knots are tight and strong and we live through this night!

Chapter 6

As dawn's feeble light comes creeping into the jungle, I peer cautiously over the edge of our hammock and gaze at the trampled grass below. I can see that the trunk of the tree is all scratched, with most of its bark gone up to a height of about ten feet. There are deep gouges in the soft wood, marks of the tiger's claws. I give out with yet another shudder. *Good Lord . . .*

I feel Ravi wriggling and his head pops up beside mine.

"I think it's gone," I whisper.

"That is to be hoped, Missy," says Ravi, looking dubious. "Tigers do come out only at night. Usually."

I give him a look. "Usually?"

He shrugs.

"Well, we can't stay up here forever," I say. "Let us break camp and be on our way."

I struggle out of the hammock and onto the tree limb. Untying the rope knots is easy, them being the sailor's friend, the bowline, a knot that never fails to untie no matter how much pressure has been put on it. If you can't tie a bowline, whether in calm or in a howling gale, then you ain't a sailor.

Getting the knots out of the canvas fabric proved a bit more difficult, but we got it done and our knapsacks repacked and back on our shoulders.

"All right, let's go," I say, beginning to climb down.

In a moment, my feet are on the ground. Ravi drops down lightly beside me.

"To the beach, Ravi, me lad," I say, clapping him on the back. "We survived the night and are not in the tummy of the tiger and—"

We both freeze at the sound of something big—something very big—rustling in the bushes behind us.

"Run!" I scream. "To the water! Run!"

Ravi needs no such encouragement. He is off like a little brown streak and I am not far behind him.

GRRRRROOOWWWWLLLLLL!

Oh, God, it's right behind me! Please, Lord, let me make it to the water.

Make it to the water we do, looking for all the world like a pair of frightened waterfowl, but it doesn't seem like it'll do us a whole lot of good, as I can hear the beast splashing into the surf right behind us.

"Get farther out!" I yell to Ravi. "Maybe he'll go back if he has to swim!"

I'm up to my chest now and pulling for the open sea. Ravi is well ahead of me. The tiger will have to swim now or else give it up. *Please, God, make him go away!*

But swim he does and give it up he does not.

I look back at him and my knees turn to jelly and my insides turn to water. His whiskered orange and black face with its big white muzzle must be two feet across!

"Nice kitty!" I shout, desperate. "Shoo! Go away!"

Swimming, he cannot bring his claws to bear, which is good, but his jaws full of teeth will get the job done just as well.

"Bad kitty! Bad kitty!"

In spite of my total terror, I manage to pull out my shiv and hold it quivering in front of me. The beast opens his mouth and I can see his pink tongue and huge yellow teeth, his bright and glistening eyes. His paw brushes my leg. In a moment he will have me and I will be lost! *Oh, Lord, he is so big! And he is on me!*

Powered by both fear and desperation, I plunge my puny little shiv into his big black nose.

GRRROOOOOWWWLLLL?

Not used to having his prey fight back, the tiger brings up his right paw to swipe at his now bleeding nose, which causes his head to sink beneath the waves for a second. It ain't much in the way of a counterattack, but it is enough for him to taste the salt and maybe think about something else for his dinner. He retreats and swims back to the shore, roaring out his displeasure. There he gives himself a mighty shake, to free his striped fur of the salt water, and then he shambles off into the forest, grumbling to himself, it seems to me. *Serves the bugger right,* I say to myself, shivering in spite of the warmness of the water. There have been many in my life who have chased me for various reasons, but this is one of the few times my pursuer actually wanted to *eat* me. 'Course there were those sharks in the Atlantic when the *Bloodhound* was going down . . . and that pack of gators on Key West, but still . . . The idea of parts of my dear body being ripped from my frame and chewed and swallowed by some ravenous beast is not a thought that sits easy on my mind. No, it is not.

"Ravi," I say, panting, my mind still in tatters. "Get up on my back and we shall wade up the shore till we are far away from here." He does it, and keeping out to my neck level makes it easy for me to bear his light weight as we slog our way north.

"Must be old tiger, Memsahib," says Ravi from his perch. "Else we now be with Brahma, enjoying eternal bliss."

I just grunt and slog on. *Eternal bliss, indeed . . . I'd settle for some temporary bliss.*

We emerge from the water still some distance from the village. It has been agreed that Ravi will venture into the town to find out what he can about the local lingo, the lay of the land, just exactly where we are, and our prospects, if any, for making some money. Meanwhile, I will hang back and hide, for I fear my appearance would seem rather bizarre to the local populace—blond hair, half-bald, with braided pigtail, to say nothing of my light skin.

As his white-clad bottom is scurrying off in the direction of the village, I climb a large, smooth-skinned tree, seat myself in a comfortable crotch, and settle back against the trunk to watch what is happening in the town.

Ravi has told me that he can speak Urdu and Hindi as well as English—sort of—having been taught my mother tongue by his late mother's employer, an Englishman known to Ravi simply as Sahib Elphy. The once wealthy man had a large household of Indian servants in Bombay, but when he had fallen on hard times, Ravi was kicked out into the mean streets. I certainly can relate to that, having been booted out into the equally tough streets of London as a young child, after the deaths of my mother, father, and younger sister. It still hurts me to think back on That Dark Day, and I am sure Ravi has similar feelings about his own loss. *Ah, well . . .*

The fishing boats that we had spotted pulled up on this shore earlier are now all gone. I guess the fishermen are out on the briny to cast their nets and tend their lines and earn their daily bread, as it were.

I settle in, feeling lazy in the sun, and snooze a bit, not having had much rest last night due to the presence of various striped beasts. I drift in and out . . . as I dream . . .

. . . and I dream that I am back in London and there I am at Saint Paul's. And once again I am small and dressed in rags and there is a great sounding of bells and trumpets, and white doves fly about as a grand wedding procession comes pouring out of the great cathedral. And there's Jaimy—oh Jaimy, yes!— at the head of it. And there's flowers all around and on his arm is his new bride and she is blond and I see her face and it glows with happiness . . . But . . . but she is not me . . . It is Clementine Jukes's face that I see, and I start to cry and tears run down my face and Rooster Charlie is suddenly at my side. He puts his hand on my shoulder and says, "Let him go, Mary, you've got to let him go . . . because you know you are dead now . . . to him you are dead and gone. Me and you now, Mary, just me and you here in the shadow land, me and you . . ." Then Clementine's face turns toward me and she smiles as she says, "I've got my darlin' boy now just like God sent him to me, and you cain't take him back, Jacky, no you cain't." And then her face turns away and when she looks at me again, her face is now that of Clarissa Worthington Howe, who winks and gives me a little finger wave and says, "Ah do believe we are even now, Jacky, you dear little thang: Jaimy for Randall,

Randall for Jaimy, fair trade, I say . . ." And I scream, "No, no, no! Not Clarissa! No, no, not that! Anybody but Clarissa! No, no, noooooooo . . ."

"Memsahib having bad dream?"

I pop open an eye and Clarissa and Jaimy and the crowd at Saint Paul's fade away into the mists of my mind as I see Ravi standing beside me, his toes hooked on a branch, looking concerned.

"I have had better dreams, boy," I say, shaking the nightmare out of my head and sitting up all groggy. "What's going on in that town? What did you learn?"

"We are in Burma, Missy. Bottom part. Big cities up north but many rivers for us to cross to get there. They do not know names. They are very simple people. One city that they do know is called Rangoon."

"Um. You could speak to them? And they understood you?"

"Mostly yes, Memsahib. Urdu works in many places."

When we were back in Bombay, Higgins had done some research, as he always does when I'm off being an irresponsible gadabout, and he informed me later that Urdu was actually a combination of Hindi and other local dialects, including some English, cobbled together by the many traders who plied the Bay of Bengal, which is what that water out there is. And so Urdu was in use in several countries that bordered the Bay, this Burma apparently being one of them, which is all that counts now.

"Who talked to you?"

"Beggar children. They were much amazed by me and most friendly."

Ah, the universal tribe of Urchindom, of which I am proud to be a charter member in good standing.

"What else?" I ask, stretching and looking out through the leafy branches of my tree. I see that the fishing fleet is returning to shore. *Hmmm . . .* Nice looking boats, all brightly painted with neatly trimmed triangular sails. If they were on the north coast of Africa, they would be called dhows. What they are called here, I do not know, but that is not important. All that is important is that they are seaworthy, and they look to be that.

"Village is all fisher folk," he goes on. "And there is much unhappiness."

"Why's that?"

The men of the boats have pulled their nets out and are drying them on racks set up by the shore. One man—a very large man with a huge black mustache—is yelling at them as they do it. Another man is gathering up the catches from all the boats and placing them at the feet of the yelling man. The backs of the other fishermen are bowed, and I am close enough to see that their faces are resigned and without expression.

"Much sadness. Three peoples of village killed by tigers in past few days. One child . . ."

I look over at the woods and know I ain't goin' there no more. So sad for those poor people . . . I know their end must have been terrible.

I see that the men have not pulled their boats far up on the beach. *Hmmm . . .* The tide must be going out, and they do not want to strand their boats too high up on the shore. The boats, though small, would still be a hard push to get them back into the surf when next they have to go out.

"And trouble of other kind, too," he says, following my gaze to the crowd of fishermen on the shore. "A *badmash* has come to the town. Big strong man. The old headman died and this one took his place. He beats upon the fishermen and takes half of each man's daily catch. Takes their young sons . . . and daughters, too . . . Much shame in village."

"Hmmm . . . That would be him, then, the *badmash*?" I ask, pointing out through the leaves at the big man. I don't have to ask what the word means.

"Yes, Missy, I think so."

"Does no one in the village stand up to him?"

"No, Missy. He is too big, and he has mighty weapons— great curving swords. He arms his followers with them and the people are afraid."

"Hmmm . . ."

"There is one, though—a young man who was to wed a girl, a beautiful girl, and he was most happy. But the bad-mash find out and say no, *he* would take the girl instead. The young man stood up against him and was beaten most harshly."

"Hmmm . . ." I muse, looking out at the fishermen stow-ing their gear. "Come, let us get closer, but let us not be seen."

We climb down from our perch, sling the packs on our backs, and make our way down the beach toward the landing spot. Before we get there, I push Ravi back into the woods and we duck down and crawl on our bellies to the edge of the brush. Leafy branches low over our heads hide us as we peer out.

That's the badmash, all right. He is free with his kicks and blows from his fists, and a large sword hangs by his side. It is plain that he has his toadies, too. Badmashes of whatever race and place always do. They grin as they carry off their master's stolen catch for sale up in the village. Poor fishermen, forced to buy their own catch with whatever meager goods they've got.

Grrrrrrr . . .

"There, Memsahib," says Ravi, pointing. "That must be the brave young man."

I follow his point and agree. He has a bandage around his head and many bruises on his face and neck and upper body. He stows his nets, his battered face impassive, showing no emotion . . . But I sense something seething within him, yes . . .

The fishermen, having put up their boats, begin to leave, trudging back to their village.

"Ravi," I whisper. "Follow that man and see if you can set up a meeting with me later tonight. Tell him I am from another land and have come to free him and his people from the badmash but will need his help to do it. Be careful, now. You can't be seen by the bad man's toadies."

"Do not worry, Missy. Ravi very good at being small and beneath notice of peoples," he says. "But what if young man is fearful of meeting with Memsahib?"

"Just ask him how much he loves his girl."

Ravi nods, and with a rustle of leaves, heads off on his mission.

I roll over and go back to watching the beach and the men upon it. Many are walking away, leaving only the bully headman and a few of his minions. Soon those toadies are gone as well—probably to go up into the village to spread terror and discord—leaving the badmash alone by his own boat, which is painted a very rich yellow. I reflect that I have always been partial to that color.

The evil man puts his fists to his hips and looks about him, gloating with great satisfaction.

Yes, badmash, you are king of your world, that's for sure— for now, anyway . . .

Chapter 7

We crawl as silently as we can under the bushes near the hut that sits at the edge of the village. Ravi gives a low birdcall in his throat and it is immediately answered by the appearance of a shadowy slender form that beckons us to hastily enter his dwelling.

We do it and are soon inside, unobserved by any evil forces, we hope.

It is a round dwelling with a small fire in the center of the floor and a hole in the ceiling to act as chimney. An older woman, wrapped in once colorful rags, works at a mortar and pestle, grinding grain, of what sort, I do not know, but whatever she is cooking smells awful good. A little girl sits by her side, her big black eyes looking at us in wonder.

I enter with a length of sailcloth wrapped around my head, so as not to startle anyone right off, and sit down next to the fire. Ravi alights by my side, ready to act as translator.

The young man who had guided us in does not sit but merely crouches across from us, his gaze level and directed at me.

I pull off my headscarf and meet his gaze.

"I am Ju kau-jing yi, beloved of the great Cheng Shih," I say, in case the latter name has any import in this area. "Who are you?"

He is plainly startled by my announcement and my appearance but does not seem overly cowed and I find that good.

"My name is Arun," he says with a slight bow of his head.

"I am pleased to meet you, Arun," I say with a bow of my own head. "Thank you for receiving me so graciously into your home."

"What I have is yours," he says, gesturing to the meager contents of the rude hut. He is plainly still guardedly feeling me and my intentions out.

"My thanks, Arun," I say, my head still down. "And what this unworthy one has is yours . . . but you can see that what I have is nothing . . ."

Then I lift my eyes and go on. "But I may still be of some use to you."

"Ah. And how is that, strange girl?"

"I have heard that you were to marry a girl of this village, and that she is young and shy and fair of face and beloved of you and beloved by you in return," I say, cutting right to the chase. "What is her name, if this stranger girl may be so bold to ask?"

His face darkens.

"Her name is Sanda."

"And . . ."

"And the headman Ohnmar will take her for his own."

"When will that happen?"

"The day after tomorrow."

I can see his fists clench and unclench over and over again in the semidarkness of the hut.

"And you will do nothing about it?"

"Do? What should I do?" he asks, his voice a strangled hiss. "I would kill him if I could, but I cannot! He is just too strong! Run away? Yes, Sanda has agreed to run with me into the jungle and hide in the bush and sleep wrapped in each other's arms, but there are tigers there. How could I protect her from them? How could I provide for her in the woods? I am a fisherman, not a woodsman. How could I—"

There is a murmur from the old woman and Arun says, plainly embarrassed, "Pardon me, Ju kau-jing yi. My mother informs me I am without manners and am being rude to a guest and she is right. Please forgive me and eat."

The woman places a single bowl before us and we each dip in our fingertips and scoop out some of the food. I bring it to my mouth and find it simple but good. *Ummm.* A mixture of grain and fish and spices gathered from the forest around us. It would probably be a lot richer if the badmash Ohnmar and his crew weren't taking their cut of the catch.

We eat and I, for one, am grateful for it. At least it's not raw clams.

Cups of coconut milk are set out and we sip it and find it good. Then I get back to business.

"Why have you not rid yourself of this man?"

"Rid the village of him? Ohnmar and his men have weapons! My friends and I have none!" He stands and glares down at me.

Ah, so you do have some friends . . .

"Oh, but I think you do have weapons, Arun. My poor

56

eyes see that you are clean-shaven. That means you at least have knives. Why have you not defended yourselves and your women?"

He looks down, ashamed, and then again he sits.

"Yes. True. We have knives. All fishermen have knives. But little knives are not broadswords. I . . . I tried to fight but . . ."

I reach out and place my hand upon his arm. "I have heard that you were very brave in standing up to Ohnmar. I did not mean to shame you."

He is quiet then, his dark eyes hooded. I observe that he is a very handsome lad, tall and straight, with glossy black hair and deep brown eyes. I suspect that Ravi will look a lot like him when he grows up.

"And you do have other weapons, friend Arun, but maybe you do not consider them such. May I tell you something of a land and the warlike games that are played there?"

He nods, and I begin . . .

"In this land, a faraway place called Roma, there are games held, very barbaric games in a great . . . open space"—I do not think he could grasp the idea of something like the Coliseum— "and men fight each other to the death and they are called gladiators. Some of these gladiators wear suits of armor and bear great broadswords, and some have bows and arrows . . . but some, dear Arun, are armed only with net and trident."

He listens, amazed. "But how can that be? They must be quickly killed!"

I know that Ravi must be having a hell of a time translating all this, but he does seem to be getting the meaning of my words across the language barrier.

"Nay, gentle Arun, they are not—they have as much chance as any other gladiator on that bloody ground."

"But how?"

"Because a well-thrown net can ensnare a sword such that it cannot be swung, and if the bearer of that sword is so entangled that he cannot move, then the simple trident becomes very deadly. You and your friends do have tridents, don't you, for the spearing of fish?"

"Yes," he says, hope beginning to dawn in his eyes.

"And nets . . . small nets?"

"Yes, our small, round cast nets that we fling over schools of fish that swim close to shore."

"The badmash Ohnmar and his men will be close to shore," I say with a level gaze at Arun's dark eyes.

He stands up and says to the little girl, who has been avidly hanging about, "Naing! Go get Nanda, Dara, and Chankrisna!"

The girl flies out the door and soon after, three young men slip into the hut and crouch about the hearth.

When all are settled, I begin to recite:

Yes, these special kind of Roman gladiators were called the Retiarii, and they fought strong armored swordsmen while they themselves were small, quick, and quite naked—no helmets, no armor, nothing but their nets, their tridents . . . and their quickness and bravery . . .

They all sit rapt and are soon firm in their resolve . . .

"It is settled, then," I say. "Give to me one of your fine cast nets and I shall make the first move. Watch for my signal. Sleep well, for tomorrow a new day will dawn."

As all fade off into the night, I wonder if they will follow through. I do not know, but tomorrow we shall certainly see.

For tonight, Ravi and I get to curl up together in a corner of the dwelling, protected, at least, from tigers.

And thank you, Mr. Yale, for your fine lectures on Ancient Rome, which so many of us at the Lawson Peabody thought were ever so boring . . .

Chapter 8

It had been decided last night, by myself and my fellow conspirators, that we would make our move in the afternoon, when the boats returned for the day, since then all the fishermen would be on the beach at once, unlike the morning, when the boats went out at irregular intervals.

Waiting for the fishing fleet to come back, I practice with the cast net I was given. The girl Naing has come along to teach me, all the boys of the village—those able to walk at least—being out with their dads on the ocean. She is very good at it, making the thing soar like an opening flower in the bright morning air. I believe that she has taken a bit of a shine to Ravi, who does not seem to have noticed.

To make the thing work, the net is arranged in neat folds and laid across the left arm, the lead weights at the bottom hanging down. A long thin line goes from the bottom of the net to the top of the net for gathering it up after it is thrown. The lower edge is picked up and placed between the teeth. One's body twists at the waist to fling it, hoping for the best. My first few tries at casting are pathetic, but I get the hang of it after a while.

After practicing on the open beach for a while, I wade into the water to try. The net flies out in a nice but not perfect circle and sinks. I even catch a few minnows. What a marvelous thing! I decide that I shall have to equip each of Faber Shipping's watercraft with some of these, should the opportunity arise and I ever get back to that side of the world.

This done, we wait for the fleet to return.

I slap the heavy turnbuckle into the palm of my hand, the buckle that Ravi and I had previously taken along with a part of the sail from the broken foremast. I do not want to bring it down on anybody's head, but it is comforting to have it handy. Although the plan does not call for its use, I carry it as backup in case things go wrong, as they so often do. Ravi, seeing me handle the deadly thing, expresses doubt.

"Sweet Missy plans something nasty? Ravi hopes not."

"Look, lad," I reply. "We've got to have a boat for lots of reasons, and I mean to get us one. Number one, we can't travel overland because of those big toothy striped devils out there in the woods. Moreover, we've got many rivers to cross on our way northward, and make our way we must." I pause as I stand to look out over the ocean, once again to see nothing. Then I continue. "Being ashore, we have no way of making money, and the sea has always provided for me. I am just not comfortable if I don't have a ship, no matter how small. And most important, we've got to help these poor people get out from under the heel of that cruel bastard."

"So Memsahib will steal boat?"

"Yes, Ravi, I plan to steal the badmash's boat. I like the color, and if things turn out as I hope, he will no longer have a use for it."

"I fear I must give up on any thought of becoming happy puppy in future life if you do this and I help you. I suspect my state will slip from happy puppy to garden slug."

"Could I perhaps write you a note addressed to Lord Ganesh, explaining that it was not your fault that you fell in with me?"

"Missy makes fun now . . ."

"I am sorry, Ravi, but I'm sure your inner good nature will win out over my evil influence when all comes to account."

"It is to be hoped, Memsahib," he answers tremulously. "Look! The boats return!"

And indeed they do.

"Right. Let's get ready, lad."

As the girl Naing scurries down the beach, ready to greet her brother's boat and help with the day's catch, Ravi and I hang the turnbuckle on a length of rope that loops about my waist such that it sits behind me on my rump, the rope being tied with a slipknot. Then I carefully arrange the cast net over my arm.

Peering out through the bushes, I see that the prow of Ohnmar's yellow boat has touched the shore and dropped its sail.

"Let's go, Ravi. You know what to do."

He nods, mumbling what I suppose to be prayers.

Taking his cue, I offer up one myself. *God, please make this work—if not for me, then for these poor people!*

We walk toward the yellow boat, where the badmash is once again laying out curses and kicks for all who are near him.

As we get closer, I turn my head to the side, putting on

an idiot's grin. Then a thought occurs to me, so I whip my pigtail around and shove it into my mouth. I chew upon it and cross my eyes and put on a severe left leg limp.

"Lay it on, Ravi," I whisper through the hair in my teeth. "Make it good." I see Arun standing ready on the beach a little ways down from us, his net and trident in hand.

Ravi runs up to the man and puts out his begging hands and lets fly a string of gibberish that I take to be an Urdu plea for alms. Ravi is good at it. His whine hits a high pitch and tears pour out of his big dark eyes while he gestures toward his unfortunate sister as she limps, cross-eyed, up to the boat. I manage to work up a bit of drool and make some moronic sounds.

All of which has no effect whatsoever on the badmash. He spits out something guttural, which I suspect translates as *Sod off, you filthy little buggers!*

That would be all right, except he is still on his boat and I cannot swing the net because the mast is in the way . . . *Damn! It's always somethin'!*

"Ravi!" I hiss. "We've got to get him out of the boat or all is lost!"

Ravi nods, takes a deep breath, then shouts, "*Kanjoos boodar!*" He then works up a good big gob of untouchable spit and lays it on the yellow prow of the badmash boat. Then he gives the boat a very disrespectful kick.

That does the trick.

Ohnmar leaps out of the boat. "*Rukhsat hona!*" he roars, swinging his big arm at Ravi. "*Rukhsat hona, naaraaz'qi!*"

His arm catches Ravi at the shoulders and the boy pitches to the ground. I take this opportunity to slip up behind the man and begin swinging my cast net.

As the badmash is aiming a kick at Ravi's belly, I let it fly and the beautiful net floats over the oppressor man and settles down, light as a feather around his head, shoulders, and then the rest of him.

He looks about, through the netting, amazed that anyone would have the nerve to—

"*AZAADI!*" I shout at the top of my lungs. "*AZAADI!*"

It means "FREEDOM!" and it is the signal that the revolt is on in earnest and there is no turning back. I am glad to hear *AZAADI!* coming from other throats farther up the beach, and am even gladder to see other cast nets blossoming in the evening air.

"Ravi! Go!" I say, tossing the lad the end of the cast net line, and as planned, he grabs it and begins running around and around the roaring bad man, further pinning him into the netting.

I look up the beach. Already several trident shafts stick straight up, quivering over horizontal, and now quite still, forms.

Well, they did have it comin' . . .

There is a shout and I turn to see that one of the toadies has gotten away from the formerly meek villagers and rushes down to help his master, his cutlass out and held over his head.

Uh-oh . . .

I whip out my shiv and crouch before him, narrowing my eyes and hissing like a snake. The sight of the knife-bearing pigtailed apparition is enough to make him pull up, amazed for a moment, but long enough for yet another billowing cast net to descend over his head, and then a trident is raised

and thrust down and he is no more trouble to me or anybody else, ever again.

I turn back to Ravi and his struggling captive, and I find
that the badmash is not yet done.

With the help of a small knife the strongman had in his
belt, he has managed to cut through the netting, enough to
free his sword arm. As Ravi passes with his entwining rope
in front of him, Ohnmar lifts his sword.

"*Halaak keerha!*" he shrieks, about to bring the blade
down on poor Ravi, who stands helpless before him.

No! Ravi! Please, God! No!

The sword comes down, but it does not come down on
Ravi. No, Arun now stands before Ohnmar, and as the sword
descends, he raises his trident and the blade is caught between its forked tines. Arun quivers with the strain of holding back the stronger man's sword, and I figure the fight
ain't quite fair, so I pull the slipknot on the rope that holds
my turnbuckle, grab the heavy thing as it falls, then bring it
down hard on the bad man's sword hand.

He howls and lets slip the sword and it falls to the sand.

Arun, seeing his chance, brings back his trident and
plunges it into the belly of Ohnmar, the badmash, former
terror of the village.

The great bully sinks to his knees and puts his hands
around the shaft of the thing that sticks out of his body . . .
But he finds, as countless fish have found, there is no pulling
out of a barb-tined trident. He gasps . . . once . . . twice . . .
and then falls over face first onto the sand.

I dash over and pick up the fallen sword and hold the
hilt out to Arun, still dazed by the heat of the battle.

"Here!" I say. "Take this, Arun, and be a good headman to your people! Protect them and make sure no other badmash comes to oppress them and make them unhappy. May you and Sanda have many fine children, and may you now summon your brothers and have them push my boat into the water!" I point to the yellow boat and then out to sea. He takes my meaning.

"Nanda! Dara! Chankrisna!"

At his call, the three young men from last night's conspiracy come pounding down the sand, huge grins on their triumphant faces.

Arun barks out the command and the yellow boat is shoved into the water.

"Hop in, Ravi!" I shout, as the boat floats in the gentle surf. I throw my leg over the gunwale.

Ravi struggles aboard and I find an oar and stick it in the water to pole us backward.

"There's another paddle there! Take it! Help me push us out!"

We continue to push until I get enough water under us to raise the sail. We have a nice alongshore breeze and that is good. I see that there is a centerboard and I shove it down. Then I grab the main haul and pull, and the sail goes up easily and fills with wind. I put the rudder down and throw over the tiller. We heel over, and we are off and away!

As we go, I wave at those who are gathered on the shore and they wave back. Then I grab Ravi and ecstatically plant kisses all over his face and exclaim, "Oh, Ravi, my brave, brave, *brave* little garden slug, we are away!"

Glory!

Chapter 9

Mr. John Higgins
Onboard the Nancy B. Alsop
Off the Coast of Siam
December 25, 1807

Mr. Ezra Pickering
Union Street
Boston, Massachusetts, USA

My Dear Mr. Pickering,
   It is with regret that I must report the apparent loss of our dear friend Miss Jacky Faber, she being swept overboard off the Lorelei Lee *during a violent storm on the South China Sea and lost. All here mourn her passing with heavy hearts.*

   I beg you to break this sad news as gently as you can to Miss Trevelyne and to Miss Faber's other friends at the Lawson Peabody School for Young Girls. I know it will be a hard task and I do not envy you the role of bearer of extremely bad news, but I see no other way. I am truly sorry.

   However, knowing Miss Faber as we did, I believe you will

agree with me that she would wish that the Corporation bearing her name to continue, since so many people now depend on Faber Shipping Worldwide for their livelihood. That being the case, please persist in your efforts to carefully manage the assets of that Corporation. It is in that spirit that I herewith bring you up to date on events here in the Bay of Bengal.

I have attached to this letter a separate account of the events—various mutinies, naval engagements, and much travail, which led to our being at this spot on the globe at this particular time—and so will not include them in the contents of this letter.

Our fleet, which was comprised of the *Lorelei Lee*, commanded by Miss Faber; the *Cerberus*, Mr. James Fletcher commanding; and HMS *Dart*, captained by Lieutenant Joseph Jared, Royal Navy, left Australia in the month of November and was proceeding north when it encountered a typhoon of horrific dimensions. I have not words to describe the awesome power of that maelstrom. Suffice it to say that it was powerful enough to tear off the foremast of the *Lorelei Lee* and, taking with it, our own dear Miss Faber.

After that fateful storm, we repaired damage as best we could and commenced a thorough search for Miss Faber, or her remains, up and down the Strait of Malacca, but we could find nothing, not a single remnant—no bones, no body, nothing. We took on translators of the various languages of the area and put into many ports inquiring as to her possible whereabouts but learned nothing. Eventually, after several weeks of fruitless search, we were forced to face the awful truth, and give up and push on.

We met the *Nancy B. Alsop* at the top of the Straits of Malacca yesterday. Yes, it is a very big world and a very large ocean, but the Straits of Malacca are narrow, and by good fortune we did manage to meet.

You will of course recall, Mr. Pickering, that I had sent a letter to Captain Liam Delaney from the port of Gibraltar some months ago, relating to him the fact that both Miss Faber and his daughter Mairead Delaney McConnaughey had been condemned to servitude in the penal colony at New South Wales and were being transported there in the *Lorelei Lee,* newly requisitioned by the East India Company, and if it was his wish, he was authorized to go to Boston and take command of the schooner *Nancy B. Alsop* to attempt a rescue. I sent a letter to you at that time, informing you of my actions in that regard. Since he appeared yesterday on the horizon in command of the *Nancy B.,* it was apparent to me that he took us up on our offer.

The joy of the reunion with former shipmates was, of course, dashed by the news of Miss Faber's demise.

As for others of Miss Faber's acquaintance, I regret to say that Mr. James Emerson Fletcher grows ever more melancholy by the day, if that is possible. He is sustained only by his fierce and all-consuming desire for revenge on those who brought Miss Faber to that fatal crossroads of her destiny. I see him standing at the rail of his ship, standing there for hours, looking out across the sea.

Others try to bring him cheer, but he does not accept it, poor man. He says only, "I live on my hatred and my rage. It eats at me, but it also sustains me. I will have my vengeance. Count on it."

Although he continues to be a competent master and commander of his ship, I do fear for the condition of his mind. In fact, I fear for his very sanity.

Lieutenant Joseph Jared grew up at sea and therefore, like others of his fatalistic seagoing ilk, is philosophical concerning life and death, since death is always very close and very present when on the unpredictable and wasteful ocean. Looking out over the waves at the scudding clouds on the horizon, he says, "We loved her, and in our hearts and our minds and our memories she will never grow any older, for whatever consolation that gives those of us left here behind. Her life was short, but she lived it as she wanted and she certainly packed a lot in to the short time she had. Jacky was given nine lives and I guess she finally used them all up. Rest in peace, Puss."

The fleet departed at dawn this morning on a northerly course, heading, for the most part, back to England. The *Lorelei Lee*, with her Irish crew, will part company with the rest at the bottom tip of Africa, and at that time will set her course for Boston to rejoin Faber Shipping Worldwide yet again.

On the *Nancy B. Alsop*, we raised anchor and headed south.

Yes, Captain Delaney has elected to make one more trip down the Straits of Malacca to search for Miss Faber, or her remains, saying, "She should have a proper burial, at least. We owe her that much. If she can be found, we will find her—and if she has to be buried on a heathen shore, then so be it. No sailor wants to be buried at sea."

He felt that the *Nancy B.*, being much smaller than the other ships in Miss Faber's former fleet, would be able to sail closer to the shore and to nip into smaller coves and inlets that would have proved dangerous to the larger ships, and so possibly gain better information as to Miss Faber's sad end and the disposition of her remains.

I heartily concurred in that and have elected to go with him. Although there is virtually no chance that she has survived, still a faint glimmer of hope remains.

No music is heard on the now somber decks of the *Nancy B.*

I grieve with you and all of Miss Faber's friends, and I am Yr most Obedient and etc.

John Higgins

Chapter 10

And so the *Eastern Star* sails up into the Bay of Bengal, with a sturdy crew of two.

Back at sea, girl, and in your own boat. Ahhh, yes!

I named my new sailing skiff the *Eastern Star* in keeping with her sister boats back in Boston, the *Morning Star* and the *Evening Star*. She is about sixteen feet long, well-found, and a good little sailor, and she's the newest addition to the fleet of Faber Shipping Worldwide. I shall have to write to Ezra Pickering and have her added to the holdings of that Corporation.

I do like the deep yellow color of her hull and the maroon of her single sail, and I love the sun on my face and the sound of the sea slipping by under the *Star's* bottom.

I was further delighted, upon commandeering this craft, to discover many fish lines and hooks stashed under the gunwales. Some jugs of water, to boot—nothing was too good for the badmash. And two of those lovely cast nets, too! Joy!

I have taught Ravi the rudiments of sailing, and he seems to enjoy it—his hand on the mainsheet, his eye on the tautness of the sail. As I lie back and let Ravi guide us on ever northward, I hook an ankle over the port gunwale and wonder how Jaimy and Jared are getting along with me being out of the way. Probably pretty good, I'll wager ... 'Course they got some things to resolve in the way of duty and male honor and all, but I do hope they'll work it out, I do. Maybe it'll be easier without my troublesome presence. Who knows? Certainly not me.

"Memsahib! Something on line!"

I jerk myself back into my present circumstances.

One of the fish lines is jerking violently, so I leap over to grab it and begin hauling it in. Whatever is on the other end is fighting mightily, but he shall not prevail. Oh, no you shan't, fishy, for Jacky Faber is too hungry for that!

After we had first taken the boat, we had sailed maybe fifteen miles up the coast. Then, as evening was about to fall, we headed into a nice little cove to dig some more clams. Both of us are heartily sick of them and think longingly of the simple meal we had at Arun's humble home, but we must eat something. We did not finish all of them but instead wrapped a goodly number in wet seaweed so as to have something with which to bait our hooks when we sailed away on the morrow. I climbed for more coconuts, as well, and we stashed some extra ones in the boat for later use. We also took the time to prepare the *Star* for the night, stretching our canvas across the lowered boom of the sail, making a very acceptable tent within the boat's hull.

We then took our sturdy little craft out into the gentle surf and threw out the anchor—yes, the badmash had one aboard, bless him. Hey, maybe the sod has earned some karma points, who knows? And then, as full night was upon us, Ravi and I, wrapped in each other's arms and lying on the hard hull of the *Eastern Star*, were rocked gently to sleep.

I yank the thrashing fish into the boat and, by God, it's a good one! About eighteen inches long, all blue and silver stripes and flashing teeth. I pick up a club that—given the amount of dried fish scales that cling to it—has been put to this use many times before, and deliver the fish a hearty *thwhack* on his head, which stops his thrashing and sends him off to wherever fishies go when they leave their water world.

"Poor fishy soul now with Brahma," whispers Ravi, appalled once again by the slaughter.

As the fish's movements subside, I whip out my shiv and open up his belly and spill out his guts.

"Ha! Now that's a good-looking liver," I crow, reaching into the mess and pulling out the bright red organ. I slap it down on the thwart and slice it neatly in half. I choose a piece and hold it over my mouth as if it is a crimson oyster and then let it slip down my throat. *Ummm . . .*

"Your turn, Ravi, do it now," I order. "It's good for you, and the *Eastern Star* must have a fit First Mate."

"To eat insides of poor creature that still quivers." Ravi shudders, shaking his head. "Hopes for garden slug in next life fading fast . . . Maybe spider . . . or lowly ant . . ." I hold the morsel over his open mouth and then drop it. He gags, but he chews and gets it down. Amazing what a little hunger will do for deciding what one will, or will not, eat.

I fillet the fish and lay pieces of the flesh on the gunwale to dry and to cook there in the fierce rays of the sun. We shall eat them later, when they turn white, and I'll wager they will be quite delicious . . . A dash of pepper and lemon would be nice, but dipped in the sea for salt, they will be just fine, and hey, this ain't exactly Buckingham Palace, now, is it?

Neptune smiles upon us and we have great good luck in fishing this day, bagging five more of the silver darlings. I unravel a length of my rope and use a strand to thread through the gills of each new arrival and tie the whole stringer over the side so that the fish will stay alive till we go to market.

We have further luck when I put the carcass of the first fish on an especially long, heavy hook and heave it over the side. Late in the afternoon, that line goes rigid and I swear the side of the *Star* heels over under the pressure of whatever is on the other end of that line. After much struggle, the blunt head of a shark appears alongside, the hook gleaming in his toothy mouth.

"Look, lad, in that cove there — it's another small town. Let's head in there and see if we can sell our catch."

Ravi puts over the tiller, I tighten the sail, and we head in, the unfortunate shark trailing meekly behind.

Good ladies and gentlemens of this lovely town, please to listen to playing of happy tunes by Sangeeta, my beloved but hideously ugly sister. Pity us, good people, and please to place alms in our poor bowl so that we might eat. Lord Krishna will bless you, yes, and thank you, good lady, thank you, good man.

I think that approximates what Ravi is saying as he dances about, passing the bowl and begging for small change. He is quite good at it, for some coins do fall—I am sure Rooster Charlie would have welcomed the lad into our company back in our old kip 'neath Blackfriars Bridge.

At our first port of call on that day of the shark, we went ashore and sold the fish we had caught. The locals seemed astonished at the size of our catch, calling us blessed by the gods of the sea, and I guess we were. *Thanks Poseidon, or whatever you are called here.* I know full well that the fishmongers cheated us, but so it goes. Ravi bargained the best he could, but at least we now had some hard coin.

So with our meager funds, we went to the small market we found in the town and bought a flint striker so we could start fires and cook our food. Then, to reward ourselves for our virtue and cunning, we bought two rice balls, all greasy and golden yellow with curry and *so* delicious. It was our first neither-clam-nor-raw-fish meal in days, and we devoured our purchase instantly and without ceremony. *Oh, so, so good . . .*

And to top it all off, we bought what would prove to be a great little moneymaker—a simple wooden flute. It had eight holes and a fipple mouthpiece and a sort of bulb at the end, and though it was not tuned to the same scale as my beloved pennywhistle, I was able to make it work. Ravi sang some of the tunes of his youth and I was able to duplicate them enough to get us by. We are now an act.

I had some concern about my safety in all this, me being a helpless young girl practically alone in a foreign land, and had bounced the idea off Ravi of retreating into the protection of boy garb. After all, we had plenty of canvas that I could cut into sashes to bind down my chest, but my young Indian consort did not think that would serve.

"Forgive poor Ravi, for what I am about to say, Memsahib, but your bottom, though not round enough to please

Burma man, still is too round to be boy. No, no. Also is abomination for girl to dress up as boy. Against the rules of nature. Ganesh not like and will bring us bad luck. Bad karma. And your face, though most dear to Ravi, is not pretty to India man—nose and lips too thin. Cheeks, too. Should be full and round like peaches. And your hair . . . please . . . is wrong color, like freak."

My hair, which had been shaved except for my pigtail at the back, was slowly growing back in. There was a light blond fuzz on my skull now, which had to look passing strange. My shiv, though sharp, was not a razor and could therefore not shave my head and keep it clean in the Chinese fashion.

"Your hair," the little rotter went on. "*Tsk!* You look like crazy woman, but maybe that is not a bad thing. Maybe we get more alms. Maybe mens leave you alone in ways of naughtiness."

For someone scarce eight years old, Ravi was certainly knowledgeable in the evil ways of the world. I'm thinkin', *Nothing like a few years spent on the street to hone up the old survival skills.*

And so it was decided that we travel up to Rangoon as boy Ravi and his mute and hideously ugly sister, Sangeeta. *Couldn't have him call me Memsahib, now, could we?* Ravi informed me that Sangeeta means "maker of music" in Hindi and so it fit . . . *but hideously ugly? I know I am no rare beauty by any means, but still there have been more than a few gents in my past who thought I was passable handsome . . . Geez . . .*

We made up a crude canvas veil to hide my ugliness. It comes to below my eyes, yet leaves my lips free to play the flute.

Ravi went on, to elaborate, "If pushy man lifts veil, you make twisted face, and he will drop veil and not bother you. See? Is good, no?"

I suppose . . . I do love being the center of attention, but not as a freak, I'm thinking. *Oh, well . . . Suck it up, lass. Sometimes a girl's gotta do what a girl's gotta do . . .*

And so we progress up the coast, going from town to town— sailing for a day or two, then stopping in the nearest port to sell our catch and do our act. We never again have such good luck in fishing, but we do all right with our street-singing bit.

My disguise as girl-too-ugly-to-ravish works. In fact, one time a crude brute made so bold as to lunge at me as I played the whistle on a corner in one of the towns where we had managed to attract a small crowd. He lifted the veil, took a beady-eyed look, and then flung it back down again. It was so sudden, I didn't even have a chance to put on my ugly face. He then said something to much laughter from the small crowd we had gathered, and then looked very satisfied with himself.

After we had collected our few copper coins and were walking back to the *Eastern Star,* I asked Ravi what the man had said.

"Oh, it was nothing," he'd answered, not meeting my gaze. "Not worthy of Sister Sangeeta."

"Come on, Ravi," I snarled. "Out with it."

He sighed and said, "Not to get mad, Missy, but he say, 'To benefit unwary, unsuspecting man, she should have *two* veils over that face.'"

"Why?" I asked.

"In case first one rips," answered Ravi sheepishly, looking for anger in my face.

Grrr . . . very funny.

So we make a few coins, we eat, we have some fun, and we get farther and farther north.

Soon, Rangoon.

Chapter 11

Aboard our *Eastern Star,* we had followed the line of fishing boats past tiny villages up what I later discovered was the Rangoon River to the city itself, and oh, what a sight it is! Glorious golden spires, dozens of them, reaching way up into the sky. I, who have seen the Cathedral of Saint Paul's, in London, and the Notre Dame, in Paris, stand awestruck at the splendor.

"What . . . what are they, Ravi?"

"I believe they are called pagodas, Sangeeta," he says. "They are the most holy shrines of the Buddhists. My master, Mr. Elphy, visit here one time and he come . . . came . . . back and told his whole household of all the glories of this city. I remember sitting before him, rapt with wonder at his tales."

The Splendor of the Orient, indeed . . .

Well, so much for sightseeing, my goggle-eyed girl, let us get on with things, shall we?

As we approach the wharf area, I spy a ship, a merchantman, flying the Union Jack and lying portside to one of the many piers. Cargo is being loaded aboard. My heart leaps to see the familiar flag once again as I pull the tiller over to head for the merchant's side.

"Ahoy, mates!" Surprised eyes peer over the side, gaping down at an apparition in ragged clothes and pigtail, speaking to them in Cockney English. "'Ave you been seein' three ships sailin' by on your way here and they was maybe flyin' the American and British colors?"

"And just who, darlin', are you?" asks the grinning rogue above me.

"Me name is Jacky Faber," I says, without thinking too hard about that. I mean, who out here would have heard of—

"Ha! Jacky Faber? Bloody Jack? Hell, Puss-in-Boots is dead ten times over, by God, and rottin' in 'er grave! Look, I gots a tattoo here to prove it!"

The sod pulls up his sleeve to show the kitten-with-sword tattoo with the word *Vengeance* writ large above it.

"See? She 'ad 'er bloody 'ead cut off by them Froggies!"

Other grinning sailors have joined him at the rail.

"Maybe so, but that weren't me," I says, pushing on, anxious to change the subject. "The ships I'm askin' 'bout, Jocko, was two merchants, the *Lorelei Lee* and the *Cerberus*, and the HMS *Dart*, a Royal Navy sloop of war. Seen 'em?"

The sods look at each other and shake their heads.

"Nay. We spotted a small ship flyin' Yankee colors a few days out of Bombay, but that's about it. Tiny ship, hardly worth the mention."

Heavy sigh by me, but I really didn't expect to see my lost fleet here. *Huh, from Commodore to common tramp in one swift fall. Oh, well . . .*

"Say, lass, how'd a nice Cockney bint loike you get all chinked up loike that, 'ey?"

"Long story, mate," I answer, pushing off with my oar. "Mayhaps you'll hear about it someday. Cheerio, lads."

We drop the sail, pick up the oars, and row the *Star* to a likely looking spot on the pier. We tie up, and Ravi barters our fish for dockage. That being settled, we head off into the wondrous city of Rangoon.

"Let's set up here," I say, pulling my flute from my sleeve. "It seems a likely place." We are in front of one of the golden temples at the corner of two streets and there are many folk about who seem to come from many different places—some who look Indian, some who look Chinese, some who look . . . what? . . . I don't know. There are saris and turbans and great mustaches and beards and pigtails and whatnot. *Hmmm* . . . It is a city in which I could thrive . . . and hide, maybe . . .

Ravi nods and holds out his bowl, and I put flute to lip and start swaying and playing and trying to work up a bit of a crowd.

We have dropped the veil bit, for blokes were always too curious to see what horror lay beneath it. Plus, as we had gotten closer to Rangoon, the towns were bigger and more cosmopolitan, less likely to be shocked by the appearance of someone from another land. So instead of the veil, I took to streaking my idiot face with dirt and acting the total fool, if it came to it. If anyone looks at me too closely, I cross my eyes and start to slobber. I'm getting rather good at working up some spit and drooling on cue. Then I point to my wet mouth with a dirty finger and make gurgling sounds. It works. I am not troubled with anything other than a pitying glance.

Ha! The very proper Amy Trevelyne should see me now . . . I have to stifle a giggle at the thought . . . *or better, yet, Miss*

Clarissa Worthington Howe, of the Virginia Howes, don'cha know—she would just die of pure vindication—"Ah told all of you that Jacky girl was nothin' but a tramp and ah was right!" I guess you were, Clarissa, after all—heavy sigh—and as for the ever-so-uptight-and-proper Jaimy, well, don't even think about it.

Anyway, I begin tootling away, and Ravi starts his rant and passes his bowl and things are going right well when I notice a tall mean-looking bloke standing off to the side, looking at me. He wears a white turban and big fierce mustache and has a stern look in his beady eyes. Do all bad-mashes have big mustaches? Did I slip up and speak English to Ravi as we were setting up? Did he hear? Did he know what it was I spoke? I hope not, but I know I can grow careless sometimes . . . *Damn!*

Things quickly go worse, with the sudden and very unwelcome arrival of several of the sailors from that English merchantman I had seen earlier.

Uh-oh . . .

"Hey, if it ain't our little Cockney bint what's got 'erself all dolled up as a ching-chong Chinaman!" says the leader of the louts. 'Tis plain they're off on some well-deserved liberty and looking for some fun, and who am I to deny them that. *But, no, not at my expense.*

"Play us a tune from the old sod," says one. "To warm our poor hearts so far from home."

I'm sweating now. *This is not going well!* I nod to Ravi and he does his routine about me being a crippled mute, and I cross my eyes and drool and limp, but it doesn't work.

"Oh, come on, we've heard her talk, by God, and we'll have no such guff! A song!"

I step out of character. "Come on, mates, let me be. You are putting me in danger here, you are. I know you mean well, but you don't understand, you—"

"*Ingrish!*"

That from the throat of the big badmash with the mustache.

He lunges toward me, grabs me by the neck, and drags me up the street. The English boys protest, but they do not pursue. Why should they? It ain't their concern what happens to some ratty-looking street singer, English or not.

I put on my big, looping limp and moan my idiot's moan, and Ravi pleads—*please, please, please, good sir, my poor sister*—in some sort of language or other, and pummels the legs of the badmash, but it doesn't do any good. I am hauled farther and farther up a dark alley toward a huge, brass-bound door at the end of it.

Time for my shiv . . .

I whip it out of my forearm sheath and thrust it into the side of my abductor . . . but it doesn't go in there. No, it doesn't because the brute has cinched a thick leather sash about his waist and I can't plunge my blade through that.

I pull back for another try at his throat, but his other hand grasps my knife hand by the wrist and I am helpless. My shiv falls to the ground and the badmash stoops to pick it up, all the time shoving me relentlessly toward that big door. He puts my shiv to my throat and I don't struggle anymore.

Oh, Lord, what now? What lies beyond this door?

My abductor takes his hand—the one coiled about my shiv, not the one wrapped around my throat—and raps three times on the massive door, then twice, then he steps back as the massive thing swings open, revealing a long, dimly lighted hallway, down which I am thrust, with the wailing Ravi right behind me. With a grunt I take to be a curse, the brute pushes me on, and then abruptly, he turns to the right and we face yet another door.

Another three raps, then two, and this door opens as well, and I am flung sprawling upon the floor.

I am lying face-down on a fine rug, heavy and thick with many fine intertwined designs woven on its surface. I raise my head and see that at the end of this room is a low dais upon which sits a very fat man on a large pillow, his silk-clad legs pulled up under him. His feet are encased in soft yellow slippers with turned-up toes that plainly were not meant for any real walking. He wears a red and gold embroidered vest, and around his big belly is a golden silk sash, into which a small curved dagger is tucked, its handle encrusted with what look to be diamonds and rubies. An abacus sits in front of him. To both his left and right sit two young girls, finely dressed in filmy silks and shiny satins. In front of them are low tables holding bowls of grapes and plums and other sweetmeats. There are bottles there, too, and cups. Were I not so scared, I would find myself quite thirsty.

I lift my head further, to look upon his face. He is plainly Chinese . . . or Korean . . . or something . . . His round head is topped with a beaded skullcap, and on his upper lip and chin are a thin mustache and a pointy beard. He wears small round spectacles and a rather bemused expression.

He says something to the badmash in a language I do not understand, whereupon that sterling personage reaches down and hauls me to my feet.

"*Ingrish!*" he says, pointing at me.

I go into my idiot act.

I lurch forward, limping, my grubby hand thrust toward the seated man. I drool, I cast my eyes to a spot to the right of his head, as if I cannot focus, and I mumble most moronically, *"Aww . . . wah . . . wah . . . gorndna . . . gawfff . . ."* with lots of spittle flying on the last nonsense syllable, for good measure.

The fat man sits silent for a while, then he quietly says—*in English!*—"My man says he heard you speaking English. Is this true?"

"Awwff . . . wah . . . wah . . . wah . . . guniffffff . . ."

The fat man considers me, his small black eyes roaming over my face. "Very well. 'Tis plain you were mistaken, Ganju Thapa," he says to the badmash. "But that is all right. I am glad you are vigilant in observing the happenings in the streets."

Hey, maybe we'll get away with this . . .

We do not.

"Ganju Thapa, take that boy there down to the boiling vats and throw him in. When his screams are ended and the flesh has completely fallen from his bones, bleach those bones such that we might sell his skeleton to the doctors. It will earn us a few coins, which I shall give to you for your diligence, such that your family shall grow in wealth."

Ganju places his arms crosswise on his chest and bows, then he reaches down for the arm of the very wide-eyed Ravi, who has understood every word of this conversation.

I heave a sigh, for I, myself, used this very tactic on a French spy back on my *Emerald.* It worked on him and it works on me. *Give it up, girl.*

"Very well," I say, standing straight. "I am English. Do not harm the boy."

The fat man chuckles. "I thought so. Fair hair and facial

features such as yours are not common in this area. Please, English girl, calm yourself, and tell me how you came to be here. It might prove amusing to me."

He beckons to the girl on his left, and a measure of what I take to be wine of some sort is poured into a cup and offered up to him. He takes a long draft and smiles.

In spite of myself, my mouth starts watering. The liquid is deep purple and looks very good.

"I will tell you who I am if you tell me who you are and how you can—"

"Ah, so you are surprised I speak your language?" He chuckles again. "You see, I was educated in your country at a place called King's College. My sponsors thought that I might prove useful to them in the ways of trade later on. They were right. I have made them very rich. Myself, too."

There is a silvery thing off to his side with a long tube leading to a smoldering bowl, containing what I smell to be vile tobacco. The fat man puts the tube in his mouth and pulls upon it, his fat cheeks thinning with the effort.

"The English in this area call me Chopstick Charlie because I am Chinese, and they cannot pronounce my real name. Not that the arrogant snobs care about that, anyway, nor do I, as long as the money keeps flowing into my coffers." He takes another drag on the pipe.

"Now, who," he asks, puffing out a perfect ring of smoke, "are you?"

I puff up my chest and say, "I am Jacky Faber, owner of Faber Shipping Worldwide. I have been shipwrecked and am desirous of being conveyed back to America wherein my enterprise is based. If you were to help me in that endeavor, you would be well rewarded."

He laughs, his great belly shaking with mirth.

"Quite impressive, Jacky Faber, owner of ships far away but none here. Two minutes ago you were a pathetic idiot and now you proclaim yourself a captain of industry. What are we to believe?"

"Believe this, Chopstick Charlie, when in these waters, I sail under the protection of the mighty Cheng Shih, the Lady of the Golden Dragon!"

The man is convulsed with laughter.

"Oh, this is just so rich! Thank you, girl, for bringing mirth to my day. The Dragon Lady, indeed!"

"It is true, Fat Charlie," I say, getting steamed. "I have upon my ships several pennants—a golden dragon on green field—which she gave me to grant safe passage!"

"Oh, please, Miss! Many have seen those flags flying and heard of the famous female pirate, commander of seven hundred ships. Surely you can't expect me to believe that one such as you—"

"How's this then, Chuck?" I ask, turning around and flipping aside my pigtail to reveal to him the golden tattoo Lee Chi had inscribed beneath it on that day back on Cheng Shih's *Divine Wind.*

He starts, then adjusts his spectacles to peer at the mark.

"Do you see it, Charlie?" I demand. "Can you read the inscription beneath the dragon? Yes? Then what does it say?"

"It says, 'If this head falls, so will yours.'" Chopstick Charlie seems a bit subdued in reading that.

"Well, what do you say to that?" I ask, crossing my arms.

He considers . . . then asks, "And so, how is our rather dangerous little lotus flower doing these days?"

"The Dragon Lady is still quite dangerous, believe me. I saw her not three weeks ago."

"And your connection?"

"I was her . . . pet."

"Ah, well . . ."

"Ah, well what?"

"I do think, Jacky Faber of Faber Shipping Worldwide, that you have just changed from being unwilling captive of Chopstick Charlie Enterprises to being that of honored guest."

"That's all very well, but why were we taken?" I ask, indignant. "Did you know that in civilized countries such things are against the law?"

"True," he agrees, a small smile on his rather tiny mouth. "But this is Rangoon. And as for why we have gathered you to our presence, my man here has standing orders to report anything that might be of interest to me. He overheard you speaking English to the boy there, and he assumed, rightly, that I would be pleased if he . . . *invited* you here to meet me. The English seem to be intent on taking over this part of the world, and as a . . . businessman . . . it is to my advantage to keep an eye on what your very busy countrymen are up to."

He takes another burbling drag on the pipe and inhales the smoke, letting it out after a moment, and then asks, "The boy, too, speaks English?"

"Yes. As well as Urdu and Hindi."

"Ummm . . . good." Chopstick Charlie mulls this over a bit, then speaks to the mightily mustachioed Ganju Thapa in a language I do not understand, but the intent is immediately clear.

The badmash goes to Ravi, grabs his arm, and begins to haul him away.

"Stop!" I shout. "He's only a little boy and has done nothing to you!"

"Do not worry, my dear, he shall not be harmed," says our host. "I have, uh, detained . . . a business associate with whom I have had some trouble communicating my desires. He speaks only Urdu and your lad will be of immense help as a translator. He could not have arrived at a better time, both for my coffers and for the as yet uncut throat of my associate.

"Now, my dear, how can *you* be of use to old Chopstick Charlie, hmmmm?" His lips, framed by his little black goatee, curl up at the ends.

"I can speak French and Spanish as well as English, not that I wish to help you in any way," I say, fuming.

"Um. It is obvious that you are educated to some degree."

"Compared to most girls, yes, I suppose."

"Then, why were you impersonating a penniless beggar?"

"Because, for now, I *am* a penniless beggar, trying to get back to my home port."

"Why did you not simply go to the British Embassy in this city and ask for assistance if, indeed, you are the owner of a shipping company? The East India Company also has a chargé d'affaires here. I'm sure they would help. Hmmm?"

Geez . . . just what I need—both the Brits and the Company finding out that Jacky Faber is not only still alive but abroad in the land.

"Uhhh . . . some sleeping dogs are best left lie," I reply, somewhat weakly.

He chuckles, his eyes twinkling with mischievous merriment. "Oh, ho? Well, we shall see about that, my mysterious guest. Inquiries will be made."

Damn! Why did I tell him my real name? Stupid!

I can curse my stupidity all I want, but what the hell, let's just see what happens . . . Plus, I'm getting hungry.

"If I am such an honored guest, then why am I not being treated as such?" I ask, gazing pointedly at the wine bottle and the rest of the food laid out upon the table.

"Why? Because you are filthy. An affront to my eyes as well as to my nose," he says, reaching for a rope and pulling it. "Here. Let us take care of that."

A bell tinkles in a nearby room, and presently a slim young woman, richly dressed in blue silk, enters through a beaded curtain.

"Yes, Father?" she says, bowing her elegantly coiffed head a bit in deference to Chopstick Charlie.

"Sidrah, my dear," he says, smiling fondly on his daughter. "Please take this creature off and clean her up . . . a bath . . . and get her into some decent clothes."

Well, that's much more like it, I must say . . .

Chapter 12

If anyone ever wants to get on the good side of Jacky Faber, just grab her, strip off whatever ratty clothing she might have on, and toss her grubby body into a good, hot bath.

Aaaaahhhhhhhhhhhhhh . . .

The girl Sidrah leads me by the hand out of Chopstick Charlie's presence, through several more beaded curtains, then out a back door. Walking through a lovely garden with hanging garlands of purple and pink flowers and smelling of jasmine and other scents I'd never before sniffed, we enter a bathhouse in the rear of the place, where great gouts of steam are issuing from cracks in the floor. I suspect there is some giant boiler hidden beneath, probably being stoked by poor abused and unseen laborers.

In the center of the room is a round pool, about twelve feet across and filled with steaming water. While the floor of the room is laid with alternating squares of teak—boards laid crosswise, then vertically—the pool itself is inlaid with a mosaic of turquoise tile, making the water within glow with a deep rich blueness. The room is dimly lit by a skylight high above, and braziers with fragrant herbs smolder in the corners of the bathhouse, giving off wondrous, heady scents that make my mind swim with the Oriental richness of it all.

Two small girls appear and divest me of my ragged Powder Monkey's garb, which has certainly seen the worse for wear. The pants, the tattered shirt, and finally my shiv's forearm sheath—yes, they all fall to the side of the pool. I am led by the two little girls—ten years old if they are a day—and I am handed down the shallow steps and into the lovely warm water . . . *Oh, yes . . .*

Sidrah, too, divests herself of her garments, letting them float to the floor, where they are quickly retrieved by other servants and whisked away. She slides into the steaming water beside me, and she unravels my pigtail and works soft soap into it as I lean back and moan with pleasure. She then rinses it and begins to comb it out.

"Mmmmm," I murmur. "Thank you, Sidrah. Such a lovely name. What does it mean?"

She smiles upon me and says, "It is short for Sidrat'ul Muntaha, which means 'The Flowering Tree That Marks the Edge of the Seventh Heaven.'"

Oh . . .

"And what means your name, Jah-kee?"

A razor appears from somewhere and my forehead is newly shaven as are my legs and under my arms, and soaps and ointments are rubbed gently all over me from head to toe and, *Oh, Lord, I love it so!*

"I am afraid that it is a common name, meaning 'Seaman,' as in 'Jack the Sailor.'"

"Ah. I think it is a fine name. I hope we shall be friends."

Me, too.

My senses are reeling, but in a most pleasant way. The skylight above lets in enough sunlight such that it filters in through the haze of steam and incense and makes lovely patterns on the surface of the water. In my contrary way, my dizzy mind again thinks of my dear friend Amy Trevelyne, back in Massachusetts—*Oh, Amy, my dearest friend, I am so far from you and an eternity away from Puritan Boston, and I am being bad, but how I wish you were here beside me, I do! Ha! Wouldn't that be a sight? You up to your nostrils in a pagan tub in a foreign land? Ha! But I know that never shall be. The cold comforts of the coast of New England for thee, Sister, forevermore, but for me all the joy and comforts of the whole wide wonderful world. Ahhhhh . . .*

I am being bad, and I know it, but I shall float here till I am boiled pink as any shrimp in all my parts, yes, I shall. Oh yes, I shall . . .

But, no, it must come to an end. Eventually I am lured out with the promise of thick, hot towels and fine raiments. They sure know how to get to the core of Jacky Faber, yes, they do, and I am helpless before them. I am completely and carefully patted dry, then dressed in the finest of silken garments. My pigtail is rebraided, and then, with Sidrah by my side, I am led back into the presence of Chopstick Charlie.

"I trust you are quite refreshed, my dear? Hmmmm?" says Chopstick Charlie, beaming his little smile down upon me.

"Quite refreshed, Sir," I reply, plunking my tail down on a plush cushion. I decide to play it cheeky. "What's the grub, then, mate?"

"Ho-ho. Very colorful. The common street English, just

as I heard it spoken in poor parts of London." He claps his small, soft hands together. "Very charming, very charming!"

A cup of the very delicious-looking purple wine is poured into a cut-glass goblet and placed in front of me. I, however, push it away. Charlie looks surprised.

"You should taste it, my dear. It is the very best plum wine, come all the way from China."

"Where is my little boy?" I ask, crossing my arms on my silk-clad chest and looking off, my expression cold and distant.

"Excuse me?"

"The little boy I had with me when I first came here."

"Ah. That one." Charlie claps his hands and Ganju Thapa appears from the shadows to the side.

Words are murmured and Ganju leaves, and soon a joyous Ravi appears.

"Memsahib!" he exclaims as he bounds over to me and plunks himself down into my lap.

"Ravi!" I exclaim, very glad to see the little fellow. He, too, has been scrubbed up and dressed in what, while not quite as fine as the golden yellow and white dress that sits lightly on the Faber frame, is probably one of the finest things he's ever had on in his young life—soft white trousers and shirt with blue trimming about the neck. Satisfied as to his safety, I lose no time in getting some of the plum wine into my mouth and down my throat.

Oh, Lord, that's good!

"What have you been up to?" I ask of the lad.

"Very unhappy man tied to chair. Ravi hopes he was able to help with the language. Man still alive when I left."

"Umm, yes," says Charlie. "That little matter was resolved to my satisfaction."

Sidrah glides gracefully down next to me as I lay into the feast that is spread before us. It all looks very good . . . Well, most of it, anyway.

"Wot's this, then?" I ask. If he likes the Cockney dialect, I'll pour it on thick for him, to be sure. I see that a pair of slender ivory sticks has been laid by my plate. Of course I am quite expert in the use of them from my time spent at Cheng Shih's table aboard the *Divine Wind,* and so I lift a piece of meat and elegantly aim it toward my open mouth.

"That is breast of peacock. Very rare, and very delicate of flavor, don't you think?"

"Mmm . . ." I say, as I stuff it in. I notice that several peacock feathers have been laid across the table. "It is good, but not all that different from common chicken."

"Ah. One who is hard to please. Then try this . . ."

I sit back. "Please, Sir . . . No monkey . . . nor dog . . ."

"Oh, no, my suddenly squeamish one."

"Nor cats . . ."

"What do you think us to be?" he says, smiling that sly smile of his. "Here, my dear, have another delicacy. This is a hundred-year egg . . . buried beneath rich soil for all that time, and unearthed just for your delectation."

I look at the gray lump lying before me. Then I take up a piece and pop it into my mouth. It may be a delicacy, but—

"It tastes like mud," I say, struggling to get the delicacy down my throat and not being very successful.

"Hmmm . . ." says Charlie. "Obviously a plebeian palate. Try this, then." He claps his hands and a new dish appears. "It is bird's nest soup . . . famous in all culinary circles."

I am handed a bowl containing a whitish crusty thing. "What is this?"

"The nest of the white swiftlet that builds its bower inside dark caves high on the limestone cliffs of Gomantong and Niah along the coast of Borneo. The white comes from the spittle of the male bird that works for over a month building the rigid nest. It is a very risky business for the persons who gather the nests in dark caves high up on the cliffs. Many die. But it is worth it, no?"

Now the Jacky Faber belly is famous for its ability to digest just about anything, but . . .

I take a sip . . . taste . . . and then declare that I'll stick with the peacock breasts, thank you, and please hold off on the nightingale tongues, but do pass the rice.

Chopstick Charlie laughs and gives up on me.

"Very well, let us dine on that which pleases us!" He claps his pudgy hands. "More plum wine for all! Yes, and some saki, too!"

My crystal goblet is refilled and a new drink is poured—this in a delicate ceramic cup—and it is warm, and, *Yum*, it is very good, too. I was a little reluctant to taste it, having vowed to never drink spirits and all, but I am assured it is only rice wine, so what could it hurt? Still, I shall have to watch myself.

The dinner being about over, I lean back, lazy as any cat, and stroke Ravi's black hair. He has eaten of the rice dishes and the vegetables, and he is now asleep, his head on my lap.

"So," says Charlie. "You say that you are a person of business—that you own a shipping company in America. Hmm? So what do you advise poor old Chops to do about these incursions of the English into his sphere of influence?"

I think about this for a moment, take another hit of that warm and heady saki, and begin:

"Tell ya what, Chopsie, old boy, what you should do is get a ship—a big one—and fill it up with all the treasures of the East and give it to me and let me sail off wi' it to old England and I'll present it to King George wi' yer compliments and you'll be made the main man in these parts, fer shrrrr . . . er . . . for sure, that is."

Watch your mouth, girl. And no more of that saki for you . . . But more is poured and, of course, I do take sips. Small ones.

"Oh-ho, my dear girl. What? You take poor old Chops for a fool?" Charlie laughs. "So very jolly a notion. Ha-ha! No, I fear that you would load that ship with all my worldly goods and never be heard from again!"

"You have my word, Charlie, that I would not do that."

"Oh, no?" He laughs, plainly enjoying this. "Listen, my devious one. While you were in your bath, I made discreet inquiries." He pulls out a sheaf of papers. "Oh, yes, I did, and I was rewarded with most interesting information. To wit."

Uh-oh . . .

"A certain Jacky Faber, condemned to life in New South Wales for crimes against the Crown of England. What do you say to that?"

"That is true, sort of, but I elected not to stay down there. The climate did not suit me."

"Did not elect . . ." Charlie chortles. "The climate? Oh, that is rich, so rich, so very rich—"

"I got a pardon from Captain Bligh, the commandant of the prison," I say, huffing up a bit. "For Services Rendered, to wit: the delivery of prisoners to the penal colony—"

"One of which was supposed to be you. Am I right?"

"Well, I had other things to do."

"I can imagine. Now, the East India Company reports that two of their ships"—he looks down at the paper— "the *Lorelei Lee* and the *Cerberus*, have gone missing. Have you any idea where they are?"

"I have no idea," I answer truthfully. "But if you were to make further inquiries, you might ask about British Intelligence and my connection there."

Charlie cocks an inquisitive eyebrow.

There is something about this Chopstick Charlie that I like—maybe it's his obvious capacity for avarice or his rampant greed, which matches mine. Yes, that and his rather jolly nature, which seems to find many things of this world not only interesting but also amusing.

Whatever it is, I take another swallow of saki and decide to tell him something of my past . . . a lot of it, actually . . .

My name is Jacky Faber and in England I was born . . .

It is much later this night when I am escorted, rather unsteadily, to a room where I sleep very soundly on pillows of the softest satin, and I do not have any nightmares, but some dreams do come, and nice ones for a change. I curl up on my side and let them take me away . . .

Jaimy appears, and he seems to be . . . what? . . . scolding me for something . . . but I ain't done nothin' wrong, Jaimy. I ain't. Maybe I did just drink a little too much o' that saki, but . . . then it's not Jaimy who is there, but . . . Lord Richard Allen, grinnin' his big white smile at me and sayin', "It's all right, Princess, you drink all that heathen stuff you want, Sweetheart, and then come over and sit here beside me. We'll get rid of those stuffy clothes and then maybe a little kiss on the back of your fine neck right on that new tattoo there." And then it's not him, but Joseph Jared, and where's he got his hot hands now? Well, it ain't hard to guess where . . . and then . . . what? Robin Raeburne? Where the 'oly 'ell did you come from? . . . and he's sayin', "Jacky, I've been lookin' for ye, my bonny wee bairn, for so long now, so long . . ." And then everything fades away into a plum-colored mist and . . .

PART II

PART II

Chapter 13

James Fletcher, Escaped Convict
Off Spithead
England

Jacky Faber, Deceased
Whereabouts of Soul, Unknown

My Dearest Jacky,

   I compose this letter to you solely in my mind, what is left of it, that is, as I lack both writing tools and the strength of will to write anything down, there being no longer any hope of delivering it to my dear lost girl.

It is in the dead of night and I am in one of HMS *Dart's* lifeboats, wrapped in a cloak and being rowed toward the dark shore of England. I am to land near Portsmouth and from there I will make my way north to London to begin to carry out my plan of vengeance against those who have brought the two of us so very low. Beyond that, I have no plans.

Our mutual friend, Lieutenant Joseph Jared, Acting Commander of HMS *Dart,* has provided me with clothing and some money, as well as clandestine transport to that lonely stretch of beach up ahead, and I bless him for it. He could have exerted his authority as a Royal Navy officer and taken me back into custody, but he did not. There are many who would think it his duty to do so, but he felt otherwise. Count on it, Jacky, you had some very good friends when you were in this world and I hope you knew that.

Your *Lorelei Lee,* which I know you loved so very much, departed our company at the southern tip of Africa, bound for the port of Boston, with your Irish crew aboard, so all will be safe from capture under the spread wings of the American Eagle. Your friend Mairead is aboard as well. I know you would be glad of that news, for you always did try to look out for your friends.

The land is drawing near—I can hear the crash of the surf on the shore. I must ready myself. Steady, now . . .

My ship, the *Cerberus,* will be returned to the East India Company, and that is fine with me, as I had no particular love for that hellhole of a vessel, nor any desire to continue seafaring of any kind.

I have been in a deep state of melancholy since your passing, and though I have tried to climb out of it, I cannot and only wallow deeper into despair. I fear that I am losing my mind.

But really, it would not be such a precious thing to lose, as it only causes me pain . . .

Yours Now & Forever,

Jaimy

Chapter 14

"And so where are my two charming girls off to to-day? Hmmm . . . ? To the bazaar again for more shopping? I swear, the two of you shall bring the House of Chen to ruin," says Charlie, as we appear before him. He sits with his ever present abacus before him, clicking. Yes, his real name is Chen . . . Chen Lee . . . *Chen-lee, Char-lee, get it? Oh, how the Brits love to bend everyone's way of speaking to suit their own . . .*

"No, Father," says Sidrah, placing a kiss upon his fat cheek. "I wish to show Jah-kee a temple several miles down the coast. A beautiful place with fine gardens, and I believe she will be pleased by the architectural proportions of the place. Jah-kee has a nice little boat and we shall sail there in it."

I have perceived that Sidrah is spoiled rotten and always gets her way with her indulgent father, and that, for me, is a good thing. Yes, Sidrah and I have become very good friends.

"Right, Charlie, old top," I say.

"This poor Chinaman perceives a certain lack of respect from an honored guest toward her host," remarks Charlie, mock-offended.

"Ah, Cholly Pops, ye knows we loves ye," says I, planting a kiss of my own on his other smooth cheek.

"Ummm."

"It is a calm day and we shall be quite safe. We are never more than a hundred yards from land in water scarce over our heads. Nothing could possibly happen . . . and you don't even have to send the two thugs with us."

But I know he will.

It has been several weeks since my arrival here, and I have been accorded a measure of freedom. Sidrah has been allowed to show me about the city—and it is, indeed, a wondrous place, with its golden pagodas and statues and, yes, shops. True, we are always accompanied by a couple of bodyguards who seem to have two main missions: the first being to protect Sidrah's body from harm and the second being to ensure that my own dear body comes back to the House of Chops, as Charlie has come to consider that particular body somewhat valuable, too. To further that end, Ravi is kept from going with us—in fact, there is a slender but strong-looking chain about his ankle, the other end being attached to the wall, should the lad think of making a run for it.

I have duties, as does Ravi, and we are kept quite busy. With five languages between us, we have proved quite useful to the empire of Chopstick Charlie. Only this morning I had helped to iron out some differences between a very angry Spanish captain and the House of Chen. All parted on good terms . . . Charlie's terms, to be sure, but finally acceptable to all concerned.

And yesterday I had sat with him in his records room,

where accountants pored over ledgers, adding and subtracting columns of figures, just like in London. Charlie has quite the operation, I have discovered, and I have continued to press my case—my plan, as it were—to do Charlie some good, and to get me out of this part of the world. Although I ran my mouth off quite a bit that first day, thanks to that evil saki, I think my idea of bearing some of Charlie's treasure as gifts to King George is a good one. Chops has got the money, the booty, the ships, and the influence. He is my way out of here and back to where I came from. I know that for certain.

"If you keep me here, what have you got?" I ask now. "Just a scrawny girl who can speak several languages."

"Yes, and one who is mildly amusing and who graces my table with her charm and her musical ability," says Charlie, chuckling.

"But if you help me return to Europe, not only will I get you into the good graces of the British Foreign Service, but I'll also make sure that you are designated as our main contact in the East for Faber Shipping Worldwide. We're planning to open up this area of the world for trade with America. That was decided at the last board meeting. And China, too . . . Don't forget, my ships have guarantees of safe passage through Cheng Shih's huge fleet. That's a big thing . . . a very big thing."

"Hmmm. True, you have been busy, but still, it makes poor Chop's blood run thin as rice water to think of entrusting you with a large amount of money. That goes against old Charlie's grain."

"Not money, Chopsie," I say, leaning in and pushing my case. "Not just money, no. Stuff. Like statues, artifacts . . .

mummies . . . cheap jewelry . . . anything as long as it's old. Brits love that stuff, believe me. They've got a big museum in London to hold it all, and their army and navy are always stealing . . . uh . . . collecting things from all over the world—Egypt and Greece and Rome and Cathay and just about everywhere. That stuff means nothing to you, but I've been there and I've seen 'em—gods and goddesses and such—whole temples, suits of armor and things. I tell ya, they eat that stuff up. They could charge admission just to look at it. Charlie, you couldn't miss! They'd love the hell out of you, and if you ever went back to England, they'd prolly make you a bloody Knight o' the Garter!"

He still looks dubious, his brow knitted as he strokes his goatee and ponders my suggestion.

"They've got a huge stone mansion over on Bloomsbury Street. I've been there. It's free to the public. Oh, sure, they chased us grubby beggars out after a while for panhandling and being filthy, but still I got to see lots of wondrous stuff. The other kids weren't much interested in it all, but I was and I still am."

I poke my finger in his big belly, which today is encased in a flowing white skirt that reaches from the bottom of his brocaded red vest to the tops of his golden silk slippers. He is standing with his hands behind him, bouncing his gold-slippered toes. He is surprisingly light on his feet despite all of his girth.

"Think of it, Pops. Vases with pictures of naked Greeks runnin' around on 'em throwin' spears at each other and wrestling and stuff, and golden masks and figurines . . . all gifts from you to the people of England. There'd be little cards next to each, tellin' where they come from and who gave 'em, and that'd be you, Charlie. Hell, you might even be thanked by Parliament for your contributions. You got lotsa stuff like that—I've seen it all over this place."

"So you would have me rob the temples of their golden treasures? So the people of Britain can gaze upon the artifacts of other lands and feel good about themselves because they do not live in such barbaric places?"

"C'mon, Chops, you've already done that. I've seen your storeroom. Hell, you could supply twenty museums with half that stuff."

"True, I do have a rather nice collection of antiquities."

His eyes take on a dreamy look and he softly says, "Sir Charles Chen, Order of the British Empire, Knight of the Garter. Oh, wouldn't that put some of those noses . . . Well, never mind," he says, shaking those thoughts out of his head. "I shall think upon your proposal. Here's Sidrah. Now off with you both."

"It is indeed a wondrous place, Sidrah. Thank you for bringing me. I wish we could have brought Ravi with us, though. I don't like the thought of his being chained up like that."

"Do not worry, Jah-kee," says Sidrah, placing her hand upon my arm, as we sit at a low table in a lush garden outside of the temple, partaking of various sweetmeats and drinks. Blossoms hang over our heads, and heady perfumes linger in the air. "Father has taken a liking to the boy. He will be fine."

Today, I have on a lovely pink silk top and a matching narrow straight-to-the-ankle skirt. I'm wearing a similar-colored shawl over my head. I figure I blend in pretty well with the crowd.

Ganju Thapa sometimes goes with us on these outings, but not today. I know the man finds escorting us a distasteful duty, and he gets out of it whenever he can. This day he sends two of his underlings, and they don't seem to like it much, either. They helped launch the *Eastern Star*, true, but did not show much joy in the outing. Perhaps they don't like being on the water. Sidrah, thoroughly enjoying herself when on the sea and marveling at my sailing skill, assigned them the task of holding parasols over our heads to guard our complexions from the sun. When we landed at the beach near the temple we were to visit, the two lugs stayed with the boat, while we proceeded through a small village to the temple grounds.

"Why do you not wear your hair like mine, Sidrah?" I ask, popping yet another olive into the ever receptive Faber mouth. There are shrimp-flavored crackers to go with them, and I crunch these with great gusto. Although they took some getting used to, I now find them quite delicious. "Your father seems to like it."

Sidrah wears her hair piled high on her head, held in place with many elaborate combs. She considers, then says, "My mother was Siamese, not Chinese. This is the way we wear our hair."

Hmmm . . . I sense she is being . . . diplomatic.

"Besides . . . ah . . . Chinese women do not always wear their hair like you have yours," she says.

"Oh . . . ?"

"No . . . Only women of certain . . . adventurous ways . . . and men, of course."

Oh-ho! I get it now! Thanks, Cheng Shih, for branding me a bad girl. Oh, well, it's been done before, and I shall live with the mark.

"Come," she says, rising to her feet. "Let us go into the presence of Gautama Buddha."

We get up and go into the quiet of the temple.

Sidrah and I kneel before the statue of the Great Buddha that is enthroned within the place—him sitting all calm and serene, gentle smile in place, with a bowl of smoldering incense at his feet. We both had bought some sticks of the stuff from a saffron-clad monk, lit them, and had placed them in the bowl. We sat there quietly for a while—Sidrah, I'm sure, praying her Buddhist prayers, and me thinking my heathen thoughts about who I am and how I got to be here in this place. *You are surely a long way from Cheapside, girl . . .*

There are other monks in the interior of this place and they sit in a circle and chant, and it is a most soothing sound. I close my eyes and let the sound and the smell of the incense take me, swaying, away.

Am I having a religious experience? My head swims and the place seems to move under me . . . *Me? Jacky Faber, the skeptic . . . the mocker, the maker of Biblical jokes. Could it be?*

No, it couldn't.

I open my eyes and look up. Among the wafts of incense smoke, I see strands of white powder, which looks like falling plaster . . . and then a grinding noise . . .

That doesn't sound very spiritual. That doesn't—

"Jah-kee!" screams Sidrah, grabbing my arm and hauling me to my feet. "Run!"

I'm mystified. *Run? Why?*

She drags me toward the portal through which we had so recently entered. She sees me confused and screams yet again . . .

"Earthquake!"

Chapter 15

My mind reeling from the feel of the earth moving in waves beneath me like some earthen sea, I struggle out of the temple. Looking down to the shore, I can see the *Eastern Star* resting quietly there despite all the pandemonium that swirls about us. Our two bodyguards begin pushing her out to sea and the cowards are manning the oars. They are probably regretting their lazy decision to let us go to the temple alone, because if anything happens to Sidrah, their lives won't be worth a farthing. Chopstick Charlie, mild though he might appear, would see to that, for sure.

Sidrah listens, head up, watching the shore intently.

"It was but a small earthquake," she says, her hand still on my arm.

Small? I shudder. It felt pretty *big* to me! I look back to the temple, which is still standing, but there are some other buildings nearby that are not—they are now piles of rubble. Piteous screams rend the sudden, uneasy silence. *Oh, Lord . . .*

"There may be aftershocks . . . but that is not the only thing to fear. Come, let us run."

All right. But she doesn't run toward the boat. She drags me in the opposite direction—inland. *What . . . ?*

"The boat's thataway, Sidrah. Why—?" I protest, stumbling along behind her.

"After earthquake," she shouts, panting, "sometimes comes the tsunami, the Great Wave . . . And look, Jah-kee, it is going to happen!"

She points to the shore. The water is fast receding and there is a great sucking sound, like it's being drawn out by some giant whirlpool far out to sea. When first we had landed in our little boat, the beach was about twenty-five yards wide. Now it is a hundred . . . now a hundred and fifty . . . The *Eastern Star* is aground on the sand, her oars now useless to the two men who still sit within her . . . Now two hundred . . . and then we can see the shoreline no more. All manner of sealife lies exposed to view. Whelks, conchs, giant clams, lobsters, all kinds of fish—all just lying there. *Oh, Lord, if we could just harvest some of these, even a few,* I'm thinking.

"Quickly, Jah-kee, as fast as you can! The wave will come fast!"

I need no further encouragement. Lifting our sheathlike skirts, we race for higher ground.

"To that tree there! It is our only chance!"

She points to a large tree with low drooping branches that sits to the left, way beyond the temple, and we pound toward it. I get there first and vault up onto the first limb, lock my legs around it, and reach back for Sidrah, as she cannot have had the experience in climbing that I do.

She goes to take my hand, but there is a cry of anguish and we both look down to see a baby, a girl, sitting naked

upon a rock next to some washing her mother had been doing, the child now plainly alone in a suddenly very cruel world.
Sidrah reaches down to scoop her up, then slings the child on
her back, and the girl wraps her arms around Sidrah's neck as
she runs to the tree. I reach under Sidrah's armpits and haul
her, and the burden on her back, up to the first branch.

"Higher!" gasps Sidrah. "We must get higher! Look!"

I look and I see it. *Good God!*

The Great Wave looms up . . . and up . . . and ever up . . .
out there on the horizon, and it is coming on like the Wall of
Doom, and judging from the masts of the boats it is devour-
ing, it's gotta be fifty feet high!

The Wave from Hell roars ever onward, sucking up whatever is in its path—boats . . . animals . . . people—sucking into
its belly whatever it does not grind to bits against the pitiless
ground.

"Higher! Higher!" shouts Sidrah, and we crawl further
into the ever thinner branches.

"But it is just a wave," I call out. "Surely it must crash
and then wash away!"

"No, Jah-kee! Look beyond the crest!" she cries, pointing with her free hand.

There is the wave itself, yes, but behind it there is no
trough like a regular wave's—like those I have dealt with all
my adult life . . . No, no simple little trough there. No, the
entire Bay of Bengal rides high behind it!

Horrified, I climb higher as the water comes relentlessly on.

Now it is at the edge of what was the beach, and from
my perch, I am amazed to see that there, midway up the wall

of water, rides the poor, doomed *Eastern Star*, its two terrified occupants still in it. And now it thunders below us, sweeping all before it.

The Devil Wave hits the helpless land and its defenseless people and their flimsy homes. It smashes into the side of the temple, surging angrily all about. The temple holds, but my *Star* hits the side of the building and shatters into a hundred yellow shards and I see no more of it.

The tree trembles, but it has seen this before, and it holds.

"Higher! There is another wave!" implores Sidrah.

I look out and see that, incredibly, there is yet another wave coming at us. This one sits *on top* of the first one! *Lord!*

We scramble higher into the top of the tree as the second wave surges by us, wetting our feet but doing us no other harm. The water swirls below for an astonishingly long time, and then slowly recedes.

It seems that angry Neptune is done with us . . . for now.

Disasters bring out the best in people . . .

We climb down and find the surviving villagers already at work trying to help the victims less lucky than they. There is much wailing and crying, but there are shouts of joy as well. Sidrah is able to hand the child she saved back to the girl's weeping mother. We join a gang digging out a man trapped by wreckage and a boy pinned by a log, and look to help others as best we can.

And disasters bring out the worst in people . . . as well as the worst people themselves . . .

In the midst of yet another rescue attempt, Sidrah

116

suddenly straightens up and looks toward the shore. She looks grim.

"What is it? Another wave?"

"No. Bad men come. Look."

I follow her gaze and see that two big launches have pulled up on the beach and rough men are pouring out of them. Beyond them, out at sea, sits a ship, and from its mast-head it flies the black colors.

Pirates!

"Out at sea they feel the sea surge below them and know that big wave will come up and strike shore. They come in to reap evil profits from unhappiness of others," explains Sidrah, the anger plain in her usually impassive face.

The seagoing marauders swarm up the beach and rage through the stricken town, and the people of the village are helpless before them. Those the pirates cannot use are struck down without mercy, and the ones they can use—those to be held hostage for ransom or to be sold as slaves—are shoved into their boats and taken back to the big ship. It is as easy as plucking apples from a tree for the heartless bastards to capture the stunned victims of the tsunami. A gang of them rampages through the temple, stealing all they can lay their hands on. The monks cry out in protest, but it does them no good, for the pirates club them down, laughing at their anguish.

"Run, Sidrah!" I shout, and run we do, but as we dash past the temple, we see with dismay that there is a high cliff to the rear of the temple, so we cannot run there. We are caught between that stone wall and the devils from the sea. *Damn! We are trapped!* They are on us in a moment.

A particularly large and smelly rogue grabs me and twists

my arm behind my back. From her cries, I suspect Sidrah has been similarly assaulted.

"Let go of me, goddamn it!" I yell, twisting in his grip.

My shiv, please, my shiv! Oh, where are you now when I need you?

"You'll pay for this, you dogs!" I threaten, but I fear in vain, for no, it does not serve. Rough hands are put on us and we are taken, the pirates plainly delighted to have snatched two girls as well dressed as we are and surely worth something in the way of very sweet ransoms.

We stand on the deck of the pirate ship, which has made sail, and we are headed south and are now out of sight of the plundered town. Most of the captives have been shoved below into what smells like the hold of a slaver, but Sidrah and I remain on deck, being examined by the grinning rogue of a captain. He is dressed in black pantaloons with a wide leather belt. His thick chest is covered with curly black hairs and crossed with two heavy straps. Above us flutters his flag, which I can now see has two crossed scimitars on a field of black, with a silver five-pointed star between the blades. Sidrah has her chin in the air, her haughtiest look on her face, and is speaking to the captain. I do not know the language, but I know what she is saying.

I am Sidrat'ul Muntaha, Daughter of the House of Chen. You would do well to treat us kindly, if you mean to keep your head.

The beast nods, happy at the news, and he replies.

That is very good, Little Chicken. Charlie-san shall pay dearly to get you back. But what is this strange creature? He hooks his thumb at me.

118

Being so addressed, I put on the Lawson Peabody School for Young Girls Look—chin up, eyes hooded, lips together, teeth apart, and gaze upon the captain as if I were looking at a toad, to which he most certainly seems to be related. I decide to speak up for myself.

"Listen, you misbegotten son of a slime worm. I am Lieutenant Jacky Faber, Royal British Navy, also known as the dread Ju kau-jing yi, beloved by Cheng Shih, Admiral of the China Sea! I sail under her protection! Look upon this, lowly eater of cockroaches, and despair!"

I whip my pigtail from off my neck and show him my Golden Dragon tattoo, my Safe Passage in these perilous waters, as it were. *So, there, pig . . .*

He laughs and brings the back of his hand across my face. I cry out and take a step back. He brings his own grisly face up to mine and exposes his yellow teeth and spits out some surly words.

"Be careful, Jah-kee!" hisses Sidrah, who had translated my bootless threat. "The arrogant fool says that he has no love for the whore Cheng Shih and he does not fear her! Especially since you, the bearer of her hated mark, will not survive this voyage if you do not curb your tongue!"

The greasy cur of a captain issues orders and I am grabbed by two burly sailors and stood up on the rail. Teetering there and looking down, I see the water swirling darkly by the ship's hull. Looking across, I see that the land is about a quarter mile off to the west.

"He says he will throw you in to drown, Jah-kee," says Sidrah, sounding very worried. "Please be careful what you say."

I look at the water. I look at the land. I look at the captain snarling next to me, and strangely I think of Jemimah Moses and one of the animal tales she used to tell me and the kids back on the *Nancy B.* as we plowed through the Caribbean last year. It had to do with Brother Rabbit and a horrid briar patch into which Brother Fox and Brother Bear were threatening to toss him.

I turn to this sleazy captain and work up a gob of spit and aim it at his eye.

"Do what you will!" I shout. "You sorry sack of monkey shit."

"Arrhhhhgash!" he roars, and I am thrown off the side, and as the water comes up to meet me, I hum . . .

Born and bred in a briar patch . . .

Chapter 16

Great, just great . . .

Here I am, sitting on yet another desolate beach, my prospects dim. The ocean lies in front of me, with the thick jungle behind, teeming with tigers, no doubt. *Well, girl, be glad you're still alive, and you'd best get on with it.* With a heavy sigh and a mighty groan, I get to my feet and stretch. I figure my best option is to walk north, to return to the devastated village to see if I can arrange some sort of passage back to Rangoon and Charlie's place.

After that unwashed cur of a captain had me tossed into the drink, I had stayed below long enough to see the hull of the pirate slip out of sight. After allowing sufficient time to lapse so that all aboard would think me drowned, I kicked to the surface and started pulling for the shore . . . *Please, Father Neptune, please hold back your toothy sharks, because I think you have handled me roughly enough this day.*

I settled into the rhythm of the strokes and soon set up a good pace, the slippery silk of my sarong not slowing me down at all as I slid through the water, my mind churning. I knew Sidrah would be ransomed, she being the daughter of the House of Chen, after all. I certainly wasn't doing her any good back on that ship, but if I can at least get back to Charlie and tell him what happened to her, he might be able to take action. As for the other poor people on that pirate ship, it was certainly the slave pens for them, as no one would ransom poor fisher folk. Aye, Sidrah would certainly be ransomed, and the others enslaved, but another thing I knew for certain: After that bastard saw the dragon mark on my neck, there was no way I was gonna leave that ship alive. I probably would have spent some interesting time below-decks with the captain and his crew before having my neck wrung and my body tossed overboard.

For me, it was the devil or the deep blue sea, and I chose the sea.

As I trudge along, keeping close to the shoreline should a hungry tiger appear with dinner on his mind, I pull the ruins of my beautiful silk sarong away from my skin, the better to dry it out. Of course, the fine pink silk is a mess, all flimsy and smeared, but I gotta wear somethin'. Oh, well, the sun feels good on my muscles after that long swim, and for that I am grateful. *Walk on, girl . . .*

I do keep walking, but I am getting hungry and thirsty and I do not have my shiv with which to dig clams or poke the eyes out of coconuts. There is a lot of ropey seaweed lying about on the beach and there are rocks around which the stuff is clustered, so I mess about in it, trying to find some luckless beast to devour, but find nothing. I do notice that the channel right here gets rather narrow and fishing craft out on the water have to come close in here. There is one rock in particular that sits a good distance out. *Would have to watch out for that one, should I be sailing,* says the mariner in me.

Well, you ain't sailing, you're walkin', so get back to it.

Within a few minutes I round a point on the shoreline and see that the channel has opened out into a wide expanse of water and there is a good deal of shipping upon it. *Well, forget about it, ain't none of it gonna do you any good. Keep walking . . . If night catches you out here, you might spend the night in a tiger's tummy, so move it and—*

Good Lord! There's a ship out there pretty close to the shore and she's flying American colors! If I can flag her down, she might help me!

I immediately run into the water and begin waving my arms about my head, shouting, "Help me! I'm an American, too!"

But I know it ain't gonna do any good because they are too far out to hear. And if any sailor aboard would train his spyglass on me, he would see what looked to him to be a demented, heathen Chinese person going mad on the shore. Certainly nothing to tell the captain about, certainly nothing to impede them from wherever they were going.

Oh, oh, oh! What to do?

Ha! I'll try semaphore! I arrange my arms and make the signals.

H . . . E . . . L . . . P . . . M . . . E . . .

No good. Not a sail is slacked, and though I see the flash of sun off a long glass lens, their course is not changed. Stupid American sailors don't know Royal Navy signals. *No, no, they're not stupid. You are! Think! It's going to get away! Think!*

In despair I see the ship approach the point I just passed. Soon it will be around it and gone.

Damn! And it is a schooner, too, and it looks like a New Englander, which might know of the *Nancy B. Damn . . . How do you get a bloody ship to stop, for chrissakes? How . . . ?*

It hits me. I know how . . . and others of my ilk know how . . . We've always known how.

The *Lorelei . . . Yes!*

I turn and pound back up the beach from whence I had just come, then round the point, the ship now being, for the moment, out of sight. Whipping off my top, I pick up a curved piece of gray driftwood and begin wading out to that rock I spotted before, the one close by the channel . . . or close enough, I hope.

Reaching the rock, I climb up on it, grabbing a good bunch of seaweed as I go. I plunk my tail down upon the top of it, wrap my sarong tightly around my legs, put my matching top about my feet in such a way as to suggest a fin, arrange the seaweed on my head such that it covers my baldness and trails down over my breast.

There.

Sailors are always telling their superstitious mates tall tales about having seen mermaids at sea, and now they're about to get one for real. I lift my piece of wood and get ready.

As I see the prow of the schooner appear from around the point and the ship heaves fully into view, I commence strumming on my driftwood lyre and begin singing. I do a high, keening *waaaaaaaillll,* as loud as I can, so it will carry out over the water, but still keeping it sad and sweet, combining the sound of an Irish wake with the Oriental tunes I had learned recently, and adding a dash of my own innate weirdness, too. And hey, how about some beckoning words as well . . .

Come all you bold sailors and listen to meeeeee
Come sit by my side at the bottom
of the seeeeea . . .
I'll kiss you and caress you and cover you
with love,
And ne'ermore you'll toil in the cruel
world above.

I'm hoping for something like the siren songs of yore, like what those naughty girls would sing, they who lured poor Greek sailors to their doom on the rocks of Scylla and Charybdis.

I think I hit it pretty close.

If a fully rigged ship of the sea could have brakes like those on a coach, then this schooner would have used them, as it suddenly screeches to a halt in its watery track. All sails go slack, there is the glint off many a telescope lens, and I see, through the strands of my seaweed hair, a boat being lowered. And, yes, it's manned, and being rowed toward me.

Ah, yes . . .

I preen a bit, moving my shoulders about, and continue to sing as I wait for the boat. I do like being the center of attention, wherever I can find it, whether it be on a stage, in a tavern, or here, perched on a rock in God-Knows-Where.

I keep up the act, seaweed in eyes and all, to preserve the illusion to the end—after all, I don't want them to come upon me and say, "Aw, it ain't no mermaid at all, it's just some scrawny little bint. Let's leave 'er 'ere," now, do I?

When the bow of the boat scrapes against my rock, I sneak a peek . . . and no . . . no . . . I don't believe it.

"Never did think much of you in the past, Jack-o, you bein' such a royal pain in the ass and all," says the grinning sailor who reaches out his hand to me.

"But I gotta admit, you got a real nice set o' tits there."

Davy . . . ?

Chapter 17

"Now you will tell me, John Higgins, just how you and the Nancy B. *and all my friends came to be here and why I am here and . . . oh, God, I am so glad to see all of you that I really don't care why! Oh, please, just hold me!"*

When I had been brought back to my dear little ship, blubbering with relief and joy at seein' Davy and John Thomas and Finn McGee in the boat, I was shocked beyond all reason to see Liam. Yes, Liam Delaney, my old sea dad, standin' there grinnin' at me and sayin', "Now ain't you a proper heathen sight, Jacky! I swear by all the saints that Moira was right. You are the worst of all possible bad influences on our daughter Mairead. For here I have to come halfway around the world to look after the two of yiz . . . but still I'm glad to see ye, lass—"

He doesn't get any further than that 'cause I rush up and throw my arms around his neck and lay my face upon his broad chest.

"Oh, Father, well met, oh, so well met!"

He pats my shaking shoulders.

"My sentiments exactly, Daughter. Mr. Higgins, might we not take our little mermaid below and get her into something a good Christian girl might wear?"

I am taken below and stripped of what little sodden clothing I have on and plunked into my dear little copper-bound tub, once again being scrubbed clean of my surface dirt and salt if not my mortal sins against God, Nature, and Good Order. Hot water is brought from the galley and poured over me . . . *ahhhhhh* . . . and Higgins gets to work on cleaning up the mess that is me.

"So, Higgins," I purr, writhing about like any slippery little eel in the sinfully warm water. "Give me the news, and tell me all. You can start with why my dear *Nancy B.* is here. Hmmm . . . ?"

"Well, Miss," says Higgins, untwining my pigtail. "You will recall that when in the port of Gibraltar, on the *Lorelei Lee,* we both dispatched letters to various people—you to your various loved ones, and me to Liam Delaney, offering him the command of the *Nancy B.* should he want to use it to pursue his lost daughter, Mairead, and her husband, Ian McConnaughey, both newly condemned to the penal colony in New South Wales. I also offered him a draft in the amount of three hundred dollars on our U.S. bank to pay his expenses."

Higgins pauses in working on my hair and says, "I hope I did not exceed my authority in this matter, Miss? I was acting in the capacity of Vice President of Faber Shipping, the President, at the time, being incapacitated. If so, I am prepared to tender my resignation as a member of the Board."

"*Incapacitated?* 'Incarcerated,' you mean, Higgins." I

laugh, for I was, at the time, a lowly convict bound for a life sentence in Australia. "No, you did absolutely the right thing, as you always do. You could've maybe told me . . . but then again, perhaps you were wise in not doing so. Anyway, let it go. Continue."

Higgins resumes his ministrations, along with his story.

"So . . . It is apparent that Liam Delaney, the enraged father, his being of Irish birth and temperament, cursed the British government straight to hell, and took us up on our offer. He immediately boarded a fast cutter from Waterford to Boston and presented my letter to Ezra Pickering, Clerk of Faber Shipping Worldwide, who, upon receipt of the letter, agreed to the terms. He was, of course, bolstered by a certain Miss Amy Trevelyne, who also wished to discover what had happened to the absent President of said Company and to aid in her possible recovery."

As I think on this, Higgins pauses in the scrubbing of my hair and curiously massages my shoulders, and though it is pleasant, I ask, "What? Is there something wrong with my shoulders?"

"Oh, no, Miss. I was checking to see if any parts of your corporeal being are actually made of cork. Like the bobbers that I believe fishermen use in pursuit of their finny prey."

"Right. Because I keep bobbing up, hey?"

"Indeed, Miss."

"Very droll, Higgins," I say, a bit huffily. "Well, if anyone ever observes me sinking into Neptune's rather damp arms, I would advise you to wait for sure evidence of my demise, as I am certain that I will die not at sea, like any good salty sailor, but shamefully on land, when it comes right down to it."

"Oh . . . ?"

"Oh, yes. When last at Dovecote, I shuddered when a goose walked over my future grave on a place called Daisy Hill. There my poor body shall ultimately lie, in a humble plot overlooking the sparkling sea. I am sure of it, so there . . . 'Home will be the sailor, home from the raging sea . . .'"

"Very poetic, Miss, if not completely rational."

"Well, so what? I have never been neither poetical nor rational . . . and furthermore, as I have always said, 'a girl what's born for hangin' ain't likely to be drowned.'"

"We hope it shall not come to that, Miss," says Higgins. "However, we have more pressing concerns. To wit: What shall we do with this . . . hair?" He lifts my poor limp and soggy and unbound pigtail twixt thumb and forefinger, with lifted eyebrows. "What to do? For once, I must confess I am at a loss."

I duck down under the water to consider this question, then come up, water streaming over my face.

"Let's keep it as it is for a while, Higgins. It might come in handy. Shock value and all. And in this part of the world, it does not at all look out of place."

"Very well, Miss," says Higgins, and he claps his hands lightly and . . .

Lee Chi!

Lee Chi, my faithful Chinese eunuch, steps into my cabin, bearing razor and scissors and a merry grin, and I am so delighted to see him!

"*Nei ho mah! Lee Chi!*" I exult. "Good day to you!" I grab his pigtail and plant one on his smooth shaven pate.

"*Nei ho mah, Ju kau-jing yi!*" he says, grinning and bowing.

"I thought it best to keep Lee Chi close to me, as he probably would be lost in the shuffle of the ships' crews. I did recall your last instruction that he be brought back to Boston and made fluent in English so as to become a valuable asset for our future trade with China. For now, he has proven useful as a steward."

"Mmm . . . Good decision," I say, as Lee Chi whips out his razor and brings it to bear on my head. My pate is soon re-shaved, smooth and gleaming.

Hmmmm . . . I feel the *Nancy B.* heel over as her course is changed, and I say to Higgins, "Would you ask Captain Delaney to step in for a moment?"

I sink down below the sudsy water as Higgins goes to the door and calls out for Liam.

"She wishes to speak to you, Sir, if you please!"

Liam ducks his head in and gives me a questioning look.

"Liam," I say. "Please continue on a southerly course, as I have business with a certain ship that passed this way recently . . . one flying a black flag bearing two crossed scimitars and a silver star. Have you seen it?"

"Aye. Yesterday. It looked like the rogue might try us, but the sight of our guns made him think twice, it seems."

"Hmmm, well, let us chase him down, shall we? And pull down our American colors and just fly the Faber Shipping blue anchor flag . . . and cover the guns with canvas. I know it goes against your grain, but make us look sloppy."

Liam grins and puts two fingers to the brim of his hat. "Back in the piratical business, eh, Jacky?"

"Even so, Liam, for there are some people aboard that ship who need rescuing, and some that need . . . a hard lesson."

"All hands aloft to make sail!" he roars as he goes back on deck.

God, how I do love the sound of that!

"So, anyway, Higgins, continue if you would. Some news of Jaimy Fletcher?"

"Ah, yes, that was a very tenuous situation—between him and Mr. Jared, Mr. Jared being a Royal Navy Officer and Mr. Fletcher now being an escaped convict. After your apparent death, however, the issue was resolved: Mr. Jared would accompany the *Cerberus*—HMS *Dart*'s original charge, you will recall—back to London, whereupon the ship would be returned to the East India Company and Mr. Fletcher would be put ashore secretly in dark of night. This was agreeable to the very gloomy Mr. Fletcher, whose sole interest in life now seems to be to exact revenge upon Mr. Flashby and Mr. Bliffil, those two gentlemen upon whom he places the blame for your untimely demise. The *Lorelei Lee* would part company when the fleet rounded the southern tip of Africa, and return to Boston, bearing your Irish crew and the sad news of your death. All felt that it would be your wish that life should go on for Faber Shipping, even in your final . . . absence."

I nod to that. *Life does go on, in spite of everything.*

"This was all decided when we met the *Nancy B.* entering the top of the Straits of Malacca. We came together and apprised the stricken crew of your fate. Liam's joy at seeing his daughter Mairead safe and in the company of her husband was tempered with news of your loss, and he decided to have one more try at locating either you or your remains. Your body could have washed ashore, you know, so it wasn't a totally hopeless quest. I elected to come with him . . . for one last search."

He pauses and reaches for a towel.

"I think it would be best if you got out now, Miss, and we'll get you dressed. I assume you will entertain your officers for dinner?"

Was that a catch in his voice? Ah, dear Higgins, you are my dearest friend.

I am dried and my hair is combed out, to be braided later when it, too, dries. One of my simple chemises is floated over me and I sprawl out on my lovely bed . . . *ahhhh* . . .

Before he leaves me, he does something that destroys any rest I might have in mind. He places a tray next to my bed, and then leaves. On the tray is a plate of cheese and biscuits and various meats and two glasses of lovely wine and . . .

Two glasses? Why two?

"I have letters, Jacky . . . from our friends in Boston," says someone entering my cabin.

Joy! I exult and reach for the letters. Then it comes to me that it was a female voice that spoke. *Wot?* There ain't supposed to be any girls here except for me . . . I look up to see just who it is handing them to me.

Damn!

"You! You're supposed to be back in school!"

"Aye," says Joannie Nichols. "And you're supposed to be in prison in Australia! Neither one of us is where we're *supposed* to be. So there!"

"I'm gonna wring your scrawny little neck!"

"No, you ain't. You, yourself, gave me orders when last you left. Remember? 'You'll get to go on the next voyage, Joannie, I promise.' So here it is, the next voyage, and here I am, as promised."

"What about the Lawson Peabody? Mistress Pimm?"

"It was all right, the school and all . . . They'll get along without me for a while. 'Specially Mistress . . . who ain't got a whole lot of use for me . . ."

I certainly know that feeling, but . . . *grrr* . . .

The door opens and Higgins enters with fresh linen for the table and for me.

"Ah, you've met our little stowaway, have you? Well, if you want me to pitch her overboard, I would be glad to accomplish that task," he says, with gimlet eye fixed upon Joannie.

She does not seem unduly worried about a watery fate.

"Stowaway?" she says. "Yes, I did stow away . . . hid down in the bilges for a whole night after Liam come aboard with the news that you was in jail again. Didn't surprise me none, you and your Cheapside ways. Didn't pop up till we were three days out. Damn hungry by then, I can tell you."

"What about Daniel Prescott? What did he think about all this, Miss Contrary-Who-Doesn't-Know-What's-Best-for-Her?" I say, placing an accusing finger on her nose.

"He was in bed. Broke his fool leg fallin' from the masthead. Doctor fixed him up," she says, her face softening. "But I didn't tell him I was goin' . . . just covered his face with kisses the night before I left." *Sniff.* "He'll be all right."

"Well, I am *not* pleased," I announce in my stern Mistress Pimm voice, with full Lawson Peabody Look in place.

"That's all very well, Jacky," she replies, a sly look on her face. "And probably you'd like me to leave . . . But then again, maybe you'd like some news of the School . . . and that Clarissa . . . hmmmm? And Martha . . . and, oh my, Dorothea and Mr. Sackett! Oh, what a scandal . . . and Rebecca and I got in just the worst trouble . . . And wait'll you hear about Dolley. You definitely want to hear about her! Oh, yes, Dolley got married and—"

"Just you come sit down here with me, you little devil," I say, making room. "Let's hear it."

I mean, what girl could resist the delicious promise of something like that, really? Not me, that's for sure. I do like my news!

Chapter 18

⚓ "Seabrook seems a good steady man and he fits well as Captain of the *Lorelei Lee*. I could have forced Padraic on as Captain of that ship," Liam Delaney is saying, "but he lacks experience. Seabrook has announced that he will leave her upon arrival in Boston. We shall have to see what happens. If I am back by then, I shall be honored to take the post. Mr. Gibson will stay on as Second, mainly, I think, in the vain hope of seeing you again, but then again he is young and stupid and of a romantic nature. He is a thoroughgoing seaman, as well, so it is good that he stays on. That boyo Arthur McBride is Third Mate, and that is fine with me so long as he does not stand on the same deck as do I. As soon as I take command, he goes."

Arthur McBride has rubbed a lot of people the wrong way in his journey through the world, I reflect. *But I rather like him—he has always brought me cheer.*

"Yes, Father, that shall be the way of it, and the *Lee* shall begin her transatlantic passenger service, as she was originally intended . . . before the last mess."

"The last mess, Daughter, that I believe you helped create."

"Yes, but I am more settled now, Liam, and I resolve to be good."

He looks up at my bald pate, which is surely glistening in the morning light, and snorts. "Right . . ."

"Ah," I say. "I hear the others arriving. Let us turn to dinner."

In troops Davy Jones, John Tinker, now Second and Third Mates of the *Nancy B.* I had been told that Jim Tanner, my usual helmsman and First Mate when I was on the little Gloucester schooner, had to remain in Boston, his wife, Clementine, being great with child and ready to give birth. "It killed him not to come, Jacky," Tink said. "But Annie and Betsey and the rest of us made him see the wisdom of it. He needs to be by his wife's side when she delivers him of a daughter or son."

John Higgins follows them into my cabin, trailed by Joannie Nichols in serving gear.

Higgins directs, and Joannie serves and does a good job of it, knowing full well that I'm watching her closely and standing ready to pounce upon any mistake. She knows how fast one can fall from being Lady-in-Training at the Lawson Peabody to lowly Cabin Girl on a small schooner—especially if she foolishly stows away on said little barky.

That was last night and now it is morning. I awaken and kick Joannie out of my bed, telling her to attend to her chores, which she does without too much complaint.

As I wash up and slip into my simple sailor's gear, I reflect on last night's dinner . . .

• • •

After we were done with the dinner and well in to the Madeira, I recounted the horror of the earthquake and the tsunami that followed it, and Sidrah's courage and concern for the poor villagers. Then I told about the crimes committed in the aftermath of that disaster by the scurvy crew of the pirate ship that we are now pursuing. *Yes, Liam . . . Higgins . . . back in the Caribbean we did plunder a few Spanish towns in company with Flaco Jimenez, but we were not nearly as vicious as these curs.*

All agreed that these pirates deserve punishment and are firmly resolved to see the job done . . . no quarter asked, nor given . . . no mercy, if it comes to it.

Grim thoughts of vengeance were put aside and we turned to song and dance, very, very happy with our lot. Me, for damn sure, considering my recent trials.

Presently Higgins comes in bearing a breakfast tray and places it on my table.

I avidly dig in.

"Oh, Higgins, you cannot know just how good this is!" I exclaim, my mouth full of eggs and bacon and biscuit.

"I am glad you enjoy it, Miss," says he. "I trust you slept well?"

"Like a baby, Higgins, like a baby in her mother's arms."

"Miss!" comes the call from above. "We have him in sight! Black flag, two crossed swords with a star above!"

I leap to my feet.

"Let's go! Hold course! Battle stations!"

"What shall you wear, Miss?"

"I think I'll go with my Chinese gear, Higgins, if you would."

Although Higgins had brought my seabag from the *Lorelei Lee* to the *Nancy B.* in the faint hope of finding me alive—and I bless him for it—I feel it best to go Oriental in this action.

My simple morning outfit is quickly stripped and replaced with the green silk trousers and tunic given to me by Cheng Shih, the back of which bears the sign of the Golden Dragon. Also on my back is strapped my two-handed Chinese sword in its sheath.

Thus armed, I run barefoot to the door and call out, "Execute Plan A!"

"Someday I'm going to get you for this, Jacky, mark me on that," growls Davy, as he pretends to swab the deck. The lad is clad in one of my bonnets, with gingham dress below.

"I think you are quite becoming, Davida, dear." I giggle. "Wait'll I tell all the folks down at the Pig and Whistle."

"*Grrrrrr . . .*"

"What, Davy? Are you saying it is all right for me to parade around dressed up as a boy, but not for you to don girl's clothing? I should think turnabout is fair play."

"It's different," snarls Davy. "It goes against my nature . . . and the nature of any man."

I, too, have a bonnet on, as does Tink, who wears one of my wigs, as well. He is red in the face but does not complain so much.

So, to any onlooker's eye, we appear to be a badly sailed, poorly rigged schooner, with an assortment of helpless females aboard. This old trick had been tried on us by the Brothers Lafitte last year off Charleston, back in the States. Didn't work for them, but it just might work for us.

The pirate craft lies off to our portside and it quickly becomes plain that he is interested . . . very interested. He has slowly decreased his speed and has altered course to close the distance between us. I have had our American colors hauled down, leaving only our little Faber Shipping blue anchor flag fluttering above. Our guns are loaded with grapeshot and covered. Liam is at the wheel, while John Thomas and Smasher McGee crouch hidden behind the rail, cutlasses drawn, many loaded pistols in their belts. The pirates are now about two hundred yards off . . .

Steady, boys, steady . . . Get close to your gun . . .

We can see them there, most on deck, some in the rigging, grinning down on us and thinking us easy prey.

. . . now about one hundred . . . now fifty . . . now twenty-five . . . now, scum, we shall see . . .

"Fire!" I shout. "Rake their decks!"

The canvas covers are ripped off the guns and the lanyards are pulled and . . .

Crrraaak!

All four cannons spit forth their deadly charges, raking the deck of the pirate. There are screams of pain from the enemy, and shouts of pure fury from my men.

"Reload with ball," I cry. "Fire when ready! Crush them!"

John Thomas gets his loaded first and . . .

Crash!

His shot is true, and a nine-pound ball of iron slams into the pirate's side, right at the waterline, and the sea begins to pour in.

Crash!

That is Finn McGee's gun, doing even more damage.

"That's enough!" I shout. "Cease fire!"

I can see still forms lying about the deck of the other ship.

"Bring us next to him, Liam! Pepper them, boys! Prepare to board!"

Davy and Tink lift their very accurate Kentucky squirrel rifles and drop two of the pirates from the rigging. The two ships come together and I leap over the rail, followed by my bully boys.

Thomas and McGee use their pistols to knock down several more pirates, then whip out their cutlasses and set about their grim, bloody work.

I go for the Captain, who stands at his wheel, shocked at seeing my return and at the turn of events. He looks up at my masthead, where I had directed Joannie, at the first sound of conflict, to raise the Golden Dragon pennant, such that the dogs would know their doom and just who was dealing it to them and strike mortal fear into the hearts of any who remain alive.

The flag twists and turns in the wind over our heads.

"So, piece of filth, you would scorn the Mark of the Dragon, eh?"

He lets go of his helm and, in desperation, pulls out his sword and raises it overhead, to bring it down upon me.

He does not get the chance. I reach back with both hands and whip out my own, and with one fluid motion, I swing it around and slash him across the belly. I have my sword back in my scabbard before he can survey the damage.

He looks down in wonder at his middle. The tip of my sword had cut the waistcord of his pants, causing them to fall to his ankles. He is aghast. Not only is his male pride wounded, as he stands there exposed to the laughter of my crew, but he's so amazed at my skill that he drops his own sword and cries out, "*Rehem!*"

I expect that means "Mercy!" but I shall give him very little.

I again whip out my sword and this time lay the razor-sharp blade right against his neck. His eyes widen and he mews and makes begging sounds.

No, I do not take his head, nor cut his throat, though I am sorely tempted. Actually, he was mistaken in his assessment of my skill with the sword, for I really was trying to disembowel him on my first swing. I just miscalculated, is all. Oh, well, all to the good, I figure, as I really don't like killing people, even curs like the one who cowers before me.

I cut my eyes to the side and see that the rest of the pirates—those who are still alive, anyway—are being herded on the fantail and stripped of their weapons.

Then I turn back to the former leader of this pirate gang and say, "So, Captain . . . Try to drown Jacky Faber, will you?"

He stares at me, uncomprehending, as I take my sword from his neck and put the point of it on his fat hairy belly and give him a poke, such that he falls back, stepping away from his fallen trousers.

"Get with the others, you scurvy dog. Now!" I shout, jerking my head in the direction of his former crewmates huddling on the stern of the sinking ship. He does not understand my words, but he surely takes my meaning as he scurries off, *sans culottes,* as it were, his flaccid buttocks jiggling in a most unmanly way.

"John Thomas!" I cry, pointing to the hatchway. "Break

that lock and let's get the captives out! This thing is sinking fast!"

He lunges forward and slams the hilt of his heavy cutlass down on the lock and it gives way. He pulls open the door and I scream down into the darkness, "Sidrah! It's me! Bring up the people! Tell them the ship is sinking and we're going to take them back to their village! Quickly, now!"

Sidrah, her dark eyes blinking, comes up into the light. "Jah-kee? Thank God!"

"My sentiments exactly, Sister. Now get these people onto my ship! The deck's almost awash!"

She shouts down into the hold and the people pour out, some of them already very wet. Davy and Tink guide them over the rail and onto the *Nancy B.*

"Liam!" I call through all the confusion. I see that the pirate ship carries a small boat—probably the same one that carried Sidrah and me to this awful ship. "Get the pirates into that boat and cast them off. Hurry!"

He looks dubious, but he does it. The boat is lowered and the pirates prodded into it and then shoved off. Amazed at their luck in not being immediately killed in horrible fashion, which is exactly what they would have done if the situation were reversed, they quickly ship oars and pull for the shore.

As they pull away, some of them, now secure in the knowledge that they will live through this day, make rude gestures and shout threats back at us. I just smile at that, for I think I remember that very shore on which they will land. I believe it is the one that Ravi and I landed on after the great storm. Yes, I believe it is. Somehow the hungry alligators of Key West come to mind. *Hmmm . . .*

When all is accomplished, Liam comes up next to me and says, "Do you think that was wise, Jacky, to let such as them live so that they might again do evil in this world?"

Sidrah, having seen the other captives taken below and settled, appears on deck to stand by my side, her face glowing in her newly regained freedom. *Oh, Sister, it is so good to see you again!*

"Liam," I say, my arm about Sidrah as we look toward the retreating boat and the rather forbidding shore beyond. "I know you have seen many old sea charts showing lands and seas through which modern sailors have not yet traveled . . . ?"

"Aye," he says, rather mystified. "I have. They are old, but we still must use them if we are in uncharted waters. What are you getting at, dear?"

"Well, then you will remember, Father, that on those charts were fanciful drawings of sea serpents and such, with 'Here There Monsters Be' penned under them?"

Liam chuckles. "Aye. I have seen those maps. At the university, last year. In Dublin. Warnings about 'falling off the edge of the world' and all that."

"Well, Captain Liam Delaney," I say, pointing with my finger to the dark, tree-lined shore. "Here there *real* monsters be—striped monsters with big yellow fangs and great appetites. Believe me, I know, firsthand. I do not think our brigands will do any more damage in this world—except maybe to upset the digestion of several honest and well-meaning tigers."

Is that deep hungry growling from the jungle? No, prolly not—we're too far out to hear that, but still . . .

Liam laughs, the sound rumbling deep in his throat. "Well, serves the buggers right, then."

"You are right, Liam," I say. "And as for right and wrong, who is good and who is bad, I say, 'Let God sort 'em out!'"

We bring the *Nancy B.* about and set her on her new course. I stand on my quarterdeck with Higgins beside me, and we watch the pirate ship slip out of sight beneath the waves, leaving only a greasy slick to mark its grave.

"Too bad," says Higgins, watching the final bubbles come up from the murky depths. "We might have sold that ship. I was going to inform you a bit later, but we are very nearly out of money and supplies."

"It was a spongy, worthless tub, weak in all its knees, else it would have not sunk so quickly," I say. "But, don't worry, John. I know where to get some money. Tell Liam to set course north . . . for Rangoon."

Chapter 19

I'm walking slowly down that same street where Ravi and I were first nabbed by that thug Ganju Thapa. My long cloak is pulled up to my neck, but my head is uncovered. I look furtively about, as if I fear capture, when actually, I am inviting it. I, of course, *know* how to get back to Chopstick Charlie's stronghold through these rabbit-warren streets, having been out and about with Sidrah many times. But finding our way there and getting into his stronghold are two different things—and I want to get in on my own terms, as well. We will need entry past that big, iron-bound door, and it is to be hoped that Ganju Thapa will provide it. Although Charlie is a genial sort, I know that both he and his household are very well guarded.

And I *do* love a dramatic entrance, as it suits my nature. *Ha! There he is . . .*

He slips out of the shadows of an alley and lopes toward me. I pretend to not see him and give out with a yelp of distress when I feel his big hand clamp on my neck.

He utters a string of guttural words, which I take to mean "Got you again, you miserable little infidel bint," or such to that effect. I struggle and wail, but it avails me not, and soon we stand in front of Charlie's big door.

Ganju Thapa knocks on it three times ... pause ... then three more ... then two ... and the door swings open to reveal yet another armed thug standing there. My escort spits out what sounds like orders to the man, but then that is the last thing Ganju Thapa says for a while as John Thomas comes up behind him and brings his belaying pin down on the back of his heathen head. As he sprawls face-first on the tiles, Smasher McGee rushes in and makes short work of the other man.

Good. They were not able to spread the alarm ...

Davy and Tink, pistols drawn, slip into the hallway and I hold my finger to my lips. They nod, and I advance to the door that I know is the entrance to Charlie's inner sanctum. Then I put my hand to the tie of my cloak and let it fall to the floor, revealing me in my full navy rig—navy blue jacket trimmed in gold braid, creamy white lace at my throat and wrists, tight white trousers tucked into shiny black boots. At my neck dangles the Trafalgar medal, and on my left breast sits Napoleon's Legion of Honor. On my face I wear the full Lawson Peabody School for Young Girls Look.

Dress to impress, I always say.

Looking back at my crew to see that all is in readiness, and satisfied as to that, I lift my right foot and kick open the door to Charlie's lair.

There he sits, in all his corpulent grandeur, his small mouth open wide in complete surprise.

I stride down the red rug and stop in front of him, give a slight bow, straighten, and with my left hand on the hilt of my sword that hangs by my side, I say, "Greetings, Honored Chen."

He gapes, and says nothing for a while . . . Then he utters one word.

"Sidrah."

Not a question. Not a plea. Just the name.

I turn and gesture to Tink, who goes out into the hall and returns with Sidrah on the arm of John Higgins.

Charlie's face undergoes a transformation. He smiles and holds out his hand to his lost daughter. She leaves Higgins's side and goes to her father and kneels before him.

"Father," she says to him.

"Beloved daughter," he answers and puts his hand on her bowed head.

"What do you want?" he asks me, his eyes glistening.

"Well, first a bit of a bite for me and my bully boys, Chops, and then we'll discuss that," I say with a wide grin.

"What's for dinner?"

Chapter 20

"Two thousand pounds sterling. Oh! Oh!" Charlie gasps for breath and clutches his chest.

"Come on, Charlie." I laugh, pointing a pheasant wishbone at him. "You know that it would have cost you twice that to get Sidrah back from those pirates, and I brought her back for nothing except for love for her and respect for the House of Chen."

We are all seated on low cushions around the table, upon which has been laid the finest of food from the East. There are goblets of fine plum wine and saki at each place and the party is warming up. Davy sits to my left and I have delighted in teasing him with the exotic nature of the dishes. *Here, Seaman Jones, try this,* I say, putting a piece of smoked peacock breast to his lips. *It is pickled monkey testicle. It is quite good . . .*

Chopstick Charlie recovers enough from his heart palpitations to inquire . . .

"And those who took my daughter?"

Sidrah sits by his side, happily chatting away with Higgins, who is not at all dismayed by the nature of the food.

I assure the rather pale Davy that what he is eating is merely a kind of chicken and then reply.

"I wish I could have brought them back to suffer your gentle chastisements, Gracious Host, but, alas, I fear they sleep with the tigers . . . or rather, *in* the tigers."

"Good," he says, a slight smile lifting the ends of his mustache, seemingly quite satisfied with that. "You speak with well-oiled tongue, Honored Guest. It would seem as if you learned the art of extortion at my very knee."

"I am sure you would have been an excellent teacher, Rotund One, but the streets of London sufficed in that capacity."

Charlie takes all the banter in good stride, as well he should. He has been introduced to my crew and all is very civil, but Davy and Tink still wear their pistols in their belts and John Thomas and Finn McGee are still very large and muscular.

"All right, so what else do you want?" he says, his eyes closed in pain. "Besides the two thousand pounds?"

"I want my little boy back—without the chain, thank you. And my knife, too, if you please."

Charlie murmurs something to the girl Mai Ling on his right and she gets up and undulates out of the room, the movement of her hips beneath her gauzy lower garment not going unnoticed by my male crew. They have been at sea a long time. Even so, I give the avidly staring Davy an elbow in the ribs and a stern look. *You be good, you. You're a married man.*

Presently a joyous Ravi bounds into the room and plunks himself down beside me.

"Very good for Ravi to see Memsahib again," he says.

"I was thinking many horrible things happening to poor dear Missy."

"Well, as you can see, my dark-eyed boy, I have not yet gone up to Brahma to be assigned another billet, which, considering the state of my karma, might be, perhaps, a post as water snake?" I say, delighted to have the little rascal by my side again.

He considers the wisdom of that and nods. "Water snakes very pretty. Would suit you, yes."

Hmmm . . .

Higgins, never the gastronomical prig, is hugely enjoying the feast, as well as the repartee with my tiny spiritual guide. I believe he figures Ravi has me nailed pretty well in the karmic sense, for sure.

"Were you surprised to see the return of your mistress, Ravi?" asks Higgins.

"No, Sahib, not totally," says the lad, expertly spearing a pink shrimp with a sharp chopstick and holding it over the small brazier of glowing coals that rests in the center of the table. "When Mai Ling come to bring me here, I see two bad-mashes in hall holding heads and moaning most piteous, so I sense gentle Missy not far away."

Higgins laughs, appreciating, I know, Ravi's fine sense of the ironic, as I say, "Hush now, Ravi. Grownups are talking."

Mai Ling has also brought me back my shiv, which I gratefully take and slide up into my forearm sheath. *Welcome back, Rooster . . . back where you belong . . .* As Mai Ling settles down on her cushion again, she lets her almond-shaped eyes travel over my crew.

"Now, Charlie, where were we?" I say, all officious. "Oh,

yes. Two thousand pounds. Well, that amount is what is needed to resupply my ship, the *Nancy B. Alsop,* which lies down at the Rangoon docks, so that we can go back to England to give King George the rich store of ancient artifacts that you are going to stuff into my hold. When those things are placed in the British Museum, you will be an honored man, believe me. Is this not so, Higgins?"

"Indeed," says Higgins. "She does know a good many very important people, in spite of her size and appearance. I, myself, am a sometime member of British Intelligence, and I believe you would do well to pay heed to her words."

Right, and a lot of those important people would like to wring my skinny neck, such that neither air nor food nor good wine like this ever travels down it again. But we shan't mention that.

"And the British government does, indeed, cast covetous eyes upon this part of the world, Mr. Chen Lee, so it would be well for an honest man of business such as yourself to place that same self in an advantageous position."

Nobody can lay it down quite like my Higgins can.

"So, Honored Guests, with your honeyed words, you clean out my treasury and then plunder my storerooms. You do know how to tear the heart out of poor Chopstick Charlie." He sighs, once again tapping his chest. "But Number One Daughter has been restored to her poor father's side, and so I will agree to your terms. Let us now enjoy the rest of the evening."

Charlie, plainly done with his dinner, holds up the mouthpiece of his smoking device and the girl to his left rises, lights a taper in the brazier, and then holds the flame to the pot of tobacco that rests on top of the thing. He puffs mightily until he gets a good blaze going. He inhales deeply and then passes the mouthpiece, which is attached to a long hose that is connected to the bottom of the . . . what? . . . oh . . . the hookah . . . to John Thomas, who sits close to his right.

John Thomas takes it and sucks avidly, making the device burble like a drowning man, and then, he, too, inhales deeply.

"Ah, thankee, Sir, and bless thee," says my good strong crewman. "Our own supplies o' that weed have done run out, and we miss it sorely."

He passes the pipe to his mate, Finn McGee, who takes it as if he were a baby and it was his mother's own dear breast upon which he was suckling.

"Well, gentlemen," says Charlie, who has clearly divined the status of all my sailors. "We shall certainly fix that tomorrow with several bales of the finest Turkish leaf."

With that, he has certainly won the love of those two coves, for sure.

As the pipe is passed around, I do not take the smoking mouthpiece, as I do not drink spirits and *certainly* do not partake of the vile weed. All the others, with the exception of Ravi, do however. Soon the smoke is all about us in swirls above our heads, mixing with the fumes from the pots of smoldering incense, and it is all, along with the saki, making me quite dizzy. I would not be surprised if our genial host had not put a little something extra into the tobacco bowl, as there is a unique scent in the mix of the smoke.

"I believe, Chopsie," I say, my head swimming, "that we must depart and return to our ship to prepare for the supplies that will be coming onboard tomorrow."

"If that must be so, then pray, Honored Guest, allow Mr. Tinker and Mr. Jones to stay for the evening and further enjoy our poor hospitality," says Charlie. "Mai Ling here, and her sister Mai Ji, have informed me that they would enjoy extending the entertainment of the House of Chen to these two fine young men."

I know a demand for hostages when I hear it, but I say, "Alas, my poor ship lies unguarded in the harbor, and I must have my men about me to protect it," I say, perfectly aware of the anguish this will cause in several male breasts. "However, I will allow Mr. John Tinker to stay the night, and I thank you for your kindness."

We rise as Mai Ling and Mai Ji, with barely suppressed giggles, lead off a happily compliant John Tinker. There is a string of low, strangled curses from a certain David Jones, but to that we pay no mind, no mind whatsoever.

You are married to my great good friend Annie, you dog, and don't you ever forget it . . .

Charlie provides us with a coach to take us back to the *Nancy B.*—sort of a coach. It seats four of us, inside, with Finn McGee and John Thomas jogging alongside, but instead of horses hauling us along, there are eight big strong men in harness, four on either side. It's still a bumpy ride, but it works. Higgins sits across from me, Davy at his side, and Ravi sits by me.

"Oh, Higgins," I warble, as we wend our way down the narrow streets. "If you could just see the beautiful bathhouse that Charlie has out back of his place! A deep pool with steamy water and blue tile all over, and I bet Tink is in it right

154

now, and Mai Ling and Mai Ji, too, and there are soaps and perfumes and sweetmeats, and oh, it is just so wondrous!"

I do not say this for the benefit of my good John Higgins, but to bring joy to a very silent David Jones . . .

Oh, I do so love torturing the lad!

Chapter 21

"And then Mistress comes in, madder than a wet hen, and Rebecca and I run screechin' out the back of the kitchen, beggin' for Peg to hide us, but it doesn't do any good and we're caught good and proper. Mistress doesn't use her famous cane anymore, but her hairbrush does the job on our poor bottoms just as well, believe me."

We're in the cabin of the *Nancy B.*, me poring over the charts on my desk and preparing for departure. Outside I hear the sounds of supplies and treasure being brought aboard, and I do love the sound of that.

"And just what were the two of you up to that earned the anger of Mistress Pimm, eh?"

"All we did was to sneak out of the school on Saturday afternoon to go down to the Pig and Whistle for a bit of fun, and geez . . . We didn't skip any classes or anything, but we did meet up with Daniel and he had a friend named Johnny with him. He and Rebecca got on tolerably well so we went walkin', you know . . . but we got caught on the way back and—"

"And Mistress didn't think it quite proper that her

charge, Miss Rebecca Adams, of the Quincy Adamses, was out mixing with the rabble? Ummm?"

"Even so, and—"

Davy pokes his head in the door and says, "Most of the stuff's on board. We should be ready to leave within the hour."

I nod and give him what I know is my infuriating little finger wave. Yes, John Tinker had come back onboard this morning smiling in a state of beatific bliss—if nothing else, he was quite scrubbed and very clean . . . *Ah, yes, that tub.* It is plain that Davy will never forgive me.

Ah, well, so be it. I turn back to the charts Charlie has so graciously provided.

Damn! I sure wish I could cut up the Red Sea and cross over Suez to Port Said and on into the Mediterranean, but no, of course, it cannot be. Charlie says there are plans for a canal to be dug there, but getting the Arabs to work together on anything is like trying to herd cats, and so it is around Africa for us, once again.

"So tell me about the divine Miss Clarissa Worthington Howe, then," I say. "Does she still think she is the queen of the school?"

"Oh, yes," says Joannie, munching on one of my breakfast biscuits. "But I am beneath her notice . . . especially since it is known that I have a connection with the wild and contrary Jacky Faber."

"Ah, same as it ever was . . ."

"Anyway, Clarissa's gotten herself engaged to a John Randolph down in Virginia, and they say he is sure to be governor of the state someday."

I look up from my study of the charts.

"The poor man," I say. "Do you think he knows what he's getting into? Ha! And could you imagine being one of the lesser ladies in Virginia society if she gets to be First Lady? By God, she'll make 'em dance to her tune, she will!"

A snort of suppressed laughter from Miss Nichols . . .

"And Dolley Frazier?" I inquire, always anxious for news of my schoolmates. "You said she married?"

"Oh, that's a good one!" says Joannie, bouncing up and down in her chair. "She left the school soon after the last time you were there and married a lawyer. Who? I dunno. Anyway, she got in the family way and then the poor man died, never having seen his child . . ."

Oh, poor Dolley, and you the best of us . . .

I leave off my study of the maps in some distress over this news, but then the girl goes on.

"She gives birth to the child—a boy—and then, having no prospects, goes to visit a friend, Mrs. Martha Washington. You know of her?"

Oh, yes . . .

"And she fixes it up so that Dolley meets this cove named . . . I forget what . . . but Dolley calls him 'Jemmy' and she is now very happy. It seems her Jemmy is now Secretary of War or somesuch down in Washington, where they built a palace for the President or something."

Well, Dolley, that's certainly better than being on your own in the world with a baby on your hip, I'd say . . .

"And Miss Amy Trevelyne?"

"Oh, yes, your dear friend Amy, how could I forget?" says Joannie with a sigh. "Every chance she got, she'd grab me and sit me down in front of her desk and make me tell her every single little bit about what happened on our trip down to the Caribbean last year, while she scribbled it all down."

Heavy sigh. Yet another book, Amy, detailing my misadventures, my lapses of feminine propriety, my greedy . . . and . . . ? Uh-oh . . .

"You didn't tell her of the gold stash we left down in the Florida waters, did you?" I ask, alarmed.

"Come on, Jacky," she says, putting on a miffed look *and* the old accent. "Just what do you take me for, mate? An easy mark, a peach, a snitch? Oi'm a rum cove from Cheapside, as well as ye, and I knows when to keep me guard up and me gob shut."

I have to smile at hearing the good old Cockney talk.

"Good. Now go on."

"Well, everybody at the school was sad that you'd been shipped off to Australia for life . . ." Joannie pauses to peek out my window at all the hustle and bustle on the wharf. I know she thinks it wondrous exciting that we're going back to England, full of the treasures of the East. Well, so do I.

"Especially Miss Amy, but she did say she hoped you might be safer in prison, rather than leading your usual life on the outside . . ."

Chopstick Charlie had come aboard earlier to make sure that the cargo was being safely stowed and had been reassured that, indeed, it was. Sidrah accompanied him and we had a nice lunch down in my cabin.

Charlie looked about him, stroking his goatee. "Hmmm . . . We pick up a dirty, mute beggar in the street and this is what it turns out like. Strange."

"Cheer up, Chops," I chirped. "It's karma, right?"

He nodded, not totally convinced.

"And don't worry about the cargo, Charlie. As I am sure you noticed, we are amply armed and my crew is well seasoned."

He cast his eyes heavenward, placed his hand on my head, and muttered what I am sure is some sort of Chinese benediction, and then, with his daughter on his arm, left somewhat mollified, I trust, as to the future of his treasure.

I regard Joannie's slight form bent over at the window, watching the loading. *Hmmm.* When first I saw Joannie again after all those months, I noticed that she had grown a bit since last I saw her. It's natural, after all, for it's been months and months. She's come out a bit on top, not much, but some, and her bottom is a bit rounder. One thing's sure, she will *not* be bedded down with Daniel Prescott anymore— not when they're on my ship, by God, proclaims the hypocrite Jacky Faber.

Joannie comes back and plunks herself down at my table and continues.

" 'Course Miss Clarissa thought that a few years in the pen would do you a lot of good. Keep you out of her hair, for sure, and for that she was grateful. I didn't believe her completely on that, but"—here Joannie sticks her nose in the air—"she is Clarissa Worthington Howe, after all, and she must keep up appearances."

Higgins comes into the cabin, bearing sheaves of papers.

"Here is the manifest of the cargo. I gave a copy to Mr. Chen and he appeared satisfied," he says, handing me the documents. "I believe we are ready to depart."

"Excellent, Higgins, then let us go."

I stride out on deck, dressed in my usual underway togs—loose white shirt, white trousers, bare feet.

Looking over the side, I see that the tide, as well as the wind, is in our favor. *Good.*

"Let's get her underway, Captain Delaney," I say to Liam, who stands looking all solid and grand on the quarterdeck.

"Aye, Miss," says Liam to me. To John Thomas, Finn McGee, and Davy Jones he calls out, "Take in the gangway, and lines one, three, four, and five. Hold number two."

As this is being accomplished, I, too, go up on the quarterdeck and stand in my usual spot, one foot to either side of the centerline, the better to feel the movement of my lovely little ship.

"Hoist the main," says Liam. He does not have to roar, though he is certainly capable of a stentorian bellow, for they all know what to do. Many pairs of hands grab the line that will haul up our mainsail, and they take a strain. The sail begins to move up.

"Rudder amidships," orders Liam, and Tink, who is at the wheel, complies.

"Take in number two."

The *Nancy B. Alsop* moves away from the dock, her mainsail filling. We are underway.

Ah, how I wish my shantyman, Enoch Lightner, with his big voice, were here to sing us off.

But—*oh, well*—I can do it myself. I raise my somewhat littler voice.

> *Haul on the Bowline, our bonny ship's a'rollin',*
> *Haul on the Bowline, the Bowline HAUL!*

Haul on the Bowline, so early in the mornin',
Haul on the Bowline, the Bowline HAUL!

On the last *HAUL!* the boys really put their backs into it, and the sail goes ever higher.

Haul on the Bowline, Davy is a married man,
Haul on the Bowline, the Bowline HAUL!
Haul on the Bowline, his Annie is in Boston Town,
Haul on the Bowline, the Bowline HAUL!

It is a simple shanty, true, but it lends itself to any lyric that might come to a simple sailor's mind, and it's fun and it gets the sails up right briskly.

Now, one more at Davy's expense . . .

Haul on the Bowline, Davy hopes she's bein' good,
Haul on the Bowline, the Bowline HAUL!

The mainsail is topped off and secured and we are pulling fast out of the harbor. The men go to the foremast line, and Davy, before I can launch into another verse, takes it up.

Haul on the Bowline, the Nancy *is a worthy craft,*
Haul on the Bowline, the Bowline HAUL!
But her Skipper's sure a pain in me ass,
Haul on the Bowline, the Bowline HAUL!

May it be ever so, Davy. I come in, exulting and laughing, for one last verse.

Haul on the Bowline, we're all bound for London Town,
Haul on the Bowline, the Bowline HAUL!
Haul on the Bowline, we'll dance a jig in Georgie's hall,
We'll haul on his Bowline, his Royal Bowline, HAUL!

And so we are off, laughing and singing, all on the bounding main.

PART III

Chapter 22

A Personal Friend of Yours
Onboard the Schooner N.B.A.
Cape Town, South Africa
May 1808

Miss Amy Trevelyne
Dovecote Farm
Quincy, Massachusetts, USA

My Dearest Amy,

I hope this letter finds you well and happy. I trust, too, that you will excuse the brevity of this letter as I must get it off quickly because the ship carrying it to you is leaving within the hour.

When the *Lorelei Lee* came in to Boston Harbor, you probably learned of my sad demise, but you should know by now, dear Sister, never to believe that Jacky Faber is dead and gone unless you see with your own eyes her lifeless and doubtless soggy form stretched out on some plank—or else hanging from a rope and no longer kicking, which is much more likely the case. You do recall those geese on Daisy Hill, do you not?

Ha-ha.

Joannie Nichols is with me, in case anyone has been wondering about the whereabouts of the little imp. You may inform Mistress of that, as she does like to keep track of her girls, even us errant ones. But please keep my continued existence in this world a secret from all except the employees of Faber Shipping Worldwide, along with those members of the Lawson Peabody whom you feel you can trust to keep it under their bonnets, at least for a while.

All here aboard our little schooner are well and in good spirits and you may inform sundry wives and sweethearts as to that happy fact. Just don't mention me.

Ha-ha. Again . . .

Seriously, though, if you would look after my dear friend Mairead McConnaughey, who has been aboard the *Lee* with her husband Ian. She has had some troubles lately and I would like it if she were restored to her former cheerful self. Perhaps Ezra can offer her some gainful employment to take her mind off her recent woes. Break the news of my resurrection to her gently, as the dear girl is of an expressive nature and in her joy is liable to break something.

Uh-oh . . . The *George Washington* is pulling in her lines and I must quickly blot this and get it sealed and over to them.

Please give my warmest regards to Mr. Pickering. John Higgins has written separately to him concerning the business dealings of Faber Shipping Worldwide, and I am sure our dear Ezra will be delighted to fill you in on happenings in that regard. Nudge, nudge, wink, wink.

Do not worry about me, Sister. I have some business to take care of in London—business that concerns my dear Mr. James Emerson Fletcher—and then I am getting back to the States as fast as I can. And I swear I shall never again leave the safety of that part of the world, which has proved so kind to a poor wandering girl.

I so look forward to many more happy days lolling about with you in that hayloft at Dovecote.

Regards to all,
Your friend,

J.

Chapter 23

Jacqueline Bouvier
Onboard the Nancy B. Alsop
Off Gravesend, England

James Emerson Fletcher
9 Brattle Street
London, England

Dearest Jaimy,

Yes, it's me, popping up yet again. Ta da! I know it must be a bit of a shock for you to find that I am still alive and back here in England, but I hope you will rejoice in that knowledge, I really do.

Father Neptune must love me some after all, for he did allow me to survive the awful storm he kicked up back when you and I were last together, there in the Straits of Malacca. You see, Jaimy, when I was swept overboard with the *Lorelei Lee's* fallen foremast and sank down with it, entangled in its rigging, the sail had enough trapped air in its belly to finally pull it back up to the surface with me clinging to it for dear life, my little Ravi clinging to me, as well. As Higgins says, I really must be part cork, as I do have a habit of bobbing back up from various troubles.

Long story short, though cast away and penniless, I resolved to bend all efforts to get back to you, dear boy, and so Ravi and I made our way up to Rangoon and there we fell into some luck. Biggest bit of that luck was meeting up with the *Nancy B.* and her crew—what joy that brought me, I cannot tell you. Will explain more about that later. Suffice it to say, my new plans concern much Oriental treasure and a possible way out of our current difficulties for the both of us. Yes, Jaimy, both you and me. We shall see.

We had a relatively uneventful journey from Rangoon to here, with only a few storms in the Bay of Bengal and some encounters with pirates off the Horn of Africa. The storms pounded us, but we managed to survive them. The pirates tried us, but those brigands came out much the worse for it when they found out, to their dismay, that our teeth were far sharper than theirs, and that we were more than willing to use them.

We made port at the Maldives, then the Seychelles, and still later Cape Town at the southern tip of Africa, and it was there that we found an American merchant ship. The *General Washington* was bound for the States and upon her I posted a quick letter to Amy Trevelyne, and I sure hope she gets it.

As for now, we are lying off Gravesend at the mouth of the Thames, waiting for the turn of the tide to take us up to London. We sailed past Sheerness in the morning, so now we have the land of England all about us. Even though Mother England has scorned me, reviled me, and condemned me, it's still good to see the land of my birth once more. I had vowed, not long ago, to never set foot on her ever again, considering what she has done to me, but England is where you are, Jaimy, so that is where I will go. I am in rather deep disguise, though, so I should be all right.

Evening is falling, so it will be tomorrow before we'll take the *Nancy B.* into the London docks. I hope with all my heart that I will see you then, or at least send this letter on its way to you. But believe me, for all my longing to be in your arms again, I will approach your family's house with great caution. I fear your mother might keep a loaded gun about the house, and if so, I am sure she would not hesitate to drop me in my tracks should she recognize me. I am also sure she greatly rejoiced over the report of my death, thanking the very heavens themselves for my demise, and would not take kindly to see me come back from the dead. But that is not your fault, Jaimy, so don't worry about it.

It has been many months, Jaimy, since I went over the side of my ship to certain doom, and you could have taken up with another girl by now, thinking me dead and gone, and if you have, I will not blame you and will instead wish you and her a long and happy life, but I really hope it will not be so, I really hope that.

Your girl forever, Jaimy . . .

With all my heart,

J.

Chapter 24

"What do you plan, Miss?" asks Higgins, as I sit cross-legged on my bed, mending my black burglar's trousers. The black jersey and watch cap that go with the pants are spread out on the coverlet, as well as other articles of clothing.

We are lying anchored in the Thames and expect to dock in London in the morning.

"I can tell you one thing for sure, Higgins," I answer with firm conviction. "I shall not go blundering blindly into London tomorrow. Each time I have done that, I have paid with the loss of my precious freedom, along with a good deal of my equally precious blood. No, thrice burned, well learned."

Joannie is also on the bed, busily sewing a black pair of pants for herself, as well. She insists on doing it, and hey, maybe she'll come in handy . . . for nighttime errands and such. She certainly knows her way around the streets that we will be traveling, that's for sure . . .

"And as for what I plan? Well, what I will do is this. I will go into the city in deep disguise as soon as we arrive and will therefore be able to get clues to the whereabouts of one Jaimy Fletcher, find the dear boy, and then give him the joyous news of my survival without being snatched up by the authorities yet again. Whereupon we will all get the bloody hell out of Britannia's waters and go back to good old Boston."

I hope the news is received joyfully by the lad and he hasn't already taken up with another girl. The last time I took my eyes off Mr. James Emerson Fletcher for a moment, that Clementine Jukes popped up. And it has been months now since he and I were parted. Hmmm . . .

"And Mr. Fletcher will agree to this?" asks Higgins.

"He must," I retort. "He is still under sentence of Transportation to the penal colony in Australia, and I am sure he would rather endure a harsh winter or two in Boston than the bleak prospect of seven years of hot and dusty captivity in New South Wales. Especially if I am by his side to keep him very, very warm."

"Ummm," murmurs Higgins, not totally convinced of that.

"Besides, Higgins," I say with a laugh, "he would not be the first sailor I have shanghaied and sent off to sea. If he must be bound and gagged and thrown into the hold of the *Nancy B.,* then so be it."

That gets a slight smile out of him. "Ah, yes," he says. "I recall the fate of the unfortunate Mr. Gulliver MacFarland."

"Even so, Friend and Former Husband Higgins."

"Well, I will again counsel you to take care. You would not want to fall back into the Admiralty's hands. You, also, are still under sentence of Transportation to the penal colony, and in your case, it is for life."

"I will be careful, Higgins," I say, and then throw the

warning back at him. "And I would urge caution on your part as well."

He raises a questioning eyebrow.

"It's true. You are well known as a friend of mine . . . and a member of Naval Intelligence. Ravi, hand me that spool."

"A much changed branch of that service, I am afraid," admits Higgins.

"Too true, too true. All our friends have moved on . . . Mr. Peel . . . Lord Grenville. And our enemies sit all smug in their place."

We had already learned, by inquiring of small Naval ships on our way in here, that Baron Mulgrave was still First Lord of the Admiralty, which was unfortunate, for he certainly is no friend of ours. And furthermore, he *is* a friend to agents Flashby and Bliffil, a pair who certainly mean me no good, having at various times in the past assaulted me, beaten me, and threatened me with much worse treatment, as well.

"So, Miss," asks Higgins. "How will you go?"

I reach over and take up my HMS *Dolphin* cap, which I had sewn as a ship's boy on that dear ship all those years ago. I cram it down low on my head and look at Higgins from under the brim.

"Why, as young Jack the Sailor, of course," I say, grinning and whipping off a snappy salute.

"Who else will serve as well in this situation?"

Chapter 25

We were lucky and got a nice berth for our little ship at Paul's Wharf, portside to and right near Blackfriars Bridge, under which was our kip when we was all members of the Rooster Charlie Gang. As soon as I popped off the *Nancy B.* this morning and headed out into the town, I checked under that same bridge, but again I found only some pathetic gin-soaked drunks. *Ah, well,* I thought. *The Golden Age of the London Gangs of Urchins is over for good, a pity in a way . . .* But I found out not too much later that I was wrong in that.

When I departed the *Nancy B.,* I had left instructions that Joannie, dressed in her Lawson Peabody School dress, should go to the London Home for Little Wanderers to inform my grandfather and the rest of the staff of my continued existence on this benighted orb. She was also to let them know the whereabouts of Mairead McConnaughey, former Mistress of Girls at the place, and now, it is to be hoped, resident in Boston, USA. John Thomas and Finn McGee, my fine Enforcers of the Faber Will, would accompany Joannie there, not only to protect her but also the three hundred pounds sterling of Chopstick Charlie's money that she was transporting to Reverend Alsop to keep the orphanage going for a bit longer. I, of course, could not visit my dear grandfather, even though I wanted to very much, for fear the place would be watched. I cannot risk being taken again.

Liam, Davy, and Tink have to stay aboard to watch the ship, with Ravi and Lee Chi as steward and cook. McGee and John Thomas, too, would be aboard, except when they were accompanying Joannie on her errands. All would have some liberty soon, but not now. I put my finger on Joannie's nose and warned her that after her mission to the orphanage, she was to return promptly to the ship and remain aboard till I got back, or her bottom will pay for it. She reluctantly agreed, though I knew she's as anxious as I to visit our old turf.

Higgins, impeccably dressed in soft gray suit and cloak, put on his matching hat and got ready to go off, as he put it, *to check his sources,* as it were.

I'm pounding up Earl Street and heading for Fleet, pigtail flying behind me, my small leather kit bag over my shoulder. I recall that the publishers of the *Shipping News* on Fleet Street generally post a registry of the ships arriving and departing in nearby ports, and I mean to check it out, first thing, before I do anything else this day. Gotta find out what's what and who's where . . . in particular, *where's Jaimy?*

Free! I exult as I tear up Bouverie and onto Fleet Street. It feels awfully good to be out and free, dressed in my sailor gear with my *Dolphin* cap crammed down on my head, my pigtail braid hanging behind it, my bald forehead covered. I love my ships, I love my men and all my mates, but sometimes it's just grand to be out and free of entanglements, at least for the moment.

I pass the newspaper print shop where, as an orphaned child, I used to sit on Hughie's broad shoulders and read out loud the broadsides pinned to the wall for the edification of the illiterate crowd in the hopes of earning a penny for my service, and where, thankfully, no one is peddling the latest installment in the Bloody Jack series of penny dreadfuls. That's a relief, anyway. I don't need anyone peerin' too close at me, or rather, *my* face. *Hmmm* . . . It seems when I get back into my old neighborhood, I tend to slip back into my old ways.

Ah, here it is. The *Shipping News* office. I pop in bold as brass and look at the ships arrival postings on the wall. I certainly don't stick out here—the place is full of sailors, officers and seamen, Royal Navy and merchantmen, all looking for news of shipmates or possible postings. The *Shipping News* also lists promotions and honors, and, in time of war, the Butcher's Bill—the listing of the dead and wounded in battle.

I have on my old *Dolphin* gear, the dress uniform I had made for myself—and for the Dread Brotherhood of Ship's Boys, to their great annoyance—four years ago when we were on that ship. The boys' uniforms no longer fit them, but mine does me. My braided pigtail sits on the blue flap in back and the loose fabric in front hides what I got in the way of female equipment—'course I've got my tight-fitting bathing suit top under it to flatten me out some, and so with the loose-fitting pants down below, I'm well rigged out as a saucy sailor boy and not worth a second glance from anybody in the room.

I work my way to the front and look up and scan the lists.

Hmmm . . . *Nothing here at the London docks. Try Plymouth . . . no.* I recognize a lot of the ships, but not the ones I want. *What's at Spithead, then . . . no . . . yes!* There's the *Dolphin!* That's something, for sure. Says here she got in three days ago. No word on when she's leaving—typical Naval secrecy—but I'll bet she'll be in for a while. Although I'd love to run down there and see Captain Hudson and my old shipmates again, there's one particular former *Dolphin* I must see, but I know he will not be there.

There is a long counter at the other side of the room, behind which sit several clerks holding pens and scribbling things. I go up to a pleasant-looking chap and say, "'Scuse me, Guv'nor," all respectful. "But can you tell me if there's any news of HMS *Dart* or the merchant ship *Cerberus*?"

He pulls a ledger over and opens it up. He has spectacles perched on his nose and he peers through them at the entries therein.

"Hmmm . . . Let's see. Ah, yes . . . The sloop of war *Dart* was in at Margate two weeks ago . . . shipped out on the sixteenth of May."

Damn! I could have used Joseph Jared's help in this. Plus, I wouldn't have minded seeing the rogue again, no I wouldn't. But enough of that . . . *Press on . . .*

"And the *Cerberus*, Sir?"

The clerk continues to peruse the columns of entries, running his finger down the page and muttering, "No . . . no . . . *Calliope* . . . no . . . *Constellation* . . . no . . . Ha! Here it is . . . *Cerberus!*"

Hope rises in my breast . . . *Jaimy!*

"*Cerberus.* Crew disbanded. Re-manned with a Captain Peterson in command. Set sail twelve days ago for India."

Hope dies . . . *Oh, Jaimy, where are you?*

The man sees my distress. "Did you hope to ship on her,

lad? Too bad. The *Hiram Walker* is taking on crew down at Hungerford Pier. You might try her."

"Thank you, Sir, I will do that." I lift my shirt and stick my finger in my money belt and fish out a coin, which I place on the counter. " 'Ere, mate, have a pint on me, for your 'elp."

He didn't ask for a bribe, but I gave him a treat, anyway, for his kindness. Not enough of that quality in this world, I figure, and it should be rewarded when found.

I bounce out of the *Shipping News* with a destination in mind. I head down Fleet till it becomes Ludgate and then turn left up Old Bailey, pressing north. I go by the Admiral Benbow and think about stopping in for a bite and a mug, but no. *Later. Push on, girl, there's business to do.* Jaimy's gotta be somewhere.

And there's Saint Paul's, where I almost got married once . . . *sniff* . . . and here's Paternoster Lane, which used to be Shanky Boys turf, back in the day, and . . .

. . . *it still is* . . .

As I pass the entrance to a side alley, three boys step out in front of me. They seem to range in age from twelve to sixteen. The biggest of the three grins a grotty grin at me and slaps a billy club in his palm.

"Well, well, what we got 'ere? A fancy little sailor boy come 'ome from sea, is it?" says the cove. "Ain't that sweet, now, lads?"

The other two sods nod their agreement.

"Just so, Grimbo." They chortle.

"And just who the 'ell are you," I spit out, angry at being stopped by this crummy trio.

"Us fine lads is members in good standin' of the Shanky

Boys Gentlemen's Club," says this Grimbo. "And now that in-tro-duck-shuns is done wit', give over that bag and ye can run home to mum and tell her how you was buggered all over the fleet from Drisco to Tim-buck-tu, whinin' *me bum is all sore, mummy, please to put some butter on it, please, mummy.*"

This bit of hilarity is met with gales of laughter from his cronies . . . *Good one, Grimbo!* . . . and the middle-sized one makes so bold as to come up to me and knock off me cap, exposing my head.

Cor! Look at that! Blimey!

After they recover from the sight, the little one puts his fingers to either side of his eyes and pulls them into slits and starts singsonging . . .

Ching Chong Chinaman, sittin' on a fence
Ching Chong Chinaman—

That's as far as he gets with that little number, as I bring up the toe of my right foot and sink it deep in his crotch. He goes *"Ooof!"* and doubles over, puking out whatever foulness is in his gut.

I whip out my shiv from my sleeve and get into a crouch, holding the blade up in front of me face.

"Shankies!" I say, and spit on the cobblestones. "Shankies? In-tro-duck-shuns ain't over yet, oh, no, you miserable scum wads! My name was Mary Faber when I ran these streets with the Rooster Charlie Gang and I was killin' Shankies for sport whilst you was still suckin' on yer mama's filthy teats. See the dried blood on the hilt of me shiv? Aye, that was prolly yer dead daddy's poxy blood that's there, and now yours'll run there, too, you poor excuses for honest footpads! Come on,

I'll cut off yer cods and stuff 'em in yer mouths! Come on and git it, you lousy pieces o'—"

They back off a bit, startled by the display and the rant. They no longer look quite so confident of an easy mark.

Thanks, Mike Fink, King of the River—I learned the value of a good brag from you.

"All right, what's this, then?" asks a voice to my right.

I twist around, my knife still at the ready, with one eye on the Shankies and the other one on a tall bloke who has appeared with two girls by him, one on either side. He wears a top hat in the current style, and coat and vest, once fine but now a bit threadbare. One girl looks to be thirteen or so, the other a mite older.

"I'm about to gut me a coupla worthless thugs," I say, panting—the blood is up in me now, for sure. "If'n yer sickened by the sight o' blood, ye'd best step off, as it's about to flow!"

The bloke smiles and says, "Did I just hear you call yourself Mary Faber of the Rooster Charlie Gang?"

"I did. What's it to you, bunghole?"

"Welcome back, Mary."

What?

"It's Toby . . . Toby Oyster, Mary," he says, the smile broadening. "Come on back to the clubhouse and let's talk."

Toby Oyster, the bloke I left in charge of the remnants of my gang when I lit out for the open sea all those years ago. What a thing . . .

With a careful eye on Grimbo and his pals, I shove my shiv back in my sheath and slap my hat back on my head and follow Toby and his crew up Paternoster to their kip, the same hole of a condemned building that I last saw when our gang fought Pigger O'Toole and his boys outside this very place.

We go in and seat ourselves about a long table. When no food or drink seems to be coming, I dig down into my money belt again and come up with a half crown, then signal to one of the girls who stand about Toby.

"Here. What's your name?"

"Gwen, Sir . . . or Miss . . ."

"It's Miss, Gwendolyn," I say, putting the coin into her paw. "Now, run up to that tavern on the corner and bring back all the bread, cheese, sausage, and wine that will buy." Her hand eagerly clasps the coin.

"And, girl, if you had any thought about runnin' off, take a look at this." With that I remove my cup and whip my pigtail from off my neck. "See that? Yes . . . That is the Mark of the Golden Dragon, and it is the sign of an organization much larger and much more cruel than any Brotherhood of Urchins. If you want to end your days screaming your life out in a tub of boiling oil, you will ignore my warning." I say that for her benefit, and for all the others gathered about.

She heeds it, and I think they do, too. In no time at all, she is back with the goods.

"So, Toby," I say, leaning back in my chair. "Tell me just how I come to be sitting here, talkin' pleasant to a bunch of lousy Shankies." I can hardly believe it myself. Back in the day, the Shankies were our mortal enemies, and here I sit in their kip. I knock back a hit of not-too-bad wine from a not-too-dirty cup and ask, "I heard from Joannie Nichols that you were taken by a press gang. True?"

Toby nods grimly. I notice that he has actually become

a good-looking young man—tall, straight, dark-haired, with only a scar across his left eye to mar his face.

"Too true, too true," he responds, ruefully. "Right after Hugh the Grand was taken, so was I. Damn stupid of me to let it happen, but it did. Prolly had me senses too full of Polly to watch out proper. Anyway, I was taken aboard the *Temeraire* and spent three miserable years in that hellhole and was almost killed at Trafalgar. But I made it through and jumped ship as soon as we were in sight of England. I came back here and convinced the lad in charge o' the Shankies that he should move on—the goddamn Royal Navy didn't do much for me, but it did teach me some fightin' skills which 'ave come in real handy."

"The *Temeraire,* eh? I got a mate on that ship," I say. "William Simpson . . . Ever hear of him?"

Toby laughs. "Hear o' him? He's the bloody Bo'sun's Mate what put this mark upon me brow!" Toby takes another drink and goes on. "But he weren't such a bad sort after all—we had a big roaring fight and he kicked the pure crap outta me, but he didn't write me up afterwards, so I didn't get tied to the grating and flogged. No, ol' Willy was all right, he was . . ."

A bit of silence, then . . .

"So you heard from Joannie . . . She's all right?"

I nod.

"Good. She was a good kid . . . And my Polly? Did you hear anything o' her? I fear that she ended up in some whorehouse, without me being 'round to protect her. I checked 'round when I got back, but found nothin' o' her."

I know this hurts him to talk of her, but it would hurt him even more to know that she's right now snugged up with

Lieutenant Randall Trevelyne, USMC, a rich young man back in Boston, so I don't tell him that. Instead I say, "Joannie heard that she went north with a company of actors and was doing quite well as an actress."

His face lights up.

"Ah, Pretty Polly, my dear, dear, sweet shining girl. I am so glad to hear that!"

Good. Maybe he will sleep easier now with that little falsehood to soothe his mind.

And now . . . it is time to go.

I stand and say, "Thank you for your hospitality, Toby— all of you—but I must be off. Here . . ."

I dig another of Chopstick Charlie's coins from my money belt and put it on the table and say, "Have another feed on me, mates. Never let it be said that Jacky Faber did not stand 'er mates to a treat when she 'ad some jingle in 'er pocket."

Toby walks me out to the street.

"If I need some help, Toby," I say. "Of maybe an irregular nature . . ."

He chuckles and presses something in my palm. I look at it and I see a small wooden disk on which is inscribed a black "S."

"For sure, Mary, anytime you need help, or a place to kip, you got it. And what you got in your hand guarantees safe passage through Cheapside. At least from my coves, if not the coppers."

I plant a kiss of thanks upon his cheek as he says with a laugh, "You Chinks got your signs, we got ours."

When I get up on Newgate, I flag down a hackney cab, flash a coin, and say, "Nine Brattle Street, if you please . . ."

Chapter 26

The hack drops me at the end of Brattle Street, and yes, I have been here before, standing in the street, looking up at Jaimy's childhood home.

The first time, I was thrown out on my ear by Jaimy's mother, who I am sure still has no use for me. The second time, poor Jaimy was wounded most grievously and did not even know me. The third time, I was ripped away from his side and sent as a spy to France.

I ask the cabbie to wait, then I approach the door with both caution and great trepidation. I take a deep breath and grasp the knocker and give it three sharp raps. Yes, I could have come to this place first, but I was afraid—afraid of what I would find, afraid of how I would be received.

Presently the door opens and a girl in a mob cap peeks out. A maid, no doubt.

"Yes?"

"Your pardon, Miss," I say, popping off a snappy naval salute. "But I 'ave here a letter for a Mr. James Fletcher. Is the gentleman at 'ome?"

"Please wait."

The door closes and I cool my heels for a while. I think I hear whispering inside. *Hmmmm.*

The door opens again and a young woman—a girl, actually, of about sixteen years—stands there. She is finely, but not ostentatiously, dressed in a mauve-gray dress with white trim. Plainly *not* another servant, and very plainly not Jaimy's mother, either. She is very pretty, with dark curls bound up with a blue velvet ribbon. *Jaimy, could you already have another girl?*

"I am sorry, boy, but my brother James is away. You may give me the letter and I will give it to him if we . . . when we see him again."

Oh. Jaimy did mention that he had sisters . . .

"I'm sorry, Miss," I say. "But me orders are to hand it to 'im personal like. Can you tell me if the gent is at 'is club?"

"No, I don't think he—"

"What's this, then, Elizabeth?"

The girl moves aside and there stands the old dragon herself—Jaimy's mother—glowering down upon me.

"The lad has a letter for Jaimy, Mother. I told him—"

"I hope you told him nothing. If I did not rejoice in the fact that the little witch was dead and gone, thank God, I would wager that it was from that guttersnipe Faber."

Uh-oh . . .

"Begone, boy! We do not discuss my son's affairs with strangers. As if we did not have enough trouble already. Go, I say!"

The door closes and I walk disconsolately back to the cab and crawl in.

I'm really not that disappointed . . . I really didn't expect to find him here . . . not really . . . *sniff* . . . But trouble? *What trouble?*

"Where to, boy?" asks the cabbie.

I compose myself and say, "The Royal College of Surgeons in Lincoln Inn Fields, if you please."

He clucks at his horse, gives the poor beast a light tap with his whip, and we are off.

Maybe Dr. Sebastian will know of Jaimy's whereabouts. He is a member of Naval Intelligence, after all.

I stand in the street, looking up at 42 Chancery Lane. I was not surprised to learn that the good doctor's house was not far from the College of Surgeons. I had inquired there and was directed to this spot not two blocks away.

Reaching into my kit bag, I pull out a small, flat sandalwood box and advance to the door with it under my arm. I knock once . . . twice . . . and before I can rap three times, the door flies open and three children stand there looking up at me.

"Uh . . . could you please tell Dr. Sebastian that there is a messenger at the door and—"

"Mama!" screams the middle-sized child, a girl it seems. "There's a sailor boy here for Papa!"

A somewhat harried-looking woman of about thirty years, trim and quite handsome, appears with an inquiring look on her face.

"Yes?"

"Pardon, Mum," I says, all respectful. "But would you please give this box to Dr. Sebastian? Tell 'im it's from a friend lately come from the South China Sea."

She nods and takes the box and says, "Come in, lad, and I will take it to him."

I step into the foyer and watch her retreating back. Naval etiquette orders that one uncovers when one goes inside, so I slip off my cap. I am rewarded by gasps from the three big-eyed kids. I think I might have won over this particular audience.

"Lord, look at that!"

"What is he?"

"A Hottentot! For sure!"

"Oh, our Papa has had such great adventures!"

I hear hurried footsteps coming down the hall. I didn't think it would take long. In the box were several perfectly preserved butterflies from Burma and several more from India. In there, as well, were carefully detailed watercolor renditions of other specimens, signed with a simple JMF penned in the corner of each.

The hall door flies open and there stands Dr. Stephen Sebastian, box in hand, mouth agape at the sight of me.

"J-Jacky! But we thought that—"

"That I was condemned for life to Australia? That I was dead? Neither one of those, you see, has turned out to be true. But what is true, dear Doctor, is that I have been halfway around the world, and oh, what wonders I have seen! And many's the time I wished to have you there beside me as we explored the natural wonders of the East. It is to be hoped that someday we shall do that but . . ."

I am beginning to tear up, but I push on.

". . . but right now I so desperately need your help. I need to get in touch with whoever might be friendly to me in the Admiralty . . . in the Intelligence Division. I have a proposition from an important man of business in the Far East, one that will benefit the Crown to a great degree in the way of treasure and the British Museum in the way of fantastic artifacts of the Orient. I might even have a way into the China trade . . . or even Japan . . . and, oh, Doctor, I need to find out where is my Jaimy Fletcher . . ."

"Come, come, my dear, let us go into my laboratory," he says, putting a welcome arm across my shoulders, "where we may talk. Amanda! Some refreshments, if you would!"

He and I are settled in the Doctor's lab, with dried specimens hanging all about us, and ongoing dissections-in-progress laid out on tables. His wife brings in a tray bearing a beaker of wine and some cakes and cheese, and I thank her and then we get down to it.

First I give him an account of my travels and travails since I last left England's shore. Then I put Chopstick Charlie's proposal to him—great treasure in exchange for his being made Britannia's chief factotum in the Far East. As I'm telling him about that, I reach in my bag and pull out an object I had brought with me for just this moment.

"Good Lord," he says, holding it up and letting the light from the window shine upon it. "What is it?"

"It is a chalice fashioned out of pure gold. Those are real diamonds and emeralds encrusted on the sides. Do not worry, I will not claim it to be the Holy Grail, as it came from Rangoon, but it is still very valuable. And there is much more in the hold of my ship."

"Indeed," he says, thinking. "However, I must tell you that I, and my associates, are currently out of favor at the Admiralty."

"I suspected as much when I heard that Baron Mulgrave was still First Lord."

"But he is not the chief problem. It is those who surround him."

"Mr. Peel?"

"Also banished from power. Mr. Higgins?"

"He is back with me and is off conducting . . . discreet inquiries."

"Good. Valuable man."

He settles back, deep in thought.

"Hmmm . . . Something might be done . . . We'll see," he says. "But what will you want from all this, aside from the eternal gratitude of your native land?"

"Not much," I say, folding my hands in my lap. "The *Lorelei Lee* restored to Faber Shipping Worldwide—we already have her back in our possession, so it would be a simple matter of a mere signature on a piece of paper—and a full pardon for me. I do have a pardon signed by Captain Bligh of the New South Wales colony in return for Services Rendered . . ."

"Sure to be an excellent forgery, if I know you," he says with a smile. "What else?"

"Pardons for all my men, and a full pardon as well for my own Lieutenant James Emerson Fletcher, and his restoration as an officer in the Royal Navy."

"Hmmm . . ." he says. "*That* might be a bit of a problem."

"Why's that?" I ask.

"Because it appears that Lieutenant James Fletcher has recently murdered Special Agent Bliffil of the very Intelligence Branch in which we will wish to curry favor."

Oh, Lord, Jaimy . . .

Chapter 27

I'm up on Whitehall, watching the Horse Guards parade by, and I must admit they look glorious astride their high-stepping horses. They wear shiny metal breastplates over their deep blue jackets with red and gold striping, high collars, white britches, black boots that come up over the knee, white sash across the chest, and all this is topped off by silver helmets with brass trim and a big black plume on top. But they ain't what I'm here for. Nay, I'm looking for the First Dragoons, and one dragoon in particular . . .

Earlier in the day, after I had recovered from my shock at the news of the death of Bliffil at Jaimy's hands, Dr. Sebastian and I got down to it.

"How did it happen, Doctor?"

"Apparently, while on an East India vessel named *Cerberus* on the way to New South Wales to begin his sentence, Mr. Fletcher managed to incite the crew to mutiny and take over the ship and—"

"Yes, yes, I know all about that. What happened later?"

"Well, as I hear it from contacts I still have at the Admiralty, HMS *Dart* regained control of the *Cerberus* in the Bay of Bengal and brought it back to England, intact, but without Mr. Fletcher as prisoner, as one would expect. It seems that when the ship neared Plymouth, Fletcher was able to make his escape, very well armed, as it turned out, and in possession of some money . . ."

Thanks, Joseph . . .

"The details of that are sketchy, but suffice to say that the fugitive purchased a good horse and made his way to London with vengeance on his mind. It is plain that he blamed the agents Bliffil and Flashby for both your death and his wrongful incarceration, and he intended to make restitution in kind."

"True enough, that. I will shed no tears over Bliffil. May the demons down in Hell scar him as he has scarred me."

"Yes, well, by day your Mr. Fletcher hung around low dives, brothels, inns frequented by soldiers and sailors and . . . intelligence agents. He let his beard grow, donned an eye-patch as disguise, and cloaked himself in a heavy black coat. He dresses all in black—black jacket, black boots, black britches, and coal-black lace at his throat and cuffs—and they call him the Black Highwayman. He was a fearsome sight on a moonlit night on Blackheath, I should imagine, with the cloak flying out behind him like the wing of a giant bat, and two gleaming pistols drawn and pointed at his victims."

You sure are getting a lot of information on this from your . . . contacts, Doctor. Hmmm . . .

"He robbed the broad highway, true, but he was searching, always searching for a way to get at either of the hated pair. As a condemned criminal, he could not call them out on the Field of Honor for neither would be required to respond to the challenge of a low felon. No, he would have to bide his time. 'Tis plain that Bliffil let his guard slip first. It was from a prostitute that Fletcher got his lead. She worked at a brothel on Carey Street, one visited often by Agent Bliffil. Apparently Bliffil enjoyed beating up the girls a bit before . . . you know . . . and this one girl didn't like that much, and when Fletcher found her at Ducks Inn, an especially low dive, and plied her with gin and found her connection to Bliffil, she agreed to supply the Highwayman, the very handsome Black Highwayman, with information as to Bliffil's movements."

Jaimy, my lad, you are getting around. But that is exactly how I would go about it, so I shall not lay blame.

"Please go on, Doctor."

"Anyway, it came to pass that one evening this girl informed Fletcher that Bliffil, the night before and well into his cups, had boasted about an important mission he had planned for the morrow—to deliver a diplomatic pouch to a ship lying at Plymouth.

"That was enough for Mr. Fletcher. He knew there was only one way down to Plymouth and that was directly through Blackheath. With grim determination, he knew he would be ready."

"But how do you know . . . ?"

"Later, Miss. Please, let me conclude, if you will."

"All right, Sir. Please go on."

"Ahem. The next day, in the early afternoon, a coach came rumbling up the Blackheath Road, heading for Plymouth, not expecting trouble but vigilant all the same. Suddenly, when they rounded a turn, there was the Black Highwayman, standing bold before them on his great black horse, both pistols drawn, black cloak swirling about him.

"'Stand and deliver!' he shouted. 'Everyone out of the coach! Quickly, if you value your lives! Coachmen, make a false move and I'll kill you where you sit.'

"The driver and the footman did not move.

"Timidly, two ladies got out, and then Bliffil, full of indignation, also stepped out.

"'Do you know who I am, you blackguard? I am an agent of the British government, and you shall pay for this!'

"The Highwayman slid out of the saddle and grinned at Bliffil. 'Oh, Sir, I know full well who you are, Mr. Bliffil. Now stand your ground, you miserable bastard.'

"'Who . . . ?'

"'You know who I am. We met, you will recall, on the *Dolphin*. Here is a pistol. Take it and stand your ground. You shall have the first shot, and I will take the second.'

"'What? I won't—'

"'Here is the pistol,' said the Highwayman, tossing the gun to the ground at Bliffil's feet. 'Take it up and stand your ground, else die like the dog you are, for I will surely kill you in cold blood on your knees if you will not stand and face me like a man.'

"Fletcher aimed his pistol at Bliffil's chest. Bliffil quivered and fell to his knees.

"'No! No, please! I beg of you!'

"The Highwayman sneered at the cowardly display and turned away, disgusted. Bliffil, seeing this, grabbed at the gun lying beside him and raised it . . .

"'Dog, am I?' he snarled. 'We'll see about that!'

"'. . . and fired."

Gasp!

"The shot took Fletcher on the right shoulder, and he

staggered forward, then slowly turned. He put his pistol in his left hand and lifted it, aiming it carefully at the crouching Bliffil.

"'You have had the first shot, and now I will take the second.'

"'Mercy!' cried Bliffil, his hands clasped before him.

"'I will be merciful,' said the Highwayman Fletcher, as he pulled the trigger.

"The pistol bucked and a neat hole appeared in Bliffil's forehead and he pitched forward into the dust.

"'That's as merciful as I can manage right now, Mr. Bliffil,' panted Fletcher, putting his pistol back in his belt and mounting, with great difficulty, his horse. 'About as much mercy as you showed my girl. Rot in Hell, Sir. Give my regards to Satan. Assure him that a Mr. Flashby will be joining him shortly. The rest of you, adieu.'"

I sit astounded. *Oh, Jaimy, how can we get you a pardon after that?*

"With that, he was gone," concludes Dr. Sebastian. He lifts the wine beaker and pours me another glass, figuring that I need it. He is right.

"But how . . . how did you come to know all this?"

"I am a doctor, expert at removing bullets from the flesh of foolish humans, as you well know, Miss."

Gasp!

"How . . . ?"

"It is simple. Wounded though he was, he cautiously made his way down to Plymouth to seek medical help. Had he asked in the usual ways, he would have been treated but then found out and arrested. Instead he held off till he found that the *Dolphin* had docked across the bay at Spithead. He hired a boat and knocked against our side, slumped over and barely conscious. I am sure he figured that he would find help there, and failing that, at least he would die among friends."

"Then you know where he is! Please!"

"No, I do not know. As soon as the bullet was removed and his shoulder bandaged, he struggled to his feet and staggered away, over our vehement protestations. But he did tell me the story before he left."

I sit silent for a while . . . then I rise and ask . . .

"Have you told anyone at the Admiralty about your caring for Mr. Fletcher's wound?"

"No. As I've said, I no longer have the ear of the First Lord."

"Then they do not know for absolute sure that the Highwayman is Jaimy Fletcher?"

"No, but I am sure that they have their suspicions."

I think on this, then rise and say, "Thank you, Doctor, for all you have done. Now, I must go. If you would continue your efforts on our behalf, I would greatly appreciate it. Please do not tell anyone at the Admiralty about treating Jaimy's wound, if you can avoid it, as the less they know about the Highwayman's identity, the better."

"Where will you go, Jacky?" he asks, rising to his own feet.

"If you would handle the politics, Sir, I will contact the military, as I am more comfortable in that sphere," I answer. "And I know that if anyone is ever sent in pursuit of highwaymen, it is always soldiers, not police, and certainly not politicos. Good day, Doctor, I shall be in touch."

The cavalrymen of the Horse Guard are done with their exercise for the day and they retreat from the field.

It's getting toward evening, so I expect there will be no more prancing around this day. Time for the lads to hit their pubs, I'm thinking, and there's a likely looking tavern right over there. Its sign proclaims it the Spur and Stirrup, and red-coated patrons are pouring in.

I bounce on in, a very small sailor boy amongst all these big, loud, coarse, foulmouthed, red-coated soldiers. Ah. There's an open-faced bloke at that table by himself. He looks pleasant enough. I head for him and plunk myself down.

He looks at me quizzically.

"What you want, swabby?"

"I wants to buy you a drink, chappy," says I, reaching into my money belt.

"Well, all right, pull out yer tin and put it on the table, lad, and you'll find a true friend in Private Thomas Patton."

A barmaid comes over and I say, "A pint fer me mate 'ere and one fer me, too . . . and one for 'im, too."

Another grinning bloke has come up and sat down and asks, "What's up, Tommy?"

"This 'ere navvy is buying us fine fellows some pints, is what," he announces.

When the mugs come, I bury my face in the foam of my mine and say, "In returns for me kindness, maybe you can help me find a fellow soldier, one who done me a good turn, onc't."

"Well, spit it out, boy. 'Oo is it?"

"Have you ever heard of Captain Richard Allen of the First Dragoons?"

"Ha! Lord Allen himself, the tyke asks after! What could you have to do wi' 'im?"

"He . . . he done a favor for me mum once."

Gales of laughter.

"So you're lookin' fer yer daddy, are you, boy. Ha! Lord Dick, as handy with a maid as with a sword, I'll own!"

Hmmmm . . .

"I already know that, Sir"—*and indeed I do*—"but if you could just tell where I could find 'im?"

"I'll wager yer mum was a pretty one, wasn't she, boy?" crows Patton, pounding the table and roaring with laughter.

"Well, give us a song or two, and we might just tell you, Richard Junior!"

Why not?

I pop up and whip out my pennywhistle and do the "British Grenadier" and then sing "The Girls Along the Road" to great hilarity, and Private Patton takes me outside and points up to a window on the barracks across the way.

"Y'see that window, lad? Well, if you see a light there tonight, then you'll know that our commanding officer, Lord Richard Allen, will be in residence."

"Thanks, Thomas, you're a good mate, you are," I say, marking well the window and the handy drainpipe that runs down alongside it. "Now let's get back to the party!"

Get back we do.

I do a few more bits on the pennywhistle. Hey, might as well make some tips while I'm at it. Someone produces a fiddle and I find myself doing a full set, far into the night.

Later, I nip outside and see with some satisfaction that there is a light in that window. I bid farewell to my new mates and I'm off.

• • •

I wrap my hands and toes around the drainpipe and work my way up. Just after I left the Spur and Stirrup I had ducked into an alley, pulled from my kit bag my black burglar's outfit, and donned it quickly—black pants, black jersey, and black hood.

As I get close to the window, I see that it is open, due to the mildness of the night.

Good.

I stick my head in and listen . . . Deep breathing . . . Only one set of lungs, it seems . . . *Good.*

I step into the room and go stand next to the bed . . .

Ah, Richard, it is so good to see you again.

His sandy blond hair is spread out on the pillow, his chest bare, the sheet below spread across his hips.

I pull off my hood and put my face close to his and sing, very low . . .

There once was a troop of British Dragoons,
Come marchin' down to Fennario,
And the Captain fell in love with a lady like a dove,
Her name and it was pretty Jacky-O . . .

His eyes pop open and look into mine.

"Princess . . . ?"

"Yes, Lord Allen . . . Now move over, for I am very, very tired."

Chapter 28

"Ummm . . ." I murmur as I snuggle deeper into the side of Captain Lord Richard Allen, as morning light slips into the room.

"It is good to see you, Princess," comes his deep voice from close beside my ear. I feel my pigtail being lifted. "I note that my simple little woodland nymph has gained a new decoration on her lovely self. A nice match for the one that sits so gaily on her hip, I must say."

"Yes, Richard, I will explain soon . . . But right now I want to sleep, just a little bit more . . . Mmmmzzzzzzzz."

I do slip back into a lovely sleep, but gradually, I reluctantly come back into full consciousness. I reflect, as my senses return, that I have never before shared simple slumber with this Richard Allen as I have done with others of my acquaintance . . . Jaimy . . . Joseph . . . Jean-Paul . . . and, well, never mind.

Hmmm . . . funny, that. Oh well, chalk up yet another bedmate to my wild and wanton ways, and I must say the past night was quite pleasant. Yes, he did kiss me and I did kiss him back, but then I did fall asleep in his fond embrace and awakened only now in that same warm entanglement of arms and legs and nearness of bodies . . . *ummmm*. And he was gentleman enough not to disturb my rest with any more questions . . . or other advances of an amorous nature . . . or I don't think he did . . . I dunno . . . I was out like a light.

Fully awake now, I feel him rise above me, resting on an elbow and gazing down. I think he means to kiss me, but, no, it is not that . . . Instead, my brow feels the touch of a gentle hand that is placed upon my smooth and shaven head.

"Ummm. It is very warm," he says.

"Aye, Richard," I say, looking up from under his hand. "I suspect it is"—as that is exactly the same comment other males have made when they have laid their hand to my shaven brow—"but there is work to be done."

I throw back the sheets and rise. Yawning, I stretch and grab for my kit bag.

"And what work is that, Princess, other than getting you out of those rather snug-fitting clothes?" says Allen, leaning back against his pillow, arms crossed over his head and looking at me with some appreciation.

"The job of rescuing Mr. James Emerson Fletcher from the gallows, and from himself, is what."

"Oh, him again," he says, also rising from the bed. "I had hoped that the primary object of your love and affection had gone off somewhere very remote."

"No, I suspect he has gone off only as far as Blackheath Moor and is in great danger of doing himself harm. Turn around and let me change, and then I shall tell you all about it."

"*Tsk*, Prettybottom, why so suddenly shy? I would re-

mind you, Princess, that I have on at least two separate occasions seen you in the lovely altogether."

I work up a blush on that.

"Yes, well, that might be true, milord, but those times
are past and this is now."

"Oh, very well. There is a washroom through that door.
I shall call down for breakfast."

"Sounds good, milord," I say, as I duck into the privy.

Hmmm . . . Good . . . a washbasin, a pitcher of clean
water . . . chamber pot . . . soap . . .

I get down to it—strip off burglar gear, do necessaries,
wash face and parts, run soapy finger over my teeth, work
up some froth and spit into basin.

I notice a bottle with a fancy curlicued label on it—
Fariña Eau de Cologne—so I uncork it to give it a bit of a
sniff. It smells wondrous good—very much like lemons and
limes—so I spread some about the Faber frame . . . Some
here, and some . . . there.

Outside, I hear Richard speaking to someone, probably
his orderly.

Then I slide back into my sailor togs, thrust cap back
on head, empty basin into chamber pot, and go back out.
Breakfast does sound good, especially in the company of my
very handsome and gallant Lord Richard Allen, who I see
has now donned a red dressing gown.

He laughs when he sees me emerge, dressed as a *Dolphin's*
ship's boy.

"Oh, Princess, you are such a delight!" he says, coming
to me and putting his hands upon my shoulders. He looks
me over, continuing to chuckle. "However, when my man

brings up our breakfast, if you could just duck behind that dressing screen there?"

"Oh?"

"Yes, dear, it would not do my reputation any good should it be found out that I had entertained a sailor *boy* overnight in my digs, now would it?"

"Why, Richard, I am surprised that the black sheep of the Allen family would care about what anyone thought," I tease, my feet doing a little sailor boy jig. "Besides, from what I hear from your men, your reputation as a . . . swordsman . . . is quite secure, you dog."

"And where did you hear that?"

"From your men, last night—Patton and Jiggs," I simper. "How else could I find out where you lived?"

"Damned loose-lipped scoundrels! Suppose—"

"Now, Richard," I purr. "Do not be too hard on your lads. After all, you *do* know that I have my ways."

He chuckles at that. "Oh, yes, you do, Princess, you certainly do."

He puts on a quizzical look and sniffs at the air, nods, and then wraps his arm around my waist, putting his face to my neck and inhaling even more deeply. "And I do believe my cologne smells better on you than on me."

"I would not be so sure of that, Lord Richard," I purr.

There is a knock on an outside door and I retreat behind the screen. Presently, I hear the sound of silverware being placed on a table and I figure I'll add to Richard's . . . standing . . . in the male community.

I take out my burglar pants and flip them across the top edge of the screen, figuring they'll look like any pair of black stockings, if one does not look too close, and then I start to sing, in a high, very feminine voice.

> *Oh, Richard is my darling,*
> *My darling, my darling,*
> *Yes, Richard is my darling,*
> *My bold Gren-a-dier!*

That oughta take care of milord Allen's precious reputation, I'll own.

Presently, my host calls me back out.

"That was choice, Princess, well done," he says. There is a table set, and he pulls out a chair for me and waves me to it.

"Think nothing of it, Lord Dick," says I, sitting down and surveying the spread—eggs, bacon, toast, butter, marmalade, kippers, and a pot of hot coffee. "Let's get down to it."

As we eat, I tell him the story of what has befallen me and mine since last he saw me at my trial in the Old Bailey . . .

". . . and thank you so much for standing up for me at that awful trial, when I was in such distress."

"I don't think you really needed any help after all, seeing that Princess Prettytail has that precious bottom warming the seat of my unworthy chair right now."

"Oh, no, Richard, if you and Captain Hudson had not used your influence, I am sure I would have been hanged."

"Oh, well, thanks accepted. Go on . . ."

. . . and over to Bombay and down the Straits of Malacca to Australia . . . the Lorelei Lee *and the mutiny on the*

Cerberus . . . and Cheng Shih and the Divine Wind *and Chopstick Charlie and the treasure of the Orient and . . . and . . . and . . . until I finally washed back up on Britannia's shore . . . only to hear of Jaimy Fletcher's new profession.*

"Quite a story, Princess," he says, mulling it all over. "Here, have some more coffee, sweet one, and tell me about Mr. Fletcher."

I accept another cup and proceed to recount what Dr. Sebastian had told me.

"Hmmm," he says, after I finish. "I had heard of the Black Highwayman and of Bliffil's demise, but I had no idea it was at the hands of the calm, orderly, and totally honorable Lieutenant James Fletcher whom I had met in America and who most impressed me at the time."

"Yes, well, that was Jaimy then. I don't know what he has become now. I . . . I . . . am worried that he might have gone . . . mad."

"Huh! Well, if anyone is going to drive a man over the brink, it is you, Jacky."

I nod.

"'Tis true." *I am so very hard on my friends!* "The poor lad has been through so much. It is a wonder he has any sanity left at all," I say, all my levity gone. "Do you think he has really lost his mind?"

"Over your death? Possibly. Over the Bliffil thing? I, myself, have been trying to kill that slippery bastard Flashby for at least three years now. Does that make me a lunatic? I don't think so."

I reach over and put my hand on his. "Dear Richard, you do give me such comfort."

He places his other hand on mine. "So what is to be done, Princess?"

I consider the question and say, "Well, the way I see it, we use the promise of Chopstick Charlie's antiquities for the British Museum to get both me and Jaimy off the hook. There's a lot of treasure there, Richard, and money generally talks."

"Hmmm . . . Well, it might be possible for you. But Mr. Fletcher . . ." He shakes his head. "Killing a government agent—that will be somewhat difficult."

"I have Mr. Higgins and Dr. Sebastian working on it from a political angle."

"Good. I am but a simple soldier and I will leave the politics to the politicos. But as for that treasure . . . hmmm . . . I have some influence, and some influential friends, yes . . . we shall see."

He leans back and smiles, then says, "I believe it would be good for you to get out into Society. Starting tonight. You shall dine with me at a fine coffeehouse I know of. All the *ton* go there, and we might find it to our advantage."

I wipe the rather greasy Faber mouth with my napkin and put it down on my now empty and quite clean plate, then stand.

"Thank you, Richard, and now I must return to my ship. There is much to be done."

He stands also and puts his arms around me, and I put my head on his chest . . . But then I push away. I take a breath and say, "Richard, I am so very, very fond of you and I would . . . you know . . . go with you, without a moment's thought, without a moment's regret . . . but I've got to find out about Jaimy Fletcher before I . . . we . . . think about things like that."

"I understand, Princess," he says planting a kiss upon my head—my shaved head does seem to be a favored point of contact twixt me and my lads. "It is why we all love you so. I shall pick you up at six."

"Thank you, Richard. I count the hours till tonight."

To avoid trouble, I go out the way I came in. I blow him a kiss from the window, then I am out and down, then back into the city.

Chapter 29

James Fletcher, Brigand
On Blackheath Moor

Dearest Jacky,

I write to you in the firm conviction that I will soon be joining you, wherever you are. If it be heaven, fine, and if it be the simple oblivion of the void, also fine. At least my raging mind will be calmed, my demons silenced. Whether my end is accomplished by a bullet or a noose or by my own hand, it does not matter.

My fear that I was losing my mind is now a certainty. On occasion I have moments of real clarity—like when I venture into the city to glean information on the whereabouts of Flashby—but now and then I black out for periods of time and cannot remember what I did during those times. Sometimes I come back to myself on the heath with gold and purses in my hand and no recollection of how they got there.

One dark night, I made the mistake of going to my family's home on Brattle Street, perhaps, in my weakness of mind, to seek some sort of solace, but found none there. Although it was good to see the old place again, and my father, too, my mother's very evident joy in hearing of your demise turned my stomach. I could not stand it and left in disgust. I shall not go there again.

The late nights are the hardest—those long hours when I writhe and toss in agony of mind. Only Bess, sweet Bess, can soothe me and finally make me fall into deep, if troubled, sleep.

I wish there was an end to this and I was with you.

Jaimy

Chapter 30

"Shankies! You sat down with Shanky Boys? Eeewww!"
Joannie is beside herself—old animosities do die hard. She points her left forefinger at me and rubs it hard with her other forefinger.

"Shame!"

"Calm yourself, Sister mine," I say. "Things have changed."

I'm back in my cabin on the *Nancy B.*, shedding my sailor boy gear and preparing for the evening. *What to wear? Let us see. The blue . . . ? The white?*

"Changed? A dirty, filthy Shanky is a dirty, filthy Shanky and—"

"Toby Oyster is the boss of the Shanky Boys now."

"What?" she asks, incredulous. "*My* Toby?"

"Indeed. *Your* Toby. He came back from the Navy and he seems to be doing a good job. His Shankies now control all the smaller gangs in Cheapside, and a general peace exists among them, which is good, as I see it."

"Coo . . . Toby Oyster, himself, back on our old turf. Imagine that."

I knew that Toby's real name was Tobias Cloister—and *cloister* being a place where they kept monks and nuns to do their prayin' and stuff and therefore not a good street name—so he becomes "Toby Oyster." Cloister-Oyster . . . "If it rhymes, it's fine in Cockney Times," the sayin' goes, and so it went, and so he became. It seemed to fit him.

"Yes. And you'll be going over there later to get more of these." I open my palm and show her the wooden disk with the crude "S" writ upon it that Toby had given me.

"What is it?" she asks.

"Safe passage through Shanky Turf is what it is, and we'll need more of 'em. At least five. And you will get 'em. Here, take this one with you, or else you might have trouble."

"When?"

"Later. When Higgins gets back."

If Higgins gets back.

"Coo . . . Can I wear my black rig?"

"Yes, but be careful. And one more thing: Do *not* tell Toby you've seen Polly Von recently. It's for his own good."

She yelps in joy as she dives for her seabag and hauls out the costume. In no time at all, she is out of white sailor gear and into burglar's black.

"Ta da!" she exults, ready to head off.

I, of course, could have gone off myself to collect those valuable tokens, but I knew I had to give her a measure of freedom, else she would have taken it for herself. She is too close to her old grounds and I know the pull of the street is strong. Plus, she has old friends out there.

Speaking of liberty, I'd better issue some, else there will be mutiny.

"Go get John Thomas and Smasher McGee," I order after she is dressed.

She darts out the door, and soon my two stalwart sailors come in, hats in hand.

I have two stacks of coin ready for them.

"Here lads, go off and have a few pints. But be back by six. You both know what we are guarding here."

In an instant the coins are scooped up and gone, as are Thomas and McGee. I sigh in hopes of seeing them back in time. *Sailors . . . I swear . . .*

As the two charge off the ship, we hear a coach approach and Joannie pokes her head out the door to see who comes.

"Higgins! Well met! Come rest yourself. Joannie, get Ravi and have him bring a glass of wine for our Mr. Higgins."

Higgins sits himself down and soon Ravi comes in with a tray bearing two glasses and a carafe of red wine. He pours and says, "Mr. Lee making the lunch right now. Be right up."

"Thank you, Ravi," I say. "Now, Higgins, what have you to report?"

He takes a sip of his wine, sighs, then says, "I have conferred with Mr. Peel. You will remember him, Miss? Yes, of course. Anyway, he was most receptive to your proposal concerning the donation to the British Museum. Although he is no longer with the Admiralty, he does still have a measure of influence. It is too bad that Mr. Pitt has recently died, but Lord Grenville is Prime Minister now—"

"Not *my* Lord Grenville?" I ask hopefully. He was First Lord of the Admiralty several years ago and was very kind to me. Joannie bounces back into the cabin and settles at my feet.

"Afraid not, Miss," says Higgins. "He is William Grenville, older brother of your Thomas Grenville, but the connection could be of use . . . Meanwhile, I did talk to Mr. Peel, whom you know well, and though he was intrigued in the treasure we carry, he was even more interested in the possibility of gaining native allies in Burma, local contacts driven more by self-interest than by nationalistic fervor. He was most enchanted with my account of Chopstick Charlie and his many-tentacled empire."

"Ummm."

"And Cheng Shih . . . and the chance of opening China, and maybe even Japan, to English influence and trade. It is most attractive to a man like Peel."

"Does he know it is me back here on British soil proposing all this?"

"I believe he suspects, Miss," says Higgins. "And if I may say so, you have proven very valuable to him in the past. It might be well to pursue that line. I know that if you were to manage to find him a way back to his former position as head of Naval Intelligence under the First Lord, he would be most . . . appreciative."

I nod, taking this in.

"And did you meet with Dr. Sebastian?"

He nods in turn, saying nothing.

"Then you know about the Highwayman of Blackheath Road?" I say.

"Indeed, Miss. A most unfortunate circumstance. Mr. Fletcher must be quite beside himself."

"Um, rather," I say, gathering my thoughts.

"I spent the night at Dr. Sebastian's. He was quite the generous host. We talked of many things, some of which I think will be to your benefit."

"Good," I say, shaking myself out of my reverie. "I myself spent the night in the company of my dear Captain Lord Richard Allen and—"

"Ha!" exults Joannie, her two forefingers again rubbing away and pointing up at me. "So *that's* where you were! 'In the company of . . .' right, in the *bed of* you mean."

I point my own forefinger down at her and say, "Out. You have your mission, Joannie. Now go do it."

She turns and heads for the door, well fitted out in her own black burglar gear. "Aye, aye, Captain!"

"And be careful! Stick to the rooftops!"

But she is gone.

I turn back to Higgins.

"And so how is our gallant and quite handsome Captain Lord Richard Allen?" asks Higgins, trying, unsuccessfully, to suppress a slight smile. Higgins, over the past few years, has given me counsel many times on matters political, financial, and social, but never on my own personal behavior in matters of . . . well . . . my affections for certain members of the male persuasion. Which is good, as I count it, since I do not think I would take advice in those matters. Certainly I haven't in the past, that's for sure. My senses tend to . . . overwhelm me.

"He is well," I answer, all prim and proper. "He is quartered with his regiment at Whitehall. They expect to decamp shortly to Portugal under the command of Lord Wellesley . . . Old Nosey, they call him."

"Ah, yes. That honored lord is supposed to possess quite

a prodigious proboscis," Higgins says, and then sighs. "The awards and honors one wins hang upon the chest, and the fleeting fame that go with them, but a nose like that hangs upon the face for the rest of one's life. Pity, that."

"But while Richard is here, he places his men at our disposal. Within reason, of course. Certainly he would never do anything treasonous, or dishonorable. But within those bounds . . ."

"Ah. There's nothing like a company of mounted heavy cavalry at one's back, is there?"

"It can lend a measure of comfort, yes," I say. "So what's your next move, Higgins?"

"Well, tomorrow I must go to Blackheath. Dr. Sebastian informs me that there are many low and disreputable inns along Blackheath Road and I mean to check them out. I am sure there will be news of Mr. Fletcher there. So I shall prepare—"

"Dear Higgins," I say, placing my hand upon his arm and smiling. "The people in those places would take you for a copper in a moment. Or at least a swell, a nob, and you would get neither information nor a safe way out. Nay, better that I should go with Liam Delaney. Both of us know how to look rough and low. Nay, best for you to pursue your aims through the perilous alleys of British Intelligence."

Higgins nods ruefully, seeing the wisdom of that. "And tonight?"

"Tonight? Well, I am having dinner this evening with Lord Allen."

"Oh? Will it be here? What shall we serve? Shall I turn back the bed?"

"No," I say, giving him a stern look. "He says he will take me to a place called the Cockpit. It is close by Whitehall."

"Forgive me, Miss, but given the name, it sounds rather like a brothel."

"It is not, O Suspicious One. It is a famous coffeehouse, I am told."

"Where more than coffee is served . . ."

"Aye. Richard informs me that it is an establishment where anything goes—it is not cheap, and the food is very good. The sporting crowd, the *ton*, goes there, and no telling whom one might meet—highborn or low. It is a place where a gent meets his friends on a level ground, and where one might take a lady . . . who might, or might not, be one's wife."

"Aha."

"And he says we just might meet someone who could do us some good in the British Museum line."

"Umm. So what shall you wear? The Empire white, the Marie Antoinette blue, the—"

"I believe, dear Higgins," I say, rising and stretching my arms above my head. "Tonight, I shall go . . . exotic."

Chapter 31

As they had promised, John Thomas and Finn McGee returned at six and Richard Allen arrived by coach shortly thereafter. He was met at the gangway by Higgins, Davy, and Tink, all of whom were known to him from our treasure hunting expedition in the Caribbean. Hearty greetings were exchanged—brothers-in-arms, and all that. As Richard was dressed in his full red-coated regimentals, introductions to my good Irish Captain Liam Delaney were somewhat stiff but cordial, I later learned.

The lads then left the *Nancy B.* and headed off for some liberty of their own. They were dressed in the fine Spanish Naval Officers uniforms they had bought in Havana last year and they looked splendid.

"You two be good now," I had warned earlier in my cabin as I gave them a bit of a brush and some good advice. "And find out what you can about the Highwayman." I figure Dr. Sebastian has his ways of finding out things and these boys have theirs. 'Twas plain they intended to hit every low dive within two miles, and who knows what they'd discover?

Ravi, dressed in his loose trousers and white turban,

then escorted Captain Lord Richard Allen down into the cabin where awaited the Dragon Lady, Western Edition, lurking in her lair.

"So what do you think, Lord Allen? Will this serve?"

I give a bit of a pirouette and hold my Chinese fan in front of the lower part of my face, my kohl-darkened eyes peeking out above. "You like, Ree-chard-san?"

He looks around my cabin, noticing, I believe, the new things I have acquired since last he was in this room—the little statue of Ganesh, for instance, that I had gotten in India. There is a little earthenware bowl in front of the jolly elephant god, and incense smolders within. My Chinese sword and sheath hang on the back wall next to Esprit, the sword given to me by my fallen comrade Bardot. And on the top of my bureau, my Golden Buddha smiles upon all within. Some frankincense burns in front of him, too. Ravi, who tends to these little fragrant offerings, is a committed Hindu, but he does try to cover all bases in the way of religion. I don't blame him for that, being something of a pantheist myself. *Yes, Father Neptune, I hear you rumbling below* . . . Then, of course, there is my Jolly Roger flag draped over *that* wall, and my Golden Dragon pennant displayed over there . . . musical instruments all over the place . . . and, of course, there's my bed—that noble structure that lies over there. Yes, his eyes play over it, but he says nothing of an amorous nature—he is a gentleman, after all.

Ravi pulls out a chair for Captain Allen and he rakes his sword to the side and sits. Ravi darts out of the room.

"Ah, yes, that simple little Indian girl I met in the forests of America . . . hmmm . . ."

"You have learned that appearances can be deceptive,

milord, and I am glad to have been a helpful teacher as regards that part of your education," I simper. "Anyway, am I properly dressed for this Cockpit?"

I have on my rich silk sarong, shimmering all blue and gold, given to me by Sidrah of the House of Chen. It is wrapped tight about my bottom and goes up to wind about my chest, leaving my belly bare. My bellybutton proudly wears an emerald taken from the treasure trove below. Hey, who could possibly think that Jacky Faber, she of the Rooster Charlie Gang and of the pirate ship *Emerald* and the *Belle of the Golden West,* yes, and even the *Santa Magdalena* salvage crew, could give *all* that treasure to some dry old museum. *Yeah, right . . . There's enough to go around,* I say. Even Ravi has a nice little red ruby stuck up on the front of his turban, of which he is most proud.

I wear the silk robe that Cheng Shih gave me, the one with the Golden Dragon on the back, over the sarong for a bit of modesty. As for my hair, I have on my brunette wig, which Higgins has pinned up with some really cunningly carved ivory pins, also from the treasure stash, to look a lot like the hairdos of Oriental women. We have seen pictures of them in the papers that protect the porcelain china that comes from the East. Some of the wrappings have lovely, delicate images on them—wood engravings, we think—and that's how we know what their ladies look like. They are very lovely, and I have saved many of the thin tissuey prints, pressing them in a heavy book. If I ever have a house, I shall frame them up for all to admire.

"Yes, Princess, I believe it will serve quite well," he says, smiling widely. "Now, why don't you come over here and sit on my lap and we will discuss plans for the evening?"

Ravi comes back into the cabin, bearing a tray with a bottle and two glasses upon it. Ravi sets it down on the table and pours the golden Porto wine.

"A glass with you, Sir, as preface to what promises to be a lovely evening. I will, however, forego the pleasure of your lap, for now."

"Ah, Princess, you slay me, you really do. Where did you learn to talk like that?"

"I have had many teachers, of whom you are one," I say, taking a glass and holding it up to him in salute.

"Well, I am honored to be named as such," he says, grasping the stem of his glass and clinking it against mine. Then he drinks from it. "Ummm. That is good."

"Yes. It is from the Douro Valley in Portugal, but we took it from a Spanish merchant on our way here from the East," I say. "It seems both our armament and our resolve were greater than his. Too bad for him that we did not know that the Spanish were once again our allies."

"Well, serves the Spanish right for being so slow coming aboard." He laughs. "I guess Napoleon's naming his brother as King of Spain was the last straw for the Dons."

Allen drains the glass and fishes out a cheroot from his vest and puts it to his lips. Ravi is right there with a glowing taper from the incense bowl.

He holds it to the cigar and Richard sucks deep on the vile weed. Soon smoke swirls about his head. Then he speaks—not to me but to Ravi.

"*Shukriya, larka.*" Then he adds in English, "Where do you come from?"

Ravi, a bit startled upon hearing a bit of Urdu spoken, answers, "From Bombay, Sahib All-en wallah."

I had forgotten that Lord Allen had served in India.

"So where did you get the little wog?" asks Richard of me.

"In India . . . Bombay, *Mr.* Allen," I reply, slightly huffily. "His name is not 'wog' but rather Ravi, which means 'Sun,' which suits him. He has proven most valuable to me and I love him very much."

"Oh, do get down from your high horse, Princess, as it does not suit you," he says, ruffling Ravi's black locks. "He seems a fine fellow to me, and if you like him, so will I. Now, I believe it is time we are off to the Cockpit."

Our coach draws up to the entrance of the place and I am handed out by a footman. I place my hand on Richard's arm and allow myself to be led in. Covering all my Oriental gear, I wear a light cloak and hood, as my escort thought it best that I save some of the surprise for later, and I agree. After all, one must think about timing in any theatrical enterprise.

We go in, and my senses are immediately assaulted by the tobacco fumes that lie in dense layers all about the place. In what's left of the air that exists in the room, there is the smell, too, of perfume and liquor, along with beer and ale, as well as sweat and clothes that need a bit of cleansing. The lighting is mostly from candles placed in front of enclosed booths wherein clusters of people huddle and laugh and raise toasts together in what appears to be great conviviality.

Richard leads me through the throng.

"Lord Allen, by God, come and have a drink with us!" *"Over here!"* And Allen is gracious, bowing and saluting, and bringing his fingers to his brow in recognition of the kind invites. *"Come, Allen, show us that bit of fluff that decorates*

your arm!" "That Allen, I swear, always with a new one!" "Here, over here!"

He pushes on, with me clinging to his arm, toward the murky depths at the back of the place.

"Yes, Princess, it would be fun to stop to lift a few with them, and it would be entertaining, as many of them are fine fellows, but we are hunting much bigger game this night. Ah, here we are . . ."

We are guided to an empty booth and we slide into it, me gathering all my layers of cloth about me.

A girl comes up and Allen orders, "Claret, two glasses—no, four glasses—and oysters, lots of them. A plate of roast beef, too . . . Yes, and some cheese, a basket of bread, also . . . and whatever else you've got that's good, bring it on!"

The girl smiles, lets her eyes travel over him . . . then me . . . and says, "Yes, milord, right away."

The food and drink are brought and I settle into Richard Allen's side, content for the moment.

There is someone far off playing a fiddle and a woman is singing, and I reflect, uncharitably, that I could do both much better, but let that go. The oysters are awfully good, and I lift one to my mouth to let it slide down, and then I hold one over Richard's open mouth and, laughing, let that one slide down there, and then—

"Steady down, Princess," says Richard. "Our quarry has arrived."

I look over the room and see a very well-dressed man coming through the crowd, receiving invitations and salutations. He seems about to sit with one group when Richard says, "Jacky. Drop the hood . . . now."

I do it, letting the whole outer cloak slip from my shoulders.

The man in question notices . . .

"Good . . . good," says Allen.

"Who is he?" I whisper, mystified.

"He is the Duke of Clarence, and the woman on his arm is the famous actress Mrs. Jordan."

The man wears a naval uniform, and the woman— a very beautiful woman—is finely dressed with a many plumed hat upon her head.

The pair is about to sit down with those who had hailed them when the man notices me preening on Richard's arm. He murmurs apologies to that group and makes his way toward us.

"Good," says Richard. "We have him."

"But who is he?" asks the stupid me.

"He is the King's youngest son, William Henry. He is third in line for the throne and does not have much chance of gaining the crown, but—"

What? The King's own son?

I sit up and thrust out my chest as the pair approaches.

"Uh . . . a little more subtle, Miss," says Richard. "Play it a little more . . . mysterious . . ."

I take the advice to heart, settle back, and wait.

The Duke of Clarence comes to our table and Lord Allen stands up and says, "Milord William Henry, so good to see you. And Mrs. Jordan, may I say how much I enjoyed your performance as Hippolyta . . . absolutely stunning."

The woman accepts the compliment, but I can see that she is used to that sort of thing and is not at all won over.

"Will you sit and have a glass with us?" asks Richard.

"My companion has a proposition that might be of interest to you . . . or to your family."

The Duke flips out his tails and plunks himself down next to me, while Mrs. Jordan seats herself next to Richard, with whom she seems to be quite familiar. She takes a plump oyster, opens her mouth, and drops it down her neck. *Hmmm.* Wine is poured and idle chatter is the order of the evening.

"So what is this, Allen?" asks the Duke, referring to me. "Quite exotic, I must say," he says, gazing at my hair with its ivory pins.

"You don't know the half of it, milord," says Richard. "She is the Lady Ju kau-jing yi, of the House of Chen, and she comes from the East with a proposition that I believe will benefit both the British Museum and the British people."

I place my fingertips together and bow my head in acknowledgment of the introduction and then Richard gives him a brief description of the proposal . . . and the treasure.

"Remarkable," says Lord Clarence. "If it is true, Father will be very interested. He does love his museum so . . . But are you sure? She seems to be but a child . . ."

I decide to attack from the left, where sits Mrs. Jordan, rather than the right. I will get to him later.

I rise enough to let the cloak slip completely off, revealing me in my silken sarong. There are several nearby gasps, which I find somewhat gratifying.

Then I reach up my forearm where rests my shiv, and pull out the necklace I had taken earlier from the stash and had placed there for just this eventuality. I hold it up to Mrs. Jordan.

Her eyes light up at the sight of the string of perfect pearls.

"My patron in Rangoon wished me to give these to you, as stories of your beauty have extended that far. If you would, my lord," I murmur, in heavily accented English, handing the pearls to the Duke.

He gets up and places the necklace upon the neck of his paramour. It looks good there, and both seem very pleased.

To top it off, I slip the wig from my head, exposing both shaven head and Golden Dragon tattoo.

Many mouths go agape.

"I hope your mistress likes the pearls," I purr. "I dove down for them myself."

Richard leans into me and whispers in my ear, "I know you are lying about that, Princess, but I do believe you have done yourself some good here. Tomorrow, you shall be famous."

The Dragon Girl hoods her eyes and nods.

I am already famous, Richard, my dear dragoon, but we shall see what comes of this . . .

Chapter 32

Early in the wee hours of the morning, after a riotous night at the Cockpit, which got even more riotous as the night went on, I was escorted back to my ship.

Yes, there had been some tabletop dancing involved—with me bare of midriff, pigtail flying, finger cymbals chiming on my fingertips, and singing songs I had learned from Ravi and Sidrah. And all the while I was slithering and swaying, approximating the sinuous moves I had seen on dancers in Siam. I must say I was a hit. The Duke of Clarence was greatly amused, and I was told that I have been promised to him the instant Lord Allen tires of me. *"You will never tire of me, Lord Dick,"* I pronounced grandly from my perch on Richard's lap, as I put yet another pink shrimp to his lips. *"I promise you that!"*

Oh, yes, the Cockpit is Jacky Faber's kind of place, that's for sure.

A quick kiss for my Lord Richard in the coach, and I made my way back to my cabin. I did not invite him down into my den. No, I did not. I still had sense enough to realize that, though I trust him to be a gentleman—and he has certainly proven that in the past—I did not entirely trust my-self, especially in my current state of . . . excitement. *Oh, it was a glorious night! And Richard is so beautiful, all red-coated and fine, such a gallant . . . enough of that, you. You're sup-posed to be saving Jaimy Fletcher from himself . . . and from an eventual noose. Steady down, girl.*

A bit later, as I was preparing for bed and dressed in my nightshirt, I heard Davy and Tink come roaring back aboard.

> *Come all ye brave fellows that follow the sea,*
> *To me, way hey, blow the man down!*
> *Now please pay attention and listen to me,*
> *Give me some time to blow the man down!*

Aye, that's me lads all right. Best send Ravi off for some coffee before they bring the night watchman down upon us.

> *'Tis larboard and starboard, on deck you'll repine,*
> *To me, way hey, blow the girl down!*
> *For it's little Jack Faber on the Blue Anchor Line,*
> *Give me some time to blow the girl down!*

Hmmm. Davy does like messin' with the lyrics—anything for a dig at me. Some things never change. He just can't get over the fact that I run the show. *Well, suck it up, boyo . . .*

They come tumbling aboard and I quiet them and hurry them below. Soon there is coffee, and cakes, and they sub-side. Higgins, also, chooses this time to return, and he comes into my cabin and lays hat and stick aside and waits to report.

"So, lads, what did you find?"

"Well, Jacky, it is plain that it is our Jaimy, no doubt about that," says Davy. "And, to be sure, his fame is growing. There are songs being made up, poems, too. Some are quite good. You could think about adding them to your act, Jack-O . . . *'Oh, the Highwayman comes riding, with his pistols held on high, 'Give me Harry Flashby!' he cries, 'And the Highwayman shall ride no more!'"*

"He always had a quick temper," says Tink. "And Bliffil certainly was no friend of ours. Bad cess to him, I say, wherever he might be."

Bliffil had been the bull midshipman on the *Dolphin* and had made every effort to make sure the lives of the junior midshipmen and us ship's boys were as miserable as possible.

Higgins speaks up.

"It is true, the legend of the Black Highwayman is growing beyond his little spat with Bliffil and Flashby. You look disbelieving, Miss, but it is a fact. The romantic press has picked up the story. Give them a good man who is wronged by base and evil men, throw in swirling black capes, rearing black stallions against a full moon on the purple moor, and you've got an avid audience."

"Oh, dear," I say, fearful. "But how can he evade capture?"

"There are many inns on Blackheath Road that cater to the highwayman class. And he has the poor people with him for he robs only the fat merchants and never anyone in want. He laughs as he robs the rich ones, and it is supposed to be a harrowing sound, but he is always courteous to the ladies, and though they faint at the sight of him, he manages to put their trembling minds at ease."

"And Flashby?" I ask.

"He has gone deep under cover and has not been heard of for a while. Dr. Sebastian hears that Flashby has doubled his bodyguards but still fears to venture out from where he is hiding."

"Serves the bastard right," I say. "I wish him troubled sleep."

"The Highwayman has not been active for a while," continues Higgins. "I surmise that he is still recovering from the wound inflicted by the cowardly Bliffil. But he must be staying somewhere. He cannot be sleeping out in the spring rains. Someone knows where he is."

"I was talkin' to this one girl," says Tink. "She says she thinks the Highwayman stops by real regular at an inn called The Blackthorn. It's midway up the Blackheath Road. And a girl there, the landlord's daughter, just might know his whereabouts. Her name is Bess."

Hmmmm . . .

"Do you think that Jaimy has gone off his mind?"

The door opens and the black-clad Joannie walks in. She places the five safe passage tokens on the table and then sits down cross-legged on the floor, saying nothing.

"Well, do you?"

"He certainly ain't been actin' real sane," says Davy. Tink nods at that, and, reluctantly, so does Higgins.

So that is it. I stand and say, "I fear that James Fletcher has, indeed, gone mad. It tears my heart out to say that, but I know it can happen to the best of us. My own poor self had to struggle to hold the tatters of my mind together after Trafalgar, and so it must be with Jaimy. And the good Lord knows I've done my part to contribute to that lunacy. But if he has really lost his sanity, I pledge that I will take care of him to the best of my ability and I *will* bring him back into the world of reason. But for me to do that, he must not be caught and hanged as a common footpad. We have got to get Jaimy out of England and to a safe place where he might rest and return to us."

Tears are trickling down my cheeks as I wring my hands and ask, "Are you with me?"

Nods all around.

"The Brotherhood Forever," say Davy and Tink in unison, and I echo the pledge, hand on hip.

The Brotherhood Forever . . .

Chapter 33

It doesn't take much for Liam Delaney to look rough—just a watch cap crammed down low on his head, leather trousers, open shirt, and heavy boots. Tink, too, will be going along today, and he is dressed a little more foppish. We're trying for a dissolute young man look for him. Me? I'm dressed as slutty as I can make it, and I can make it pretty slutty, believe me, as I have had practice. I have on my low-cut blue dress, the one I'd sewn for myself back on the *Dolphin* in imitation of a frock I had seen on a Mrs. Roundtree, practitioner of the World's Oldest Profession. *Hey, what did I know? I was just a kid!* I top off my outfit with my outrageous red wig and my black lace mantilla thrown over my bare shoulders, *for modesty, don'cha know.* I slather too much rouge on my cheeks and lots and lots of white powder on my chest. Higgins shudders as the preparations are made, but we get it done.

At last we are ready and head out onto the pier. Higgins, impeccably dressed as always, of course, in gray suit and cloak, climbs into a hackney cab to go to meet again with Mr. Peel, my old controller at Naval Intelligence, to see how things lie in that direction, while Joannie Nichols bounds across Upper Thames Street toward Paternoster and the den of the Shankies, of which gang she is now a full-fledged member. *"Me a Shanky! Can you believe it?"* she exclaims. Her mission: to use the underworld gang network to find out where the frightened fox Lieutenant Harry Flashby has gone to ground, giving, as I see it, the brave and noble foxes a bad name.

Liam, Tink, and I get into a coach-and-four and clatter over Blackfriars Bridge and on to the moorlands south of London.

Coming off the bridge we make our way down Blackfriars Road to London Road, thence onto the Kent Road and then New Cross Road and on and on. The city has been steadily thinning out, turning into pastureland and meadow, with some sections of woods.

As we clatter along, I think grumpily how much I would prefer a good horse under me, rather than this stuffy, rattling, jarring coach, but the plan must be served. I amuse myself in teasing Tink about Concepcion Mendoza, the Havana innkeeper's daughter he had met on our treasure hunting voyage last year. It seems the *Nancy B.* had made other trips to Cuba on the rum-molasses-granite trade, after my departure, and Tink had revisited her each time.

"Huh!" I say, all contemptuous. "If I'd been along, you'd be married to Ric's daughter by now, and happy as any clam, with your head now resting on Concepcion's ample bosom, her belly big with child."

"Aye, now wouldn't that be sweet, instead of bein' shaken half to death on a cold, drafty day on the moors of England, chasing a phantom?"

"Well, when we get Jaimy back and safe, I'll do what I can to make it happen, and I *do* have my ways."

If we get Jaimy back . . .

Then I turn to Liam and start reminiscing with him about when the *Lorelei Lee* had met up with the *Nancy B. Alsop* in Rangoon, and his reunion with his daughter, my very good friend Mairead Delaney McConnaughey . . .

"Yeah, so I stuck my finger in the young rascal's face and said, 'Ian McConnaughey, you low-livin' poltroon, ye got me daughter in a pack o' trouble, and I blame ye for it. So now ye'd better be takin' her over to America where she'll be safe, and if I ever have to come after the pair o' ye again, it's her I'll be savin' and you I'll be drownin'! Do ye take my meaning?'"

Apparently, Ian took his meaning and debarked on the *Lee* with his wife, bound for America . . . or Amer-i-kay, as the Irish would have it.

"Do not worry about her, Father, as she and I have many friends there and she will be well cared for," I reassure him, my hand on his arm. "And Ian is a very good man."

Liam Delaney responds with a grunt. "Good man? Right. I have to chase halfway around the world, through heathen seas, to get her back . . . You, too."

We turn, finally, onto Blackheath Road, and the landscape changes. We are definitely in the moors. The earth itself is black, and the few and solitary trees are stark against the gray sky.

"It was my fault, Father," I say, snuggling into his side, looking out into the bleak surroundings and taking comfort from his solid presence. "Not Ian's."

"Aye," he responds with a short laugh. "But we forgive the lasses, don't we? But not the lads who should know better and take better care of their girls . . . and in this case, *my* girls."

"Ah, Liam, there's more o' it than that . . . and, oh! There's an inn up ahead! Let us stop and see what we can learn."

"Driver! Stop!"

We do, indeed, pull to a stop and get out. We go in, take welcome refreshment, and learn nothing. We press on.

The landscape grows darker and ever more gloomy. It starts to rain, a dismal, relentless downpour. We pass a pair of gateposts whereon is inscribed the name "Bask . . . Basker . . . ville . . ." or something. Whether it is a town name or the title of an estate, I do not know, but it is all very much lacking in cheer. From far off across the moor, a hound howls, low and mournful. *Ahooooooo . . . Ahoooooo . . .* I give a shiver and snug down even further twixt my friends. The road is now a glistening ribbon of highway in the gloom.

"There! There's another one!" I say, leaning out and pointing at the inn's sign swaying in the wind. "And it is the Blackthorne! The one we heard about!" The old inn looms out of the mist, its timbers black against the white of the upper structure. In the past, Higgins has informed me that this style is called Tudor, after old King Henry and his bunch. This particular structure looks like it might just have been built back in Henry the Eighth's time. It certainly seems intent on settling back into the black earth.

We pull up and the coachman sees to the panting horses as we enter the place. Through the smoke that hangs heavy in the air of the main room, we see that there are many low types seated about long tables, and me and my lads head for an empty one and plunk ourselves down to wait for service. While we wait, I burrow into Tink's side, giggling as if I'm a common tart with a good mark in my sights.

Tink plays along, while Liam pounds the table and roars out, "Bring us strong ale and be quick about it! And something to eat, too, by gawd!"

A girl appears. She is quite beautiful, as I was certain she would be. Dark ringlets frame the flawless skin of her face. She is dressed in serving gear with a loose linen white top, brown vest gathered about her lower ribs, and a full black skirt flowing from her trim waist to the tops of her tiny feet. She bears three tankards of foaming ale along with a basket of bread and cheese.

"Good afternoon, gentlemen . . . and lady," she says, cocking a knowing eye at me. "Welcome to the Blackthorne."

"Thankee, Miss," I say, picking up one of the mugs and throwing back a healthy slug. "And what might your name be then, dearie?"

"Then and now, it's just Bess," she says saucily, then turns away.

Ha! The landlord's daughter!

We fall to the ale and food, and when the lads have downed their glasses, I pop into Tink's lap and wriggle around a little bit and begin giggling and nuzzling his neck with my nose.

"I know you're just play-actin', Jacky," says Tink, reddening and beginning to breathe a bit hard. "But you're still a girl, and—"

I laugh and give him a peck on the cheek. "Hey, any old port in a storm, John Tinker. Ain't that what all you randy sailors say?"

"Ummm . . ."

I catch the eye of the observant Bess, who is missing none of this.

"'Ere, Miss, let's 'ave us another round of pints." In a moment she is over with a pitcher of ale and I toss a purse on the table, letting a good quantity of coins spill out. The girl takes thruppence for the fare so far. "Ah, that's good of ye, it 'tis . . . and 'ere's a shiny copper fer you," I say, pushing the coin toward her. "Now, you be tellin' us what ye know about this 'ere 'ighwayman. We hears yer right tight wi' 'im. Coo, right romantic and all, 'im being so dashin' and brave and all. I'm so bloody envious, I can't tell ye."

"I don't know what you mean, Miss." The girl sniffs, refilling our tankards from her pitcher. I note the red ribbon twined in her hair. It is a love knot, and I've got a feeling I know who it's for. He may be a lunatic, but he sure didn't waste any time. "Will that be all? Good." She turns and walks away, her hips swaying.

Nay, that won't be all, bitch, you will tell me . . .

Liam sees me redden, about to pounce on the girl, and presses his hand on my arm, holding me down.

"Easy, Jacky," he says. "You will gain nothing by threatening the girl."

"But she's seen Jaimy, I just know it!" I hiss, steaming. I note that the girl has gone through a door, probably back to the kitchen. I rise and follow.

The girl stands in a hallway, surprised to see me there.

"Sorry, Miss, but the privy's out back, around—"

"Here," I say, going up to her and pushing two guineas into her palm. "This is for you. I don't expect you to tell me where he is, but just do this for me, will you? Tell him you

237

have seen Jacky Faber, and that this Jacky is not dead. Will you do that?"

A knowing look comes over her face and she gazes at me with those black eyes and says, "Seems you've lost your cute little accent, haven't you, *dearie*?" She reaches over and pulls out the top of my bodice and drops the coins in. "Here. Save your money 'cause I got nothin' to tell you."

Defeated, I slump back against the wall. This girl ain't gonna tell him anything. I know that now. But I also know for sure that she has seen him. Otherwise she would have taken the money and laughed at my foolishness.

"Will you answer me this, then?" I ask, dropping all pretense. "He was wounded. Is he all right? Please tell me." My eyes mist up, and my lower lip trembles.

I believe she sees the genuine concern on my face, and hers softens and she answers, "It is said hereabouts that the Black Highwayman will soon be back on the heath."

I let out a heartfelt sigh. At least that is good news. I decide to press my luck:

"Could . . . could you at least *say* the name Jacky Faber to him? He . . . Jacky . . . is a mutual friend . . . It could do no harm."

The girl gives me a deep look, then shrugs and turns to wait on customers.

I know she won't . . . But I'm sure that she has heard the name Jacky recently . . . perhaps muttered in someone's sleep. I don't like to think it, but I believe it is true.

"Shall we push on further, Miss?" asks Liam when I return to the table.

"Nay, we shall go back to the ship. We have met the one we came to see, and further exploration will avail us nothing.

She will not tell us anything, nor will she tell Jaimy, but we must not spook her. We must pursue this in other ways."

We settle up and head out, me giving the girl Bess one last look. As I climb back into the coach and we start off, I think I hear a rattle of hooves at the back of the inn.

Could it be that Bess, the landlord's daughter, is back warmly receiving whoever has just arrived at the old inn door?

Damn . . .

Chapter 34

It is the next day and we are gathered back on the *Nancy B.* to discuss our plans.

" 'Tis plain the girl will tell us nothing, nor will she convey any message from me to him. In his current state of mind, he probably wouldn't believe it, anyway," I announce, having just told all gathered about of our visit to the Blackthorne Inn. It is breakfast, and Ravi is pouring coffee all around. Let us get on with it.

Late last night Joannie had come in while I was still up finishing a letter to Ezra Pickering concerning matters of international shipping. I had also acquainted him with the Jaimy Fletcher situation and my guess as to the current state of Jaimy's mind and the causes thereof. I asked Ezra if he would make discreet inquiries into finding a suitable home for Jaimy to begin recuperation should we succeed in getting him shipped safely back to the States. I was in my nightshirt and sealing the letter when she came in, chock-full of herself and bursting with news.

I listened with great interest to her report as she changed into her own nightshirt, washed up, and crawled into bed, heaving great dramatic sighs. I smiled in recognition of a fellow theatrical type, then blew out the lamp and climb in beside her.

Yes, as the only two females aboard, and both unattached to any male at the moment, we have been sharing my bed at night. Anyone who knows me at all recalls that I don't like sleeping alone. It's because of the screaming nightmares I am liable to have when curled up in the dark. The presence of another warm and breathing body beside me always seems to soothe those fears.

Plus, I do have to keep an eye on her . . .

"That was very good work, Joannie, and I am proud of you," I murmur. "Now, get over here and keep my back from the cold." It is, after all, still early spring and it gets damp and chilly out here on the Thames. I know the lads have the pot-bellied stove lit down in the galley, and they hang their hammocks about it for warmth. If it gets much colder in here, we'll be joining them down there. But for now, this is fine.

She flips over and I feel her small form hugged against me. Yes, this is just fine . . . but I need to say some things . . .

"Joannie," I say. "You know that you are now old enough to get in trouble of a different sort, if you catch my meaning . . . ?"

"Aye." She snorts. "And don't worry, Jacky, I've got me head on me shoulders and ain't likely to fall into any of that, not 'ere anyway, and 'specially not wi' any of them Shankies— 'cept maybe Toby, but he's already got a girl, and, of course, I got me a boy back in Boston, named Daniel."

"Well, that's good, Sister," I answer, noting that she, too, falls into the old way of speakin' when she's once again back on her home turf.

She stifles giggles, then says, "You do know, Jacky, don't you, that my good pal Rebecca Adams takes great delight in retelling the speech you gave to the Lawson Peabody girls back on the *Bloodhound*, 'The Nature of Things Twixt a Man With a Maid or . . . Things Your Own Mothers Should Have Told You But Plainly Did Not'?"

More giggles, then she says, "It is a very popular performance and she is very good at it with dramatic gestures and all."

I can just imagine, Rebecca, you little ham.

"And it is attended not only by the youngers, but also some of the older girls, them that wasn't on the *Bloodhound* cruise."

Hmmm . . .

"Well, I'm glad I was a source of amusement," I say, not very glad at all.

"Oh, Jacky." She chuckles, giving me a poke. "You cannot possibly know what a badge of honor it is at the school to have been one of the Original *Bloodhound* Thirty! And, oh, how I wish I could have been along on that journey!"

"No, you don't, you little fool. It only seems glorious and romantic 'cause everything worked out all right and we all got back safe. If things had gone differently, I'd be in some awful sultan's harem right now and you'd still be in the streets, bound for a life of shame and degradation."

"Don't be so sure of that, Jacky. You don't know me all that well," she says, her breath warm on the back of my neck.

"Besides, bein' in a sultan's harem don't sound so bad, eatin' grapes and them pomy-gran-ates."

"It's what else you've got to do in return for those grapes and pomegranates that's the problem, Miss," I reply. "Being a slave in any of its forms ain't no fun, believe me, girl, no matter how pleasant it might seem, 'cause I know."

"Aye. I've been pumpin' Ravi about you and that Cheng Shih, I have, but he won't say much. He only gives out with winks and giggles about his 'wicked, wicked Missy Memsahib.'"

Joannie gives me another poke in the ribs. "One of these days you'll tell me what went on between you and her, you bad thing, you."

"One of these days, young one, you shall hear of it, although you should not concern yourself with the actions of your betters. Right now, though, let us go to sleep."

That was last night. This is today. Joannie, dressed again in her sailor gear, sits anxiously at my side, her belly full of Mr. Lee Chi's fine breakfast, ready to tell her tale.

Let her fidget, I'm thinking. *Let's hear from Higgins first.*

"Mr. Higgins," I say, tossing in yet another bit of buttered toast. "I trust you had an interesting day?"

"Indeed, Miss, the good Dr. Sebastian was able to set up a clandestine meeting with the Doctor, Mr. Peel, former head of Naval Intelligence, and myself, of course, at his club. It was a most agreeable place, well appointed and exquisitely furnished. The service was impeccable, I might add . . ."

Get to it, Higgins.

". . . and another meeting has been set up for tomorrow

morning at the same place, to discuss the possible donation of great treasure to the British Museum . . . that and the subsequent advancement of Mr. Peel's rather stalled career. He is most interested, I might add."

"As well he should be," I retort. "Does he know I am involved?"

"Not yet, but as I've said, he might have his suspicions. He is a very intelligent man, and seeing both Dr. Sebastian and myself together, he might well draw his conclusions."

"Ummm. All right. That is all to the good," I say, putting napkin to lips. "Now, you have already heard of our visit to the Blackthorne Inn yesterday. So let us now hear from our street representative, Miss Nichols."

Joannie pops up straight in her chair and begins.

"Me and the Shankies have found that this 'ere bloke 'Arry Flashby—"

"Speak correctly, dear," I say, hearing the rush of her words. "There's plenty of time."

"This man, Harry Flashby, has taken rooms somewhere north of Cheapside. We do not know just where—right now, anyway—but we do have scouts out searchin'," she says, looking sly. "And we are certain of one thing. Flashby is afraid to come out of his rooms till the Black Highwayman is taken. Until then, he contents himself with fine feasts and . . . with carefully chosen . . . er, um . . . female company."

Ah . . . ever the lusty one, eh, Flashby? We'll see about that.

"We also know who gets these girls for him," she continues. "He's a pimp named Benjamin Crespo, otherwise known as Benny the Creepo. He goes through the whorehouses and chooses those girls he thinks Flashby would like. It's said that he selects the more exotic types: Negroes, mulattos, Creole, French, Spanish, and the like. And it's all done very secretly, too. The girls are taken by coach in dark of night and are blindfolded on the way there and back so they won't be able to tell where his hidey-hole is."

"Where can this Benny the Creepo be found?"

"Usually at a brothel called Mrs. Featherstone's. It's on Ludgate."

"Well, then, we'll have to pay that fine establishment a visit then, shan't we?" I say, rising. "Ravi, go get Mr. Lee and have him bring his razor. My head needs a bit of a touchup. Oh, and get your turban . . . and your curly-toed slippers, too, as you will be going with me. Joannie, into your sailor-boy gear . . ."

"Aye, aye, Sir!" she chirps, diving for her seabag.

". . . and Higgins, if you would be so kind as to continue your inquiries? Good. Davy and Tink, to the taverns to pick up what you can. We must know when the Highwayman resumes operations. All set? Then, let's do it."

The coach pulls up in front of Mrs. Featherstone's Fine Emporium and I wait for the coachman to open my door to hand me out.

"Joannie, you stay here, out of sight. Ravi, you will pick up the back hem of my garment and follow me in. Got it? Good."

The door opens and we get out in all our splendor.

Ravi has on his white turban with the ruby in the center of it, and loose white trousers gathered at the waist and ankles. His brown chest is bare and his feet are encased in golden silk shoes with upturned toes.

I have my green and gold sarong wrapped about my

hips and chest, leaving my midriff naked except for the emerald that sits in my bellybutton. Silk slippers are on my feet, as well, with my light silk cloak wrapped around all.

The well-tipped and eager-to-please coachman bounds up the steps and opens the door for me, and we enter, me first, with Ravi behind, holding up my silken train.

Surprised female eyes look up at us as we sweep into the foyer. The ladies are in various stages of undress, with much black lace and brightly feathered boas in evidence.

"I am the Lotus Blossom and I am here to see a Meester Creespo. You are to go geet heem, pleez."

One of the girls gets up and darts out of the room. Presently Benny the Creepo enters the room, an inquiring look on his face.

He is small, round of belly, and bald of head. On me, baldness looks good, but on him it does not. He affects a greasy mustache and beard, and he is dressed in a garish, foppish fashion. A smirk creeps over Crespo's full, purplish lips.

"What have we here?" he asks.

"I am called Lotus Blossom," I purr, letting the cloak slip from my head and shoulders to stand before him in all my Eastern finery. If this ain't exotic, I don't know what is. His eyebrows go up in appreciation.

"And I hear that you make assignations of a certain sort for gentlemen of very refined tastes," I continue, turning myself about slowly so that he might appreciate all my charms. I make sure that my braid is brushed to the side so that he might view my Golden Dragon tattoo. "Ess thees true?"

"Might be," he says. "What have you got to offer?"

"What I have to offer is a youth spent in the Willow World of the East studying the sensual arts," I softly say, looking up through my kohl-rimmed eyes. "I know ... theengs ... techniques ... your gentlemen have never heard of. I know they will be delighted and will reward you handsomely for bringing me to them."

"All, right, dearie," he says, rubbing his hands together and looking me over most avidly. "Let's just step back into my room and see what you've got."

I throw on a look of supreme contempt. "One such as Lotus Blossom is not for one such as you." I snap my fingers and Ravi scoops up my fallen cloak and drapes it about me again. "She is for *finest* of gentlemen. I shall send my slave around tomorrow to see what you have arranged. Oh, and yes, the price is fifty pounds, not a penny less. Goodbye."

With that I sweep back out, leaving an astonished Benjamin Crespo behind me.

"Driver, pull down the street a bit and wait," I order, as Ravi and I climb back in. He does it and we sit and wait.

We do not linger long. In a few minutes Benny the Creepo comes out and hurries down the street.

"All right, Joannie, go!"

Joannie, now Johnny Nichols, sailor boy, leaps out of the cab and follows the pimp down the lane. I see her make a signal wave, and up on the rooftops I see figures outlined against the sky, making the thumbs-up sign.

Our little pimp is going to have an avid following.

Chapter 35

The next morning, I receive several messages.

The first one is from Dr. Sebastian, reaffirming our appointment for a meeting at one o'clock with Mr. Peel at his club on Bishops Gate. Both Higgins and I will attend.

The second is from Richard Allen:

Princess—

Please forgive my not delivering this note in person as I am detained on military matters. Do please honor me with your presence tonight at the Cockpit. A coach will be sent for you at six. I promise you a good time.

Oh, yes . . . Please invite John Higgins to join us as there will be a person in attendance tonight whom I think it would be advantageous for both you and our worthy Higgins to meet.

Cheers,

Richard

I fold each note and put them both aside on my breakfast table. I take another sip of coffee. *Mmm.* Ah, yes, Mr. Lee Chi has finally mastered the art of making a more than acceptable brew.

Joannie Nichols is beside me, tucking into her own hearty breakfast and bringing me up to date on her investigative missions through the rough neighborhoods of Cheapside.

"We followed Crespo halfway 'cross London, but after a bit he pulled up on Chiswell Street, where it seems our Mr. Flashby has his hideout. He's got rooms on the top floor, four stories up. His window faces an alley and there ain't no drainpipes or anything like that to climb up on, so we'll have to come down over the top on ropes tied to the chimneys."

"Good work," I say. "Here, try this orange marmalade. What else?"

"That's about it."

"Well, tomorrow night you and I shall go up to case it out further."

"Tomorrow?"

"Yes. Busy today," I say, putting away another tasty little biscuit. "And tonight the mysterious and exotic Lotus Blossom dines with the very handsome and gallant Lord Richard Allen," I announce with a broad wink at my very able sidekick.

Mr. Peel's club is very well appointed, what I have seen of it, anyway. Women, of course, are not allowed into the inner sanctums of the place—not even wives. But there is a nice reception room, furnished in red leather and dark wood paneling, and it is to that spot that Higgins and I are led.

As we are made comfortable by a liveried butler, Dr.

Sebastian and Mr. Peel enter the room. I am dressed somewhat more modestly than usual—brunette wig, black Lawson Peabody School dress, with my black mantilla over my head.

Higgins rises and shakes hands, while I remain seated. I slip the black lace from my hair and gaze up at Mr. Peel, the former head of Naval Intelligence, the man who had sent me on various dangerous assignments in both France and the Caribbean, without too much concern for my safety . . . or my virtue.

I offer up my hand and he takes it. At that, I rise and make a small curtsy.

"So good to see you again, Sir."

He does not register much surprise.

"Ah, Miss Faber," he says with a slight bow. "I suspected you were somehow involved in all this. Please, do be seated and let us talk about the . . . situation as Dr. Sebastian has outlined it to me."

The conversation then turns to the task at hand.

"It all boils down to this, Sir," I say. "I have a great treasure to give to the British Museum." Here I withdraw the pendant made of a gold Roman coin, bearing the image of Augustus Caesar, and hand it to Peel.

"Very nice," he says. "And what will you want in return?"

"The thanks of the British people would be too much to ask for, I suppose. So I merely request a full pardon for myself and for Lieutenant James Fletcher."

"Hmm. So where is this treasure?"

"In a very safe spot, you may be assured, Sir," I murmur. "And I have already made the acquaintance of the Duke of Clarence and have enlisted his help in this matter."

That gets a response from the man. He looks sharply at Higgins.

"The King's son?" he asks of him, his eyebrows raised.

"She does stay busy, Sir," says Higgins.

"Indeed. Quite remarkable."

"Yes, I had lunch with him several days ago . . . and I am invited to a cotillion on Saturday. I am greatly looking forward to it."

"Hmmm," says Peel, hand on chin, regarding me intently. "As I am out of favor and out of office, I cannot possibly see what part I might play in this."

"Perhaps I can help in that way, Sir, having the Duke's ear, as it were," I reply. "Now, tell me just who has taken your place at the Admiralty?"

A cloud goes over his face.

"A very disagreeable chap named Durward Smollett, a cheap bureaucrat and toady who has kissed his way to the top. First Lord Mulgrave is not a bad sort, but he has surrounded himself with some very marginal people."

"Hmm. Is this Smollett married? Has he a mistress?" I inquire, thinking maybe to attack this person in that direction.

"He is married. His wife is an avid social climber. It is she who has helped him advance."

"Well, we shall see about that," I say, smiling slightly.

"Oh?"

"Yes, I am about to make Mrs. Durward Smollett very happy."

"And how's that?"

"Why, she and her husband are about to receive an invitation to the Duke of Clarence's fine cotillion."

Chapter 36

I whisper in Lord Allen's ear, "Richard, get out of the game, and do it *now*."

We have been sitting at this gaming table for some time now, and Milord Allen has been steadily losing to a very affable and fussy gent who sits across from us, chuckling over his winnings as if he were blessed in all his incompetence at cards by Lady Luck. But I don't think so . . .

I have become something of a fixture at Lord Allen's side here at the Cockpit . . . and . . . the object of much discussion . . .

Who the hell is she, anyway, this so-called Dragon Girl? No one seems to know, but she surely has Lord Allen in thrall, don't she? Nah, to him she's just the tart-of-the-month, you'll see. He'll have a new one soon and she'll be out in the streets again. Some say she is Eurasian—half English, half Japanese or somesuch . . . Tsk! That's what happens when you send silly missionaries into those un-Christian lands. The heathens knock up the preacher's daughter and they still go unconverted, the swine. Best not call her a filthy wog, though—not in Lord Allen's hearing, anyway. He's got a hair-trigger temper, as you well know. Oh, yes, I know that . . . hmmm . . . Nice ass, though, and she sure don't mind swinging it around, do she? Look at that—looks like her backbone's got a swivel hinge on the lower end, don't it? Ha! You are right . . . and she sure don't cover that rump with much cloth, either. I swear you can see right through that thin silk . . . Man, I sure wouldn't mind being in Allen's shoes for a few . . .

And those are just the *male* voices I hear murmuring in the gloom. There are female voices in the chorus, too . . .

Damned uppity arrogant little bitch. Did you know she had dinner with the Duke of Clarence? Yes, it's true, I saw them right here, not two days ago. No! Yes, I did, and it's rumored she's going to be presented to the King, himself. Something about museum knickknacks she brought back with her from God-knows-where. I know the King is a bit off his wig, but . . . A scandal is what I call it—under all that jewelry and makeup and silk, you'll find just a common tramp. You can mark me on that . . .

You may be mean-spirited harpies, ladies, but you are absolutely right—even though you don't know it for sure. I am just an ordinary Cheapside scammer, lookin' for the main chance and playin' my cards as they are dealt to me . . . Well, sort of as they are dealt.

. . . and she brings that little nigra boy with her all the time, as her servant. You know, the wog with the turban? Disgusting! Well, I don't think it's quite right, don'cha know, the way this place is run and . . . Look at that! George Gordon has just brought that big smelly dog of his in here again. God! How can we stand it all? Well, Allen's a lord and Gordon's a lord and they're all bloody lords so they get away with it and with all . . .

Yes, gossip is grist for the Cockpit's mill, that's for sure. But I must say I like the place—smoke hanging in layers to the ceilings, intrigue, plots, loud swirl of talk-talk-talk, constant talk . . . reputations enhanced . . . and destroyed, revolutions planned and then crushed, plans made, plots laid . . .

Yep, my kind of place.

"Get out of the game gracefully, Richard," I whisper as the seemingly hapless winner turns aside to talk to an acquaintance who has stopped by to observe the card play. "Do it now."

"But why?"

"Because he has been dealing seconds . . . and I believe the deck is shaved . . . and probably marked, as well. Like any good magician, he distracts you at just the right moment. But he does not divert *my* attention. You have lost enough, for now." There is a stack of gold coin, formerly owned by my good Lord Richard Allen, that now rests in front of the seemingly happy but nonplussed winner.

"Well, by God, I'll kill—" Lord Allen snarls, about to rise and grab for his sword in righteous anger.

"No, dear one," I softly say, still playing the compliant courtesan whispering sweet nothings in my lord and master's ear and pushing him back down. "What you should do is issue compliments all around, then rise and go. Sometime later tonight, pick up a few decks of the Cockpit's own house cards and give them to me. The next time we sit down to play with this cheat, we will trim him, and trim him good. Trust me, Richard. Don't you remember my mentor and teacher Yancy Beauregard Cantrell, back there on the *Belle of the Golden West*? That very smooth and skillful gambling man who delivered the promise of a particular kiss into your hands? Hmmm?"

I see Richard recalling the Incident of the Famous Wagered Kiss back there on the Mississippi, which ended with my paying off the wager. It was for a mere kiss—to the winner—which, of course, was Cavalry Captain Lord Richard Allen. So in a quiet pool of clear cool water on that same river, where we were both quite free of any clothing, I kissed him. And just as I did, we were visited by a very unexpected guest . . .

"Very well," he says, smiling at the recollection and rising with me on his arm, his anger stifled, for the moment, anyway. "Gentlemen, I bid you good night. Thank you for your company." He bows, I cast a few dark glances about, and we leave the table.

As we're wending our way back through the crowd, I hear the same mumblings . . . *There's the little hussy . . . Who does she think she is . . . ?*

And when we get to our booth, who do I find but my good John Higgins, who had accompanied me here on Richard's rather mysterious invitation, deep in conversation with a very handsome, elegant, and languid young man. At the man's side is a very big black dog.

"Princess," says Richard, upon our arrival. "May I present my good friend George Gordon and his companion, Boatswain, both fellow schoolmates at Harrow. Boatswain was, by far, the better scholar among the three of us!"

"Right you are, Allen," says the gent, rising and extending his hand to me. "As Boatswain majored in Faithful Service, and we majored in Sloth, Drunkenness, and Lechery. Charmed, my dear." He bows and kisses my hand.

"*Enchanté, m'sieur,*" I murmur, not quite knowing how to handle this and figuring that hiding behind my French would be best.

"My word, Allen, she is quite remarkable. Does it speak

English?" From his calling Richard like that, so familiar, I assume that this Gordon shares a similar peerage. It turns out I am right.

"Yes, she has a passing familiarity with our native tongue," says Richard, with a laugh, putting me into the booth such that I slide next to this Lord What's-His-Name Gordon. "I met her as a Shawnee princess in the wilds of America, and she has proved most fascinating in all her aspects." The dog wriggles and thrusts his massive head twixt my knees and looks up at me with big brown eyes.

"Ah, a girl of many parts, then?"

"Many, *many* parts, George, you may rest assured."

The men prattle on about my supposed virtues while I take the dog's face in my hands. I cannot resist a good dog, no matter what the place or the circumstances, and I drop some of my pretense.

"What a fine fellow he is, Sir," I say, petting the dog's broad brow and thinking of my faithful Millie back at Dovecote.

"Yes," says Gordon, reaching over and affectionately stroking the dog. "He, like many dogs, possesses Beauty without Vanity, Strength without Insolence, and . . . yes . . . Courage without Ferocity."

"Well put, Sir," I murmur, as I receive a big, wet kiss from Boatswain's tongue. "He is so much more sweet than any actual Bo'sun I have ever met."

"And well said, Miss," says Gordon. "All the Virtues of Man without his Vices, as it were."

"Ha!" Allen laughs, his arm comfortably about my neck. "You must hear this one. When we were at Harrow, the old schoolmasters refused to let any dogs on the premises, and so poor Boatswain was banished. So challenged, old Gordon here went out and got himself a bear . . . yes, an actual bear cub, and brought him into our rooms! Ha! That put those school-marmish noses into a bit of a twist, not having the foresight to banish bears as well as dogs from their holy environs."

"Truth be told," says George Gordon. "Little Hugo was quite a delight."

"Yes, he was," agrees Allen, somewhat ruefully. "Till the brute got big enough to eat us out of house and home."

"Right. And big enough to beat either of us to a draw in the way of wrestling. Now he bothers the chickens and geese up at Newstead Abbey, happy as any bruin on this earth."

"Good old Hugo," says Allen, raising his glass. "To a noble bear."

"Hear, hear!" and the toast is drunk to an absent bear.

"Now, Allen," says Gordon. "Back to your little friend here."

At that, I snuggle deeper into Richard's side, put on the big eyes, and wait.

"Has Samuel seen her? I must suspect he has. Tell me, dear, do you play a dulcimer? Do you know a Kubla Khan? And are you an Abyssinian maid?"

What? I am confused.

Higgins, seated on the other side of this George fellow, comes to my rescue.

"I'm afraid, Sir," he says with a slight cough, "that Mr. Coleridge has been sent off to Malta . . . for reasons of health, and really cannot have been acquainted with our young miss here, however apt the allusions might be."

"Reasons of Health! Ha!" exclaims Gordon. "They're just trying to dry out the poor sod. It's said he's up to two quarts of laudanum a week now!"

Two quarts of tincture of opium! Good Lord, is the man a racehorse? Has he any mind left at all?

"Yes, it is a shame," agrees Higgins, who has been my good guide through the perilous waters of temptation these many years when my weak self was sometimes prone to fall under the baleful influence of various substances offered to me. "I have seen many wasted lives."

"Well, it shan't get us, shall it, John?" says Gordon, rising and bowing to those assembled. "It grows late and it seems the place is quieting down. May I ask that your Mr. Higgins be allowed to accompany me back to my rooms, as we have much to discuss in the way of poetry, philosophy, and mutual friends?"

I nod, with a knowing look at Higgins. His returning look says, *This man is well known in the arts and letters world. He could be very, very valuable to us in our current endeavors.*

"Of course, George," says Allen. "I shall be delighted to see the young lady back to her ship."

Have fun, Higgins . . .

Chapter 37

"So how do you know all these people, Higgins?" I ask. We are taking our supper together in my cabin. He's dressed to the nines for he will be going out on the town later, and I am dressed in my black burglar's garb because I will be going out on the town, too . . . or, more precisely, on *top* of the town. "This Lord Gordon you went off with last night and . . . and this Cold-Ridge person you both spoke of at our table . . . ?"

"Ah, yes . . . well, George Gordon—Thank you, Ravi—Ahem . . . well, yes, he is more often referred to as Lord Byron, for, indeed, he holds that title. And as for knowing them . . . Well, Miss, you know I once was employed in Lord Hollingsworth's household . . ."

I nod at that, eyebrows raised.

". . . and in that capacity, when it was time for young York Hollingsworth to go off to school at Harrow, I was sent along as valet to the young man, and I must say I enjoyed our time there most immensely."

"Yes," I comment, a bit sardonically. "Nothing like letting the lads off the farm for a bit of frolic in the city to get the young blood going."

"True, Miss," Higgins says, smiling at the recollection. "The future Lord Byron was there, as well as many others. Percy Shelley, for one, though not at that particular school, was part of the literary life of London, and a glittery life it was. It was a very liberal gathering of minds, and I was not excluded from the . . . conversations."

"And how, my dear Higgins, did you manage to attain such an education so that you were able to hold your own with these young literary lions? Hmmm?"

"Well might you ask, Miss. You see, Lord Hollingsworth had an extensive library at his estate, and by the time I was twelve, I had read just about every volume in it. I was translating Cicero when the good Lord Hollingsworth died."

"Did you ever do any actual work?" asks the ever practical me, cocking a knowing eye at him.

"I was, Miss, indulged, you might say, and given special privileges, due to my aptitude for learning."

"Ah."

"The taste for the high life in London was probably the cause of my rather ill-considered decision to apply for a post as steward for the wretched Captain Scroggs of the *Wolverine,* following the death of Lord Hollingsworth. After the good lord's death, I had the choice of remaining in a rather dull post at Hollingsworth Manor, tending to the needs of the young daughters of the house, who, though delightful young ladies, would soon, I knew, be heading off into marriage and leaving the estate quite bereft of any joy and excitement. I stupidly thought that a life at sea might lead to a life of some adventure."

"It did do that, Higgins," I say, laughing. "After we both had a dose of some very good luck."

"That is true, Miss. Luck that you made happen."

"Oh, bother that, Higgins, you have saved my hide many more times than I have saved yours. So anyway, what is this Kubla Khan stuff? It seems I should be familiar with it."

"Ah. Well. You have been gone from the London scene for quite some time now and it might take a while to bring you up to speed in a poetical way. I took the liberty of obtaining some copies of Mr. Coleridge's work. Here they are," he says, laying some sheets of paper on the table. "The bit that Lord Byron was referring to goes like this, if you will pardon my rather inept recitation . . ."

> *In Xanadu did Kubla Khan*
> *A stately pleasure-dome decree:*
> *Where Alph, the sacred river, ran*
> *Through caverns measureless to man*
> *Down to a sunless sea.*

"Sounds good to me, Higgins, as I'm all for pleasure, though I don't know about those 'sunless seas' as I rather like my seas warm and comfortable, but sing on, Orpheo," I say, grandly waving a bread stick. "Sing on . . ."

"Yes, Miss . . . ahem . . . this from later in the poem, and more to the point of which Lord Byron was referring in relation to you the other night . . ."

> *A damsel with a dulcimer*
> *In a vision once I saw:*
> *It was an Abyssinian maid,*

And on her dulcimer she played,
Singing of Mount Abora . . .

"That is good. I like it. Yet another mountain to sing of. I already do 'The Mountains of Mourne' and 'Kilgarry Mountain,' so that should fit right in."

"Indeed, Miss," says Higgins. "I had thought, given your current mode of dress and . . . coiffure, you might profitably add a version of the poem to your act."

"You bet, Higgins, it's already in there, even as we speak. Now, what is a dulcimer and where can I get one? And where the hell is Abyssinia?"

"A dulcimer is a form of the classical zither. There are many about. I shall find one for you," he replies. "And Abyssinia is very close to Ethiopia, I believe."

"Ah. And this Mr. Coleridge has been there and gazed upon these Abyssinian maidens frolicking about?"

"Only in his dreams, I'm afraid. It is said that he composed the poem in an opium trance, and I do not doubt it. He was well on his way to full addiction when I knew of him back in those days." Higgins pauses to dab his napkin at his mouth. "Mr. Coleridge is now on the island of Malta. You see, Miss, it is common practice for the young men of fine families to be sent off on the Grand Tour of Europe to cure them of what the families perceive to be various personal . . . eccentricities."

"Oh?"

"Yes, I have observed that it seldom works . . . not as intended, at least. Generally, it makes those eccentricities more pronounced."

"And your Lord Byron?"

"Alas, yes. He, too, is to be sent off soon, as well, as an antidote to what his family perceives to be his rather wicked ways."

"Soon, Higgins?" I ask with a smile and a wink at him over the top edge of my wineglass.

"Yes, Miss, soon, but not yet . . ." he replies with a secret smile of his own.

There is a tap on the door, and I say, "Come in."

A dark-suited gent, unknown to both Higgins and me, enters and bows. My hand goes to my shiv and Higgins's hand slips under the lapel of his jacket to rest, I'm sure, on the grip of one of the small pistols he wears there.

"Your pardon, Miss," says this man, holding out a letter. "But I bear a message from Mr. Peel."

I relax and take the proffered letter. The man bows again and leaves. I crack the seal to open the letter . . .

My Dear Miss Faber,

I regret to inform you that the Black Highwayman is back on the High Road, and plying his former profession. Yesterday, he stopped the Plymouth Coach at the Kent Road and, at gunpoint, bade the gentlemen within to step out. There were two merchants, and of these he relieved them of their purses. The third was a Naval officer, a Post Captain Oliver. Of him he was most respectful and demanded of him only the gentleman's sword, which was tendered to the Highwayman, who then disappeared in a cloud of dust, the merchants' money in his sack, the Naval officer's sword slung over his back. That same sword reappeared this morning, stuck through a torn piece of paper

*and thrust into the front door of the Admiralty itself. The paper,
obviously taken from a broadside sheet, showed the Puss-in-Boots
tattoo with the word "Vengeance!" under it ... and below that
was lettered two names:*

<del>Lieutenant Alexander Bliffil</del>

Lieutenant Henry Flashby

*The Bliffil name was crudely crossed out in red ink. That
was the extent of it, but all concerned believe the message was
quite clear.*

P.

After reading the note, I pass it on to Higgins. He takes
it and reads, then leans back, thinking.

"Hmmm. I suppose the tattooists must be taking their
pattern from somewhere, the image being rather standard."

*Oh, Jaimy, what if we cannot get you back in time? What
if you are taken? What if . . . ?*

Higgins gazes at me, knowing exactly what I am
thinking.

"What if we cannot bring Mr. Fletcher back?" he asks
gently. "To both safety and sanity? Have you given any
thought to that eventuality? You must think of your own
future as well. We cannot know how all of this will turn out,
and life will go on."

Heavy sigh.

"Of course I have thought of that awful possibility,
Higgins. I'd be a fool not to." I take a deep breath, then say,
"I could renew my vow to live single all my life."

Higgins raises an eyebrow. "And devote yourself to good
works, I suppose, from the confines of some worthy con-

vent," he says with a slight smile. "Knowing you as I do, I consider that a highly unlikely prospect."

And I, too, certainly know myself better than that.

"Well, for now, all I can think of is rescuing Jaimy and getting him back, hale and hearty, to stand by my side, where he belongs."

"We can only hope that will be the outcome."

"Indeed. We will hope . . . and we will put things in motion as well."

Higgins takes a sip of his wine and does not ask me what I mean by that, no doubt figuring I have something disastrous in mind. Instead he asks, "And Lord Allen? You two seem to be sharing very close company of late."

Again I heave a heartfelt sigh and say, "Although I would mourn Jaimy Fletcher all my days, the prospect of being Richard Allen's bedmate is not at all distasteful to me."

"That might not be an ill-considered choice, Miss," says Higgins, considering this. "The protection of a landed lord would be very helpful to you if you do not succeed in gaining a pardon for yourself through the antiquities gambit."

"Richard certainly couldn't actually marry me, being, as you say, a landed lord. The British Empire would totter and fall."

Higgins chuckles at the thought. "But, then again, he seems extremely fond of you."

"And I of him," I say, smiling.

"I have observed that Lord Allen is a bit of a reckless sort," muses Higgins. "He might well defy convention and make you Lady Allen in spite of it."

The possible Lady Allen gives out with a ladylike snort and reflects, "You know, Higgins, Richard has sometimes viewed me as an object of desire—though I can't imagine why—and I certainly get worked up myself when I am with him in intimate circumstances. But I think he mostly views me as . . . well . . . an amusing child. He is, after all, a good ten years older than me. Being a gentleman, he has held off, for the most part, on the lusty stuff, knowing as he does my continued commitment to Jaimy. But . . . oh, Higgins, as usual I don't know anything about anything and can only let things play out as they will and drift along on the tide."

"Indeed, Miss. That is all any of us can do, when it comes down to it."

There is a light tap on the door and Joannie comes in, dressed in her black rig.

"You ready?"

"I am," I say, rising.

I don the my black watch cap and black gloves and strap my long glass across my back.

"Good night, Higgins. Pray have a good time. My regards to Lord Byron. Joannie, let's go!"

We take to the streets, loping along in the pale moonlight like any two black-clad gazelles. We stick to the shadows, the side streets and alleyways, pounding through the town. And oh, Lord, it feels so good to be out here running through our old turf, chest heaving, with cold air tearing down my throat and into my lungs as I'm dashing through the night with purpose and determination, my worries and troubles falling, for the moment, from my mind.

When we get above Fore Street, we clamber up to the rooftops and work our way through the maze of chimneys, leaping from roof to roof till we come to a spot directly across the street from Flashby's rooms on Chiswell Street.

"There! See?" Joannie points in the gloom at a window glowing in the night. "That's his bedroom. He's got a couple of blokes stationed down below and they check everyone goin' in. Sometimes it's girls, sometimes it's coves in black suits."

"Aye. Those gents would be his contacts in the Intelligence Service. I guess he's still got to do his job, in spite of it all," I say, squinting at the window.

"When Crespo brings a girl, she is hooded and given over to them thugs, who take 'er up to Flashby. Creepo comes back with the coach at midnight and picks up the girl," Joannie says, then falls silent. I can hear her breathing in the dark.

Then she says, "One time *two* girls were brought . . . and another time the girl had to be carried back to the carriage."

Joannie and her Shankies have been keeping a close eye on the blighter.

"All right, Joannie, you been doin' a real good job," I say softly. "It's gonna be a real pleasure bringing this bastard down."

"Jacky," says Joannie, tapping my arm and looking down. "It looks like we're just in time for another one."

A hackney cab has pulled up below and Benny Crespo steps out, followed by a female figure wearing a hood. Creepo grabs her arm and leads her inside. In a moment, he is escorted back out by two very large men. He climbs back into the cab and is gone.

I squat down and bring my long glass around to my eye, resting my elbows on my knees for steadiness. I train the glass on the brightly lit window and focus the lens.

Presently I am startled to see Flashby's face appear in the window. *You son of a bitch,* I hiss under my breath. I see that he is still handsome and continues to wear his big mustachio. *I am sure Satan is good-looking, too, you devil, and I hope you'll be meetin' him soon!* He opens the sash and peers out, looking up and down the street. If I had my pistol with me, I could've put him away right then and there with a bullet through his bloody brain, but I don't want to do that. No, I don't . . . *You've got an appointment to keep, you cur, and you're gonna keep it.*

Flashby starts and looks over his shoulder. I suspect he has heard a rap at his door. That will be the girl being delivered.

A smile breaks over his face. He reaches up and slams down the window. With his right hand he latches it, then turns away to the nasty business at hand.

I keep my glass trained on the window, not to watch Flashby's performance but to examine the latch.

It is a simple but effective lever-type lock, easily thrown open or engaged.

Hmmm.

The bed seems to be located across the room. Probably Flashby doesn't want to worry about an assassin drawing a bead on his hairy butt when he's takin' his pleasure.

Well, that will all have to be taken into consideration, I'm thinking, as I close up my long glass and rise. I look to the rooftop above his room and see that there are many handy chimneys there. *Good.*

"Come on, Joannie," I say. "Let's go back. Our work here is done. For tonight, anyway."

We leap across the rooftops and head back to the *Nancy B.*

And a good night's work it was, indeed.

Chapter 38

"Missy Memsahib!" calls my little Ravi, bursting unannounced into my cabin and waving a piece of paper above his head. "A message from Sahib Creespo!"

He bounces up on the bed as I groan and sit up.

"Give it over, lad," I say, reaching out a hand. My bedmate, Joannie, is a silent lump off to my left side. No, actually, we had not returned directly to the *Nancy B.* last night after we had completed our nocturnal reconnaissance of Flashby's lair. No, on our way back, when we passed by the Admiral Benbow Tavern and music and laughter were pouring out, we just had to stop in. We did not stick out. We were just two more black-clad footpads jammed in the crowd. And, of course, our money was good and so no questions were asked. The fiddler was excellent, with a fine strong voice. He reminded me of my Shantyman, Enoch Lightner, now back in Boston on the *Lorelei Lee.*

We got back *very* late, and so we were sleeping in.

I open the note Ravi has given me and read.

To the Person known as Lotus Blossom, Greetings:

One of the particular gentlemen of whom we spoke at our last meeting has agreed to meet with you on the night of Wednesday next. Please present yourself ready at Mrs. Featherstone's at eight in the evening. The gentleman is a very secretive sort, so expect to be conveyed to him under cover. I trust you will not mind a blindfold. Your terms for payment will be met.

Benj. Crespo

I refold the note and lay it aside.

"How did it go at that place, Ravi?" I ask of the little fellow.

"Oh, very well, Memsahib," he says. "The ladies there much kind to Ravi. Many pettings of his unworthy person."

"I'll bet," I say, smiling and giving him a pet of my own.

"Sahib Creespo ask Ravi if he would like to earn some money . . ."

Aha . . . I figured something of the sort would happen. That's why when I left orders with the watch last night that Ravi was to be sent to the brothel in the morning to see if anything was up with Creepo, I added that the very large and forbidding John Thomas should go with him as protection, in case anyone tried to pull something nasty with him. Ravi is such a very pretty little boy.

". . . but I told the Sahib that I was very happy in the employ of Memsahib Blossom of Lotus Tree."

"Well, good on you, Ravi," I say, laughing. "Now go tell Mr. Lee Chi that we are ready for our breakfast."

As he pops off the bed and scurries out, I give Joannie a poke.

"Up, you lazy slug," I say. "My Lord Richard Allen is taking us all on a ride in the country today."

Later in the morning, as we are out on deck and preparing to leave, Davy and Tink come up before me. Davy, looking serious, says, "We gotta talk."

"So talk, Davy," I say, adjusting my bonnet and looking off for the approach of Lord Allen's carriage. "What's on what passes for your mind?"

Davy, with Tink by his side, pokes his finger at my nose and demands, "Why don't we just grab this Creepo and make him tell us where your man Flashby is? He don't sound like a really noble type and prolly would faint at the sight of your shiv held to his throat. Then we'd storm the place with Liam, Thomas, McGee, Tink, and me, and take the bugger and hand him over to Jaimy. Then we'd all sing 'Ring around the Rosy' and go back to Boston, me to snug up with Annie, and you with Jaimy, if he could still stand the sight o' you. Strong stomach he's gotta have, as I sees it."

I consider this, starting to get a bit steamed. I give a bit of a tug of my snowy white gloves, setting them just right, and say, "Which is why I'm the boss and you're the seaman, Mr. David Jones. It's because Flashby and Creepo ain't wanted for nothing and if we took 'em, we'd be the criminals, not them. The coppers would be after us in a flash, is why, then they'd stuff us down in Newgate and we wouldn't be able to do anyone any good then."

"All right, then," responds the ever reasonable Davy, his face in mine. "But whyn't you just keep takin' coaches through

272

Blackheath Road, every day and night, like—dressed maybe as Jacky Faber for a change—you do remember her, Miss Elegant Jumped-up Jewel of the Orient, don't you? A little bit of an English girl from Cheapside she was. Small and no-account, annoying for sure, but still loyal to her friends—till Jaimy finally stops your coach and out you pops and cries, *'Jaimy! Oh, Jaimy love!'* or some such drivel. Then he picks up your scrawny ass and it's all *kissy, kissy, joy, joy, oh Jaimy, oh Jacky* when he sweeps you up and takes you somewhere to . . . and then we all go back home to Boston, happy as clams. What's the matter with *that* plan, Jack-O?"

Tink nods solemn assent to that.

"I would remind you, Davy, that I am an escaped convict and if I leave off the disguise and am recognized and taken again, I would surely be hanged, and I would do Jaimy Fletcher or anybody else scant good dangling from the gallows!"

"All right. So send me and Tink. We'll find him."

Grrrr . . .

"I would further remind you both that press gangs are still abroad in the land and two seasoned sailors such as yourselves would be a prime prize. And you might recall, Seaman Jones, that you are still in the Royal Navy, never having been discharged after the *Santa Magdalena* expedition, and could well be charged and hanged for desertion!"

I poke my own finger into his chest. "How would you like that, pudding-for-brains? Besides, that girl Bess inspects all the coaches stoppin' at her daddy's inn, and she sure wouldn't put the Black Highwayman on to robbin' any coach I was in, that's for sure. I've got a real strong feeling that girl wants Jaimy for herself. Besides, I don't think Jaimy's gonna rest till he nails Flashby's bloody hide to the front door of the Admiralty, whether or not he knows I'm still around!"

Davy steps back, crosses his arms on his chest, and regards me.

"Fine words, Jacky. Real logical and all," he says, his eyes hooded and his tone not at all friendly. "But could it be what you really like is hangin' about with Lord High Muckety-Muck and all those other lords you been goin' about with? Hmmm? That you care more about the high life you been livin' than you do about rescuin' our poor brother Jaimy? Could it be that you're draggin' your feet?"

Wot?

Stung by the accusation, I spin around and stick my gloved finger in his eye and snarl, "I ain't draggin' me feet. I got plans, Davy, good plans, and I've put things in motion and—"

"We ain't seen nothin' of those plans. Alls we seen is you prancin' about twitchin' your ass and cozyin' up to nobs."

"How could you say that to me, Davy, the Brotherhood—?"

"Ah, yes, the Brotherhood," says Davy, looking up off into the sky. "The Holy Brotherhood . . . Aye, we still believe in that, Tink and me. After all, we left our wives and sweethearts to come halfway around the world to find you, Jacky, and we'd go all the way around the world for Jaimy, too. But what about you, eh?"

"What about me?" I demand, beginning to tear up.

"How far around the world would you go for Jaimy, Jacky?" he asks, quiet and serious. "Only as far as the next pretty boy?"

I stand stunned.

"But . . . but Richard Allen is only a dear friend. He's m-my—" I stutter.

"You seem to have lots of 'dear friends,' Jacky. Mostly male, I notice," continues Davy, relentless. "You know they gotta lot of words for girls like that, girls like you, Jacky, girls what's got lotsa men 'friends' . . . rough, ugly words."

Tears are now running through the kohl that rims my eyes.

"All right, Davy," says Tink. "That's enough. You got her cryin'. You've made your point."

"Right," Davy says as he turns away from me. "Anyway, here's her fine lord come to fetch our little lass. Have a good day . . . my lady."

Dimly, I hear the clatter of hooves on the pier.

I recover enough to spit after him, "Ain't nobody gonna tell Jacky Faber how to live her life! 'Specially not you, Davy Jones! You remember that! And you can just sod off and go to hell!"

He shrugs and goes below.

Damn!

I fume in righteous indignation as Richard alights from his coach to lead us off for a fine day in the countryside.

And what a glorious day it is—we see a scientific exposition, lay wagers at a horse race, exclaim at the beauty of the summer flowers, and eat at an excellent country tavern. I chatter, I sing, I sparkle, and all are joyous . . .

. . . but in the lower depths of my mind, I find that much of my joy is gone. It nags at me . . .

Could Davy be right?

Chapter 39

I enter on Richard Allen's arm, dressed in my Orien-tal garb, head up, newly shaved and shiny, eyes hooded at half-mast, with Ravi in train, and collect the *ooh*s and *aah*s that are my due, nodding grandly to the right and to the left. I see Mr. Peel off in a group of men, and I tip my head to him in acknowledgment of his presence, but we do not go to meet him. Oh, no, not yet . . .

Ah, yes, back in the belly of the Cockpit, and, indeed, it is my kind of place! The country hath its charms, but I am a city girl at heart!

And yes, the Pit is a veritable hotbed of intrigue . . .

Groups of men smoking and drinking and laughing, sometimes jolly, sometimes deep in serious conversation. And there are the pipes, always the pipes, with the tobacco smoldering and glowing in the bowls, saturating the air with their heavy fumes.

I hate to admit that I've become quite used to the nox-ious weed, and I hope I'm not becoming surreptitiously ad-dicted to the stuff.

There are some ladies, to be sure, hanging on various

arms, but they are merely decorations. The serious work of deceit is being done by the men.

Ever since King George suffered his latest lapse into madness several years ago, the intrigue continues. Who shall be Regent if the King has another relapse? True, he seems to have come out of it, but who knows? He may slip yet again and who shall . . . and so on and on . . .

Can that be my old guardians Carr and Boyd seated over there, close by the door, nursing a couple of ales while scanning the crowd? No doubt they're reporting on someone . . . Who . . . ? I don't know, but I certainly keep my face covered when I'm in their field of vision, that's for sure. I suspect that, deep down, they are decent fellows, but I also know they follow their orders and their current instructions more likely come from Smollett, not from Peel.

Richard leads me to the gaming table where sits our former adversary, the seeming country bumpkin who had divested Richard of some of his money on our previous meeting. The man's name turns out to be Upton . . . Squire Upton. Of what country parish the red-faced and jolly fellow is squire of, we do not know, but let that be, for now.

We sit, pleasantries are exchanged, and then Richard says, "I hope you don't mind, gents, my bringing my little piece of Oriental jade with me to play. She does not know much about card playing, but she does . . . amuse me."

He hugs me to him, and I play it up for all I am worth.

Hale and hearty male laughter all around. *But of course, Sir, let her play!* Knowing looks are passed around, too, as Richard lays out a mound of gold pieces. But we shall see, gents, we shall see.

We sit and Squire Upton, chuckling, shuffles the cards—

his cards, I know—and announces, "Dealer's Choice. Oh my stars and garters, this is so exciting. What shall it be? Oh, yes, the choice shall be Five Card Monte, one card down, four up, with a bet on each card. Are we agreed? Good, then here we go . . . Ante up, gentlemen, if you would . . ."

The cards are dealt, one to each player, face-down, and the bets are laid. Without turning it over, I am sure it is a king.

The last time we had sat at the gaming table with this Squire Upton, I feigned disinterest—boredom, even, with several ill-concealed yawns thrown in and my head lying sleepily on Richard's shoulder. Actually, though, I had been carefully scanning the backs of the cards for any irregularities and I eventually found them. *Ha!* There, a very slight extension of a curlicue up in that corner. I'll bet it is a face card . . . and yes . . . it turns out to be a queen. A little while later I had ciphered out his system and directed Richard to get up and leave the game, sadly a loser, for another time. *That time has come now, Squire . . .*

I reach over and lift up our down card. It is, indeed, a king . . . a good card, but I do not think this Squire Upton has placed it there for our advantage, no, I do not. Our next card up is a ten of hearts. I make a bit of a fuss, putting my fingertips on the cards and pretending to be the utter fool . . . *"And thees ees a king? Oh my, yes, he looks so royal with hees crown and that is his queen, no?"* and so on.

Amidst all this tomfoolery, I lean over and whisper in Richard's ear, *"Bet very lightly, dear one, for we will lose this one . . ."*

Sure enough, we end up with two kings and the Squire,

again blessing his stars and garters, shows his two aces, so we lose. Pity that. The deal passes to another gent and we are allowed to win a small pot. Our country squire is, of course, setting us up for the big score.

Then the deck passes to us.

I pick up the deck in my right hand and then exclaim, "Oh!" and reach up for the bejeweled clasp that holds up the top of my sari. *It appears to have come loose, the silly thing.*

"Ravi," I say to the turbaned lad who stands by my side. *"Champa gabeesh guptil na."*

"Jee han, Memsahib," murmurs Ravi in response to my line of gibberish, and as planned, he begins to unwind my sari from my shoulder and then my upper chest.

Ravi has long ago given up any hope of being reincarnated as anything higher than a carpet beetle, should his death come while in my employ, and so goes about his duties. These, at the moment, consist of disrobing a young female in what he would consider a den of the worst iniquity—with a certain air of karmic resignation.

When he gets the cloth unwrapped to such a degree that a good deal of my left breast is exposed, I say, *"Kaafee,"* which does, actually, mean "enough." He then rewinds it and fastens the clasp once again, and steps back.

It was then, of course, that I had switched the decks. With all male eyes attentive on my little charade, I slipped my deck from the garter just above my left knee, and holding the Squire's deck between my knees, I slid my deck onto the table, ready to cause havoc.

"Thee same game," I say, clumsily shuffling the cards and presenting them to Squire Upton to cut. In addition to my exotic dress, I am also drenched in enough jasmine perfume to fell any poor bloodhound with a sensitive nose. Hey, it will further cloud the unsuspecting human male mind.

He cuts, I reassemble the deck and deal. And yes, my deck was shaved. Several of the more important cards had their edges sanded such that I could put the deck back together as I wanted it, after the cut.

I had purposely, when marking my deck, made the marks very similar to those of the Squire—except that my little squiggles marked very different cards.

I deal each player one card down. The other two participants get insignificant cards—a trey and a seven—but the Squire gets a queen of diamonds. I know it and he knows it, too, without even looking, because I had left the queens' markings the same as his . . . almost the same. The queen of spades got an entirely different mark, but he does not know that . . . not yet.

Our hole card is a jack of spades.

Pretending to be interested only in nuzzling the very handsome Lord Allen, I whisper in his ear, *"Bet everything on this one. He will become suspicious and leave after this. Let's break him!"*

Richard smiles and nods, and reaches for his pile.

"Five pounds is the bet," he says, pushing out that amount.

The Squire covers the bet, but the other two drop out. *"Too rich for my blood,"* says one.

I deal again, one card up for our opponent. For him, the queen of clubs, and for us, the jack of diamonds. Squire Upton licks his lips.

"High card bets ten pounds," he says.

"Ten pounds it is," says Richard. "And I call."

Good move, milord. We musn't spook him.

I deal another two cards up. A queen of hearts for him. There is a slight gasp from onlookers. *Two queens showing!* And onlookers there are, because this bumpkin of a squire has won a great deal of money at this place. And a poor eight of hearts for us.

The Squire is again high hand.

"*Twenty* pounds, my lord," says Upton, shoving the amount forward.

Allen appears to hesitate. *Good lad, I know there is an actor in you!*

"Twenty pounds it is," he says, covering the bet and looking a bit grim. "Deal."

I do it.

The next set is a ten of hearts for our opponent, and a jack of clubs for us. Another intake of breath from the crowd. This is getting good! Two queens face up against two jacks showing. What can they have under?

Richard smiles and shoves a pile of coins. . . and paper bills . . . into the pot.

"The bet is fifty pounds."

The Squire looks at the top card and knows it is coming to him. He cannot suppress a slight smarmy smile, as he sees it is marked as a queen, the queen of spades. I take my hand from the deck to make sure he sees it.

He does. He puts out the money.

"Beggin' your pardon, my lord, but I will see your fifty pounds and raise you one hundred pounds."

A gasp. There is now two hundred and seventy pounds in the pot.

Richard sits, staring at the cards. Finally he takes a deep breath.

"I will see you, Sir," says Lord Allen, his voice thick with contempt on the *Sir*. "And raise you five hundred pounds."

The entire place is watching now. *Five hundred pounds! The yearly pay of a Post Captain in the Royal Navy is three hundred pounds! Good Lord!*

Squire Upton considers, then says, "You will take my marker, Sir?"

"I will," says Allen coldly.

"Then I will see your five hundred and raise you another five hundred."

"Done," says Richard. "I assume my marker is good, as well."

"Yes, my lord."

"Good. Then I call."

Everyone holds their breath as I again pick up the deck and prepare to deal out the last two cards. Secure in his knowledge, the Squire flips over his hole card, the third queen.

Nonchalantly, Richard does the same, revealing our hidden jack.

Three queens up, versus three jacks up! Oh, glory!

Squire Upton settles back, ready to exult in the victory of a lifetime, as I deal out his card.

The biggest gasp of all comes from the Squire as I flip over a deuce onto his pile. His face registers the most supreme shock, as he sees his queen of spades magically transformed into the lowly deuce of clubs, by the rules of some games, the lowest card in the deck.

I then deliver the jack of hearts—*you grinning knave!*—to our own hand.

The place erupts. *A pot of two thousand pounds! Four jacks over three queens! A record at the Cockpit!*

During the hullabaloo, I slip my deck back into my garter—and the Squire's as well. There's no sense in anybody bringing up anything improper in the future, I say . . .

We rise and Richard escorts the destroyed Squire to the door—*so that we might discuss the question of your marker, Sirrah.* I place my hand on the arm of Mr. Peel, who has wisely stayed close by, and we find a relatively quiet corner booth.

"Well, that was quite something, I must say," murmurs Mr. Peel.

"Yes, an amusing diversion, Mr. Peel," I simper. "Now, if you would stay by my side for the rest of this evening, that would be good."

"Oh, really?"

"Yes, it might be to your benefit. Now, is this Mr. Smollett here?"

Peel's face darkens.

"Yes, he's right over there, surrounded by his toadies."

I look across the room and see a scrubby little man dressed in black, as they all are, talking energetically to a small group of very attentive subordinates. He is narrow in the shoulders, somewhat wide in the hips, with thin shanks for calves. I have heard that haberdashers supply "calf-enhancers" for gentlemen deficient in that regard to wear under their stockings, and this Mr. Smollett certainly could have used them to his advantage.

"Umm," I say, thinking . . . "You must stay attentive, Mr. Peel, for anything can happen."

"What do you mean? You wouldn't . . . ?"

"No, Sir, I am not a murderess, Sir, no matter what they might say of me."

"Not that I'd mind overmuch," he says through gritted teeth, looking across at the despised Smollett.

"I merely mean, Mr. Peel, that you must keep your eye on the main chance," I say. "Bide your time and wait for opportunity to present itself. Now, I assume you got your invite to the Duke's Ball?"

"Ahem. Yes," he says. "I suppose you arranged that, too."

"Yes. I sent along a manifest of our treasure cargo, as well as a trinket for the Duke, himself, and a request that you and your wife be added to the guest list."

"Um, I cannot say my wife was displeased to receive the invitation," says Peel with a short bark of a laugh. "I even believe she loves me again. However, the price of that new dress . . ." He shudders.

"Ah, here is my Lord Allen, back to claim my poor self," I say, as Richard comes back into view. "I assume all went well with Squire Upton?"

"Yes," answers Richard, somewhat testily, as he slides in next to me. "Rest assured that man will never come in this place again. I am afraid I dirtied the toe of my boot in sending his ass off into the night."

"Ever my most gracious lord," I murmur, with not much sympathy for Squire Upton's sore bum.

"Yes, and for his marker, my dear, I believe we have won a very nice little country estate not far from here," he says, his arm once again encircling my waist. "Would you not consider taking up residence in it, to warm me with your presence when I am back from campaign?"

"Oh, good sir, if I am to understand—you would be off

giving good and noble service to the King and country as the gallant cavalry officer you most certainly are, and then you would, when the notion took you, come back and . . . service me?"

"That is *exactly* what I have in mind, Princess," says the rogue, burying his face in my neck.

"Well, Lord Dick, that shall have to wait awhile, I'm afraid," I say. "Now, let me introduce you to my very good friend, Mr. David Peel, late of our Naval Intelligence Service."

"Ahem, oh yes," says Allen, noticing Peel for the first time. "Charmed. Richard Allen, here," he says sticking out his hand. "Any friend of Jacky is a friend of mine."

I give Peel a bit of an elbow. "And speaking of friends, stand ready now," I say as I notice the Duke of Clarence enter the Pit, his mistress, Mrs. Jordan, on his arm. I also note that she is wearing the string of pearls I had given her.

The Duke, without any sign from us, which would have been unpardonably rude on our part and probably never forgiven, comes over to our table, and room is made for him and his lady. I think I hear Peel gasp a bit, which is somewhat gratifying to me.

"I must tell you, Miss," the Duke says, after greetings are made and acknowledged. "The British Museum is *most* interested in your . . . offerings. Thank you for the accounting . . . and for this . . ."

I had sent over our manifest, written out by Chopstick Charlie himself, to the Duke's secretary, along with another golden coin, very similar to the one I had given to Mr. Peel earlier in this endeavor—*hey, I've got a whole box of 'em.* I am gratified to see it resting outside his pocket as a fob for his beloved watch, as I had hoped it would be.

He pulls it out for all to admire. The image of Augustus Caesar glows upon the coin.

"Looks rather like Dad, doesn't it?" laughs the Duke, and from what I have seen of images of the King, I have to admit it does.

"Anyway, things are in train as to that," he says. "Have you a representative, Miss? I cannot see you messing in sordid politics."

At this, Mrs. Jordan gives me a level look. I sense that she knows me for a fraud, and as sordid as they come, but she does not let on. The Sisterhood of Thespians and all . . .

"Yes, my lord, he is right here," I softly say. "My very good friend Mr. David Peel of the Intelligence Service. You might know of him from your time in that Service?"

The Duke had, indeed, been in the Royal Navy and had attained the rank of Post Captain. It was not all patronage, for Lord Nelson had some very good things to say about him as a seaman, and Nelson did not give out that kind of praise without due consideration.

"Oh, yes, well," says the Duke. "We might well have met in the service of our country. Now, we must be off. Allen, Peel, Miss, adieu. We shall see you all at the Ball? Yes? Good. Till then."

I settle back against both Peel and Allen.

"*Quite a piece of work, indeed . . .*" I hear someone murmur.

Chapter 40

The other night at the Pit, after Squire Upton had been properly dispatched and I had left Mr. Peel to his many intrigues, I asked Richard, "Do you think I should go Oriental to the Duke's Ball? My saris and sarongs and all?"

He considered, then answered, "No, I think you've already firmly established yourself as a genuine exotic, so you needn't go any further in that direction. Since this will be an extremely formal occasion, you'd best pull out all the stops, Princess. Knock 'em dead, as I know you can."

Today, with that advice in mind, I went to my seabag and discovered that I had absolutely nothing at all to wear, don'cha know, so I sallied forth to shop for a smashing new ball gown. I figured it was my duty, after all. The Empire style is still being worn, so my new gown is high in the waist with a low-draped bodice, all white with pastel accents and the most cunning little row of lavender flowers embroidered across the top. *Oh, yes!* I already have Empire dresses, but they are not ball gowns. This one is extravagantly expensive and very elaborate. I figure that I deserve it, and furthermore,

I didn't have to pay for it. That expense had been taken care of by the greedy but now broken Squire Upton. Richard had insisted that I should have half the table stakes from our little game of not-very-much-chance. I protested that not only was it his money at risk but also that I could have messed up or have been found out as a cheat. If that had happened, milord Allen would be out right now pawning his sword. But, of course, he would have none of it. We'll settle up the marker later. I cast eyes heavenward once again. *Thank you, Mr. Yancy Beauregard Cantrell, Mississippi Gambler Extraordinaire, for teaching me the Black Art of Card Playing. Yes, yet another rotter has bitten the dust . . .*

"Deep breath, Miss."

I suck it in and Higgins gives a good strong pull to the corset cords, drawing the thing tight about my waist.

"You do not really need this," observes Higgins, tying the fasteners tight. I exhale with a sigh of relief. It is true. Ever since the late and unlamented Bliffil had broken my bottom ribs with his boot when I was but a child back on HMS *Dolphin,* my middle has been uncommonly narrow. I have found that to be all to the good, as I have suffered no lasting ill effects, and many are the males who have commented on the slenderness of my waist, Lord Allen being one of them.

"True, Higgins," I say. "But why not maximize an asset, I always say."

"Well, in that regard, thank God the larger bustle has gone out of style," he says, wrapping a sausage-shaped roll of cloth around my hips, beneath my petticoats, "and this has replaced that horrid wire contraption, in the supposed enhancement of the female bottom."

"I think I would have looked just smashing in it, Higgins."

"I am sure," says Higgins. "Rather like the rear part of a unicorn. There. I believe we are done. Please give my regards to Lord Byron tonight. Here, stockings now."

"Oh, will he be there tonight?" I ask, all innocent, presenting the lower limbs for encasement in the silken hose.

"Yes, he shall," says Higgins, snapping up the garters without much grace. "And I shall not."

"Poor Higgins," I simper. I lean over and give him a kiss. "It is too bad that you were not born to the purple, as were all those other men."

"Ummm . . ." he murmurs, putting out the ever-so-delicate pumps that will adorn the not-so-delicate Faber feet.

"I know that many others of my sex will be in attendance tonight who were not born to that purple either," I tease. "But then, again, we have other . . . ass-ets." I give my bum a bit of a wiggle on that one, along with my foxy, open-mouthed grin.

That gets a laugh from my dear Higgins.

"And, Higgins, I have not the slightest doubt that Mr. George Gordon will make a quick exit from that party to rejoin you for . . . poetical discussions. Prose and poesy and all that. Must be awfully interesting."

"That might well be so, Miss. We shall see," says Higgins, holding up my white Marie Antoinette hairpiece. "Let's get this on, shall we?"

Higgins does not approve of my many wigs, but he knows I have no choice in this matter, having very little actual hair of my own upon my head.

He settles it in and then places upon it the most beautiful

little tiara I had borrowed from the treasure trove. It's silver with inlaid diamonds and, of course, my favorites, emeralds. I know I'll have to give it back when the deal is made. Chopstick Charlie does have an inventory, after all, and woe be to me if it comes up short, I know that. Although I realize that he's half a world away, I would not want to cross him. It's not too fanciful a thought to wake up some morning with Ganju Thapa standing at my bed-foot, curved sword in hand and unforgiving look upon his swarthy face. No, a strict accounting will be made of all of the treasure, Chops, you can count on that. But right now, Jacky Faber shall wear the jeweled headband.

All done, and now I hear that Cavalry Captain Lord Richard Allen has come to call . . . and I bounce up to go greet him. I do hope he likes what he sees.

"Good Lord, Princess," he exclaims upon seeing me sashay down the gangplank in all my finery. "How do all your innards fit in there?"

"My insides are not a proper subject for discussion, Sir," I say, giving him my hand, all prim and proper. "Shall we be off to the merry dance?"

He laughs and hands me up into the coach, and we are, indeed, off.

All of the men wear powdered wigs on formal occasions, of which this is certainly one, but Richard, having a good, thick head of hair of his own, merely pulls it back, has it powdered all white, then binds it with a blue ribbon. He is wearing his full-dress regimentals: rich scarlet coat with blinding white turnouts and tails, tight white hose, shiny black boots . . .

Oh, my God, he's gorgeous . . .

Yes, we go past all the places of my youth: Blackfriars Bridge, the Admiral Benbow, Saint Paul's, Paternoster Lane. Yet again I think of all that has happened since I scurried along these same streets as a child, wild and free. Ah, well . . . things change, don't they?

We alight from the carriage and Richard puts his left hand out, fingers pointing forward at about my shoulder height. I place my hand lightly on top of his, for that is how it is done, and we make our entrance between the lines of liveried footmen and the hundreds of glittering lanterns set out to guide our way, into Bushy House and the Duke of Clarence's magnificent Ball.

We enter, to find a receiving line with the Duke of Clarence at the end of it, his Mrs. Jordan at his side. There are bows and smiles and much kissing of hands.

"I am with the best-looking man here, and that's no lie," I whisper in Richard's ear as we advance down the line.

"And I could not be with a lovelier consort, Princess," comments Richard. "However, I could use a drink."

"Patience, dear Richard, we are almost to the end," I caution. "Ah, here's our Mr. Peel and his lovely wife." We bow and curtsy and introductions are made. Mrs. Peel is just as bubbly and charming as Peel himself is reserved. She looks positively dazzled by all this spectacle and seems supremely happy. I don't blame her, what with all the glamour: the blazing chandeliers, the chamber orchestra sawing away back in the corner, the tables set with name cards and laden with wondrous food and drink, liveried servants all about, to attend to any need. Mr. Peel has informed me that the Duke is deep in debt, and it is no wonder, I think, as I gaze upon all this. I do not feel glad about that news, but it is good to know. It might make him somewhat more receptive to our . . . offerings.

"Does not the Duke look fine tonight?" I ask of Mr. Peel, while my Richard gallantly engages Mrs. Peel in light conversation. The Duke of Clarence, dressed in full Royal Navy dress uniform, is certainly a splendid sight: navy blue jacket with tails and gold turnouts, a golden epaulet or swab on each shoulder with matching stripes on his cuffs, pure white breeches and hose, and black pumps on his feet. He wears a wide forest green satin sash across his chest—probably 'cause he's also the Duke of St. Andrews—his sword by his side, and a white wig upon his head.

"Milord Clarence is proud of his Naval service?" I murmur.

"Indeed," says Mr. Peel. "He was Captain of HMS *Pegasus,* in Nelson's Caribbean campaign back in '86, and HMS *Andromeda* in '88, and the *Valiant* the following year, and was elevated to the rank of Vice Admiral while there. The Great Lord Nelson had only good things to say about our prince."

"A distinguished career, indeed," I say, as we grow ever nearer our host . . . and hostess. Mrs. Jordan stands by the Duke's side, looking serene and radiant.

"True, but I'm afraid that career has hit rocky shoals since."

"Oh . . . ?"

"Yes. When the war with France broke out in '93, he asked for a commission, anxious to serve his country, but was not given one."

"Wot? They denied the King's own son a ship? How could that be?" I ask, me the commoner aghast at such a notion. "If I were King, I'd have given my son some ratty old ship, if only to shut him up."

"Politics, my dear. The Duke made an ill-considered speech against the war in the House of Lords, and . . . well . . . politics. As you know, the King has not been well, and there are many anti-monarchists around."

"Ah," I say. "Politics . . . a field best left to the politicians, I suppose."

"Spoken like a true and simple soldier," says Peel, nodding.

"Umm . . ." I murmur, not committing totally to that notion.

"Doesn't Mrs. Jordan look fine?" I ask of him.

"Oh yes," agrees the ever practical Peel. "She is in very good shape, considering she has had a distinguished stage career *and* borne the Duke ten children . . . all illegitimate, of course."

"*Ten?*" I exclaim. "And I worry about birthing even *one*? When did she ever find the time?"

He chuckles at that, then says, "Here we are . . . come dear." He hands me back to Richard Allen and takes his bedazzled wife up to meet the Duke of Clarence. She shakes Mrs. Jordan's hand—and both say, "Charmed"—and then does a very acceptable curtsy in front of the Duke, one that I am certain the poor woman has been practicing over and over for the past few days. Then they pass on, relieved, I am sure, that this part of the evening is over.

Our turn now.

"Ha! Richard! So good to see you! And your lovely consort, too!" says the Duke, shaking Richard's hand vigorously.

"Milord," says Richard, bowing. "Mrs. Jordan . . ."

I myself drop down into my very best Lawson Peabody curtsy—and a fine thing it is to witness, too—and come up with hooded eyes.

"My lord," I murmur. "Mrs. Jordan, so kind . . ."

The Duke of Clarence gives the back of my hand a kiss and Mrs. Jordan gives me a level look. I can just imagine the pillow talk between the two. *If you think for one moment, Willie, that girl is anything like what she appears, then I fear for your sanity.* Then we, too, pass on.

But before we go on by, I whisper to Mr. Peel, "Stay close now, and be attentive. Especially when the Scotch reel is announced."

I had seen, very much gratified, that the Duke of Clarence had once again his faithful watch in his waistcoat pocket, and to it was attached the golden Roman fob I had given him. *We shall see . . .*

Richard leads me out onto the floor, and the Minuet in G is struck up by the orchestra. Yes, the dance is very formal, all bows and curtsies and light touching of hands, but it is still enjoyable. Me? I would rather have a good country dance, with female hands clasped ardently in male ones and arms wrapped around waists and skirts spinning about flashing legs, but so be it. *Enjoy what you got, girl, and don't complain.* Besides, the rhythm nearly always picks up following a slow number.

The minuet is over and, sure enough, the Scotch reel is announced. It is a dance very much like the Virginia reel I had seen—and, of course, had danced—back at Dovecote in Massachusetts. In both reels, there are two parallel lines, men on one side, ladies on the other, and when the music starts, the first pair in each line bow to each other and commence a promenade up the center. At the top, the couple separates and the next two couples repeat the same move. The purpose of the whole thing is that every single male in each line comes in contact, at least for a fleeting moment, with every single female.

It is dances like these, I have found, that make the world go 'round. It is how glances are exchanged, alliances are made, vows sworn, and, ultimately, how babies finally get born.

Richard and I advance down the lines, he at the bottom of one, me at the foot of the other. The band strikes up, we join hands and dance up between the lines. When we reach the end, Richard hands me off to the male at the top of that line, and he takes up the hand of the facing female, and so on down the line . . . easier, I'm thinkin', in the dancing than in the explaining.

My next partner is a nice young man and I enjoy his company for the few moments we have together, and then I am passed off to another man . . . and another . . . and then . . .

I find myself with the Duke of Clarence. He takes my hand, we do the dance, and I am about to go to another when I see that Mr. Smollett is three more down the line . . .

Good . . .

I lean into the Duke, perhaps a bit too much, but then again I have been playing the Oriental exotic to the hilt, and so I am not noticed in doing this. I reach in, grab Augustus Caesar by his golden head and, ever so gently, ease the Duke of Clarence's beloved watch out of his pocket and into my hand. I was an accomplished pickpocket back in my days with the Rooster Charlie Gang and renowned in the criminal dens of Cheapside for my skill.

We separate, I slip the watch into my sleeve and let myself into the embrace of the next male in line ... and the next ... and ...

... and now Mr. Smollett.

He takes up my hand and stiffly puts his hand on the small of my back, but he is not interested in me, oh, no ... His eyes roam over the crowd to see what profitable contacts he might yet make this evening.

While he is doing that, I slip the watch into his waistcoat pocket, making sure that the golden Augustus stays on the outside, gleaming in the light of the chandeliers. It looks right good there, I'm thinking.

I catch Mr. Peel's eye—he is farther down in the line—and give him a look that I hope conveys, *Get ready—all hell's about to break loose.*

Break loose it does.

The Duke, releasing his last partner, goes to tap his watch, as he often does, I have noticed ... and he stops dead.

And when the Duke stops, the music grinds pathetically to a stop, as well.

"What ... ? What ... ? What has become of my watch?" asks the befuddled royal, looking about.

Eyes are cast about the now quite still dancers. Each looks at the others, uncomprehending.

Peel picks it up.

"There!" he shouts, pointing at the fob hanging out of the pocket of the unfortunate Mr. Smollett. "There it is!"

Mr. Smollett gazes down at the damning thing, dumbfounded. "Wot . . . ? Wot . . . ?" is all he is able to get out, his lower lip quivering, eyes wild.

"Most irregular!" shouts the Duke, incensed. "Most irregular!"

People are flying about, aghast at the turn of events, but the levelheaded Peel is on the spot.

"Let us take care of this, Your Highness," he says, directing the men he had stationed about. *Could it be Carr and Boyd? Yes, it is! Lay on, lads!*

Smollett is grabbed by his arms and relieved of the watch that rests most damning in his pocket. He is then hustled out without ceremony, his poor wife wailing behind him.

Mr. Peel looks *very* satisfied, very gratified, indeed.

When things quiet down and the music resumes, Richard takes my hand and leads me to a table where glasses of fine wine are arrayed. He gives me one and I place it to the lips.

"Umm?" I ask, since his look is quite intense. "Wot?"

"One of these days, Princess," he says, looking at me rather sternly. "You are going to find that slender little neck of yours in a noose that it won't be able to wriggle out of."

"It is true, milord, I have always feared that the rope would be my ultimate fate, but let us not speak of that now."

"What would you have done if that plan of yours had gone awry and you had been caught picking the Duke's pocket?" he persists.

"Me? I would have done nothing except put the back of my hand to my forehead and gone into a swoon, whereupon my gallant Captain Lord Richard Allen would have scooped me up in his arms, drawn his mighty sword, waved it about, roaring out something incredibly romantic, like, 'Back you dogs, you shall not touch one hair on this fair head!' Then we would have crashed through that window there in a fine shower of crystal, mounted your fiery stallion with my frail self clutched to your chest, and pounded off into the night, on the road to even more splendid adventures."

"Hah. Well, I am rather glad it did not come to that, Prettybottom," he says, grinning in spite of himself. "It is very possible you underestimate my good sense, and overestimate my bravery."

"Your good common sense, maybe, Lord Dick, but your bravery . . . ? Never!"

I put out my lily-white hand . . .

"Shall we dance?"

Chapter 41

"I don't know about makin' common cause with the Shankies like this," grumbles Davy. "Me, of course, bein' an upstandin' member of the King's Own Cavaliers. Worked my way up the ranks till I was Third in Command, Officer in Charge of Procurement, I was. Still got some of that old Cavalier pride, y'know."

Pride, I say to myself. *Pride in being a dirty little urchin in a dirty little street gang. Ah, well, I had a certain pride in bein' one of Charlie's bunch, I did, so I know, Davy, I know . . . and old animosities do die hard.*

"Well, the Cavaliers ain't no more, Davy," I say. "And the Royal Street Rounders ain't neither, Tink, in case you were about to say you were the warlord of that mob. And what's left of the Rooster Charlie Gang is standin' right here." Joannie, dressed in her black rig, nods at that. "All what remains in the way of the old street gangs is the Shanky Boys, and we got to work with 'em. Are we ready?"

There are murmurs of assent all around.

We are all in my cabin, suiting up. Davy has a coil of rope around his shoulder and Tink carries a medium-sized block and tackle, a pulley, as it were. They are both dressed in as dark clothing as we could manage to put together. I am dressed in my full Oriental splendor: sari wrapped tight about me, silken shawl on head, and a light veil draped across my nose, hiding my lower face. Higgins, mercifully, is off with Lord Byron, no doubt advancing our efforts—and maybe his own, too—and so is not here to worry about me or to admonish me to be careful, which I certainly will be, anyway. I am not as rash in my actions as many people think.

Captain Liam Delaney, well-armed and resolute, is left to guard the ship and her cargo, and I know the *Nancy B.* is in good hands. I believe he is rather glad to be left out of what is going to happen tonight, as it is sure to be beneath his dignity. He is right on that, I'll own.

"Then, let's go. Davy and Tink, follow Joannie. She knows where to go and how to get there. Ravi, you're with me. John Thomas, McGee, you know what to do. Everyone, be careful."

And with that, we are out into the night. Davy and Tink lope off down the street, Thomas and McGee disappear down Fore Street, and Ravi and I climb into a cab.

When we are settled and on our way, Ravi says, "Missy Memsahib going to do some more naughtiness."

He does not even put it as a question.

"It might look like it, Ravi, dear," I say, giving his hand a reassuring pat. "But if everyone does their part, yours included, everything should go all right."

"We go now to the place of many ladies?" he asks, plainly not quite convinced as to the "all-rightness" of this expedition. He is quite nicely turned out in his snowy white turban and pantaloons.

"Yes, Ravi," I answer. "And here we are." I hand him the

train of my dress as we alight from the carriage, then enter Mrs. Featherstone's Fine Emporium.

The door to that illustrious establishment is opened for us and we enter to find Mr. Benjamin Crespo waiting for us, rubbing his hands in anticipation of a lucrative evening.

"Ah. The Lotus Blossom her own self." He smiles, showing an unpleasant set of yellow teeth. "Are you ready to go?"

I stick out my hand. "As soon as I receive one half upfront. Twenty-five pounds sterling now, the rest . . . after . . . as agreed, Mr. Creespo?"

Benny the Creepo reaches into his pocket and pulls out the required coins and drops them into my outstretched palm. As I slip them into the tiny beaded purse that hangs at my hip, I reflect that I have already made considerable money at prostitution. First it was my gallant French artillery major, whom I took back to my room at 127 Rue de Londres in Paris, and now this. All the while, I've remained . . . well . . . a maiden . . . sort of.

"You'd better be worth it, sweetheart, or your ass will pay," warns the ever pleasant Creepo, gesturing me toward a waiting carriage. "My client is not a forgiving sort."

I frost him with a look, then get in, with Ravi following close behind.

The pimp whips out a linen hood and goes to put it on my head. "Tell the little wog to lie on the floor so he can't see where we're going."

I nod for Ravi to follow his order, but shake my head at the hood. I pull from my sleeve a silken scarf.

I am actually somewhat relieved to see the hood being brought out—it ensures that we are going to Flashby himself. I mean, Crespo could have had some other client in mind, and had that happened, I would have feigned sudden sickness and brought things to a quick halt. But, no, it's Flashby for sure.

"Take your filthy cloth away, whoremaster," I say, wrapping my scarf around my eyes and tying it behind my head. "I will do it myself. There. Satisfied?"

He checks the blindfold to make sure I cannot see out and then calls to the driver to proceed.

Oh, don't worry, scum, my eyes are quite blind—but then, again, I do not have to see, for I know exactly where we are going.

As we clatter along, Crespo cannot resist making pointed remarks about how he and I might get together after, as he puts it, *"my client has broken you in, as it were."*

I maintain a stony silence until we arrive at our destination.

"All right, you can take off the blindfold," says Crespo, as the coach comes to a stop. "Get out."

I pull off the scarf and, without moving, give him a kick in the shins.

"You will open zee door for zee Lotus Blossom, pig."

He grunts and reluctantly gets out and holds the door for me, and I climb out and down, followed by a silent, and I know very worried, Ravi.

"Later," says Creepo, under his foul breath. "Then we shall see."

Yes, we shall, Mr. Crespo, oh yes, we certainly shall . . .

We are escorted to the door and, after a few hard raps of the knocker, it is opened by a big surly ruffian showing a lot of muscle and not much in the way of forehead or neck. I make sure my veil is securely in place.

"Here is tonight's offering for our Mr. X," announces my slimy escort, smiling and handing me in.

"Awroight," says the thug. "Getcherself gone, pimp."

The door closes behind me and I am led up the stairs. I notice, on my way, that there are several more guards on station, each one looking more brutal than the last. Harry Flashby is being *very* careful. I notice also that the guard finds Ravi's presence unremarkable—there must have been many rather bizarre combinations of visitors to these rooms in the past—and much more bizarre than the mere addition of a little boy to this evening's . . . entertainment.

When we get to the fourth floor, the brute shoves me to the wall and begins frisking me for hidden weapons . . . *very* thoroughly inspecting me . . . His hand goes up the inside of my leg.

Expecting this, I did not wear my shiv this night, and feeling miffed at being so handled, I bring the back of my hand across my abuser's face and hiss, "Hands off, churl!"

He starts back and then snarls, "Listen, bitch, I'll—"

Just then I hear a latch thrown and a door opens behind me. I turn my veiled face and there stands Lieutenant Henry Flashby, glowing cigar clenched in his teeth, his mouth framed by his luxurious mustachio. I force myself to be calm and not leap upon the bastard and claw out his eyes.

"Now, Randolph, you shall have her back later, and on her knees . . . just like the others . . . Just be patient, hmmm . . . ?"

The guard retreats, fixing me with his gaze, as Flashby bows and waves me into his room. I enter, with Ravi right behind me.

The room is laid out just as Joannie and I had observed

when we had trained our long glass from the rooftop. The bed is in the center of the room with the window beyond. There is a washstand, a wardrobe, and a bureau upon which sits a lit lamp. Good . . . no chairs . . . The only place to sit is on the bed.

"Ha! I get you and the little wog, too! Capital! He can watch and see how Englishmen do the job!" Flashby puts his arms about me, ready to get down to business right away, but I push him gently away, murmuring, "Please, Honorable Master, if we take this slowly, it will be much more pleasurable for you. The Lotus Blossom promises many, *many* fine things . . . Things you will never forget . . . Please to sit, and she will now dance for you."

"Very well, let's see what you've got." He plunks his rump down on the bed, grinning in anticipation. There is a small table next to him and on it is a bottle of gin and several glasses. He takes a drink from the nearest glass, draining it. He is dressed only in breeches and white undershirt. It is plain that he does not stand on ceremony. "Here, have a drink, Lotus Bottom, or whatever it is you call yourself."

"I prefer," I reply, shaking my head, all demure—"when I am with such a handsome man, not to dull my senses so that I will be better able to enjoy his tender touch."

I let slip the silken shawl that covers my head and it floats to the floor, exposing not only my smooth head, but also my bare midriff, which has my emerald firmly implanted in my bellybutton.

"Good Lord, look at that," breathes Flashby. "I gotta feeling you're gonna be worth every cent, girl."

"This girl hopes she pleases you," I whisper, hands together, big eyes gazing at him over the top edge of the veil. "What shall this humble one call you, Master?"

"Master's good," he says. "I rather like that. However, the name's Henry, but you can call me Sir Harry," he says, leering, his lips rolling the cigar around twixt his teeth. "Now let me see your face."

"Honorable Sir Harry-san. I will show you my face in a very little while, and then the rest of my poor self, too . . . But now this worthless one shall dance for you. I know you will enjoy. Ravi?" I say, and nod to the lad. He puts the Indian flute—the one we had gotten in Burma, the one with the bulbous end—to his lips and begins to softly play the simple but exotic sounding melody I had taught him over the past few days. Yes, it is that time-honored tune: *There's a place in France where the ladies wear no pants. And the dance they do is called the hootchy-kootchy-koo.* And yes, I begin doing a version of that old hootchy-koo dance. It has served girls like me in good stead in the past, and it serves me well now.

"Oh, you bet your sweet, sweet ass!" exclaims my gallant consort. "Dance on!"

Out in the hall I had put on my finger cymbals, and now, putting palms together over my head and gently chiming the things, I begin to dance, swaying myself and my hips as sinuously as I can. When I was at Chopstick Charlie's place, I had observed several performances of Arabic belly-dancing, and had picked up a few of the moves from the girls residing there. It's enough to get by with this lustful bastard, anyway.

I twitch the belly muscles enough to make the emerald jump around a bit, anyway, turn around and shake the tail, and then turn around again. This time, as I gyrate about, I reach up for the brooch on my shoulder and unfasten it. The top of my sari immediately loosens and begins to fall away, unwrapping swath by swath, fold by fold.

Looking over Flashby's head, I see a pair of feet appear in the window, and then knees, and then the rest of Davy Jones being lowered from above in a Bo'sun's chair. When his face is full in the window, I nod to Ravi, who redoubles his blowing of the flute, while I bring my finger cymbals to either side of Flashby's head, one by each ear to cover any sound of the window being opened.

Flashby reaches up and takes the end of the silken cloth that is slowly slipping from my body. The sari has now completely fallen from my chest and is bunched about my waist. Flashby, breathing a bit more labored now, begins unwinding the rest of the garment and I move ever closer to him as he does it, my finger cymbals ringing in his ears, my voice still singing.

When the sari is fully unwound and lies on the floor leaving me completely unclothed, I nod to Ravi, who trails off his piping and goes silently to the window to open the latch. Flashby is otherwise engaged and does not notice.

I keep the finger cymbals clanging as I see Davy slowly lift the window sash and then climb into the room, belaying pin in his belt.

Flashby now has a hand firmly on each of my buttocks, with objective plainly in sight, and is about to bury his nose where it don't belong when he happens to glance to the side and notices my HMS *Dolphin* blue anchor tattoo sitting on my hip. He jerks back, and I can see memory tugging at his jasmine- and lust-fogged brain.

"Wot? . . . You . . . ? No . . ."

"Yes, it's me, you rotten son of a bitch!" I snarl, yanking the veil aside.

He stares incredulously into my face and is about to cry out when Davy slams the belaying pin down on the back of his head.

Joannie follows Davy into the room, with Tink and Toby right behind them. Joannie flips me the bag containing my black burglar's gear. I rip it open and dump out its contents.

"Quick! Get him bound up before he wakes up! And quiet!" I hiss. "Shhhh! There's a guard right outside that door!"

Tink and Toby bend to their task while Davy wraps a gag around Flashby's mouth and cinches it behind his head. Just in time, too, for the captive is starting to wake up. His eyes look about, dazed, and then focus on me . . . His stunned look is replaced by one of sheer terror.

I sit on the floor to pull on the black pants and jersey and cram the watch cap down on my head. Then I get up and see that they have done an excellent job of trussing up our Flashby, just like any Christmas goose. His hands are tied behind him and strands of good thick rope are coiled tightly about his legs. Ah, yes, trust seasoned sailors to know how to go about these things!

Toby goes to the open window and signals to the Shankies on the roof and presently a large iron hook at the end of a rope is lowered and brought inside to be affixed to the ropes that bind Flashby's ankles.

His head back inside, Toby quietly says, "All right, lads, take a strain."

The slack goes out of the line and Flashby is taken, wriggling for all he is worth, out the window, to dangle upside down in the night air.

I go to the window and look down. Sure enough, a wagon drawn by two horses and driven by John Thomas, with Finn McGee beside him, has pulled up below.

Flashby's face, which hangs on a level with mine, is flushed bright red, partly from the blood rushing to his head on account of his being upside down and part from fury.

I reach out and tap him on his nose.

"You like your Lotus Blossom, Sir Harry-san?" I say. "You velly happy man, now? Good." Then I gesture to those on the roof. "Lower him down."

And lower him they do.

After we've ascertained that Finn McGee has gathered Sir Harry, none too gently, into the wagon, Joannie and Tink slide down the rope. Then it is Davy, with Ravi clinging to his neck, and then, finally, me.

When I am in, I give the rope two jerks and the dangling block and tackle is drawn up. The Shankies will dispose of the rope, the pulley, and the Bo'sun's chair, and all evidence of our being there will have disappeared.

We head joyously back to the *Nancy B.*, all of us singing away in the London night, with our feet firmly planted upon the recumbent form of Lieutenant Harry Flashby, late of the Naval Intelligence Service, and soon to be the bait for a certain Black Highwayman.

Chapter 42

If there's one thing the crew of the *Nancy B.* knows how to do, it's how to celebrate, and celebrate we do after we bring our struggling captive aboard and plunk him down in a chair in my cabin.

Wine, rum, and ale are passed all around, along with trays of spicy snacks brought up from the galley by Lee Chi. We all fall to, delighted with the spread and with our own cunning and daring in bringing our quarry to bay.

Poor Flashby is still bound tight—hands, arms, and feet—and his mouth is gagged, so he cannot, alas, join in the festivities. It's unfortunate, because he is the guest of honor, after all.

There are not enough places for everyone to sit in my small cabin, so Davy and Tink grab two of the chairs and Liam yet another, while Joannie and Ravi sit on the bed. Seamen Thomas and McGee squat by the door, clubs in hand. No sense in allowing ourselves to be caught unawares, is there?

I, myself, plump the black-clad Faber tail down on the unfortunate Flashby's lap and place my finger on his nose, his mustache sticking out over the top of the gag, all bristly and comical. "This is where you wanted the Lotus Blossom to be, isn't it, Sir Harry-san? Well, here she is. It's too bad that this will probably be the last female bottom to sit in your lap before you are taken off to be thrown into the fires of Hell. Perhaps Satan will give you a loathsome female demon all slimy and scaly and stinking of brimstone to cuddle with. I trust you will find her charming."

Laughter all around. Flashby is not particularly loved by this company, and all are greatly enjoying his discomfiture.

His eyes wide with fear, he tries to speak, but all that comes out is an incoherent mumble.

"Our ever-so-charming Mr. Flashby is being uncharacteristically quiet, do you not all agree?" I ask with raised eyebrows. "I do believe he wants to speak. Shall we loosen his tongue? John Thomas, please bring your club over here." John Thomas gets up and goes to the side of Harry Flashby.

"Show him your club, John."

John Thomas, grinning, dangles his belaying pin before Flashby's eyes. He taps the club lightly on the bridge of the captive's nose.

"Mr. Flashby. We are going to remove your gag so that you might speak to those of us gathered here. You know we are your friends, but if you should even consider for one moment crying out for help, Seaman Thomas there will bring his bludgeon down upon your face, smashing your nose and probably a good many of your teeth. Do you understand that, Mr. Flashby?"

Flashby nods.

"Ravi. Please relieve our guest of his mouthpiece."

Ravi bounces down off the bed and goes behind

Flashby's head and unties the gag, casting aside the limp and soggy rag in disgust.

While Flashby coughs and clears his throat, I run my finger lightly down the side of his face and ask, "What is it you want to say, noble Flashby?"

"I . . . I've got to relieve myself."

"Oh? Hmmm . . . I have noticed, dear one, that you have to do that a lot when you are in some danger," I say, thinking back to our time on the Mississippi, when I had Flashby walk the plank, and he did not present a very noble figure.

I jump off his lap and look toward the chamber pot that sits in the corner. Then I glance at his bound arms and laugh. "If you think for one minute, Harry Flashby, that I'm going to pull that thing out and hold it for you while you are eased of your discomfort, then you are sadly mistaken."

Coarse laughter all around.

"Joannie, do you want to help out our guest in his time of need?" I tease.

"Eeeeeww," she squeals and dives behind my bed.

"Oh, well," I say, ruffling Flashby's hair. "We cannot have you messing up the cushion of my fine chair, now can we? We'd never get rid of the stench. John Thomas, Finn, please take our guest back up to the head, and do what you can."

Thomas and McGee come over to grab our captive and carry him away.

"Don't worry, Cap'n," grunts McGee. "We knows what to do with the sod."

They carry him out and I say, "Give us a song, Davy, to celebrate this fine day!"

And we do "Hearts of Oak" and "The Bonny Ship the

Diamond" with much gusto and great acclaim, and presently the bound form of Harry Flashby is brought back into my cabin.

"And how did you manage the task, my fine fellows?" I ask of Thomas and McGee as they dump their burden back in his chair.

"Aw," says John Thomas. "We just pulled down his drawers and throwed him on a hole and made him piss like a girl, is all. He did it."

More raucous laughter, all at Flashby's expense.

I had pondered earlier about sending my two crushers, Thomas and McGee, over to Chiswell Street to meet Benny Crespo when he came back thinking to pick up the much-soiled Lotus Blossom, and to lay some well-deserved punches upon him, but then I thought, *Nay, let that Randolph and his fellow thugs take care of the Creepo when they find both the Lotus Blossom and their master gone from that room, without a trace.* Well, actually, there was a trace. I had left my silk veil neatly folded on the unrumpled bed as a token of remembrance. I am sure that Benjamin Crespo has come to rue the day he ever set eyes upon the Jewel of the East, and well he should.

"Doesn't do much for your manly esteem, does it, Flashby?" I chortle, plopping back into his lap.

He stares straight forward.

"Cat got your tongue, Sir?" I tease.

"So you mean to kill me, then?" he asks, his voice shaking.

"Oh, do be a man, Flashby. Bear up, my lad. Others have faced execution. I certainly have, and I am sure you, too, will face yours bravely. Well, actually, I'm not sure of that at all, knowing you as I do."

"I have money," he says.

"Of course you do, you lyin' son of a bitch. But you do not have enough money to buy yourself off, Flashbutt. Not this time," I say.

I stand and point my finger between his eyes. I drop the bantering tone and my voice hardens. "You tried to rape me when I was but thirteen. You tortured me when I was fifteen. You kidnapped me from my wedding when I was sixteen. And you bore false witness against me and James Fletcher last year, thinking to get both of us hanged. But it didn't happen, did it, you sorry bastard? No, it did not. It only served to get me condemned to life imprisonment in a foul penal colony and to drive James Fletcher to the edge of madness and beyond."

"Do not kill me, please," he whimpers.

"Kill you? Nay, though that would be a real pleasure, I shall not kill you," I purr. "No, what we are going to do is to deliver you to the Black Highwayman. Any mercy you might plead, you must beg of him!"

Flashby slumps in the chair at that news. *Well, let him suffer,* I say. *Just let him . . .*

"Skipper," says John Thomas from the door. "Someone's comin'. It's Mr. Higgins . . . with a friend."

Hmmmm . . . I consider this, then I jump up and order, "Get the gag back on him, quick now!"

The soggy gag is stuffed back in Flashby's mouth as I pick up my napkin to wrap it around his eyes, effectively blinding him. Then I go to the door to welcome the visitors.

I give Higgins a look and hold my finger to my lips, signaling that care is to be taken.

Higgins ducks his head to enter and I see him immediately appraise the situation.

"No last names, gentlemen," I warn. "While it's true that Mr. Flashby here, late of the Naval Intelligence Service, is not likely to be alive to tell tales in a few days, one can never tell. And it does not hurt to be cautious, hmm?"

"Leave you alone for a moment, Miss," says Higgins, "and no telling what one will find upon one's return."

Higgins is followed into the cabin by George Gordon, also known as Lord Byron.

Gordon surveys the scene. He sees both me and Joannie in black burglar's garb, many rough sailors scattered about, a small brown boy in a turban, and a bound, gagged, and blindfolded man weeping in a chair. His eye travels further, taking in my skull and crossbones Jolly Roger flag, my various trophies, like my swords, Buddha statues, my Ganesh, the Golden Dragon pennant, and oh, just all my glorious stuff. His gazing about is interrupted by Lee Chi coming in again, bearing another tray of Oriental delights.

Upon Lord Byron's entrance, I signal for McGee to toss Flashby onto the deck, which he hastily and roughly does, while I wave the poet to the now vacant chair.

"Come, my lord, and share our humble hospitality," I murmur, and bow my shaven head.

"My word," remarks Lord Byron. "I'll say it again, friend John. You do have some very interesting friends. 'Tis a shame I'm to be shipped off tomorrow. A great pity, indeed."

We do aim to please, my lord, in the way of Romantic Tableaux.

Chapter 43

Busy, busy, busy . . . so much to do, so little time . . .

Tonight we attend a performance of *A Midsummer Night's Dream* at the Theatre Royal, Drury Lane. Someone else is trying to reprise Mrs. Jordan's role as Hippolyta, but I doubt that she'll even come close. I am, however, looking forward to listening to Mrs. Jordan's comments on the actress's vain attempts to emulate her. And I'm anticipating the Royal Museum people's coming here tomorrow to inventory Charlie Chen's treasure trove, thanks to Lord Clarence's efforts on our behalf. Then, of course, there are other important tasks for me to accomplish, such as the disposal of Lieutenant Harry-the-Bastard Flashby chained up down below, the rescuing of my Lieutenant James Emerson Fletcher, and the refitting and supplying of my *Nancy B.* for another transatlantic voyage.

Oh, my, yes. So much to do . . . But as for right now, I am ensconced in my lovely cabin, enjoying a nice leisurely lunch with my good friend John Higgins. He has just returned from seeing off his boon companion down at Tower Wharf, George Gordon having been bundled off by his family on a Grand Tour of Europe, for his own good, of course . . . and to protect the good name of the family.

"Lord B. took it all with good grace?" I ask.

"Oh, yes, never let it be said that George ever lacked grace," replies Higgins. "No, he sailed off, waving his hat in the breeze, his long dark hair blowing in the wind, a budding poem, I am sure, being formed in his mind." Higgins breathes a wistful sigh. "And, speaking of poems, he left this for you."

Higgins hands me a folded note. I open it and read . . .

Maid of the Orient,
Ere we part,
Give me, oh, give me,
Back my heart!

There is a discreet *G.G.* initialed at the bottom. I smile and refold the paper. "Very nice. I am honored," I say, tucking it into my bodice. Later I shall add some flower motifs to the border and have it framed to add to my collection of treasured things. "However, I think that *I* am not the one to be returning hearts."

A small laugh and a faraway look at that, but no reply.

"Do you think the trip will change our Lord Byron's . . . ways?" I ask.

This time, I get a secret smile from the very reserved John Higgins. "I certainly hope not, Miss . . . And frankly, I do not think it will be so."

I consider this and say, "You could have gone with him, you know. You are certainly rich enough."

"Yes, I could have, and as a matter of fact, he did invite me along. 'Come John,' he said. 'Let's be off to great adventures, fine deeds, noble causes, and we will leave the dull world and all its cares behind and blaze new paths of glory . . .' But when all was said and done, I had to admit that I had . . . responsibilities, and that it would be best that we part."

My eyes mist up at that and I look fondly upon my very best friend and place my hand on his arm.

"Dearest John . . . there will be other friends."

"I know, Miss, but he was so . . . never mind," says Higgins, clearing his throat. "Now, what are your plans concerning our unwilling tenant?"

"The prisoner below, you mean?"

"Yes, Miss, him."

"Well, it is all very simple. As soon as we reach an agreement with the Crown concerning various pardons and reinstatements, and dispose of the treasure lying below, we will tip off those who lie in wait at the Blackthorn Inn. In particular, we'll inform Bess, the landlord's daughter, that one day soon, a certain Sir Henry Flashby will be on the evening coach from Northampton bound for Plymouth. She will inform the Highwayman, of course, and all will be in train."

"And . . . ?"

I sniffle, draw in a breath, and continue, none too steady. "And then the Highwayman will stop the coach, and we'll deliver Flashby to his fate. Jaimy will probably put a hole in him, whereupon I shall reveal myself and, of course, Jaimy will be amazed. Then he'll sweep me up onto his mighty steed and we shall pound off to the *Nancy B.*, locked in each other's arms. We'll set sail for America and we will be married at long last and there we shall stay until our names are cleared of all disgrace. The Royal Navy will reinstate Jaimy and I shall be permitted to pursue my interests unencumbered."

"Very neat, Miss. I hope it happens in such a way," says Higgins with some doubt in his voice. "And Lord Allen?"

I smile at the thought of that particular rogue settling down to any kind of stable married life. "Ah, my dear, dear Richard. My dashing Captain of Cavalry . . . Alas, I fear domestic bliss is not in the cards for you. There are lots and lots of girls and many fine adventures in your future, of that I am sure. You will get over one Jacky Faber very quickly, as a little of her goes a long, long way, as we all know . . ."

But I will never get over you, dear Richard, never . . .

I shake thoughts of the gallant Lord Allen out of my easily befuddled mind.

"And the girl, Bess," continues Higgins relentlessly. "The landlord's undeniably beautiful daughter . . . ?"

That brings a frown to the Faber forehead, but I answer evenly, without malice, "I have gathered a pouch of gold for the girl, which will hold her in good stead, in payment for her . . . service to Jaimy in his time of distress. I am sure she will find that adequate compensation," I say, ardently wishing the subject would change. Mercifully, it does.

"Very good of you, Miss. I hope it will serve."

"Umm."

"Now, as to the unfortunate Mr. Flashby's current condition . . . I trust you are not abusing him, Miss?"

"No, I am not, though the temptation is strong. I have directed Lee Chi to provide Mr. Flashby with all the fresh water he requires. Also I have described the kind of foul gruel I was given in Newgate where I was confined because of the same Mr. Flashby, and our very clever Mr. Lee has cooked up a similar concoction. It has been served to our guest and I hope he enjoys it."

"Umm. Cruel punishment, indeed, especially since he knows just who is dishing it out."

"Yes, that makes it all the better . . . Indeed, it is true. Vengeance is sweet . . . and best, as they say, served cold, as cold as Flashby's lunch. Here, Higgins, have some of this goose liver pâté. It is quite good on a nice puffy biscuit . . . and the oysters are very plump and fresh. Ravi, Mr. Higgins's glass, if you would?"

"Thank you, I shall," says Higgins, falling to the excellent repast. "And thank you, too, Ravi. This is all very nice. I am surprised we are not to eat it in front of Lieutenant Flashby."

"Well, that would certainly be fun, but it would have been too much trouble bringing him up, and I certainly wouldn't want to eat down in the bilges."

The *Nancy B.* is a clean ship, but as for the bilges, well, they stink on any ship and mine is no exception. Having neither time nor inclination to build an actual cell to accommodate our hostage, his ankles and wrists, which are encased in good stout chains, are merely shackled to the bulkhead. He sits on a little platform above the sloshing water that has leaked or sweated through our hull. With the stench of a dead rat or two floating in the mess, it is very much like Hell . . . Not quite, but it will serve for Mr. Flashby till he can be delivered to the real one.

We continue eating and discussing the many charms of London town, which we are both very much enjoying, when there is, yet again, a discreet knock on the door.

"Come in," I call, and Liam Delaney's large form fills the doorway.

"Liam! Come join us!" I exclaim upon seeing my dear old sea dad.

"Maybe later, Jacky," says Liam. "But right now, it's best you come out on deck. We have a visitor."

Wot?

I put napkin to lips and dash out to scan the harbor. I am amazed to see what looks like a Chinese junk being rowed up the Thames. From its masthead flies the Golden Dragon pennant. But, no, it is not Cheng Shih on the *Divine Wind.* No, it is smaller than that, and as it approaches and pulls in beside us, I am shocked to see a very fat man dressed in Oriental finery, seated in a palanquin on the deck of the ship with a very familiar female figure beside him.

The fat man lifts the mouthpiece of the hookah he has been smoking and gestures to me.

"*Neih hou,* my dear little envoy. I have come to see what joy my presents to the British Empire have brought!"

Chopstick Charlie . . . ?

Chapter 44

"But how did you ever get here so quickly, Charlie? Surely we left far ahead of you." It is early evening and we are riding in Chopstick Charlie's palanquin, an ornate box affixed with sets of poles, held by eight strong men, four on each side. They carry us along at waist level when the way is clear, and hoist the whole thing up to their shoulders when the crowd gets dense. *Very convenient*, I'm thinkin', for it works really well. It gets us a lot of strange looks, that's for certain. Charlie is in one seat, and facing him are Sidrah and me, side by side, looking very fine, I must say. She's in her Rangoon best, black hair combed and pinned up high with jeweled combs, and me in my usual knock-'em-dead Oriental garb, my head newly shaved and polished and my blue-green sari wrapped all about me.

Ravi sits atop the palanquin, grandly giving directions to the men who carry us through the London streets . . . and to two others who escort us—Ganju Thapa and his fellow Gurkha, each of them with their wicked, inward curved *khukuris*.

We are taking a brief tour of the neighborhood, and

then we are going to the Cockpit. I have arranged for us to meet Richard Allen there. Just how we will be received, looking as we do, I do not know. But hey, I've been thrown out of better places.

"It is really very simple, my dear," says Charlie, gazing about at the passing city. "While you took the long way around the southern tip of Africa, I merely took a shortcut. I sailed my little ship, well protected by Ganju Thapa and twelve of his fellow Gurkhas, around India and up the Gulf of Aden and through the Red Sea to Suez. There is a canal there, you know."

I frown. "Hmmm . . . I recollect from my time in the Mediterranean that the canal did not go all the way through to Port Said." I had learned from Dr. Sebastian that . . . *yes, the canal is almost completely cut through that last bit of desert . . . A pity, for it would shorten the time to get to the rich Orient by many weeks. And it would not take them long, considering all the slave labor they have. But you know those Arabs . . . renowned in mathematics and science, but when it comes to digging a simple ditch, they just cannot get together on that. The phrase "trying to herd cats," I believe, was coined when dealing with Arab politics . . .*

"Ah, too true, too true, but merely a minor inconvenience. When we got to the end of that canal, I simply hired a contractor who rigged a cradle for our small ship to which was attached many stout poles. There were a number of slaves assigned to each cross-pole and we were *carried* across the land and deposited into the Mediterranean Sea. You see?"

"*Carried?* Your whole ship?" I ask incredulous.

"Slaves work cheap, you know. A little gruel at the end of the day and they are, if not happy, at least allowed to live another day. If one stumbles and falls, another is whipped into his place."

"That's awful, Charlie!" I exclaim.

"It was not awful at all. In fact, it was quite smooth and comfortable—much better than the sea. I did not even have to get out of my palanquin."

"That's not what I meant, Chops. Those poor men."

"It is a cruel world, child, and . . . Oh, look, there's Hyde Park. I used to go there often when I was but a slip of a schoolboy."

Looking at Charlie's jolly face and present girth, it is hard to imagine him as a skinny boy, alone and afraid in a strange land.

"But the Arab lands are rife with bandits, Charlie. Did you not fear you would be taken?"

"With my Gurkhas by my side? Surely you jest. One Gurkha is worth a hundred other men. The Gurkha war cry is *'Jai Mahakali, ayo Gorkhali,'* which means 'Glory be to the Goddess of War, here come the Gurkhas!' Ha!"

Gazing fondly about at the scenes of his young manhood, Charlie continues the account of his journey here:

"As a consequence of sailing through the Mediterranean, I was able to stop off in Greece to pick up a few more things, such as some very nice statues of comely young maidens that I thought the King might enjoy. Knocked them off this porch thing on a place they called the Cropolis or something. No one seemed to mind. The whole place was a wreck, anyway. Nobody said anything to my Gurkhas, at least when they were chiseling the things off."

"You would not call it plundering, Honored Father? Stealing another country's cultural heritage?" I ask.

"Ha! Listen to her talking of 'cultural heritage,' she who has been, by her own account, beggar, thief, pirate, and buccaneer in the not-so-distant past! No, I think of it more as 'protective custody' for those cultures that cannot manage their own affairs."

"Ummm," I murmur, not entirely convinced of the ethics of the thing, nor of the selfless nobility of Charlie's "protective custody." But he is right, of course—just who is Jacky Faber, Hypocrite First-Class, to cast aspersions on the motives of others, when she has acted as she has?

Earlier, we had received Charlie Chen on the *Nancy B.* and had gone down in the hold to go over the inventory of items *very* thoroughly. Old Chops is no fool. He did not become rich by being careless with his goods. I gave him a list of whatever favors had been given out and he approved wholeheartedly. *We must grease the wheels, mustn't we, dear?*

On our way down into the hold, we heard a rattle of chains and a low moan. Charlie lifted his eyebrows in question.

"Oh, just an old enemy, Chops. Think nothing of it," I said. "He is soon to be disposed of. The day after tomorrow, as a matter of fact."

"Umm . . . you are becoming more Eastern in your outlook every day, my child. I believe I have been a good influence on you," commented Charlie, chuckling in approval.

As we went over the stuff, I filled him in on the social situation: the Cockpit, the Duke of Clarence, and all, and how the disposition of his treasure is going. He pronounced himself most satisfied.

• • •

Sidrah, though she sits silently with her hand in mine, as befits a Burmese maid in the presence of her father, is clearly entranced with the new city she finds herself in, giving out only an occasional *oh!* and *ah!* London may not have golden temples and such, but we do have our charms.

"I find this oh-so-delicious, you know," says Chopstick Charlie. "When I was here as a lad, I was treated rather abominably by many of the sons of the ruling class—like not being allowed to attend certain functions or to go in the front door of various clubs. They thought it was not quite right, you see, my being a mere Chinaman. Oh, but things are different now, much different!"

"Very true, Honored Sir of Yellow Hue. And there," I say, pointing to a large building, "is the British Museum, where your collection of antiquities will rest for the edification of all good Britons. The House of Chen will be well remembered for its generosity."

"Well, good," says Charlie. "My ancestors will be pleased, as will I."

We pull up to the front door of the Cockpit and pile out of the palanquin. The Gurkhas line up on either side as we approach the door. Can't say we don't make a splendid entrance.

A hush falls over the place as we grandly enter. Although Sidrah and I are dressed Oriental, Charlie is not. No, we had spent a good part of the morning at my tailor's and he is dressed top-to-toe in the latest fashion. Whether it will carry him through, I don't know, but it turns out I underestimated him.

Going down the aisle, chin up and little goatee pointing forward, Charlie looks about and suddenly grabs a very surprised man by the shoulders and exclaims, "Stinky! Stinky Beans!"

Wot?

The so-named Stinky Beans gapes in horror at the apparition in front of him.

"Stinky! Stanley Bernard! Don't you remember? It's Chinese Charlie, from back at good old King's College. Ha! The Old School Tie, eh, what? And is this your fine mistress, Stinky? Oh, so very fine! Ho-ho-ho! A lot better than your constant consort at our dear old school. You remember, Mrs. Palmer and Her Five Beautiful Daughters!" Charlie lifts his right palm and wiggles his fingers suggestively.

"Oh, and who do we have here? Why, it's none other than Reginald Rothenbottom. Yes! Oh, good old golden school days! Reading and writing and roasting fags! Yes, I do recall how you did roast me. Oh, yes, I do! Tell me, Reggie, how's your bank balance? Oh, well, come talk to me and we'll see what we can do about that!

"And who's this?" *Gasp!* "Why, it's . . ."

I, myself, sidle away from all this Old School nonsense and drag Sidrah over to a table where I spy Richard and the Duke of Clarence sitting. I shove Sidrah into the booth next to Richard and I hear him say, "My, my, look at this . . . Where did you come from, now, dear?"

I immediately think better of my proposed seating arrangements and yank Sidrah back out and plunk myself into her place on the bench and pull her in after me.

Yes, I know . . . Although I am totally dedicated to getting my Jaimy Fletcher back into my arms where he belongs, I have appreciated Lord Allen's company, having sailed into many a fine establishment when on his arm, and I do feel a certain proprietary interest in this gallant cavalry officer. Unwarranted, I know, but still . . .

Introductions are made, and then Charlie, himself, joins us and pulls off the greatest feat of all . . .

"Willie, old top!" he says, standing in front of the astounded Duke of Clarence.

Oh, God, it's all over, I'm thinkin' in despair. *We are ruined* . . .

"Oh, the halcyon days at Kew! Were they not glorious, Willie? Ah, the simple joys of youth!"

I am amazed to see the Duke of Clarence, the youngest son of George III, by the Grace of God, King of England, rise to his feet and say . . .

"Good Lord, Chinese Charlie . . . ? Yes, yes, it is, indeed, you. Do sit down, sit down . . ."

Later, when all hubbub has died away, I whisper in Charlie's ear, "So how did you pull this off, Chops?"

He laughs and says, "You see, little one, I own many of these people, for all their fine airs. I have been keeping an eye on them through my contacts in India, in Ceylon, in Malta, in Italy, and yes, in London, too—their financial dealings, their banking . . . their very extensive gambling debts. You see, I own half the stock in the Bank of Norfolk, and a few others, so . . ."

"I know," I say, laughing and poking him in the ribs. "Money talks, and all else walks . . ."

"Indeed, little one, indeed."

I turn my attention back to Cavalry Captain Lord Richard Allen, who once again has his hand on that of my very good friend Sidrah.

"Ahem, Lord Allen, need I remind you of our appointment tomorrow?" I give him a look.

"What, Princess?" he asks, distracted.

Grrrrrr . . .

"We have a date for a picnic, you might recall . . ."

"Oh, yes . . ."

"And a bit of church, too," I say, "which, I think, will do both of us a world of good."

Chapter 45

"What are you thinking about, Princess?"

I am sitting cross-legged on the blanket we had spread out on the grass of Lincoln's Inn Fields, a lovely open spot of greenery rimmed with daffodils and tulips overlooking the Thames, glittering down below. Lord Richard Allen is lying on his back, his booted ankles crossed, his scarlet jacket opened, his lovely head on my lap. It is an absolutely gorgeous day and the city, in all its glory, lies spread out all around us.

I am dressed modestly, for a change—a simple pink and white frock to mirror the beautiful spring day—and we have been to church, after all, and I had to be somewhat chaste in the way of attire. It is rather too warm for one of my wigs, so I have donned a soft bonnet to hide my somewhat outrageous head. My black mantilla rests on my shoulders as well. Although I generally crave to be the center of attention in most situations, I don't always like to be stared at.

Yes, we went to services at Saint Paul's Cathedral this morning. Although I am not always a faithful churchgoing type, I did wish to go today, and I dragged a very unwilling Richard Allen with me. Ravi, too.

It is the Sin of Pride, I know, but I do like going in the front door of that grand place, a privilege that was denied me when I was a starving and undeniably filthy street urchin. I especially like going in dressed all fine and on the arm of an extremely handsome young cavalry officer. Yes, I know, Pride Goeth Before a Fall, but still . . .

"Is very grand temple, Memsahib," says Ravi, his dark eyes wide in all the splendor. "Where do we go?"

The smell of incense is sure to be familiar to the lad, but scant else in this place would be. We have made up a nice little white linen suit for him—neat trousers and jacket buttoned up to the neck. His loincloth and turban are banished for this day, as are his golden slippers. Today, he wears black leather pumps on his feet, which I am sure he finds most uncomfortable.

"Just follow us and do what I do. You'll see." Richard leads the way to a pew and we slide in and sit down.

"But where is Ganesha?" whispers Ravi in the hush of the place. "I wish to make small offering."

"Uh, he's out in the hall. Quiet, now, Ravi," I say, suppressing a smile at the thought of the jolly Indian elephant god dancing out in the anteroom of this Anglican fortress. "Kneel down when I do and fold your hands and look pious."

He does as I tell him and so does Richard. The service begins with a procession down the main aisle and when all the robed clerics are in place, the service begins.

We recite the prayers, take the sermon to heart, mostly, and listen to the music . . . the glorious music. It's the Mass in C by a new fellow, Beethoven, who I hear is getting a lot of play lately. German, of course. I listen to the *kyries* swirling about the interior of the dome, and decide that I like it. *Sing on, Ludwig van . . .*

The place was awe inspiring, as always, and brought back many memories, not all of them pleasant. I recalled some terrifying times clutching Rooster Charlie's hand as we made our way through the catacombs beneath this place, a deceased churchman's dried-out, hollow-eyed corpse on every hand.

Eventually, all the prayers are said, the last benediction is bestowed upon our unworthy brows, the last thundering chorus is sung, and it is over.

As we leave, I say to Richard, "Please, Richard, give us a minute. We'll meet you outside."

He nods and bows as I lead Ravi into a side room.

"Ganesha?" asks Ravi, gazing at rows of lit candles in the dimly lit room.

"No, dear," I reply, taking a few coins from my purse and handing them to the old woman who sits within. I buy two candles and give one to Ravi. "But, here, lad, take this and you can light it in front of Ganesha when we get back to the ship. Be sure to put in a good word for me. Now, scoot on out to Lord Allen. I want to be alone for a moment."

He scurries out and I take my remaining candle and light it from the wick of one of the lit candles, one that is guttering down and almost extinguished. I know that each of the candles have been placed there by someone with heartfelt prayers for the sick, the needy, or the departed. I add mine to those on the small altar, pull up my mantilla to cover my head, and kneel down on the narrow pad below the rows of flickering lights that is provided for supplicants. I put my hands together and say . . .

Lord, I don't even know if I should be talking to You because I know I got a lot of things to answer for in this life of mine, and we both realize that I come prayin' to You only when I'm in a mess and not when things are goin' good for me, but You gotta know Jaimy is in such deep trouble right now and a lot of it's my fault. Maybe I shouldn't even be asking this of You, but I am, I am, Lord, for Jaimy is a good boy and my cockeyed plan to rescue him is so full of "what ifs?" that things might go so awfully wrong when it all comes down, but I pray that they won't. I don't even know if You're listening, but if You are, please watch out for him a little, at least till I can get him back and straighten him out. Oh, I don't even know what I'm sayin' and I'm crying now and I gotta stop, but I think You know what I mean by all this whimpering and whining, I do. . . . Amen.

I stand, collect myself as best I can, and go back out to Lord Allen and Ravi. They stand waiting on the steps. Richard presents his arm, and I wipe at my eyes and take it.

Well, I don't know if that did any good, but I do know it couldn't hurt.

I had bought a kite for Ravi to use on this fine day, and after he has set out the fine luncheon made up for us by Mr. Lee, he runs off joyously to fly it.

Watching him go, I reply to Richard's question, "Well, for one thing, milord, I'm thinking about my meeting with Mr. Peel yesterday outside the office of Baron Mulgrave, the First Lord of the Admiralty. I think it went rather well . . ."

At that meeting I had been dressed in as military fashion as I could manage—that is, just short of outright scandal—my navy blue lieutenant's jacket with white turnouts and gold braid, white lace at throat and wrists, white skirt pleated at front with small bustle roll at back. I had worn my Trafalgar medal about my neck *and* my Legion of Honor adorned my left breast. My white-gloved hand had rested upon the arm of Mr. Charles Chen, of the House of Chen. He, too, was dressed to the nines in the best that the tailors on Savile Row could supply. He beamed merrily about, looking every bit like the cat that swallowed the canary . . . any number of unfortunate canaries, as a matter of fact. Under the arm that did not bear my hand rested rolled-up pieces of what appeared to be parchment.

"All is going well for your pardon, Miss," Peel informs me as we wait for our summons. "But as for Fletcher, well, it is rumored that he did kill one of our operatives, a Mr. Bliffil, who, I believe, was of your acquaintance. I don't know if Fletcher's pardon will fly, but we are working on the problem. We shall see. Ah, shall we go in?"

A man has appeared at the now open door and we are beckoned inside.

We enter, introductions are made—*Lord Mulgrave, Miss Faber, Mr. Chen, charmed, enchanté, and all*—and we sit down.

Once again, a man sits at a desk going through papers that no doubt concern me.

"Hmmm. Mr. Peel here seems to think a lot of you, Miss Faber," says Baron Mulgrave, First Lord of the Admiralty.

"Indeed, Sir, she has been invaluable in the past . . . the matter of the *Santa Magdalena* gold, chief among them," says Mr. Peel. "Over a million pounds sterling into the Treasury, you know . . ."

Peel has, indeed, been restored to his former position as Chief Adviser on Matters of Naval Intelligence. The unfortunate Mr. Smollett, last holder of that position, is off somewhere in the wilderness of banishment and ill-favor, trying to explain away what has become known as The Affair of the Duke's Watch.

"Hmmm . . ." muses Baron Mulgrave, mulling over the contents of the papers. "While there are some who extol your virtues, Miss Faber, there are others who wonder why you are not yet hanged."

"I have determined that hanging would not suit my constitution, Sir, so I have tried to avoid it."

A short bark of a laugh at that.

"Yes, rather . . . But from what I have read of your behavior, it seems you have not gone out of your way to avoid that particular fate." He looks me up and down. "Still, it would be a pity to see that dangle . . ."

I put on a modified version of the big eyes, looking helpless in the presence of the big, strong man.

"Ahem. Well, we'll have to see about you later," he stammers. "Now, Mr. Chen, I hear you bring us great riches."

"Ah, yes, Honorable One," says Charlie, grinning and opening up his charts and laying them out. "And I bring you much more than mere trinkets. You see, here is the layout of the fortifications of Rangoon . . . and here, the principal ethnic peoples' areas of influence . . . and the plan of Singapore harbor . . ."

Mr. Peel's eyes gleam, and he and Lord Mulgrave lean over the maps.

I take this opportunity to excuse myself, but nobody seems to notice.

As I leave, I hear Charlie say, "I believe I could be of very much use to the Crown. And yes, I should like to meet the King . . ."

Ha! Good old Chops! You tell 'em!

My mind once again comes back to the greensward of Lincoln's Inn Fields. I reach down and pull a tendril of light brown hair from Richard's face. It had worked its way out of the tie that holds the mass of his thick hair back upon his neck.

"Don't you dare fall asleep on me, Richard," I say sternly.

"How could I possibly do that," he murmurs sleepily, "when my poor unworthy head rests in such a holy hollow?"

"Stuff and nonsense," I say. "I shall recite to you a poem, so you will remember this day. Ahem . . ."

> *A book of verses 'neath the bough,*
> *A loaf of bread, and thou,*
> *Beside me singing in the wilderness,*
> *Ah, wilderness, thou art Paradise enow!*

"How did you like that, milord?" I chirp. "You get to be the 'thou' in that one. First 'thou,' anyway."

"I like it very much, Princess. Did you learn that from your new poetical friends—Lord Byron and that bunch?"

"Nay, Sidrah taught it to me, back in Rangoon. It's by a man they called Omar the Tentmaker, a Persian, written a long time ago. Rather nice, don't you think?"

"Yes, and so is the lovely Sidrah. I squired her about a bit this morning . . . showed her the sights and all."

"I'll bet you did," I say, giving him a poke in the ribs.

He laughs. "A bit jealous, Jacky, I hope?"

"Not a bit, you rascal, as I have no claim on thee . . . or thou . . . as I am promised to another."

That gets another chuckle from the very pretty Lord Allen. "And you are as loyal as the sky is blue."

Another poke and I look over and see that Ravi is not having much success in flying his kite. The breeze, though pleasant, is just too strong. As he runs along holding his string, his kite dips and dives in crazy arcs before crashing into the ground.

The other kids on the green are not having any more luck at kite flying than Ravi, and I know how to fix that, but . . .

Uh-oh . . .

I hear the words *wog* and *nigra* being tossed around. The words are coming not from the children, but rather from some of the adults scattered about the green. And it ain't hard to figure just who they're talkin' about. Ravi hears and gathers up his fallen kite and walks away from the other kids, disconsolate, his joy gone. I know the word *untouchable* is going through his mind. Holding his kite at his side, he comes back to our little encampment.

Grrr . . .

"Here, Ravi," I say. "What you need is a tail. Richard, up with you." Lord Allen groans and sits up.

When my legs are freed, I flip up my dress a bit, exposing one of my petticoats. Then I whip out my shiv from my forearm sheath and make a cut in the bottom hem. That accomplished, I rip off a good three inches of it, maybe six feet long. Hey, I've got lots of petticoats—got three on right now, in fact.

"Here, Ravi. Give me your kite."

He holds it out to me and I tie the strip of cloth to the bottom point of it and hand it back to Ravi.

"There. Now try that."

He runs off, trailing the newly tailed kite. It, of course, rises smoothly into the air, to the wonder of all.

"Very nice, Princess," says Allen. "I had no idea you were so expert in the science of aerodynamics."

"We used to fly kites every March in Boston, when I was at the Lawson Peabody School for Young Girls. It was a very merry time, winter coming to a close after all, and, with the wind off Massachusetts Bay, well, it necessitated tails."

Ravi whoops with joy and comes back to our blanket.

"Look, Memsahib, it is flying!"

"Indeed it is, lad," I say, reaching out. "Come, hand me the string and I'll show you some tricks."

He does, and I say, "See, if you pull it this way, it will make the kite swoop down . . . That way and the kite swoops in the other direction. See? Now watch that bloke over there . . ."

I let the line go slack and the kite comes floating down . . . down . . . down . . . and when it almost reaches the ground, I pull it up sharply and it takes the wind and buzzes by the head of one of those men who called Ravi those things. I almost succeed in taking his hat off and he must duck to avoid our vengeful kite.

Take that, you mean bastard . . .

"Well done, Princess," says Richard, beaming. "You truly are a piece of work. Even kite flying falls within your expertise."

"Yes, well, one time I even went up into the air myself, riding a big kite. It almost killed me."

"Yes, Jacky, I know . . . I can read, you know, simple soldier though I am."

"So you've read those books?" I ask, working up a maidenly blush. It's getting harder and harder for me to do that.

"Oh, yes, and enjoyed them hugely."

"Even the naughty bits?"

"*Especially* the naughty bits," says the rogue, grinning, his teeth gleaming white in the sunlight of the day. "I think I came out rather well in the Mississippi thing."

"Umm . . . Well, Amy Trevelyne tends to exaggerate a bit."

Hmmm . . . I notice that one of the little boys who was having trouble flying his kite has come up next to Ravi.

Uh-oh . . . Trouble . . . ?

But no. The boy merely says, "My name's Tom. Can you show us how to do that?"

Ravi, warily, says, "Yes, Tom, for certain."

"Good. Then, what's your name?" The lad seems to be a pleasant sort, for a boy.

"Ravi."

"Just Ravi? No last name?"

"No, I-I am Untouch—"

"His last name is Faber," I finish for him, loud and firm. "Ravi Faber."

I reach up under my dress and pull off the petticoat I had previously torn and toss it to Ravi, whose luminous dark eyes are brimming now, not with shame but with pride. Then I reach in my sleeve and flip him my shiv, which he expertly catches on the fly.

"There . . . my son . . . Cut tails for everyone's kite so that we might all decorate God's blue sky on this beautiful day."

Soon all the kites of Lincoln's Inn Fields are aloft and flying.

"My turn now, Richard. Up you go now, lad," I say, sitting him up and squirming around to plop my head into his lap. By turning my face, I can look out over the river. Boats on the Thames—mostly commercial coal barges—work their slow way up and down the river and suchlike, but there are some that are out for the mere pleasure of sailing a small boat on a glorious day.

"Does the offer of a ladyship still go?" I tease.

He leans down and plants one on my forehead.

"Yes, Princess, it does."

"Right, Lord Allen. You'd be tossed out of the House of Lords on your wellborn ear if you married something like me."

"I would not care. They're just a bunch of puffed-up old coots, anyway. I can barely stay awake when the House is in session. Which is why I'm a soldier and not a politician."

"Being a politico is a lot safer than being a soldier, Richard. I'd hate to see you hurt."

"Ah, well, nothing much happening now, so don't worry," he says. "No, at the moment, it's all parades and fine uniforms and impressing the ladies."

"Yes, but I hear Lord Wellesley is taking on Napoleon down in Portugal. You could be sent there."

"True, but it ain't happened yet, so not to worry."

"Right." I sigh. "Live in the moment, I always say, and the moment right now is truly fine."

"Indeed, Princess, an excellent motto, and one to which I fully subscribe." He makes so bold as to lean down and place a light kiss upon my lips. I should protest, but I do not really mind.

"Lady Allen, Jacky Faber, herself," I say, laughing. "Look down there, Richard. Do you see that muddy patch of open shore next to Blackfriars Bridge? You do? Good. It is mostly gravelly mud, but still a beach . . . sort of . . . Well, anyway, when she was a kid, the grand Lady Allen used to swim there in summers with the other street kids. It was neutral territory between the gangs, like."

"Ah yes, the youth of London, frolicking in bucolic splendor."

"Well, no, it wasn't quite like that, milord, no—a bit more squalid. For one thing, the water was dirty and muddy, with things floatin' in it."

I sink back into remembrance.

"Shall I tell you a tale of Cheapside you ain't yet read in any of those books?"

"Please do, Princess."

"All right," I say, and I begin . . .

"We had back then what we called 'chicken fights'—they were gladiatorial contests, actually. How to explain? Well, here's how Rooster Charlie, our gang leader, used to describe the game. 'Y'see, gents, we 'ave the Bulls and the Chicks. The Chicks, bein' the girls, ride the shoulders of the Bulls—the big lads, like—into the water, about waist deep, and the object of the contest is to topple the opposin' team. The rules, as they was developed over the centuries, Sirs, was this: The Bull cannot hold the Chick onto his shoulders—the Chick has to do that by clamping her legs about the Bull's neck as hard as she can and holding on to his hair. The Chicks can do whatever they want to the other Chicks—bite, scratch, pull hair—and the Bulls can wrassle with each other but can't touch the Chicks. The battle is won when one team's Chick topples off into the water, or mud, which is more likely to be the case. Oh, sirs, you ought to see it, when four or more teams stride into the water, ready to engage, well, it's a Battle Royale, I can tell you. Tomorrow, twelve noon, when Big Ben strikes, you'll be in for a treat! The mud and water shall fly!'"

I have to chuckle when I think back to Rooster Charlie explainin' the game to the local sportin' toffs—he did have a way with words, our Charlie did, I recall fondly.

"'What's the scam, Charlie?' asked the leaders of the other gangs when we all gathered under a flag of truce.

"'The scam is this,' says Charlie. 'The toffs bet on the fights, I collects the bets and takes ten percent off the top and divides it up later twixt the gangs. Got it? Hey, it's better than beggin', and it's legal and ain't about to get you hanged, neither. Now, every gang should put t'gether at least two teams . . . and yes, there'll be prizes for winners, too. Got it? Tomorrow noon.'"

"And you, of course, were a Chick," interrupts Lord Allen.

"Yes, of course," I reply. "Me and Hughie made quite a team, too." Hugh the Grand we called him—the biggest, strongest, bravest, and sweetest member of our gang. He was simple, but he was good, and some of the happiest times I've ever had in my life was in riding his broad shoulders, whether to be high enough to read the broadsides on Fleet Street or riding into gang battles on the rough streets or in the Chicken Fights on the Thames. We used to have Hughie fight the prizefighters what would come into Cheapside with the autumn fairs, takin' on all comers, but I hated to see him hurt, even though he won most times, to our benefit. But still, wiping the blood from his face afterward . . . I just didn't like it. I liked the chicken fights a lot better. At least it wasn't Hughie what got pounded.

"Anyway, the next noon we had maybe twenty spectators at the foot of Blackfriars Bridge, and we got down to it. Charlie got up first to announce the matches.

"'Step right up, gents, and place your bets! We have five fine teams here for the first bout—the Royal Cavaliers, the Rounders, the Lords, the Shankies, and, of course, my very own Blackfriars Bridge Crew. You can be sure we don't throw no fights like them pugilists sometimes do, no sir. Nay, we're honest to the core. And throw a fight to a Shanky? Why, Guv'nor, we'd rather die, we would. Step right up, gents, and place your bets. Hurry up, now, the first match is about to begin . . . Go!'

"With the Bulls bellowing, we waded into the first bout and my good Bull and I went for Toby Oyster's team first, as they seemed the weakest. 'Over there, Hughie, hit 'em hard!' and he did. The girl Toby had up was game, but she didn't last long. I got her by the hair and twisted her about so's I could get my arm around her neck and squeeze till she made gargling noises and dropped off into the water without further protest, and Hughie and I swung around to confront the next challenge . . . It was from the Shankies, but they didn't field their best team, I knew, 'cause Pigger O'Toole wasn't the Bull. Not yet, he wasn't . . .

"And that was just the first round. Bruises and cuts were addressed, fresh Chicks were put up, and the battles resumed.

'Course us Chicks didn't wear nothin', being just kids and all, and why give the enemy Chick somethin' to grab on to other than your hair, which you couldn't do nothin' about? We could've cropped our hair, but even though us Chicks were gutter girls, we still had some pride about our appearance. And so the teams gained some renown. As we went down the bank to battle, it became common for the Chicks to stand on the shoulders of their Bulls and hurl taunts at their enemies, further garnering the cheers of the crowds that came down to watch us. It was actually a pretty fine time.

"Yes, we had many Battle Royales in the days after that— we fought the Shanks, the Cavs, the Rounders, and the Lords, and we came up winners most times, thanks mostly to Hughie. But some we lost, me ending up with my face in the mud. But money was waged and gradually odds were made and Hughie and I ended up among the favorites . . . and then Pigger O'Toole himself entered the fray as a Bull, and then—"

"Hello. What's this?" says Allen suddenly, looking off over my recumbent form.

Startled, I sit up to see Dragoon Cavalry Sergeant Enoch Bailey, Richard's good right-hand man, come striding purposefully across the green.

Uh-oh . . .

He approaches, salutes, and says, "Pardon, Sor. Mum. A message from the General. Thought you ought to see it right away."

He hands Richard a note, who opens it and reads as I say, my voice full of trepidation, "So good to see you again, Sergeant Bailey."

"Mutual, Miss," says the stolid Bailey. I do not know how

much he means that, considering the fact that I was instrumental in peppering his hide with a good dose of rock salt fired from one of my guns on the *Belle of the Golden West*. He steps away, respectfully out of hearing, to await further orders.

"Is it orders for Portugal, Richard? Is it . . . ?" I ask, breathless.

He looks out over my head, deep in thought.

"No, Jacky, it is not that."

"Then, what news?"

He takes my hand and says, "The town fathers of London have deemed its local constabulary to be either corrupt or incompetent. I suspect they are both. Whatever the reason, I have been ordered to take my troop of Dragoons out onto the heath and not come back until I have captured the Black Highwayman."

Oh, no . . .

"I know, Princess, I know. I will try to take him alive . . . and unhurt, if I can."

"When do you go?" I ask, trembling, the joy of the day gone.

"Today is Sunday. We ride out on Thursday."

"Thank you for telling me, Richard," I say, wrapping my arms about him, putting my face to his chest. "Now I think it best we go back and prepare for what it is we both have to do. Ravi, come!"

I have been lax in my duty to Jaimy. I know that. Because he has been inactive on the moor, I have relaxed and let my affection for Richard Allen guide my days and my actions. No more. We must set things in train . . . and we must do it now . . .

Chapter 46

"Yes, Sir," I say, all respectful like, with a neat little curtsy.
"My name is Mary Alsop, and I'm writing a piece on the
Black Highwayman. I hope to write a book about it. I heard
that you were most cruelly robbed, Sir, and if you would be so
kind, Sir, can you describe your experience for me?"

Earlier in the day I had gone back to the *Shipping News* office on Fleet Street. With the help of my friend who had been so helpful the last time I'd gone looking for information, we pulled out as many eyewitness accounts of the Black Highwayman as we could find. I wrote down the addresses of those who lived nearby, thanking my friend in my usual way, with a hefty tip. Hey, always make 'em glad to see you comin', I say. I went on my way to seek out these witnesses to hear what they had to say.

"Women on Grub Street? By God, it's an abomination!"
Didn't get far with that bloke, no I didn't. He was a cheese merchant down on Earl Street. He looked me up and down and then tossed me out even though I was dressed all prim and

proper. Wasn't worth my time to point out to the sod that many women were workin' the literary trade now. Grub Street was where most of 'em worked, male or female. Grub Street Hacks, they were called, and I'd be proud to be named as a member. If ever I were to work on land in England, I'd work there. Yes, I would. And I'd drag Amy Trevelyne over here, too. Can't get published in Puritan America? Well, try Grub Street, m'lass, and I am sure you would prosper. That little play I wrote back there on the Mississippi? Yes, the one I named "The Villain Pursues Fair Maiden" is now most often titled "The Villain Pursues Her." I hear that it has been performed many times and in many places, and that gratifies me, even though I ain't made a dime off that epic since coming off the Big Muddy, but so it goes. Hey, anyone, lad or lass, can lift a pen and make up stuff, and the money ain't bad sometimes, neither. *So good day and bad cess to you, Sir. I'm glad the Highwayman got your gold. May your cheese turn as sour as your disposition. Grrr . . .*

By and large, I have better luck with the ladies . . .

"Yes, Missus," I say, with a curtsy and my eyes cast down. "My name is Mary Alsop, and I'm writing a piece on the Black Highwayman. I hope to turn it into a book later on. Can you describe your encounter for me, such that my readers might experience for themselves some of the dreadful feelings your own poor self must have gone through in that ordeal. Hmmm?"

Yes, I had much better luck with the women. They tended to be better witnesses, anyway, not being half drunk at the time of the robbery, as most of the men generally were. My best source was a Winifred Beasley, a seamstress, wife of a hackney driver, who had gone down to Plymouth to visit her aged mum and had been in the coach with her daughter one evening when it was stopped by the Black Highwayman.

"Oh, Miss, it was just so 'orrible! He comes roaring up on this great black horse, which I swears was breathin' fire out o' its nostrils!"

Her daughter, who sat excitedly by her side, had a slightly different opinion . . .

"Oh, he was ever so dashing, Miss!" she says, clasping her hands and looking off, her eyes shining at the memory. "His horse rearing up, his black cape swirling around him, a sword on his hip, and a pistol in his hand! 'Stand and deliver!' he shouted. 'Everyone out of the coach!'"

"Aye, and we did get out, you may be sure, Miss," continues Mrs. Beasley, looking a bit askance at her daughter.

"Now don't you go getting all romantical, Griselda," says the mother, disapprovingly. "After all, he is a robber and a brigand."

"Yes, but he was so gallant . . . at least to us ladies. He told us we were not to be fearful because his business was not with us," says this Griselda. "But he did stand the men in a line in front of him and he looked in each face . . . and in each of their purses. From the rich blokes, he stole their gold . . . From the poor, nothing. Oh, what a noble outlaw!"

The mother gives the daughter a gentle swat. "You calm down, you!"

"Did you see the color of his eyes?" I ask of them both. Griselda shakes her head.

Mrs. Beasley looks at me curiously. "His eyes? Miss, when

you are looking down the barrel of a gun, you most certainly do *not* notice the gun toter's eye color. Dear me, no, you do not!"

"Oh, it must have been horrible for you, Missus, just horrible," I simper, then thank them for their time. I stand and prepare to leave. "Aside from the black boots, trousers, and cape, is there any other thing you might remember about the Highwayman? Some small detail?"

The woman thinks for a moment and then adds, "The mask he wore that covered his lower face . . . it was silk, and it had little gathers in the top where it went across his nose, you know, like this." She points to the tucks at the top of her bodice.

Hmmm . . . Trust a seamstress to notice that.

She turned out to be the most reliable witness, but even she did not notice the color of his eyes, nor did her awe-struck daughter.

Which is good, I'm figuring.

The other witnesses I interviewed were no better at describing the Highwayman. Their accounts varied wildly. 'Course when you stand there in fear for your life, your mind can play tricks on you.

One thing the men were good at . . . recounting exactly *where* the Highwayman stopped them. It was almost always at a sharp turn of the road near the crossing of Gallywall Road and Halfpenny Lane, where the coaches are forced, by the curve and the roughness of the road, to slow to a crawl. There are fens, pools of dark water, all about, and woods, the former being treacherous for horses, the latter making for good hiding places for highwaymen . . . and maybe others.

Which might be good. We shall see, for this afternoon I shall go there to scout it out.

On my way back to the *Nancy B.,* I spy a sign outside a rather shabby shop—it shows three balls arranged in a triangle, proclaiming it a pawnshop, a place for people who need a quick bit of money. They put up personal articles as security for loans. If they pay back the loan on time, they get back their stuff; if not, the shopkeeper puts it up for sale.

I duck in and buy a handful of jewelry—nothing really worthy, just some cheap, glittery stuff . . . but it will serve.

"Joannie. Put on some decent clothes. I want you to go up to the Horse Guards' barracks and deliver this note to Captain Richard Allen. Thanks, Joannie. Here's cab fare. Now, scoot."

She darts out and I turn to Higgins.

"Things are afoot, Higgins, and we must be quick. Here is a list of things we will need, and now I shall tell you of my plan . . ."

Richard Allen arrives by horseback in the early afternoon with a great clatter of hooves and rattle of spurs. He dismounts and hands off the reins to Ravi, who has bounded down the gangway to meet him.

"Richard," I call from my quarterdeck. "Please come up and attend me. Things are comin' to a head and we must be quick. I have something to show you. And then I will tell you of my plan."

"I'd rather hoped you were finally inviting me to your bower, Princess," answers the very forward but nonetheless very beautiful cavalry hound upon gaining my quarterdeck

and looking toward my cabin door with a certain male longing. "Pity, that . . ."

"Not yet, you dog," I say taking him by the sleeve and
guiding him toward my main hatchway. "Follow me."

*Geez . . . There's serious work to be done and he thinks of
that. Men, I swear . . .*

We descend into the gloom of the lower decks. As we
go, our eyes become more accustomed to the dim light, and
at the bottom of the lower ladder we come upon . . .

"My God!" exclaims Allen, upon seeing Flashby chained
to the wall. "You've got the rascal!" He explodes into delighted laughter. "Oh, you have been busy, Jacky!"

Flashby is *not* laughing. I have had him gagged once more
to prevent his making a disturbance upon seeing Richard
Allen again. So now he can only rattle his chains and moan,
his eyes rolling about, both furious and fearful at seeing his
old adversary looming joyfully above him.

"So why have you presented him in such a state to me?"
demands Allen. "You want him dead and do not quite have
the stomach for it, so you want me to do it? No, that can't be
it . . . I seem to remember the Dread Pirate Faber quite
cheerfully putting a bullet in that Spanish officer on the
deck of the *San Cristobal* last spring."

"That was in self-defense and you know it. No matter
what they say about me," I protest, "I have never killed anybody in cold blood."

"Hmmm . . . I'm sure that is cold comfort to those you
have dispatched to the netherworld in . . . warm blood, as it
were," replies Lord Allen.

"Well, they had it comin'."

"I'm sure they did, my gentle Princess," he says, leaning

down to peer directly into Flashby's eyes. "And, except in battle, I have not killed anyone, either. But in this case I might make an exception. I believe putting a hole in this particular piece of meat would not overtax the Allen conscience. What say you to that, Flashbutt? Hmmm . . . ?"

Flashby recoils and moans, but nothing intelligible gets by the gag.

"You will now tell me, my delicate little muffin, just how you came by this . . . um . . . piece of goods."

So I settle down with my back leaning against the bulkhead and Richard sitting beside me as I recount the tale of the Taking of Harry Flashby. My good Ravi comes down with mugs of mulled wine to soothe the Faber throat as I tell the tale, replete with songs and humorous descriptions— *and there he was, hanging upside down outside his window and able to watch as I rifled through his drawers and seized all his money and papers before we lowered him down . . .*

Lord Richard Plantagenet Allen, Earl of Northcumberland, pounds the deck with his fist in glee at the telling of it.

When he recovers, he wipes tears from his eyes and says, "Oh, that was choice, that was really choice." And then he asks, "Why did you not tell me you had the cur, my deceptive little seagoing nymph?"

"Because I know you for a man of honor, despite your protestations to the contrary. And Flashby, while he is a vile bastard, remains in the supposed service of His Majesty, as do you. So I thought that might cause a problem."

"No problem, Prettytail, no problem at all. So what are you going to do with it?" asks Richard, unable to wipe the grin from his face as he gives the prisoner a none-too-gentle nudge with the toe of his boot. "I would expect an anchor and chain wrapped around its neck, followed by a discreet splash over the side, and then the noble Flashby gargles his last."

"No, milord, I am going to use it as bait," I say, and tell him of my plan . . .

". . . and then you and your men will ride out from your hiding place to capture the Black Highwayman alive."

"My duty is such that I must bring down the Highwayman, Princess, whoever he might be," warns Richard. "Even if it be your Mr. Fletcher."

"Oh, do not worry, milord, you will do that. Trust me."

"Very well, then," says Richard, getting to his feet. "It could be fun. Be seeing you on Thursday, then, Flashbutt." He reaches to pat Flashby on the head, and is rewarded with a glare of the purest hatred.

Lord Allen reaches out his hand for me, and I take it and rise.

"A last glass of wine with you, Jacky, in your cabin, hmmm . . . ?"

Sure, why not . . . ?

Late in the afternoon of this very busy Monday, Liam, Tink, and I take a coach to go back out to the Blackthorne Inn to speak once more with Bess, the landlord's daughter.

"You three again," she says upon seeing us enter and sit down. She is not at all friendly.

I speak right up and get to the point immediately.

"Harry Flashby will be on the Plymouth coach Thursday night."

"What's that to me?"

"I think it will be of interest to a mutual friend."

"I don't know what you mean. Do you want something to eat or drink? If not, move on." Her dark eyes hold my gaze, telling me she ain't gonna be tellin' Jaimy nothin'.

"Show him this," I say, as I slap Flashby's identification papers on the table. "Please do it."

She looks down but does not move. I press on.

"Listen, Miss. You know your Highwayman eventually will be caught and hanged. All of them have been, you know, and it will happen to him, too. He has been lucky so far."

Probably because you've been selecting his targets for him.

She still does not move, but her eyes grow more uncertain.

"There is a way out for him . . . and for you, too," I continue. "If he is allowed to settle his score with this Flashby, I believe he will cease his outlaw ways and the Black Highwayman will ride no more."

Her eyes flash.

"And you?" she asks. "What about you?"

I take a breath.

"If you do this, I will not interfere anymore. I shall not reveal myself to him. He will be yours. You can both leave and start a new life. I'm sure you have enough money for that. If not, I'll give you some."

She glances down at the papers.

"Please, Miss," I say, my eyes welling up and begging her to do it.

Abruptly, she nods, snatches up the papers, and turns away.

I let out a breath of relief.

Tink puts his hand on mine.

"So, Jacky," he asks gently. "You really love him so much that you would give him up?"

I nod, letting the tears flow freely.

Yes, I do . . . and yes, I would.

Chapter 47

We enter the Great Hall of the British Museum, Sidrah on the arm of her father, Charlie of the House of Chen, and I on the arm of Cavalry Captain Richard Allen, all of us looking splendid. Sidrah and I are dressed in our Oriental finery, and Charlie in his Savile Row best. Ravi stays alongside us, ready to pick up any silken train that might trail in the dust. I'm thinking that this will be the last time I'll be appearing in this guise and I intend to enjoy it. Once inside, I doff my silk shawl and am rewarded with a great number of gasps from the crowd. This bunch sure ain't the usual Cockpit crowd. I twirl about a bit so they can properly appreciate, and oh, I do love it so! I know it is sinful of me, but I do!

"I must hand it to you, Princess," observes Lord Allen as we proceed into the Hall. "For a self-proclaimed guttersnipe, you have managed to get poor Richard Allen into some *very* interesting places. It is rumored that King George, himself, will attend today."

"I hear that is possible, milord," I say, smiling my winning smile all about.

"Well, that will be rare company, indeed, for a poor cavalry captain."

I cut the arrogant but undeniably charming rogue a look as we proceed down the aisle.

"A poor cavalry captain who is also the fifty-first Earl of North-whatever-land. Poor little fellow, indeed."

"Ha. Well put." His face takes on a false dreamy look. "Oh, Fabled Northcumberland, place of my birth . . . Truth to tell, it is actually a rather shabby little estate located in the north of England. Dreadfully cold and rainy. We are forced to run around in kilts much of the time . . . and those god-awful bagpipes wailing away. Quite poor. You wouldn't like it at all."

"Poor, eh? Only a thousand or so serfs for you to order about?"

"We prefer to call them 'tenants,' dear one. They seem to shoulder their burdens better being named that. Gives 'em a bit more dignity, like. And you should know we have only a mere hundred or so, at last count. They do keep having babies, against all sense, so the number might be higher now."

That gets a bit of a rise out of the commoner Jacky Faber. I puff up and say, "So, when the Revolution comes, Lord Richard Plantagenet Allen—"

"On that glorious day, I will be out there leading the mob, Princess. Count on it."

"I do not doubt that, milord." I laugh. "Your kind always rises to the top, doesn't it?"

"I certainly hope so, Miss . . . Ah, here we are . . ."

There is quite a number of people in the hallowed marble halls of the museum, probably due to the rumor that the King might attend this opening of the new Oriental collection. I look about with a bit of pride, because the place looks a lot grander now thanks to Charlie . . . and me.

There are serene Buddhas sitting in front of glowing bowls of incense, and the Grecian maidens are lined in an elegant row over there, and to Ravi's delight, there's a golden elephantine Ganesh bestowing good will upon all. There's also golden jewelry from every corner of the East, along with Chinese dragons and fierce suits of armor from Japan . . . and a whole line of Grecian urns.

Richard and I pause in front of the large pottery jars. They were probably made to hold wine or olive oil and are quite well proportioned and elegant. They are black and have white lines etched on them depicting Greek soldiers fighting with sword and shield, and Greek wrestlers wrestling with . . . *ahem* . . . nothing on. *Nude* Greek soldiers and wrestlers . . .

I point at one of the fighting ones and say, "Funny how even in battle, their little . . . dangly bits . . . point up all jaunty. Could that be so, my Lord Allen? You have been in battle and you are a man, so you would know."

A short snort of a laugh from my escort.

"No, my inquisitive little nymph who always asks the most impertinent and outlandish questions, an emphatic *no*. In the heat of battle, I assure you that Little Dickie Allen was very quiet. He was lying low, as it were. Very low."

"During that time on the Mississippi when we had our little bit of a swim, I do not recall him being all that . . . little." I give Richard the big, innocent eyes.

"You do know how to flatter a man's vanity, do you not, my little minx?"

"Umm. I have found that, as a group, you men are all rather easy in that regard."

"Ha! I am sure of that." Richard laughs. "Before your formidable charms, we are all as mere beamish boys and . . . ah, wait . . . What's this?"

There is a commotion at the door, and every head swings in that direction.

"I believe the King is coming, Richard," I say, suddenly breathless in spite of myself. "Let us rejoin Charlie."

A few quick steps and I am beside Chopstick Charlie. Sidrah, looking radiant, stands on his other side, while Richard guards my left flank. The rest of the museum goers are lined up against the wall, facing the entrance. You do not ever, *ever,* show Royalty your backside.

We wait, but we do not wait long. Presently, a man walks in, hits a brace, and announces, "His Majesty, King George, by the Grace of God, King of England, Scotland, and Wales!" and . . .

And there he is! Imagine that.

He is a large man, rather tall and dressed quite simply—for a king. He wears a scarlet jacket with a large medal on it, white breeches, and black boots. It appears as if he might have just come in from a ride, though I doubt that. His prominent brow and nose and rather fleshy chin are softened a bit by his powdered wig. He looks, in fact, very much like the coins that have been struck in his honor. He gazes about him with hooded eyes and a half smile on his face. He gives a slight wave and proclaims to the crowd, "Come, dear friends, please be at your ease. This is not a state visit. Let us not stand on ceremony, but rather savor the treasures of this place."

I'll wager there are many here who wish he *would*

"stand on ceremony," which would mean that they would be presented to the King and thus would have something to tell all their descendants.

Alas, they shall not have that pleasure . . . but it turns out that we will.

The King, who is escorted by his son, the Duke of Clarence, strides across the floor directly toward us.

Oh, my . . .

When he gets close, Sidrah falls to her knees in the Oriental fashion and puts her forehead to the floor. Since I am dressed in similar garb, I, too, drop to the floor, my pigtail swinging to the side of my shaven head. I would not have been able to perform an acceptable curtsy in this tight-fitting sari, anyway. Although I cannot see them, since the tiles are only a few inches from my nose, I know that Charlie has bowed very low, and that Richard has done the same.

"Up, please, both of you, and let us see. Oh, how wonderfully exotic . . . and a little Hottentot, too!" The royal eye had undoubtedly fallen upon Ravi, who is probably cowering on the floor behind me in a very similar posture.

"How marvelous! William, please introduce us!"

"Certainly, Father," says the Duke of Clarence. "May I present Mr. Charles of the House of Chen—"

"Delighted, Sir!" says the King. "On behalf of the people of Britain, we thank you for this incomparable treasure!"

"How good of you to honor my poor House," says Charlie, his hands clasped in front of him. "May I present my Number One Daughter Sidrat'ul Muntaha, and my Number Two Daughter Ju kau-jing yi?"

"How lovely, both of you. Welcome to England."

Sidrah bows her perfectly coiffed head and I bow my

pigtailed one, and my spinning mind, uncontrollable beast that it is, thinks, *Thanks, Georgie, it's good to be back!*

"Now, perhaps, Mr. Chen, you will show us your wonderful collection," says our monarch, and Charlie smoothly waves him over to a display.

Crazed mind of Little Mary Faber of the Rooster Charlie Gang quickly composes a letter to Amy Trevelyne and the girls of the Lawson Peabody: Oh, by the way, dear Sisters, I met King George the other day . . . yes, that King George. Now that I have met the two main combatants in this war, the King of England and Emperor Napoleon Bonaparte, dear Amy, if you could please arrange for me to meet your President Jefferson when next I land on your shore, I shall pronounce myself satisfied.

"Please tell me what this is," I hear the King demanding of Chopstick Charlie.

"It is a porcelain dragon from the Ming Dynasty, Your Grace, and this is a suit of armor that belonged to Genghis Khan."

"Quite impressive. Should hate to meet anyone wearing *that* on a battlefield."

"Indeed, Your Majesty, it was designed to intimidate. Now, over here, I think you will find this particularly interesting . . . I have heard that Your Highness is of a scientific bent? Yes, this is the astrolabe that might have been devised by the Greek mathematician Eratosthenes, who first figured out the circumference of the world back in, by your reckoning, around 200 BC."

"My word!" exclaims the King. "The one who figured it out by looking down a well? I cannot believe it!"

"Yes, Majesty . . . and over here we have . . ."

The two drift off in earnest conversation.

"Hard to believe that pleasant man is the one who lost our American colonies," I say to Richard.

He cocks an eye at me.

"*Our . . . ?*"

"Faber Shipping has a certain proprietary interest in things of that nature. When I am in England, I am English. When I'm abroad, I fly whatever colors suit me."

"Spoken like a true pirate," he says, with an affectionate smile. "Well, if you must know, it wasn't the King who lost 'em. It was his ministers . . . Pitt and that rotten crew."

"Oh," I respond. "Politics from you, Richard? I thought such a simple soldier did not mess with that sort of thing." I give him a poke.

"Umm. Well, it appears the King is leaving," he says, looking over at the entrance where the King's party is exiting.

He turns and graciously gives a small royal wave to the crowd and then is gone. There is a great hubbub as people congratulate each other on having been in the presence of the King of England, Scotland, and Wales.

We rejoin Charlie and Sidrah after the crowd around them disperses.

"I think I shall return home soon," says Charlie. "I have done what I came to do. I have met the King of England. I have been named Special Trade Representative of His Majesty, a title that I believe will hold me in very good stead." He chuckles. "*And* I have had the delight of seeing many former classmates grovel at my feet. Yes, most satisfying, but time to be off."

"When will you go, Charlie?"

"On Friday. I have several dinner engagements planned."

"I will be sorry to see you go, Chops," I say, laying my hand upon his arm.

"Ah, well, I must get back. I am sure my enemies have made much of my absence and will need to be chastised," he says, patting my hand. "Perhaps we shall meet again, dear. After all, you *do* get around."

"I am sure of it, Charlie," I say. "And thank you for adopting me, Father. Does that mean I shall be in your will?"

He laughs. "We will have to negotiate that part of your adoption."

"That we shall," I say. "Now, let us all be off for one last night at the Cockpit, for this week we will have work, and I fear it will be hot work, indeed."

I put my hand on Lord Allen's arm.

"Come, my gallant Hotspur, I am feeling apprehensive and in need of some cheer."

At least I will get to see you soon, Jaimy, and I pray that all goes well . . . but I just don't know . . .

Chapter 48

James Fletcher, Highwayman
In the Saddle and Waiting
On Blackheath Moor

Jacky!

I have received reliable word that Harry Flashby, yes, that despicable bastard who has brought us both so low, will be on the Plymouth coach this night. How long I have waited, oh, how so very long! But now the base coward will be brought to bay. At last!

My pistols are primed, my sword is sharp. You will be avenged this night, dear girl, I promise it!

Jaimy

Chapter 49

We've managed to get a coach very much like the regular London-to-Plymouth carriage, and we are heading down Blackheath Road toward the Blackthorne Inn, probably for the last time, for better or for worse. Liam is driving the team of four horses, his hat pulled low over his face in case Jaimy is capable of recognizing anybody in his current state of madness.

On the seat across from me in the coach, Harry Flashby sits, well bound up and glaring. We have given him a decent shave. And, oh, how I shall always remember the look on his face as the smiling Mr. Lee Chi approached him with a gleaming straight razor in his hand. We have dressed Flashby in new black trousers, black shirt, and boots. After all, when first we took him, he was wearing only his underclothes. We have his gag in place and the curtains are drawn because we do not want him attracting attention. Night has fallen, but there is a very bright moon rising, with ghostly clouds scudding across its pale and pitted face.

Next to Flashby are Davy and Tink, and beside me sits

Captain Richard Allen, a dark gray cloak hiding his scarlet regimental uniform.

I am too nervous to make much small talk on this journey. A knot of worry is gnawing at the pit of my stomach . . . *Oh, Jaimy, what if things should go wrong, horribly wrong?*

But if I am too full of dread and apprehension to make cheerful conversation as we clatter along, Richard most assuredly is not.

"There is a very good chance you will be killed this night, Flashby, old boy, and we do hope you will make a good show of it. After all, you have the reputation of the Black Highwayman to uphold," says Lord Allen to the gagged and moaning Flashby.

"We don't want future romantics to think he met his end as a groveling, sniveling coward, now, do we?" continues Allen, plainly enjoying Flashby's discomfort.

More grunts from Flashby, who finds his tormentor not finished quite yet. I know that Richard senses my unease and is doing this to cheer me, and, admittedly, it does help . . . a little.

"For the love of God, Flashbutt, hold up your head! Don't you realize that stories and poems will be written about you? Yes, it is true!" he proclaims. "Think of it . . . dewy young girls heaving great palpitating sighs and hugging their well-worn and tearstained copies of the sacred poem to their breasts, and all you have to do, for your part, is to perish nobly. Not too much to ask, is it, old top?"

On we go along the road that is now a pale ribbon of light under the glowing moon.

"Now there *is* a slight chance you might survive this

night, in which case you will certainly be hanged at Newgate as fast as that can be arranged. Enough proof has been planted on you to ensure that, I promise you . . . Yes, the evidence will be circumstantial, but it should prove damning. I can see it now—'Oh, the Highwayman stood on the gallows, his head on high, and proclaimed . . .' et cetera, et cetera. You know, all those things noble characters say when their noble necks are about to be stretched."

Flashby's face has by now turned a rather unsightly shade of pale, as he finally realizes just what is planned for him. I take the opportunity to remove the black silk mask from my purse, the one with the gathers so well described by Mrs. Beasley, the very observant seamstress, and tie it about Flashby's neck so that it will be ready to be yanked up into place when the time comes. And yes, I had stuffed all that cheap jewelry I had purchased at that pawnshop into Flashby's pockets, making sure that some spilled out so that all could take note.

That done, I draw back the curtain and stick my head out the window to look down the road we have just traveled. There is a cloud of dust back there, and I know it has been raised by Richard's company of Royal red-coated Dragoons, who are trailing us by a quarter mile. They bear orders to stay out of sight behind that hillock at the turn of the Black-heath Road until they are called. They lead Richard's horse and a few extra mounts.

Hmmm . . . I'm thinkin' . . . they'd better stay in the rear. It won't do for them to be spotted. Hey, what's that? High on the crest of a hill I see a boy, framed by the rising moon, standing beside a horse, looking back from whence we had just come.

366

Uh-oh . . . Could it be that Bess, the landlord's daughter, who has so far proved herself most cautious, has allies in her enterprise? *God, I hope not* . . .

Hope or not, the boy bounds into the saddle and pounds off to the south. Maybe it's nothing . . . but maybe he's headin' to the inn . . . Maybe he will tell . . . *Oh, Lord, let us beat him to the spot* . . .

I pull my head back in.

"We're gettin' close. Everybody ready? Remember, we must stay hidden. We don't want to spook him and send him flying off after all this trouble we've gone to. Got that? Good."

All nod, with Davy and Tink each putting their hands on a Flashby arm, and holding him upright. Richard loosens his pistol in its holster and says, "Ready, Princess. Let's get to it."

Liam leads the coach around the treacherous tight turn and there . . . there . . . there in the moonlight on his great black horse, stands the Black Highwayman of Blackheath Road, his mount rearing, his black cloak swirling around him.

"Stand!" he roars, pulling out his pistols. "Stand and deliver to me the base coward I know rests within that coach! Bring out Harry Flashby now!"

"Tink! Davy!" I hiss, yanking the gag from Flashby's mouth and pulling up the mask. "Put him out!" My shiv is already in my hand and I use it to cut the bonds that bind his wrists.

Davy kicks open the door and Flashby is tossed out to lie squalling and writhing in the dirt.

"No! Fletcher, please! Don't do it," croaks Flashby, now on his knees. "I beg of you! Mercy!"

The Highwayman looks down upon him, ignoring the rest of us.

"Take this pistol. You shall have the first shot." He tosses the pistol to the ground in front of Flashby.

I jump out of the coach and pull back the hood from my head.

"No, Jaimy, don't do this," I plead. "He's not worth it! He's—"

There is the sound of approaching hoofbeats, the sound of a horse being ridden desperately hard.

"NO, JAMES! WATCH OUT! IT'S A TRAP! RUN! RUN!"

The Highwayman's head jerks up to see Bess, the landlord's daughter, come pounding toward him.

"THERE'S A BAND OF REDCOATS BEYOND THAT HILL!" she screams. "YOU MUST FLEE! RUN!"

The girl jumps down from her horse and runs to his side and wraps her arms about him.

The Highwayman, confused, looks down upon her, his remaining pistol still in his hand.

"Jaimy! No!" I yell. "It's me, Jacky! Put down the gun! We can work this out!"

But it turns out we cannot work this out. Not now, not ever . . .

Flashby, now unbound and seeing confusion all about, reaches down to pick up the pistol that was tossed to him. To my horror, he aims and fires. Following the flash, I see the bullet find its mark. No, it doesn't penetrate the dear body of the Black Highwayman but instead goes straight into the chest of Bess, the landlord's raven-haired daughter.

She jerks and slumps to the ground.

Flashby, realizing that he has missed his target and can

only expect a bullet in return, jumps up and runs away, up the road and toward the safety of London.

The Highwayman drops his pistol and sinks to his knees in the dirt beside his stricken girl, gasping as her heart's blood flows out of her. He gathers her to his own chest and holds her.

"James . . ." she whispers. "I . . ."

"Hush, dear Bess," says Jaimy, for it is now plain that it is he, the mask having dropped from his stricken face. He buries his face in the thick mass of her long black hair. "Just you rest now . . ."

I come up to him. Maybe I shouldn't, but I do.

"Jaimy . . . please . . . we must fly from here, we must . . ."

But he does not see me. His mind is closed to all but the girl who lies dying in his arms.

He places a kiss upon her brow as she gasps her last breath on this Earth and slumps lifeless against his chest.

"All I ever loved . . ." whispers Jaimy. "Jacky . . . and now Bess. All I ever loved in this world . . . gone . . . taken from me . . ."

His left hand holds the girl's body, while his right searches through the dust and finds the unfired pistol. He fits it into his fist and lifts it . . .

Wait, Jaimy! Flashby's gone. You can't hope to hit him! You can't . . .

But it ain't Flashby he's aiming to shoot . . . no, it ain't . . .

He lifts the gun and points the barrel to his own head, his eyes dead.

"NO!" I scream, and throw myself over the pistol. His

finger tightens and the gun fires, tearing a hole in my shirt and a narrow burning groove in the skin of my belly. "JAIMY! DON'T YOU KNOW US? WE'RE YOUR FRIENDS! THERE'S LIAM, AND DAVY, AND TINK . . . THE *DOLPHIN*! THE FORETOP! OH, DON'T YOU KNOW US, JAIMY?"

But he doesn't know us. No, he doesn't . . .

He gently lays the girl's body down and rises into a crouch, facing me.

"Demons . . . all of you. Jacky's dead. My Bess is dead . . . They're all dead . . . and you have come here to torment me, you hellish fiends, you . . ."

Jaimy, his face a mask of pure insane rage, fixes his mad gaze upon me.

"No, Jaimy, it ain't like that, it ain't!" I plead. "We're your friends! I'm your girl, I am—"

What I am is standing there pleading with him as his fist comes rounding about and slams into the side of my face.

Oh, God! The shock, the pain!

I fall back and my head hits something hard and my senses cloud and I . . . I can't get up, I can't . . . I swim in and out of consciousness. Through the thudding pounding of my brain, I hear shouts . . .

Here, Delaney, get this rag over his face! That's it. Don't breathe it yourself, man, it'll knock you on your ass. Ah, yes, Mr. Fletcher, be calm now, that's it, relax . . . just relax . . . Everything's gonna be all right. Good. He's out. Jones, Tinker, get him in the coach.

I groan and roll over in the dirt.

Christ! She's got blood on her front! Here, hold her!

I feel my dress being ripped open.

Thank God, it looks superficial! Get her into the coach!

I am lifted up and my swirling senses slowly return to me. I find I am leaning against Richard Allen and being held up by his right arm.

"No . . . wait," I manage to say, still weaving on my pins. "Jaimy . . . ?"

"He is all right, Princess," says Allen. "Don't worry. Now, as for you . . ."

Just then the red-coated Private Archie MacDuff bursts into our little circle of dim moonlight, followed by the rest of the Dragoons, with a struggling Lieutenant Harry Flashby secure in the burly arms of Sergeant Bailey. He had run off only to shortly find himself locked in that firm and quite unfriendly embrace.

"We nabbed 'im roight off, Sor," announces Bailey. "He's the Highwayman, roight, Sor?"

"He is, indeed, Sergeant," says Allen, who goes up and puts his face in Flashby's. Leaning down and picking up Jaimy's wide-brimmed hat, he claps it on Flashby's head. He then pulls the little silken mask up over his nose and taps it down securely.

"Take him back, Sergeant, and parade him through the streets of London for the delight of the mob. Let them hoot and holler at him, as he's got it coming," says the grinning Lord Allen. "That'll be a bit of fun, won't it, Flashby, before the rather grim stuff to come? Yes, I hear, Mr. William Brunskill is the hangman at Newgate and he favors the short drop, don'cha know . . . the one you had planned for Jacky, remember? Cheerio, now, old top. Sergeant, take him to Newgate and dump him there, on my authority. Make sure his accommodations are of the very worst."

"Aye, Sor."

Flashby, wild-eyed, is dragged away as Richard leads me, still woozy, off to the coach.

"Here, Princess, up with you. There. I shall ride behind you."

I am put up and placed within, as Lord Allen mounts up to follow.

In the coach, Tink and Davy have Jaimy between them, trying to bring him around.

"C'mon, Jaimy, we're back on the foretop o' the *Dolphin*, don'cha remember? C'mon, mate, good times then, eh?"

"Nay, lads," I say, still trying to clear my battered mind. "Don't do that. Here, let me over." And I move over to take Tink's place, such that Jaimy's head is lowered into my lap.

I take my hand and smooth his hair from his face and look down upon him.

Poor Jaimy, that you had to go through all this for me . . . and I am so unworthy of it all, you know. Me, Jacky Faber, just a scrap of skin and hair and bone and that's all there is to it when all is said and done. So much better for you, lad, if you had never got on the Dolphin *and I had stayed in the streets of London. I don't know what leads us on our paths to whatever destiny awaits . . . Sometimes I think it's just a flip of the coin, a turn of the card . . . I just dunno . . .*

Jaimy gives a bit of a moan, a shudder goes through him, and then he subsides again.

That's it, Jaimy, just rest. Don't worry, things will get better, you'll see, you'll see . . .

I lean over and lift his head and place his face on my breast and hold it there and let the tears drip from my eyes.

Oh, Jaimy, this world was not of our making, why do we have to suffer through it so?

As we ride on through the night, I know that I should be rejoicing because we were successful in rescuing Jaimy from the gallows. Here he is, after all, in my very lap, safe for the moment from the authorities and maybe from himself, but I am not joyful, no . . . I can only think of that poor, loyal, and loving heart left lying back there on the road . . . back in the waning moonlight . . . blood on her shattered breast, the red love knot that had been twined in her hair, now trailing in the dust . . .

Chapter 50

I am again seated in the office of the First Lord of the Admiralty, the unworthy Faber bottom once more pressed into a very fine chair. The Faber ears are listening, once again, to Mr. Peel speak to matters of Naval Intelligence. Mr. Peel is standing, while Baron Mulgrave, the First Lord himself, sits with his hands clasped over his belly. He does not seem to be at all favorably disposed toward my poor self. But that's all right . . . I sit with my hands demurely folded on my lap, with chin up and the Lawson Peabody Look firmly upon my face. I am dressed fairly military, as I believe befits the moment. I'm wearing the blue jacket, white skirt, and all, and I sit and listen.

"Now as to your status, Miss Faber," Mr. Peel intones. "The amount of historical treasure you have very ingeniously managed to obtain from the East has been very well received by the Crown and we are directed to act kindly toward you . . . and yours . . ."

And you, too, Mr. Peel, should be well disposed to be kind to me and mine as I got your job back for you . . . the Affair of the Misplaced Watch, you will recall . . .

It turns out that Mr. Peel is, indeed, well disposed toward me for all that.

". . . and it has been decided that Lieutenant James Fletcher, whereabouts unknown, shall be restored to his full rank in the Royal Navy—that is, of course, if he should ever turn up again. It has been determined that his conviction at court-martial was tainted by the testimony of false witnesses."

"That is good, Sir," I say. "Mr. Fletcher is entirely devoted to the Service, no matter what aspersions might have been cast against his good name."

"You mean the charge that he led a mutiny on an East India Company ship?" growls the First Lord, speaking up for the first time.

"That was the *East India Company,* Sir," I purr. "Not the *Royal Navy.* And, you will recall, he was serving out an unjust sentence."

"As opposed to your very just sentence to life in the penal colony at New South Wales for your own crimes against the Crown?"

"Whatever you say, my lord," I murmur, eyes cast modestly down. "If you want to dispose of me, then just do it. I have always tried to serve my country to the best of my ability."

That gets a slight cough of disbelief from Mr. Peel, but he soldiers on.

"However, for all your good work, you have done some damage to this Branch of the Service. Agents Moseley and Bliffil are now gone and Agent Flashby is . . . indisposed."

Indisposed? Ha! I'll bet he is, trying to talk his way out of that one!

"You shouldn't hire such lowlifes to work for you," I say

evenly. I cast an eye on the agents Carr and Boyd, who stand guard at the door. They aren't so bad, but they do follow orders from the top, and I'm not anywhere near the top . . . but we'll see . . .

Last night, when Jaimy, all bound up, had been brought down to the wharf, he was taken not to the Nancy B., *but rather to the* Celestial Light, *where Chopstick Charlie Chen waited.*

"Leave him to us," said Charlie, upon my breathless arrival. He was once again clad in his Oriental garb. "We will take care of him. We have herbs, potions, curatives . . . We have our ways. As a matter of fact, we have just given him a dose to calm him down. He is now very quiet and you can see him if you wish."

I did so wish, and went down into the cabin where Jaimy lay on a pallet, Sidrah beside him, placing a cool compress to his forehead.

I crouched beside him.

He stirred a bit, his legs thrashing about.

"Jaimy . . . dear . . . Everything's all right now . . . Just rest . . ." Tears welled up and ran down my face as I brushed the hair from his wild eyes.

"Bess?" he said, looking about.

"No, Jaimy . . . not Bess," I said, choking, thinking of the poor soul left lying back there in the dirt. "It's Jacky."

"Jacky? No . . . you're dead . . ."

"No, I'm not, Jaimy, I—"

Davy sticks his head in the door.

"Ready to go, Jack. We'd best get moving."

"Right. I'll be only a second . . ."

I stand after placing a kiss upon Jaimy's brow.

"Get well, Jaimy. I'll be back, I will. I promise."

I feel Charlie's arm on mine.

"Do not worry, Little One. We will cure him and bring him back to you."

"Thank you, Charlie. Please, do what you can."

"Farewell, Small Round-Eyed Barbarian. We leave within the hour. I shall give your regards to Cheng Shih when next I see her. I am sure she will be full of inquiries about you and your well-being."

"Please do . . . Oh, Charlie . . . Sidrah . . ." *I cry, the tears streaming down my face.* "I so hate to see you go!"

A shake of the head and I am back in the First Lord's office.

"All right," continues Peel. "To sum it up, Mr. Fletcher shall be pardoned and your own life sentence has been overturned . . . under the following condition."

I sit up straight and wait for it.

"You shall remain as an agent of Naval Intelligence. Lord Wellesley has been dispatched to Portugal as head of His Majesty's Army. Spain has joined our side. Apparently the Dons did not like Napoleon's installing his brother as King of Spain. It is rumored that Wellesley will soon be named Duke of Wellington for his service to the Crown. He will attack Boney's army from the south. You will be assigned to his staff as translator, your being fluent in both French and Spanish."

"And as Fly-on-the-Wall for Royal Naval Intelligence in the very heart of the Royal Army," I say, stating the obvious.

"Even so," says Peel.

"Very well," I say, rising. "I agree. May I go now?"

"Yes, you may. Prepare yourself. You leave in two days."

I leave the office to find Captain Richard Allen in the hallway, leaning against the wall, waiting.

He stands up straight, and I go over and place my hand upon his red-coated arm.

"To Portugal, Princess?" he asks, taking my hand and smiling that roguish smile of his.

"Yes, my lord, to Portugal," I say, and softly sing as we walk off toward whatever awaits us . . .

Over the hills and over the Main
To Flanders, Portugal, and Spain.
King George commands and we must obey,
Over the hills and far away . . .